"Infused with . . . fresh detail. Between the sweetness of the relationship and the summery beach setting, romance fans will find this a warming winter read."

—*Publishers Weekly*

"Fans will love the frank honesty of her characters. [Beck's] scenery is richly detailed and the story engaging."

—RT Book Reviews

"[A] realistic and heartwarming story of redemption and love . . . Beck's understanding of interpersonal relationships and her flawless prose make for a believable romance and an entertaining read."

—*Booklist*

PRAISE FOR *WORTH THE WAIT*

"[A] poignant and heartwarming story of young love and redemption and will literally make your heart ache . . . Jamie Beck has a real talent for making the reader feel the sorrow, regret, and yearning of this young character."

—*Fresh Fiction*

PRAISE FOR *WORTH THE TROUBLE*

"Beck takes readers on a journey of self-reinvention and risky investments, in love and in life . . . With strong family ties, loyalty, playful banter, and sexual tension, Beck has crafted a beautiful second-chances story."

—*Publishers Weekly* (starred review)

PRAISE FOR *SECRETLY HERS*

"[I]n Beck's ambitious, uplifting second Sterling Canyon contemporary... [c]onflicting views and family drama lay the foundation for emotional development in this strong Colorado-set contemporary."

—*Publishers Weekly*

"Witty banter and the deepening of the characters and their relationship, along with some unexpected plot twists and a lovable supporting cast . . . will keep the reader hooked . . . A smart, fun, sexy, and very contemporary romance."

—*Kirkus Reviews*

PRAISE FOR *WORTH THE RISK*

"An emotional read that will leave you reeling at times and hopeful at others."

—*Books and Boys Book Blog*

PRAISE FOR *UNEXPECTEDLY HERS*

"Character-driven, sweet, and chock-full of interesting secondary characters."

—*Kirkus Reviews*

PRAISE FOR *BEFORE I KNEW*

"A tender romance rises from the tragedy of two families—a must read!"

—Robyn Carr, #1 *New York Times* bestselling author

"Jamie Beck's deeply felt novel hits all the right notes, celebrating the power of forgiveness, the sweetness of second chances, and the heady joy of reaching for a dream. Don't miss this one!"

—Susan Wiggs, #1 *New York Times* bestselling author

"*Before I Knew* kept me totally enthralled as two compassionate, relatable characters, each in search of forgiveness and fulfillment, turn a recipe for heartache into a story of love, hope, and some really good menus!"

—Shelley Noble, *New York Times* bestselling author of *Whisper Beach*

PRAISE FOR *ALL WE KNEW*

"A moving story about the flux of life and the steadfastness of family."

—*Publishers Weekly*

"An impressively crafted and deftly entertaining read from first page to last."

—Midwest Book Review

"*All We Knew* is compelling, heartbreaking, and emotional."

—*Harlequin Junkie*

PRAISE FOR *JOYFULLY HIS*

"A quick and sweet read that is perfect for the holidays."

—*Harlequin Junkie*

PRAISE FOR *WHEN YOU KNEW*

"[A]n opposites-attract romance with heart."

—*Harlequin Junkie*

PRAISE FOR *THE MEMORY OF YOU*

"[Beck] deepens a typical story about first loves reuniting by exploring the aftermath of a violent act. Readers will root for an ending that repairs this couple's past hurt."

—*Booklist*

"Beck's portrayals of divorce and trauma are keen . . . Readers will be caught up in their journey toward healing and romance."

—*Publishers Weekly*

"*The Memory of You* is heartbreaking, emotional, entertaining, and a unique second-chance romance."

—*Harlequin Junkie*

PRAISE FOR *THE PROMISE OF US*

"Beck's depiction of trauma, loss, friendship, and family resonates deeply. A low-key small-town romance unflinching in its portrayal of the complexities of friendship and family, and the joys and sorrows they bring."

—*Kirkus Reviews*

"A fully absorbing and unfailingly entertaining read."

—Midwest Book Review

PRAISE FOR *THE WONDER OF NOW*

"*The Wonder of Now* is emotional, it is uplifting, it is heartbreaking, but ultimately shows the reader the best of humanity in a heartfelt story."

—The Nerd Daily

PRAISE FOR *IF YOU MUST KNOW*

"Beck expertly captures the bickering between sisters, the pain of regret, and the thorny path to forgiveness. With well-realized secondary characters . . . and believable surprises peppered throughout, Beck's emotional tale rings true."

—*Publishers Weekly*

"[Beck's] heartwarming novel explores the sisterly bond with a touch of romance and mystery."

—*Booklist*

PRAISE FOR *TRUTH OF THE MATTER*

"Beck spins a poignant, multigenerational coming-of-age tale as these three women navigate their identities, dreams, and love lives. Complex and introspective, this is by turns heart-wrenching and infectiously hopeful."

—*Publishers Weekly* (starred review)

PRAISE FOR *FOR ALL SHE KNOWS*

"Women's fiction readers and series fans will be pleased with this story of friendship, family, and forgiveness."

—*Publishers Weekly*

"Like *Little Fires Everywhere* and *Big Little Lies*, this novel tackles the complicated dynamic between mothers."

—The Hollywood Reporter

"An inherently reader-engaging and impressively original story of friendship, hardship, love, tragedy, and redemption."

—Midwest Book Review

"*For All She Knows* is a must-read for book clubs! Jamie Beck's latest novel is both an insightful examination of modern-day parenting mores, and a poignant reminder of the importance of friendship and forgiveness."

—Brenda Novak, *New York Times* bestselling author

"Jamie Beck deftly crafts a riveting tale of parenthood, marriage, and friendship around a tragic event that unravels the threads that hold everything dear for two friends: their families and each other. As heart-wrenching as it is inspiring, *For All She Knows* reminds us that forgiveness is the first step to heal and Beck captures this brilliantly. A spring read every book club should pick up!"

—Kerry Lonsdale, *Wall Street Journal* and *Washington Post* bestselling author

PRAISE FOR *THE HAPPY ACCIDENTS*

"This story is an ode to girl power, making mistakes, and following your dreams. We'll race you to the bookstore."

—SheKnows

"Beautifully moving, masterful storytelling that weaves the nuances of relationships and finding yourself while facing the intricacies of life-changing decisions and their consequences."

—Priscilla Oliveras, *USA Today* bestselling author

"Jamie Beck has moved from a heavy hitter in romance to a sure thing in women's fiction, and *The Happy Accidents* shows why she can do both. In this novel, three old friends make a pact that changes everything . . . and may just be the best decision they ever made. You won't regret *your* decision to one-click this book."

—Liz Talley, *USA Today* bestselling author

take it
from
me

ALSO BY JAMIE BECK

The St. James Novels

Worth the Wait
Worth the Trouble
Worth the Risk

The Sterling Canyon Novels

Accidentally Hers
Secretly Hers
Unexpectedly Hers
Joyfully His

The Cabot Novels

Before I Knew
All We Knew
When You Knew

The Sanctuary Sound Novels

The Memory of You
The Promise of Us
The Wonder of Now

The Potomac Point Novels

If You Must Know
Truth of the Matter
For All She Knows

Stand-Alone Novels

In the Cards
The Happy Accidents

take it from me

A NOVEL

JAMIE BECK

 Montlake

Text copyright © 2022 by Write Ideas, LLC
All rights reserved.

Published by Montlake, Seattle

www.apub.com

Amazon, the Amazon logo, and Montlake are trademarks of Amazon.com, Inc., or its affiliates.

ISBN-13: 9781542032391
ISBN-10: 1542032393

Cover design by Caroline Teagle Johnson

Printed in the United States of America

*To my beloved children, Kayla and Ford,
with the hope that they remain open to surprising
friendships and differing perspectives.*

CHAPTER ONE

WENDY

A Saturday morning in early October
New Canaan, Connecticut

While my husband is upstairs sleeping in, I climb onto the second shelf of the built-in unit flanking the living room fireplace and peer through the quarter-round window to spy on whoever is moving into the Durbins' house today. Discovering other people's secrets doesn't make mine less shameful, but it does make me feel less alone. Intimate knowledge forms a bond even when the other person remains unaware. Of course, my husband knows of mine, but even he doesn't know everything. And, God willing, he never will.

Nevertheless, I can't say I'll miss George Durbin. He isn't neighborly—always seeking a way to extricate himself from conversations with me. Joe and I invited him to our Christmas open house and a summer cocktail party this past year, but he wasn't interested. Come to think of it, George has never been interested in much, which is probably why his wife, Peg—whom I do miss terribly—ran all the way to California last year.

Peg's sarcasm made me laugh. She was also the queen of unplanned get-togethers. The first time she asked me over, she didn't put on airs like so many others. She simply kicked off her shoes, uncorked a bottle of inexpensive wine, handed me a glass, then proceeded to gossip about the insurance company office where she worked—conversations that, over time, we called episodes of *As the Policies Turn*. The important point is that Peg was a true friend, not a casual acquaintance from one of my volunteer committees. A true friend is a rare and precious thing.

The November day she told me she was leaving was dark in more ways than one. Her declaration landed like a fist to my jaw—a rejection of me as much as of George. I'd thought I knew her, but apparently she'd held something back just as I'd been doing. Envy deepened the bruise. Not that I want to flee my home, but her courage at our stage of life cracked open something uneasy in me.

I blame that and the second bottle of wine we guzzled for sparking my compulsive urge, a constant source of turmoil that I've had to manage since my late teens. Until Peg's announcement, I'd rarely slipped up since quitting therapy years ago. Yet suddenly there I was, sneaking the wineglass charm into my purse when she wasn't looking. That little item is now tucked away in the drawer beneath my feet—hidden but tangible, just like my shame.

I'm about to give up my lookout when two youngish women and a long-haired young man tumble out of the large U-Haul, each straining to carry a rolled carpet. Cupping my hands around my face, I press my nose to the glass to get a closer look. We've never had renters on this street. What kind of people would lease a home with peeling paint and neglected flower beds littered with dead rhododendron? Such a shame, that. It'd take so little effort for that Cape to look charming, with its expansive front porch and antique shutters.

"Whatcha you doin' up there, Wendy?" my husband asks, yawning.

"Oh, Joe!" Startled, I fall backward against the end table that belonged to my great-grandmother, nearly knocking over our son Billy's high school graduation photograph. My cheeks are hot as I tighten my silk robe's belt. "You shouldn't sneak up on people."

"Hm." He bestows a warm smile. "Interesting advice coming from the neighborhood spy."

His genial wink eases the sting of embarrassment. He's never judged my peccadilloes. They amuse him, which isn't the worst thing. After all, no marriage survives without humor.

"I'm hardly spying." I skirt around the end table to cross the living room. "I'm just curious. Did George tell you about his tenants? Are they a family?"

Children's laughter would offset the otherwise dubious rental situation. How I miss those busy, happy days. The endless sticky hands and kisses. The invigorating rise and fall of my heart with each of my son's victories and setbacks.

Now there is such silence.

Joe walks toward the kitchen, his iPad in hand, ready for his ninety-minute Saturday-morning ritual of downing three cups of coffee while reading the paper. "He didn't say."

Translation: Joe didn't ask.

Eager for company, I follow him, although I've already had my coffee, eaten breakfast, and cleaned up my mess. We've been married twenty years, so he's used to being shadowed. I'm a tracker. I like to ensure that he and Billy are safe, comfortable, and have what they need.

"Can I pour you a cup, too, hon?" he asks.

"No thanks." I grab the sugar bowl, a teaspoon, and the creamer, and set them on the kitchen table while he finds a mug and pours his coffee. "Would you like some eggs?"

"Not hungry yet, thanks." Joe sits and sweetens his drink, then turns his iPad cover into a stand for the device and proceeds to open the *New York Times* app. Before he begins reading, he asks, "What's on your agenda today?"

It's been roughly six weeks since we dropped Billy off at Colgate University. Forty-one days that feel like as many months. Not that Joe seems as affected by his absence. Then again, Joe's life hasn't undergone a wholesale change like mine.

Older friends swore that we'd revel in reclaiming our lives and spontaneity. I'm still waiting for that promise—one I clung to when hugging my son goodbye—to come true. While the details of our life before Billy are hazy, I treasure my early encounters with Joe's effortless love and comfortable companionship—an ease that was a first for me.

"Want to drive up to Litchfield? We could hike around Lake Waramaug and then hit that winery." I rest my chin on my fist.

"Would that make you happy?" He sips his drink, brows rising in question.

Happier than sitting here all day. "The leaves should be gorgeous."

"Okay. We'll drive up after lunch." He nods and then turns his attention to the screen in front of him, falling silent.

I flex my hand and stare at my manicure, which is chipping thanks to the refinishing work I did on the Levys' armoire last week, determined to brush aside the nagging thought that keeps poking at my figurative ribs. *Is this all there is?* How many times have I overheard women whining about one sort of midlife crisis or another and sworn to myself it wouldn't happen to me? Sworn that I'd always be grateful that my married life was so much better than my childhood. And yet here I am, pestered by that irksome question for which I don't have even a rhetorical answer.

With a sigh, I place my hands in my lap. Maybe I'll swing through Burtis Nails after dropping my son's care package at the post office; then perhaps I'll pick up a small welcome gift for the new neighbors.

My gaze wanders back to my husband, whose forty-ninth birthday is coming up, not that you'd know it. Regular exercise keeps him trim. He has all his hair, too, although it's graying pleasingly around the edges. The only change to those deep brown eyes—the kindest eyes I know—is that they're bracketed now by deep smile lines.

He's a content man. An honest and committed one who accepts our restricted social lives to help me avoid triggers. He first learned of my problem during our engagement, after I was arrested for palming a sample tube of lipstick at Nordstrom. I was sure the horror would send him running. When he bailed me out of jail, compassionately listened to my teary explanation of my compulsion, and then suggested therapy, I knew he was a keeper. Although I was fearful that confessing would lead to additional arrests, I was more afraid that Joe might end our engagement if I didn't get help.

I should count myself lucky with him. I do, too, except for one recent and troubling change.

Glancing down at my nightgown—a pretty periwinkle silk negligee trimmed in cream-colored lace—I commit to seduction. As subtly as possible, I loosen the robe's neckline to expose my pajamas' lacy bodice as well as my cleavage. Twining a shoulder-length, highlighted lock of hair around my finger, I stretch my foot out beneath the table until it makes contact with Joe and then run it playfully up his shin.

He looks up, confused. "Did you ask something?"

"No." I aim for a sensual pose, feeling simultaneously vulnerable yet daring. We're alone. Nothing on the calendar and all the time in the world. "Wanna have a little fun?"

Joe pats my foot, all the while wearing a pleasant smile. "I'm reading, hon."

I maintain an equally pleasant expression despite the burn of rejection. Not even a twinkle in his eye or a "maybe later" to pacify me. It's been this way for a few months—as if he woke up one morning without any libido. Worse, he doesn't seem to miss it. I try not to take it personally or let my mind tumble down the rabbit holes spawned by a community that's seen its fair share of affairs.

I've never before doubted Joe's love for me, even though gravity and a flagging metabolism have begun to grab hold of my butt, my tummy, and my boobs despite the many long walks, yoga classes, and facials I endure. He delights in my kindness, as well as my effort spent improving everything from our home to the community. And he patiently helps me handle my mother, which is more than my father could muster. Joe couldn't fake that affection, could he?

Sighing, I rise to go get dressed. "I'm hitting the post office soon. Would you like to add a note to Billy's care package?"

Joe looks up again. "Isn't that, like, the fifth box you've sent?"

"I know. I'm falling behind." Last week's stomach bug ruined my plan to send them weekly.

"Getting care packages from 'Mommy' every week could be a little embarrassing." He eyes me over his coffee cup.

My mouth falls open. "Those boys love the goodies." My son and his roommate, Craig, live in a shoebox posing as a dorm room, eating mediocre cafeteria food. There's no way they don't look forward to my treats. "Just because he's growing up doesn't mean he doesn't appreciate reminders that he's loved. Everyone likes reassurances."

"Okey dokey." Joe shows no sign of picking up on my hint. Before returning his attention to the news, he says, "If we get home in time, maybe we'll hit a movie."

I nod. There's almost no risk of my impulse causing trouble in a theater since there's nothing in the lobby to take. "Sounds good."

On that note, I wander out of the kitchen and down the hallway to the base of the stairs, passing a wall of family photos. Some people have trophies. Others display diplomas and certificates. My family is my legacy. I've given my all to these two men, which might explain my growing sense of emptiness.

I've daydreamed about turning my refinishing hobby into a business. The before-and-after videos that so-called pros post on Instagram and TikTok confirm I'm as good as any. But working with clients, particularly if working in their homes, makes it too dicey.

Those boundaries became clear during my real estate broker days. When Billy was three, I swiped a drink coaster from an open house. It was a cheap-looking gold-beaded cloth with a mesmerizing royal-blue evil eye in its center. Unbeknownst to me, the set had been a gift from a deceased relative. The homeowners called my agency to complain about the missing one, assuming one of the potential buyers had stolen it. I managed to slip it back the next day, relocating it to a table in another room as if someone had simply misplaced it. Regrettably, it wasn't the first random item I'd taken from a client's home.

Horrified, I confessed to Joe, quit my job, and doubled down on therapy sessions for a couple of years with great success. Since then, I've arranged my life to minimize triggering and stressful situations. Until last year I'd lost control only a handful of times. Two handfuls, tops.

Upstairs, I hang my robe on its hook and thumb through my closet, which is neatly arranged by color and type. The bathroom sparkles and smells faintly of the Ocean Mist–scented candle set on the ledge of the tub. Peaceful. Pretty. Orderly. If only the rest of the world were as easy to manage.

I change into my favorite pair of dark jeans, a crisp white button-down shirt, and a leather-and-turquoise belt, then fasten my hair into a low twist. When it comes to makeup at my age, less is more. A swipe of pale pink lip gloss and a dash of mascara is enough. I choose silver hoops for my ears, take one last look, then return downstairs to the kitchen pantry, where the care package remains open.

It's stuffed with brownies baked fresh last night, jalapeño potato chips, Clif bars, a fresh pack of Billy's favorite mechanical pencils, and a card with a surprise check for fifty dollars. After taping and addressing the package, I pass Joe, who is still seated at the table.

"See you later." I plant a peck on his head and then grab my car keys from the tray in the small mudroom just off the kitchen.

"Mm," he grunts as I breeze through the back door.

While pulling out of the driveway, I crane my neck to look for movement next door. The ragtag group is taking a brief water break at the rear of their truck, laughing about something. The only sign of the new occupants is a bright blue MINI Cooper.

Hm. Not a family, then. Dashed hope deflates my lungs.

After mailing the package—where a postal worker named Vicky ribs me about my frequent visits—I swing through the grocery store to pick up a few things, including fresh-cut gerbera daisies. They have roses and lilies, but nothing beats the bright cheeriness of the gerberas. I also pick up a lovely mix of sunflowers, orange roses, and gold cushion poms for my new neighbors. They'll probably be too tired from the move to cook, so I grab a container of store-made butternut squash soup, which is as good as my own, and a rotisserie chicken. My gesture should make them feel welcomed.

The potential for change—a new friend—excites me. I jiggle my keys, revved and anxious, and hurry down the paper-goods aisle toward the checkout counter. Awareness of the crowd of shoppers in the line should keep me from slipping, but this brewing energy is a warning sign. The urge has struck more frequently since Billy left—a departure that brought about a swift and unceremonious end to my volunteer work at the high school and with the lacrosse board. An abundance of free time and the anxiety of worrying about his transition have increased the threat to my family's reputation and possibly to my freedom. For now, I shove my hands in my pockets to be safe.

By the time I return home, the U-Haul is gone. Joe is also out—probably on a run. Good news, actually.

I beeline to the living room, open the bottom drawer of the built-in cabinet, and kneel beside it to pick through the various items I've "collected" throughout the years. My secret stash.

Kleptomania—a label I hate to own, but there it is. A much ridiculed and misunderstood condition. My therapist once tried to offset my shame by explaining the difference between it and shoplifting. Shoplifters take something they don't want to pay for. Kleptomaniacs are compelled to filch things in their immediate vicinity that usually have little to no monetary value. The chance of having this rare impulse control disorder is greater if one's parent suffers from it or a closely related one. Not great news for Billy, but so far I haven't detected any hint of trouble in him.

Aside from the initial euphoria of giving in to the urge, I live with immediate remorse. Cognitive behavioral therapy and medication helped, but there's no cure. I was told it could lessen with age, but my recent behavior suggests that my earlier success was the result not of maturity but rather of my structuring a meticulously buttoned-up life.

Unfortunately, Joe believes I've been in complete control since I quit therapy a decade ago—a belief I've never corrected. It's bad enough that I winnow the scope of our lives. Why force him to live on pins and needles about slipups? Constant worry could drive him to bolt like my father did when he tired of my mother's crippling OCD.

It takes a second to find what I'm looking for—a squatty, square, orange-glass vase—wedged in the back of the drawer. My mother's, taken six years ago after a particularly unpleasant visit. Now it will be a gift instead of a reminder.

In the kitchen, I fill it with cold water and plant food, then snip the ends of the stems and arrange the flowers to their best advantage. I return to the kitchen pantry shelf that houses my wrapping papers and ribbons. Among the many varieties is a wide, yellow organza wire one that I fashion into a classic bow around the vase. Perfect.

Before I leave the house, it occurs to me that my neighbors will be busy unpacking. Not an ideal time to chat. I pull out a sheet of embossed stationery from the kitchen desk.

Welcome to the neighborhood! We hope these small gifts make your day a little easier. Looking forward to meeting you once you're settled.

Fondly,

Your next-door neighbors, Wendy and Joe Moore

After taping the note to the soup container and packing the food into a recyclable bag, I check my reflection in the microwave's glass door and then slip out the back with the goodies in hand.

It feels as if I'm floating across the yard as fantasies about whoever has moved in begin to spin. Maybe they'll be empty nesters like Joe and me, possibly from someplace interesting like Montreal or London. Maybe the wife will be into yoga or paddle tennis. Maybe they'll enjoy hanging out with us, and by this time next year we'll be true friends.

Smiling to myself, I trot up the porch stairs, prepared to hand over the goodies and allow them their space.

Resisting the desire to step inside the wide-open door, I ring the bell while a mild pang for Peg tightens my chest. We often sat here commiserating over childhood stories. I would seek advice about dealing with my mom, and she'd lament about her alcoholic father. We bonded in part through the scars and childhood embarrassment our sick parents caused us. Luckily, I've spared my son that fate. Ten seconds later, a young woman—thirty-five, tops—comes into the foyer. My pipe dreams scatter like dead leaves in the wind.

She's quite out of sorts. Her hair—a plain shade of brown that could use both highlights and lowlights—sticks out at all angles, doing nothing at all to complement her sparkling cornflower-blue eyes. Compactly built, she's dressed in ratty jean shorts and a snug black-and-white long-sleeved T-shirt that says THIS IS WHAT A FEMINIST

LOOKS LIKE. She tips her head to the left and flashes a winning, broad grin. "Hello there."

"Hi," I say dumbly, tearing my gaze from that shirt. "I'm Wendy, from next door." I gesture with my head while holding up the gifts. "I thought you might appreciate a little food and a welcome gift."

"Well, that's unexpected. Thanks." Her statement almost sounds like a question. She takes the gifts, then can't shake my hand because hers are full. "I'm Harper. It's nice to meet you."

"Same to you." A fly buzzes between us. "I know you're busy, so I won't keep you."

She sets the bag and bouquet on a table just inside the door and steps onto the porch, clasping her arms behind her and stretching. "I've got a minute."

"Oh." I'm not prepared for a conversation, but I smile. "So, are you on your own or do you have a, um, partner?"

She crosses her arms, her gaze trailing off. "On my own. Moved from the city."

People from Manhattan refer to it as "the" city, as if it's the only one on the planet.

"This'll certainly be a change of pace." Although only seventy-five minutes by direct train to Grand Central, New Canaan's the opposite of that bustling metropolis. I'm curious about her choice, but it'd be rude to question her so quickly. "We're a small but mighty community. If you'd like, I'll give you a list of the best doctors, dentists, and salons in the area."

"Is everyone here as helpful as you?" Her expression is as enigmatic as her tone.

I choose to treat her question as sincere. "Not always, but this is a friendly street. Peaceful too."

"Perfect." Harper lets her hands fall to her sides. "Thanks again for the thoughtful gifts."

"You're welcome." I pause, then add, "You should consider joining the Newcomers' Club. It's a great way to meet people in your situation—new to town, I mean."

It then occurs to me that she'll stick out in this family-oriented community, populated primarily by married folks with small children and older folks who've been here forever. Despite the multitude of restaurants and few bars uptown, there isn't much of a singles scene, especially if you exclude older divorcées.

"Maybe I will," she says, glancing over her shoulder through the open door. "I should probably get back to work now, Wendy. Have a good day."

"Same to you." I nod. "I look forward to getting to know you better."

Her expression is friendly as she waves goodbye, then she strides inside where I can't see her anymore.

When I return to my kitchen, Joe is there, glistening with sweat and gulping down water. "Saw you over at the Durbins'."

Why didn't he come introduce himself as well? "I took a little welcome gift to our new neighbor."

He sets the glass in the sink and wipes his forehead with the hem of his shirt. "Neighbor—singular?"

"Yes. A younger woman. Harper."

His expression reflects my same sort of surprised curiosity about that fact. "Let's hope she's quiet."

I snicker. It's such a Joe thing to seek the quiet. He can spend hours in his hammock or puttering around the garden humming to himself, content with whatever the day brings. "I guess we'll find out."

He busses me on the cheek. "Gonna go shower." Sadly, it's not an invitation. "Then we'll head to the lake."

Once he's gone, I dab his sweat from my face and think about Harper. She's not what I expected, but perhaps the unexpected is what's needed to shake off my doldrums. She looks like someone who'll need help to learn the ropes around here. Someone to perk up her style a little, too. Maybe even to play matchmaker.

I tap my finger to my lips, making a mental list of some of the single men in Joe's office.

Yes. By Christmas, Harper will be telling everyone that moving next door to us was the best decision she ever made.

CHAPTER TWO

HARPER

The same Saturday evening

I ladle some of the butternut squash soup Wendy brought me into a bowl and pop it in the microwave before checking my phone for the tenth time. There it is—the email from my agent that I've been waiting for and dreading in equal measure. Her notes on the third proposal I've sent her after my editor, Tessa, rejected the contracted manuscript I recently delivered. That massive blow came soon after my damn third book—*The Hypocritical Oath*—suffered a humbling release flop.

When Tessa rejected the follow-up manuscript, she "suggested" a new direction in my storytelling: *"Harper, you might not earn out the advance on your last book, so I can't risk accepting another story in that same vein."*

In other words, no more books about single millennials, even though my first two books sold more than a million copies and led to the fat advance for two more books. Sadly, my agent is now mimicking Tessa's flagging enthusiasm for my work.

I count to three before opening the email, then cower while reading it as if I'm watching a horror flick.

Harper,

I read your pages, and while there might be some elements here to play with, this synopsis lacks a high concept. "Empty nester" isn't enough. We need to come up with something unique, with more conflict, and possibly a quirky take on a socially relevant topic. But also something universal.

If you want to jump on the phone and brainstorm a bit, I'm happy to do that, but we need to get something to Tessa ASAP.

Regards-

Cassandra

Setting my phone aside, I bang my forehead against a cabinet like a baby having a tantrum, which is basically what I'm doing. If I don't pull my head out of my ass soon, my career is over. My editor has been more than patient, but my publisher won't indefinitely hold a publication date for me without an accepted proposal.

I can't retire at thirty-two, especially after blowing a good chunk of change on some fabulous trips and then sinking the rest and half of the next advance into buying my SoHo condo. Signing that deed before my thirtieth birthday validated every choice and sacrifice I'd made to get there. It has been the testament to my talent and ambition. To the fact that I competed and came out on top in a highly subjective and competitive industry despite my creative writing professor's dissing most of the female students' relationship-driven stories (including mine) as "unoriginal and uninspiring."

Or rather, it has been until recently.

Selling the condo now is a painful reality, but the humiliation of another potential failure would be worse. I can already envision my brothers' subtle wisecracks, the worry in my mother's voice, the "told you so" in my father's eyes, and the pity from my colleagues. And God spare me more crushing reviews.

"But I've got an idea," Tessa had said. *"One of the most vibrant reading markets is the forty-plus-year-old woman. Readers also remain fascinated by the secret lives of the affluent, from* The Great Gatsby *to* The Nanny Diaries *to* Little Fires Everywhere. *It might be beneficial if you spent some time in an affluent suburb—like a writing retreat slash research opportunity—and see if you can't come up with a fresh idea."*

While neither a command nor an ultimatum, *"It might be beneficial"* was something rather close. I couldn't say no when my agent didn't even protest. Neither of them knows of my general aversion to suburban culture, much less why I feel that way. I was in no position to argue, either. The failed book and rejected manuscript prove I'm a writer who no longer can write, after all.

Tessa gave me a five-month extension to complete a new novel.

That clock is ticking. Like a bomb.

A cool breeze carrying the moldering scent of dead leaves slips through the open window above the kitchen sink. That whiff sends me back to suburban Ohio circa 1995, where my friends and I ran through piles of crunchy leaves on fall evenings. It's one of my fonder memories of home, before I was old enough to resent the biased rules and expectations our parents imposed on me versus my brothers.

There could be unfortunate similarities between that time of my life and this reserved village. Not that my middle-class hometown teems with houses the size of small hotels or Ivy League parents competing to get their kids into the best boarding schools.

At least the tranquility here might help me focus. In SoHo, truck engines, Uber horns, police sirens, neighbors arguing overhead—as well as some bad memories—interfere with my concentration and sleep.

Conversely, it's quiet here tonight even with the windows open. Only the faintest hint of the Metro-North train whistle moans in the distance of this peaceful cul-de-sac. A place where my mind can stretch and wander and hopefully unlock the prison that's held my creativity captive for nearly two years.

The town's proximity to my agent and publisher in Manhattan also makes it a convenient choice. And though it's quite beautiful on the surface, it's been the setting of a few noteworthy scandals—the grisly Dulos murder, the cafeteria worker who stole half a million bucks, a CEO showing up on Page Six for an affair with squash coaches. Shit goes down in this town. The kind of trouble that could spark an intriguing plot bunny.

I reread my agent's note. "High concept"—technically it means a story with a clear, easily understood premise or hook. I hate the term, mostly because it's subjective. Half the time a ripped-off retread of an old TV show or movie suffices as high concept. That's not exactly original or authentic, but whatever. My bad attitude isn't helping.

The microwave beeps.

After moving two open boxes to clear a small table space, I take the bowl from the microwave, grab a spoon, and sit at the table. Soft notes of curry and brown sugar tempt me despite my lackluster appetite. I blow on a spoonful before swallowing. The complex flavor and warm, rich texture taste even better than its aroma, prompting a swell of gratitude. No one has pampered me in a long time.

My neighbor Wendy's starched shirt and blonde bob are straight off the *Stepford Wives* set—ironically, she might've been an extra in the remake of that movie, which was filmed here—but her kindness seems genuine. Under other circumstances, I might welcome the overture. But having been raised by a well-intentioned busybody, I recognize the signs of someone poised to micromanage my life.

I can't let her learn my identity when the entire point of coming here is for research. People won't let their guard down if they know what

I'm up to. There's also my landlord's warning to consider. What did he say when handing over the keys? *"It's a nice neighborhood, but you might want to steer clear of Wendy Moore. She's a few fries short of a Happy Meal."* He then twirled his finger near his head, making a "cuckoo" gesture.

"How so?" I'd asked.

"Wound tight, like she's hiding something. My ex mentioned that Wendy's mom has serious mental problems, and trust me, that apple didn't fall far from the tree."

I left his clichés at that, figuring he didn't know anything specific and merely gleaned his conclusion from their interactions over the years.

My text notification pings. I wince, hoping it isn't Cassandra again, then peek. Mandy—my cousin and closest friend—who now lives in Baltimore with her husband, Jeff, and their toddler, Becca, while juggling the roles of mother, wife, and preschool teacher.

Checking in. Hoping the move went well.

Rather than text back, I hit "Call" and turn on the speakerphone.

"Wow! To what do I owe the honor of an actual phone call?" Mandy, the perkiest optimist I know, seems years younger than me although we're the same age. We grew up one town apart and saw each other most weekends. Throughout the years, her sunny-side-up attitude has offset my cynicism, bringing me closer to what I imagine a normal person's outlook might be.

"Can't use my thumbs while I'm eating." I sip more soup, my thoughts still parsing Cassandra's dismissal of that last proposal.

"Should I call back later?"

"Only if you can't stand the slurping." I slurp extra loud in jest.

"Such a sophisticate." Always a joke with us. She was more genteel by fourteen than I've ever been. Following a brief pause, she asks, "So you and your things got there in one piece?"

18

I glance around at the dozens of boxes scattered across floors and tabletops. My only fragile valuables are an array of colorful handblown tea light–size votives my father has made for me for each birthday, which are wrapped in inches-thick air-bubble wrap. "My body's here . . . The brain is still catching up. As for my stuff, most cartons are still taped shut, but none look damaged."

The boxes depress me. I never wanted to sell the condo. I listed it out of fear that my next manuscript could get rejected, too. If that happens and I have to return the advance, it'll leave me totally strapped for cash. So it would've been stupid not to accept the full-price offer after setting a sky-high price. If all goes well, we'll close in fifty-two days.

"Excellent." Mandy pauses to say something to Becca before getting back on the line. "I hope this helps you bust through your writer's block."

She means well, but her words cause my shoulders to tense. No one was more shocked than I was by my last book's abysmal launch, which resulted in a titanic set of doubts and depression that apparently plagued me while writing the recently rejected manuscript. If I can't judge the quality of my work anymore, how do I go forward? "If not, I'm screwed."

"You know, being surrounded by what you went to New York to escape could help more than your career."

"Tell me you didn't give my parents my new address," I joke, scraping the last bit of soup from the bottom of the bowl.

Mandy never chafed against our patriarchal upbringing. Perhaps having only sisters made it less obvious that men get many advantages for no reason other than the fact of their penises. While sharing many of my views, she's managed to carve out a conventional lifestyle that doesn't make her feel oppressed. It helps that her husband shares the housework. He even joined the 2018 #metoo march in DC with her, though I suspect he wanted to "protect" her as much as he hoped to advance the cause.

"Ha ha. But seriously, what's your first impression of the town?"

"Jaywalking is probably the most common crime." Despite my sarcasm, I could leave my first-floor windows open all night in relative safety for the first time in a decade. Even I can't turn that into a negative. "Also, my neighbor is a buttinsky."

A gentle snicker comes through the line. "Why do you think that?"

"She brought me food and flowers before the moving van pulled away." A slight exaggeration, but it makes for a better story.

The blooms do brighten this old kitchen. Despite my landlord's opinion, I could've done worse—a handsy widower, or a family with noisy kids.

"That's so nice." Always a glass half-full with Mandy, whose sing-song voice is like a warm hug.

"It was nice." If a bit uncomfortable. I'm not looking for friends. Or, God forbid, a surrogate mother. One of those is enough. I'm an adult with no need of "good advice" from older women who don't understand my perspective. All I want from my neighbors is an insider's peek into what makes them tick, what scares them, and, most critically, what they hide. "To be honest, I got the feeling she was assessing me and plotting something."

"How so?"

Granted, the plotting part may be a reaction to George Durbin's commentary. "She was subtle, but she cataloged everything—my clothes, my hair . . . She even tried to peek around me to see inside the house."

"Aw, you're being silly. She's probably trying to start off on a good foot. Maybe she's a little lonely, too. Be nice. Who knows? She could be the key to your next great novel."

I laugh aloud because it is better than crying. Writers are champion-level eavesdroppers and observers—always stealing bits and pieces from people and places and storing them away for when they might be useful. But it's degrading to acknowledge that my *New York Times* bestselling writing career now hinges on whether my neighbor or other women here inspire a compelling narrative. And even if Wendy is hiding something, getting her to reveal that on my accelerated timeline could prove a challenge. Four months, three weeks, and five days . . . Shit.

"It's a blow to have sunk so low." Pride attempts to flare in denial, but it's been doused by scores of negative reviews on my last release, including a crucifixion in the *New York Times* and an offhand, biting sting by a *Good Morning America* host on a show where some of the "highly anticipated" releases were discussed.

A beat passes before Mandy replies.

"Instead of focusing solely on work, try making friends with people there. Reevaluating your preconceptions about marriage and suburbia could spark an idea." Mandy's ability to stake out neutral ground between opposing views is why she makes friends easily, and also why she still tries to fold me tighter into our family.

Still, my inner rebel braces. No doubt I'll meet folks who, like my parents, employ subtle and not-so-subtle methods of keeping unconventional people, particularly progressive women, in check. In no time, the resentment from being ostracized within my family—my mom's disapproval of the neon hair streak in ninth grade, my father's disappointment at my going on the pill in college despite having tossed condoms at my brothers in high school, my oldest brother's ridicule of my joining the vocal minority protesting the war in Iraq—burns. I stare ahead. As far as I'm concerned, there's not much to reevaluate, because I'll never stifle my beliefs just to make peace.

"I'm here to mine data for an idea, period. My next book is a make-or-break one for me."

Her silence—an acknowledgment of the truth of my claim—makes me wince. Then, with uncharacteristic derision, Mandy says, "I see Ellen Griffin's new book is making a big splash. I don't get it. Her voice is so flat."

Ellen and I met in a writing workshop before we were published. We enjoyed a friendly rapport and did some beta reading for each other in the early days. Cheered each other along on social media with other unpublished writers in the face of query rejections and the like. Once in a while we'd meet up at another workshop and share a meal. We landed different agents in the same year, and our debut novels came out with the same publishing imprint in the same year. Then my career took off like a shot while hers has enjoyed a slow but steady build, which initially introduced a different dynamic—me withholding so as not to sound like a braggart, her being somewhat deferential, which also made me uncomfortable. Now our roles have reversed.

"Lots of readers like her spare writing style. Her stories are compelling, too, and story always trumps prose." That's what I tell myself to feel better about the endless hours spent honing each sentence on each page of that turd that released in April to too many reviews like *One star: another among the many tiresome books of this ilk, featuring shitty, self-indulgent characters navigating even shittier relationships.*

Criticism is part of this job, but that book was personal. The story had been loosely based on elements of my own life, if somewhat distorted and distanced and featuring a younger protagonist: a twentysomething feminist in the city, striving for success amid corruption on Wall Street, navigating sexism and ethics in the workplace, and coping with disillusionment after discovering her lover's hypocrisy.

In contrast, Ellen's third book, which features a triad of suburban female friends, hit the *New York Times* list in July and has stuck there for thirteen weeks and counting. Yay for her. I let the soup spoon drop and give myself a mental shake. Ellen is perfectly nice and talented. We've helped each other throughout our careers and enjoyed laughs over drinks now and then. I do not hate her for her success. I will not let professional envy make me find fault with a fellow female author.

"Your stories are compelling, too," Mandy says, cheering me on with the same tone she employs when potty training Becca. Next thing I know, she'll be making me a sticker chart for motivation.

Talking about my stalled-out career has literally given me hives. I hate that my family might enjoy a touch of schadenfreude if I fall on my face again. *"I'm all for creative hobbies, but how will you support yourself? Get a real job like me, and then you can fiddle around with your stories on the side,"* my father had said when I compared my passion for writing to his glassblowing. Nothing would be more humbling than proving them right.

I push the empty bowl and spoon away. "Let's change the subject. What are you up to?"

A bored sigh. "Nothing much. Still having trouble getting pregnant. Last time was so easy—I don't get it." I picture her sitting alone on her steps, chin in one hand. Her wistful tone makes me want to hug her even though I can't relate to her desperation for another baby.

Children bring all the conventional trappings—a husband, a house, a 401(k), and a 529 plan. My ex, Calvin, and I enjoyed an unconstrained lifestyle and an open, provocative seven-years-long love affair. Of course, that didn't end so well for me. At thirty-two, my window for reconsidering having children is only starting to close, but I can't see myself as a mother. "I'm sorry, Mandy, but it'll happen. Maybe don't focus on it. Stay relaxed."

"Good advice for both of us, I suppose." Mandy pauses. "Well, I'll let you get back to unpacking."

"Give Jeff and Becca a kiss from me."

"I will. Take care."

"Thanks for checking in. Good night." I hit "End" and set the phone aside, tightening my short ponytail and blowing air through my mouth to make my lips flutter. *We need to come up with something unique, with more conflict and possibly a quirky take on a socially relevant topic. But also something universal.*

Ugh. Stop overthinking. Just be present. Take a breath, for shit's sake.

When I slip off the stool, the floor creaks beneath my feet. I shift my weight back and forth to re-create the squeak. That might drive some crazy, but the cozy quirk wrings a smile. It makes the home feel alive with the sort of company that won't distract me. My condo association didn't allow pets, but this rental does. I could get a cat or two or ten. Another heartbeat between these walls wouldn't be the worst idea.

I lug one of the heavier boxes—one filled with books—from the hallway into the living room, tear it open, and begin unpacking. For most of my life, storyland has exceeded reality, thus my hundreds of books. And while it might not be very authorly of me, mine are arranged by color rather than title, author name, or genre.

Like old friends, I greet each with a smile: Austen, Díaz, Ng, Atwood, Patchett, Moyes, Weiner, Picoult, Thorne, de Beauvoir, and many, many more. Every book opened my eyes to something new and took me far away from my parents' old-fashioned ideas and disparate rules for me and my brothers. The spines are cracked and worn from dozens of readings—some for pleasure, others to study what precisely it was in a book that moved me and how the author executed it so well.

Sometimes I miss my earliest reader days—the ones before I understood or worried about craft. Before comparisons cropped up like dandelions to hinder my ability to fall headlong into a story. Before envy of another's gorgeous prose made me doubt every word I typed, and impostor syndrome encased my imagination in ice. *One star: I got this book as a gift, but it felt more like a punishment. I repent. I repent!*

"Argh," I bark into the silence.

After arranging the books on the built-in shelves surrounding the brick fireplace, I turn off the overhead lights in favor of a single lamp and slump onto the sofa. The rest can wait.

Outside, the crickets and cicadas produce a rhythmic chorus. With my eyes closed, I take several deep breaths. Each one invites a new thought—about the scent of cardboard and dust that reminds me of my gram's old house, about what to expect from the coming weeks, about how the road that led me here began when Calvin and I parted ways.

I open my eyes but can still picture his face, though not as sharply these days. On the larger side with a bold nose, he had a masculine appeal. The kind of escort who made you feel safe in an alley in Chelsea after midnight. A Penguin Random House editor who loved poetry slams, cupcakes, and motorcycles, Calvin defied labels. For seven years we happily lived our take on the American dream—enjoying a grade A sex life and wide-ranging debates while giving each other plenty of space to pursue careers and hobbies and the occasional one-night stand with an attractive stranger.

It remained fiery and interesting because it wasn't bogged down by expectations or forced monogamy. Every minute spent together was a choice, not an obligation. A perfect arrangement that should've lasted forever because we didn't curtail or try to change each other. I was utterly and happily in love . . . until the day he told me he'd met someone.

At first I didn't get his meaning. But unlike prior one-offs—the infrequent hookups we'd each had the freedom to explore—this new someone had bewitched him in a way that surprised me. Surprised him, too, I suppose. Calvin grabbed his personal things from my place and walked out my door for the last time while I was in the middle of drafting that doomed "one star" book.

He gave up me *and* freedom for *her*. Talk about a double-whammy rejection. Here's the mortifying truth: for all my talk about being my own woman—a tried-and-true feminist who doesn't need a man or any of the trappings of marriage—losing Calvin—particularly losing him to another woman and a monogamous relationship—snapped me in half. Not that I shared my brokenheartedness with anyone but Mandy. I was questioning myself enough without giving other people fuel for gossip. Mostly I coped alone with bourbon and random Tinder booty calls.

As that book's deadline approached, it seemed that my rage, resentment, and a fair amount of self-doubt left me with only the worst words and most clichéd ideas. The result? A steaming pile of sarcasm and self-indulgence that even my brilliant editor couldn't save. For proof, refer back to the poor reviews and sales.

While I cringe at the thought of my peers' and publisher's opinions about my spectacular flameout, what's worse is wondering whether Calvin read the book, and what he thought of it. He didn't call or write—not even a sympathy card, which would've made me laugh because that kind of joke would've fit his sense of humor and made me feel better.

But letting him be any part of the reason my career peters out would be the final straw—the true death of who I think I am: an independent, untraditional woman of the world. I mean, really. Have I become my mother—someone who defines herself by her relationship to others: a wife, a mother, a volunteer—when I wasn't looking? Screw that. I won't let my lifestyle or career die, full stop. I've worked too hard and overcome too many obstacles to allow Calvin's rejection, Ellen's success, and my own missteps to knock me out.

I lever off the sofa and return to the kitchen to clean up from dinner, trying to shake off bad memories. While I'm loading the empty soup bowl into the dishwasher, Mandy's advice drifts back: Stay open. Let my neighbor in. Confront the past.

If my landlord is right, perhaps Wendy could be my muse. Secrets are perfect fodder for fictional characters, and if hers are juicy, it could give a midlife-crisis story a fresh twist. I suppose there's little to lose by cozying up to my nosy neighbor to forage for a secret or two.

CHAPTER THREE

WENDY

Tuesday morning

I turn down my street on my way home from Elise Landscapes & Nursery, thinking about Billy. He hasn't returned last night's text or the one I sent two hours ago asking if the care package had arrived. If I don't hear back by lunchtime, I'll text his roommate.

Pacified by that plan, I pull into my driveway, which is adjacent to the Durbins'—er, Harper's—yard. Our aster and helenium blooms sway in the breeze, offering a lively burst of autumn color on this overcast day. Perfection if you ignore the barren clay pots on the porch stairs, which I emptied of their withering begonias last week.

Rather than go to the detached garage behind the house, I park in the driveway and pop open the hatchback. Removing the mums requires a bit of oomph, but I line them up on the grass without toppling.

"Need help?" Harper calls out, startling me. I haven't seen her leave the house since she moved in.

I glance over the roof of my car. She's sitting on her porch with a cup of coffee and an iPad in hand. It's nearly ten thirty, yet she looks as if she's only recently gotten out of bed.

Nice of her to offer, though—an improvement over George. I'm glad she's friendly. Joe cautioned me not to overwhelm her, so I simply wave. "I'm fine, thanks."

I drag the buckets of flowers and bags of potting soil across the lawn to the porch, then climb into my car to pull it into the garage, where I grab my basket of gardening tools and gloves before returning to the front yard. Across the way, Harper lingers on her porch, feet up on the rail, sipping her coffee and reading. The last time I lazed outside with a beverage and relished a crisp autumn morning might've been with Peg.

Frowning, I tear open the potting soil. Perhaps my industriousness will inspire Harper to do something about the Durbins' neglected flower beds. A small goal is better than none, so I let hope rise.

Suddenly it strikes—that pesky wave of heat that starts at my feet and rises to my scalp, where it clings like the humidity in New Orleans for sixty seconds before receding. I fan myself with both hands, feeling ten years older thanks to menopause. Or perimenopause. Either way, it's another reminder that I'm continually losing pieces of myself: the chance of becoming a new mother dwindling at the same time mothering Billy is waning—not that I want an infant at this stage of life. That's not the point. Losing control over my own body is undignified. You'd think that, given I have to cope with a mental illness that affects every facet of my life, God might've at least spared me hot flashes.

I dab my forehead with the back of my arm.

"Are you hot?" Harper asks, having sneaked up on me. Her hair is tangled and bunched up on the left side. The stretched-out cardigan she's using like a robe sports a dollop of egg yolk. She doesn't appear to be wearing a bra, either. Boobs that large should always have support. Did she grow up without a mother?

I raise my gaze to meet hers, covering the truth: "It's just the exertion."

"Pretty colors." Harper surveys my gold-and-plum bounty, then adds with some humor, "You obviously enjoy gardening a lot more than Mr. Durbin did."

"Mm. George didn't much care for maintenance of any kind. Too bad, too. His house would be much cuter with a little TLC." I wrinkle my nose, thinking of the pride Peg took in keeping the house up. Gardening was a pastime we shared, often trading tips and tidbits about nursery sales and such. But maybe Harper has an interest in her yard. I couldn't have planned this any better. Still, Joe's warning repeats in my head, urging restraint—something I've never been good at.

"Did you know George well?" She cocks her head, watching me intently.

"I was very close with his wife—his ex-wife—Peg. I also used to watch their daughter, Judy, sometimes, too, when their after-school sitter canceled or Judy had to stay home sick. Peg and I hung out a lot. She enjoyed the company since George wasn't chatty."

Harper folds her arms under her bountiful chest. "Sounds like you miss her."

"I do." I fall silent, remembering waving from my porch as Peg's Touareg pulled out of the driveway for the last time, condemning me to a lonelier life. I went through half a box of tissues that morning. After a mental shake, I beam at Harper, who seems engaging. "But now you're here. And I happen to know that Weed & Duryea is running a sale on plants this week. For less than a hundred bucks and a few hours' effort, you could transform those front beds."

She screws up her face, which makes her look even younger. "I know squat about gardening. A perk of city living."

I wave that excuse away, determined to persuade her. Even Joe would agree that those beds need to be addressed. "I'm happy to help. In fact, we could start now. I'll take care of my pots later."

Her eyes widen as she sputters, "Don't I need the flowers first?"

"We'll weed the beds and prune the shrubs." The yolk stain catches my eye again. "After you get yourself dressed, you can pick up mums or whatever plants you like. I'll help you get them in the ground tomorrow."

"Yes, ma'am." Harper mock salutes me, which makes my cheeks flush worse than that hot flash did. I don't mean to be commanding. Controlling my environment while keeping in motion helps me manage my not-so-little problem. Not that I can explain that. I must have stiffened, because she says, "Just kidding. I'd love the help if you don't mind."

Mind? I'd pay her to let me at those unkempt beds. "Terrific."

With my arm threaded through the gardening basket handle, I abandon my yard to follow Harper to hers with a decided spring in my step.

Making a new friend who has nothing to do with the schools and my son makes me want to skip around. Perhaps we'll pick up where Peg left off, with Harper sharing her work stories and giving me a peek into a world I left behind. A younger friend might also be exactly the boost I need at this point in my life. A clean slate with someone who doesn't appear to be judgmental, either.

Up close, George's flower beds look even worse, overrun with crabgrass, thistle, and wood sorrel. I scrape one branch of a rhododendron, looking for green flesh beneath.

"Would you rather prune or weed?" I ask.

"I'm only qualified to yank stuff out of the ground."

"Be careful with that thistle." I hand her the gloves and garden fork from my basket. "This will help you dig out stubborn roots, and these will protect your hands from the prickers and dirt. Let me get my wheelbarrow and some lawn bags so cleanup is easy. Be right back."

I trot back to my garage, buzzing with energy. My wish is coming true, and I didn't even have to push my way in. Not much, anyway.

When I return, Harper's sitting cross-legged on the ground, scrolling through her phone, still in that filthy sweater. Not that I'm well dressed, but my gardening joggers and shirt are clean, and my hair is combed. Her slovenliness might be some kind of statement—a middle finger to basic expectations or something. If so, I don't get it. Taking a hot shower first thing each day is like giving myself the gift of a clean start.

"Whoa!" She eyes my green-and-red wheelbarrow. "You mean business."

Well, yes. I do. If you plan to do something, do it right, especially if you have only one shot. With so many matters beyond one's control, why not master what you can? I smile rather than defend myself.

"We'll throw all the weeds and cuttings in here so it's easy to bag everything at the end." I pull out the pruning shears and begin to shape an old rhododendron, cutting away at the dead branches. Plants bring such cheer to any yard. My favorites are those that thrive in shade, like foxglove. They offer hope that people like me who live partly in the shadows can still experience the beauty of life. "Your yard will look a thousand times better even before you plant anything colorful."

"Where'd you learn to garden?" Harper asks, limply digging out a weed and holding it by the tip as if it might bite her. If she doesn't do a better job, they'll grow right back. She doesn't strike me as someone who will keep after these beds.

"My mother loved flowers but couldn't do the work, so she hired a neighbor to keep our yard pristine. Mrs. Higgins taught me what she knew until I could take over."

My mom. A woman stuck in an endless mental war and who lives as if the world will crash upon her if she relaxes her vigilance. One whose acute germophobia dictated every facet of our lives. It was easier to avoid all her triggers than to deal with stressing her out. Her behavior—whether doing the same load of laundry six times, making us wash our hands and doorknobs and any other things we touched when entering the house, or her crying jags from the agony of obsessive thoughts—drove my father so far away I rarely saw him after my fourteenth birthday.

"Are you close?" Harper eyes me keenly while tossing another weed into the wheelbarrow.

I avert my gaze. "Yes, but she lives in Rhode Island, so I don't see her that often." True enough. I love her, yet each visit is a painful exercise in patience. I hardly lack empathy for the anxiety caused by life with an impulse control disorder, but her continued suffering is a constant reminder that mine will never go away. For years, I've made excuses—Billy's games, committee work, Joe's needs—to put off visits. Most of those obligations have now ended, leaving me plenty of free time, a fact that drives home how isolated she's always been. I sigh. "We speak three times a week."

Mondays, Thursdays, and Saturdays, 9:40 a.m. sharp—the way she requires. That timing allows her to perform her many morning rituals intended to ward off danger for the day before we catch up.

"Wow. Now I feel bad." Despite Harper's words, her expression is hardly that of a person saddled with guilt.

I snip another dead branch, deceptively nonchalant despite raging curiosity. "Why?"

"My mom and I speak only when necessary." Harper frowns, digging the next weed with new intensity, like she didn't mean to make that confession.

Several questions cross my mind when she doesn't elaborate, but I take the hint and drop it for now.

"Mother-daughter relationships can be tricky. Luckily, I've got a son." I smile at the mental picture of Billy's face. A perfect blend of Joe and me, with Joe's darker hair and my square jaw and sharp cheekbones. It's then that I remember he still hasn't returned my texts.

"Oh?" Harper finally looks at me, this time with some surprise. "I haven't seen him around."

"He's at college. *Colgate.*" I'm probably beaming.

"Good school." She doesn't gush or congratulate him or me like other neighbors and acquaintances usually do.

Not everyone cares as much about these things, yet I can't deny my pride. Although naturally bright, Billy worked hard to earn his spot there, excelling despite a rigorous curriculum. Sure, anxieties would flare before big tests or games, especially during his junior year. I watched for signs of my mother's or my issues, and did everything possible to ease the pressure—fixing his favorite meals, keeping track of his schedule on Schoology, managing his extracurriculars. Fortunately, it all worked out as we hoped.

"I miss him so much. It's been an adjustment." I snap off another branch, missing being needed. This subject might be boring for a single woman who can't relate to a mother's dilemma. "Of course, now Joe and I have free time for other things."

What "other things" won't pose a challenge for me is unclear, but I've never been a quitter. We'll figure it out eventually. From the night we met at a mutual friend's party twenty-two years ago, Joe has been on my side. We've built a good life and family. Far better than I expected given my condition and my parents' divorce. That's what matters most. This current sense of being at loose ends will fade soon enough, I'm sure.

Harper waggles her brows. "A second honeymoon, perhaps."

Her saucy gaze strikes like a bucking horse, making me cough. I gather myself, hoping I'm not blushing. Imagine if anyone learned the truth about my current sex life.

"Mm" is all I can manage. A nonanswer, but not a lie. Single women probably still talk about sex often, but the topic makes me want to change the subject. "So, did you go to college?"

She nods, scooching over to another patch of weeds, and resumes her work. "Oberlin, in Ohio."

"Oh, yes. A very fine school." One with a strong liberal rep. Must be where she ditched her bras. "Are you from the Midwest?"

"Small town in the Buckeye State. Now you know why I escaped to New York." She snickers.

Lots of people dream of big-city life. I prefer visiting cities to living in them. But her statement is strange given her current address. "Yet here you are in our little village."

"Touché." She shakes her head as if even she can't believe it.

Time to pry a little. "What took you to New York in the first place?"

She rakes the dirt without intention, like a child playing at working. "A need to flee double standards, not that anyone back there would admit to them."

"You think those don't exist in Manhattan?" I raise a brow.

"It's less tolerated. At home everyone preached the same tired ideals. Boys were pushed into STEM careers and assertiveness while girls were steered toward teaching and expected to be accommodating. Even my own parents saved more money for my brothers' educations than mine because—and I quote—'the boys need to work forever, but someday you'll get married and raise kids.'" She seems finished with her rant, then adds, "Meanwhile, they then criticized working mothers who didn't help the PTA, saying nothing about men's long work hours, weekend golf outings, and lack of help around the house. Worst of all were the patronizing remarks like 'settle down' or 'don't get riled up' or 'you'll understand someday' whenever I'd point this stuff out. I understood perfectly well, though." Her voice takes on a haughty edge. "Hey, boomer, the twenty-first century is calling!"

So her T-shirt from the other day is a commitment, not just a fashion choice. Her reddened cheeks and split focus suggest there's more to the story, but I've got enough of the picture for now.

As an only child, I didn't face that double standard at home, and the real estate brokerage firm employed mostly women. Not that I examined gender roles too closely. I was too busy learning to clean to my mother's exacting standards and seeking quiet places at home to study or relax that wouldn't aggravate her condition. Too troubled by my parents' arguments. Too hurt by my dad's abandonment and lonely from being forbidden to invite friends over because of spreading germs. And in my later teens and twenties, too preoccupied with my own burgeoning problem to care much about societal matters well beyond my control.

"Did I offend you, Wendy?" Harper asks, interrupting my train of thought.

"Not at all. I'm just considering your perspective." I flush when caught daydreaming. "I can see how that was a real problem, especially for career-minded women. Of course, girls around here study STEM, so things are changing. But I'm not one to force my politics on other parents or people. Everyone will eventually choose their own path."

Harper crinkles her nose as if she's not quite sure she believes me.

"You disagree?" I ask.

"I think it's easy for someone like you to be blasé, but not everyone shares the same options and opportunities."

Someone like me? As if she knows anything about my life and how it shaped my options. The lack of parental guidance and support didn't open any doors. My mother was too mired in her own illness to get me help for mine, even though I got caught stealing twice as a minor. My life got easier only after I graduated from college and met Joe. I'd floated home from that party on a cloud of hope for something better than I'd ever known. Once we married, my primary goal was to build a stronger family than the one I'd been born into—so I embraced the housework and childcare and threw myself into therapy and volunteer work. If my gender limited me, I didn't notice or care. I set my course, and I've been happier than someone with my history has dared to dream.

"Maybe not, but I doubt a simple change of geography solves everything." I believed it when I was younger, though.

When we moved to New Canaan, I assumed distance from my mother would magically improve my life. I even briefly thought it would resolve my illness and lessen the pain around my childhood disappointments. Distance provided some buffer, but my mother's affliction still affects my life, and my own is a constant shadow over everything.

"I had more freedom in New York than I ever did in Ohio," Harper says.

"Isn't that freedom largely a state of mind? There are probably as many women who feel trapped in New York as anywhere else. But anyway, why'd you leave if that's how you feel?" I purposely keep my gaze on the shrub I'm pruning after putting her on the spot.

Harper's voice is unnaturally even. "Sometimes shit happens that makes a big change the only way to move forward."

Ah. Suffering a major disruption is something I understand and can help her with if she'll let me. "Do you still work there? Let me guess, a lawyer for the ACLU." I raise my index finger.

"No." Harper digs at another patch of weeds, waiting a few beats before she replies. "I'm between jobs at the moment."

Being alone in one's thirties, out of work, and looking down an uncertain road is certainly free, but hardly sounds ideal. In fact, it sounds terrifying. Yet she doesn't look worried. Maybe she has family money or a divorce settlement? At this point, another change of topic seems in order—something light and fun. "What about romance? Any love interest in your life?"

"Love interest?" She chuckles, which instantly puts our age difference front and center. Of course, I also chose that term because I've no idea if she prefers men, women, both, or neither. "Guess I'm in between men at the moment, too."

Men. Okay, although her caustic tone suggests a bad breakup—perhaps the "shit" that drove her here. Lucky for her I'm a consummate matchmaker. Volunteering often provided an ideal position not only to meet a lot of single parents but also to observe their personalities. The secret to my success has been pairing opposites who possess complementary traits. I'm three for three so far, perhaps soon to be four for four.

"Well, I know tons of people around here. What kind of guy do you like? A cinnamon roll, an alpha . . ." I narrow my eyes, wagging a finger. "Or do you go for the bad boys and rebels?"

She fixes an impish smile in place. "Are you reading romance novels, Wendy?"

That she recognizes the lingo tells me that she reads them, too, so I don't bother defending myself like I must with the women in my book club. Who can't appreciate a good love story, especially lately, when my real life has lost a certain kind of titillation? "Sometimes. I love the hopeful themes, don't you?"

Her dubious expression answers before she does. "The messaging's not very realistic."

My goodness, the messaging is the best part. I stop cutting and stare at her. "Which part? Love? Hope?"

"The whole redemptive power of love—like love cures all problems." Her eye roll is unnecessary because the sarcastic tone did the job on its own. "It's just more brainwashing to keep women fantasizing about how they'll only be truly happy when they find the right partner."

I move on to the third shrub, affronted although I can't say why. It's not like I write those novels. But her dismissive attitude about them—about love and hope—nettles. If I didn't believe in those things, I'd never leave the house.

What would make a young woman that cynical? And then it hits me. "I see."

"What do you think you see?" Despite hands full of weeds, she's eyeing me intently.

She seems to appreciate frankness, so I blurt my thoughts. "People get jaded when they get hurt, so I'm guessing someone really hurt you.

But love—real love and acceptance—*is* redemptive." I know this thanks to Joe, whose devotion made me feel valued and beautiful for the first time in my life. Whose acceptance of my demon motivates me to control it—mostly, anyway. "You get more than you give up, too. When you meet the right person, you'll see."

"Now you sound like my mom, but trust me, Disney-style love stories aren't for me. I like orgasms, but no man or marriage will make my life whole. That's up to me. Besides, there aren't many men looking for a strong, unapologetically opinionated woman."

I continue pruning while some of her attitudes settle uncomfortably around my thoughts. She's not entirely wrong. People should find happiness within, and no one should forgo his or her values for another. But you can't have a genuine relationship with another human being without giving up some bit of autonomy and freedom. Compromise is the glue that keeps *all* relationships going.

"Are you perturbed by my views?" Harper asks, crawling forward to reach for weeds between a shrub and the porch.

Talk about assumptions.

"Nope. It's your life. I just disagree with broad statements—like an entire institution isn't for you. How do you know if you've never given it a chance?" I shrug, clipping another branch. "Call me provincial, but I like being part of things bigger than myself—part of a couple, a family, a community."

Harper swallows, saying nothing as she gazes out to the street. At that moment, my phone rings, so I peek at the screen. "Excuse me. It's my son."

She nods, waving for me to answer.

"Hi, honey. Did you get the latest care package?" I turn away from Harper and cover my free ear with my palm to better hear him.

"I got a D on my lit paper," he grouses without answering my question.

"A D?" I repeat aloud without thinking, then more quietly ask, "What happened?"

"The professor screwed me, Mom. He's totally unreasonable."

I flinch at his tone and word choice. Sadly, this isn't the first time Billy's butted up against difficult teachers, either. Throughout high school we had to run interference with a few of them—those on power trips or with inflexible rules that seemed more focused on punishment than on learning. In any case, being needed again feels good. "In what way?"

"He docked it two grades because I turned it in one day late, and he won't let me do anything for extra credit."

"Why'd you turn it in late?" Has he been sick, and if so, why didn't I know? Illness should be grounds for an extension.

"I put it on my calendar wrong. It was an honest mistake, so I don't know why he's being so cold."

Oh. Not sick. An honest mistake. "Let me talk to your father to see if we can help. In the meantime, double-check your calendar of due dates against the syllabus so this doesn't happen again." Remembering that I have an audience, I say, "Honey, I'm not at home now, so I'll call you later, hopefully with a solution."

"Fine. Bye." He hangs up without a thank-you for either my offer of help or the care package.

I stare at the phone, wondering if he'll lose all his manners while living away from home. After I tuck it back into my pocket, I mumble, "Sorry about that."

"No worries." Harper throws the last of the weeds in the wheelbarrow and removes her gloves, returning them to the basket. "I couldn't help but overhear. It's not my business, but he won't learn from his fuckup if you step in."

I clench my jaw. Today is not the day for parenting advice from an unmarried, childless feminist who hardly speaks to her own mother. In fact, no day will be that day. With a tight smile, I toss the final dead branch into the wheelbarrow and return my shears to the basket.

"Thanks for the advice, but Joe and I have gotten Billy this far, so I think we can handle him ourselves." I grip the wheelbarrow, biting back a remark about how she should focus on getting herself a job or at least putting on a bra. Sarcasm is my go-to defense when I'm upset or feeling judged, not that I often let it out. "Now that we've finished clearing these, you probably want to shower and get about your day. Hope you're happier with your beds now." I know I am.

With a sharp nod and forced smile, I begin to wheel away.

"Sorry if I offended you, Wendy," Harper says to my back.

Waving one hand overhead, I make sure my voice doesn't wobble. "It's fine, Harper. Let me know if you want help planting new flowers."

I keep moving forward without looking back—the best way to do most things, I've found. Her apology is appreciated, but the reproach lingers. Almost everything she said today felt like a jab at some part of my life. Worse, she made it sound like women like me are too obtuse to know if we're truly happy or not. Whatever my problems, I'm more content than she seems to be.

After setting the wheelbarrow at the base of the porch steps, I slip inside to collect myself. Joe is at work, so he can't talk me out of this tailspin.

I kneel beside my drawer of shame and paw through some of the items: the single black chopstick I swiped during Miné Oka's neighborhood party six years ago, when my mother was in the hospital for colon cancer surgery; the pocket-size metal spray bottle of freesia-scented air freshener I took from Tish Barrett's powder room during the high school graduation party she threw this past summer, at which everyone was talking about life without the kids. In both cases, CBT training failed me. It's why I keep most people at arm's length and prefer to invite them here rather than go elsewhere.

Revisiting these items is dangerous, yet I can't bring myself to throw them away. Luckily Joe never opens a cabinet, preferring to rely on me to locate everything he needs. I slam the drawer shut and pace the room, feeling worse than when I first came inside.

I collapse on the sofa and take some deep breaths, forcing myself to picture Harper's smiling face when she'd come over to compliment my garden. She'd seemed genuinely friendly, so I doubt she meant to hurt my feelings. She thought she was being helpful. Differences of opinion can make life more interesting, I suppose.

On that note, I return to my front yard to plant my new mums. Harper is no longer on the porch. A bittersweet twinge passes through me, but her absence allows me to relax. While I transfer my perky little flowers to clay pots, a light drizzle begins to fall. Perfect weather for my lingering pessimism.

I cast a wary gaze toward Harper's house, curious about what she's doing in there. She seems too different from me to think we could become real friends, yet that attitude reeks of failure. A little space is best today, but I'll be cordial the next time we cross paths.

———

Joe walks through the back door and hangs his overcoat in the cubby before coming into the kitchen. He gives me a kiss on the cheek while loosening his tie. "Smells delicious, and your flowerpots look perfect, hon."

"Thank you." My husband's keen observations make me feel seen and appreciated. Another way in which I'm luckier than women who complain that their husbands never notice anything. "Why don't you clean up while I put dinner on the table?"

He goes to the sink to wash his hands while I plate garlic butter–baked salmon, rice, and seared zucchini.

"Wine?" I ask, biding time before sharing the bad news about Billy's grade.

Joe shakes his head and grabs two water glasses, filling them from the pitcher of filtered water. After he sits, he heaves a satisfied sigh and smiles at me as he picks up his knife and fork. "So, how was your day?"

Leading with pleasantries, I recount addressing George Durbin's neglected beds and the crumbs of additional personal information I learned about Harper, confirming her single status. He listens while eating his dinner.

When I fall silent, he says, "We had a day at the office. Software snafu—"

"Is Nate Johnson still single?" I interrupt.

Nate is in his thirties and works for Joe. We've talked at work-related holiday parties and sometimes when I swing by Joe's office on an errand. He's a handsome man with a good sense of style and humor. His conventional bent and even-tempered nature are exactly the opposites-attract things that might click for him and Harper. It's also my favorite romance trope, so there's that.

"Far as I know. Why? Are you aiming to meddle in his private life?" He's wincing.

"'Meddling' sounds ugly. Matchmaking is a kindness." Ask Allison Westover from the lacrosse board, whom I introduced to Art Walker last year after her divorce. He's sure to propose any week now, and she won't even need to toss her monogrammed glassware. Besides, I wouldn't be obvious with Nate and Wendy. It's a simple matter of inviting them both to a small cocktail party and letting nature do the rest.

I'll check availability with a few folks later—maybe the Wheelers and the Varmas, who get along well. I met the wives through school activities. Last winter they invited me to join their book club. Going from acquaintances to social friends was a welcome, if slightly scary, step. I hesitated to join, but we mostly meet on weekday mornings at Rosie's Café. I'm always careful to bring my smallest purse and wear clothes with no pockets to make it almost impossible to take something. Since joining that book group, we've enjoyed dinner a few times as couples, too. I clasped my hands on my lap throughout much of those meals, but I'll be safe in my own home.

"As long as you don't ask me to play go-between." He shakes his head in surrender.

With that subject closed, I turn to the bad news. "I hate to ruin dinner, but Billy called with a problem."

He pauses, his face tightening with mild concern. "What's happened?"

I relate my earlier conversation with Billy. "I'm at a loss. How can we help?"

"We can't." He shrugs, cutting into his salmon again. "Hopefully he'll learn from this."

"Joe." I set my palms on the table, tension wrenching all my muscles. "He's really upset, and a D makes it nearly impossible to get an A for the semester."

"Probably." Joe nods nonchalantly, scooping a spoonful of rice.

I scowl. "I can't believe you aren't more upset or helping me come up with a solution."

"I'm not surprised this happened, Wendy." Frustration creeps into his tone. "He'll never become a man who can manage his own life if we keep fixing his mistakes."

"Are you blaming me?" It's like Harper all over again, except worse because it's Joe criticizing me. My stomach threatens to upchuck everything I've eaten.

"It's not about blame, but you've hardly ever listened to my opinions." He takes another bite of dinner, unaware of how spousal grousing twists me up thanks to reminders of my father's attitude before he left.

"That's not true." I always discuss Billy with Joe.

He pauses eating, holding his knife and fork upright on the table. "Anytime I made a suggestion, you'd cite this child study or that one until I'd give up. Honestly, I would've pulled back a couple years ago and let him sink or swim."

My hands become fists. I only step in to support Billy. Loving guidance helps kids navigate the world. My life would've been a lot happier if either of my parents had taken more interest in me. "If you felt so strongly, why didn't you try harder to persuade me then, rather than sit back and make me the scapegoat?"

"I just told you why. But now that he's at college, it seems like a good time for a change."

Fighting about the past won't resolve anything. "You're really not going to help?"

"No. And I hope you don't, either." Joe gives me a stern look. An expression so rare I should stand down in the face of it.

And yet I can't. "If the D ruins his GPA, it'll affect his internship options this summer, and possibly even his graduate school applications down the road."

"But he'll never turn in another late paper. Managing the professor only teaches Billy that he can talk his way in or out of anything, which isn't the way the world works. And imagine how little respect the teacher would have for Billy if we jump in." Joe pats my hand, wearing a sympathetic smile. "Your heart is in the right place, but it's time to let go."

My entire body prickles. "We worked so hard to help get him into a good school, and now you want to wipe our hands clean?"

"*We* shouldn't be working hard to get him anywhere. He needs to do that on his own so he learns what he's made of. When we rush in, we're basically reinforcing that he can't do it on his own."

I sit stiffly, rooted in my chair while blinking repeatedly.

"Honey, I know how close you two are and how much pride you took in raising him. His turning to you probably feels good, but I don't think what you need is what's best for him at this point. We have to trust him so he can trust himself."

Joe's words burn like ropes strapping me to a chair while I'm made to watch my kid suffer. "Well, then, you be the one to tell him he's on his own."

"Happy to," he says before eating the last bite of food on his plate. Apparently, his stomach is not awash in acid like mine. "I'll load the dishwasher."

"No, let me," I huff, needing to keep busy.

Joe rises, gently massaging my shoulders. "Okay. I'm going to change into something more comfortable."

Nothing in his tone carries a hint of flirtation or teasing, so I know what we won't be doing next. Not that I'm in the mood now anyway. I gather the dishes and rinse them in the sink, staring out the window into the backyard at the steady rain, feeling my world getting smaller and colder by the minute.

My head is pounding.

Then Harper's back porch light flicks on. I turn off the faucet and watch as she—still in that same dirty sweater—walks out into the yard, spreads her arms, raises her face, and turns in a circle.

What in the world?

She stops and glances over at my house, so I duck out of sight, my pulse rising. It's not like I meant to spy. I'm doing dishes and she's right there in the open, acting like a fool.

This whole day has run off the rails. A normal person might go to a mall to window-shop to blow off steam, but that's a big risk for someone with my affliction.

I think of my mother sitting alone in Rhode Island. Will that eventually be my fate, too? I shiver as if I'm the one outside dancing in the rain.

CHAPTER FOUR

Harper

Wednesday

The village of New Canaan is as quaint as any New England town I could conjure. Rock walls and white picket fences adorn the yards along South Avenue, the main thoroughfare lined with large colonial homes that leads to the heart of the town. Once there, you're greeted by herringbone brick sidewalks that boast lampposts with hanging flower baskets, and meticulous storefronts and restaurants, each with overflowing planters to beckon you inside. Adjacent to the business district sits God's Acre—a triangular, grassy plot of land adjacent to the Congregational church and flanked by two others, where many New Canaan settlers are believed to be buried.

The town's sidewalks remain litter-free, save the rare smear of old bubble gum. Baby strollers, not homeless people, huddle in the shopping district's corners. Citizens smile at each other, and many seem to know each other, too. Every cliché about this place appears to be true, from the fit yoga pants–wearing yummy mummies to the Vineyard Vines–attired prepsters. I, with my ringless left hand, my lack of classic hairstyle, and my SATAN MADE ME DO IT T-shirt, am an alien.

An outsider. An oddity.

Of course, all this impeccable beauty could still hide ugly things, like the whole mess that happened in my hometown with my friend Linda, who was sexually assaulted at a high school party by my oldest brother Rick's friend Kevin, then victimized again by a community bent on blaming her clothes, her drinking, and whatever else they thought mitigated Kevin's responsibility. Society has finally begun to see those arguments for the bullshit they are, but I bet there are some parents here who, like my own, default to victim shaming. I shudder at the memory of those dinner conversations.

Reminding myself that I'm here to research, I snap a few photos and dictate my observations before fixing a smile on my face and heading into Elm Street Books, a proper independent bookstore. Given this town's family demographics, the large children's literature department at the rear of the store is no surprise. Naturally, the bestsellers shelves are in the front of the store. Striking cover art calls to me, as does the smell of all the paper. While I enjoy the practicality of adjusting font sizes on an e-reader, nothing beats holding a real book.

Of course, this excursion is not without risks. The first blow to my ego strikes from the window display of Ellen's latest book, *Same New Story*. Its cover—a vivid turquoise field splattered with thick pastel brushstrokes and finished off with a fat handwritten-styled font—sets it apart. A "staff pick" card is also taped to the display. My breathing shifts uncomfortably as my ribs seem to tighten around my lungs. Words like "charming," "terrifically blunt," and "poignant" leap off the notecard, stirring my worst insecurities.

"Are you interested in this one?" A disembodied voice cuts through the high-pitched ringing in my ears.

I swivel to find a pleasant-looking woman with red-rimmed glasses staring at me expectantly. "Oh, no. I was just browsing." As I step back, the wood floor beneath me creaks accusatorily. I should support my friend and buy her book, even if I never read it. I absolutely will. Just not when my own wounds are still gaping and sore.

"Well, if you're in the mood for a fresh take on a fish-out-of-water story, it's quite a fun read." She smiles, then her eyes narrow before her expression bursts into a knowing smile. She touches my forearm. "Ohmigod, are you H. E. Ross?"

Shit on a shingle. I hunch a bit and quietly reply, "I'd rather not call attention to myself."

"This is so exciting. I'm Anne, by the way." She extends her hand, oblivious to my body language. She hasn't even lowered her voice. "I adored *If You Say So.*"

My debut and personal favorite. A coming-of-age tale that, in retrospect, was loosely based on my earliest days in Manhattan—an era of excitement and hope. Everyone adored that book, including Ellen. Mine was the "sparkling new voice" then. Funny how all that praise got buried by recent criticism. I shake her hand. "Thank you very much, Anne."

"What are you doing in town? I don't recall seeing you on the library events calendar."

"Oh, no, I'm not here for an event. Actually, I'm here working on a new project, so I'm keeping a low profile."

"Exciting." Her intrigued expression softens as she gestures around the shelves with both hands. "Welcome to our store. Is there something I can help you find?"

"Yes, actually. I'm looking for informal handbooks for college students. You know, the sort of 'college hacks' self-help books that make a nice gift." I walk deeper into the store before the uranium effect Ellen's book has on my psyche may turn me into a Hulk-like beast that topples the display.

Anne waves for me to follow her. "Come this way."

She leads me to an aisle with everything from SAT prep guides to the types of materials I asked about. Before leaving me alone, she points to one. "This one is fairly popular."

"Thank you." I pull *The Freshman Survival Guide* off the shelf and read the back-cover copy before thumbing through it and skimming some passages. This could help get me back into Wendy's good graces. Whether she'll be a gold mine of material for the antagonist in my next book is uncertain, but she can definitely introduce me to other women in town. More important, her obvious hurt when she took my suggestion as criticism made me feel . . . shitty. Despite her can-do spirit and her comfort with verbal sparring (a pleasant surprise), there's something fragile about her. The reason for that frailty is what most interests me as a writer, but as a regular human being, I also want to apologize and smooth her ruffled feathers.

Satisfied with the college-hack recommendation, I wander into the adult self-help section and find another book, *Empty Nest, Full Life*, but decide Wendy would view that as more criticism. I don't know her well enough to judge how she manages her life, but my fondness for self-help books knows no bounds.

Wendy is probably fifteen years my senior, and my own mother is about an equal number of years older than my neighbor. There might be something important about that symmetry, although I can't put my finger on what that could be.

I push the empty-nester book back into place.

On my way to the register, my inner masochist steers me toward the general fiction shelves—organized alphabetically by surname, of course. My gaze skims the books: Redfern, Rice, Riordan, Robb, Ross. One lone unloved copy of *The Hypocritical Oath* by H. E. Ross—Harper Elizabeth Ross to those who know me—is here. I chose the androgynous pen name to minimize any gender bias of my publisher and readers. My latest release sits spine—not cover—facing out. No "staff pick" or even review card touting its brilliance. Its "freshness."

I pull my book from the shelf. In my mind, spotlights flood the aisle and the entire staff snickers from a polite distance. My peripheral vision narrows as I reread the copy, hoping the reason it didn't help sell the story will become apparent this time. Perspiration oozes from every pore.

Another patron comes into the aisle, so I quickly return the book to the shelf and make my way to the cash register. How different from yesteryear, when I would've signed all the store's copies and shamelessly self-promoted my work to anyone in the vicinity. I've got to bolt before I drown in flop sweat.

"Will this be all?" a different salesclerk asks as she scans the barcode.

"This too." I grab a small note card from the desk and hand it to her.

While she's putting my purchases in a paper bag along with a free bookmark, I stick my credit card into the machine and dash off my name, eager to bolt before this clerk recognizes me from my author photo. Not that I've ever resembled the polished woman in that photo other than on the day of the photo shoot.

Once outside, I can breathe again. While my pulse resumes a normal rhythm, I dab my forehead with the back of my arm and then begin the three-quarter-mile walk to my cul-de-sac. Along the way, a man in colorful, skin-tight red, black, and yellow clothing races by on a bicycle. Several people and their dogs pass me, too. The elderly woman pushing a double stroller beneath a canopy of vibrant leaves must be a nanny or grandparent.

People say "good morning" as we cross paths, so I mumble greetings in reply. New Yorkers are usually too invested in their phones to pay much attention to the people around them. Polite friendliness without the negative memories of my hometown makes this suburb at once familiar yet strange. These people cannot all be as happy as they appear, and yet we smile and wave. Will I miss the abundance of congenial behavior when I return, triumphant, to the city? *If* I return triumphant, whines the mean little voice in my head.

I want to write out the gift card before dropping the parcel in Wendy's mailbox, so I go into my house and rummage around for a pen that works. Pink ink. Some other author's conference swag, but it'll do the job.

Wendy,

I hope you and Joe were able to help your son last night. I saw this today at the bookstore and thought of him. Maybe it will help with the big transition.

Best,

Harper

Mentioning her husband reminds me that I've yet to see Joe, let alone meet him. I shouldn't ignore the men here, and Joe will be an important piece of better understanding Wendy. I wish George Durbin had offered more specific details when I got the keys. If I call to inquire now, it'll be weird. Crass, even.

My mom's name flashes on the screen when my phone rings. I let it go to voice mail and then play the message.

"Hi, honey. Checking in to see how you like your new home. Have you made any friends? I know you're there for your book, but maybe you'll meet some financial bigwig and be able to live on easy street. Dad says hi. Love you. Call us later."

She doesn't mean to undermine me, but really! Her lack of faith in my talent is obvious if she thinks my best chance at happiness is to marry a rich guy. I've never once heard her encourage either of my brothers to marry rich girls so they could live off those women. Worst of all is knowing, no matter that my first novel sold a million copies in its first year, she'll never think my life complete or successful until I have a ring on my finger—never mind that I'm not looking for one.

I'll call her back when my exasperation subsides, which could take a while.

Wendy brought me welcome gifts wrapped in ribbons, with a note on monogrammed stationery. My apology gift is in the bookstore's rumpled paper bag, my note dashed off on a generic card. Sums us up rather neatly, doesn't it? With a shrug, I take the package outside and place it in her mailbox, which is at the end of her driveway on a white post surrounded by ornamental grasses.

The contrast between our yards—mine a rental, with boring, empty beds and Wendy's handsome lawn—and the work we did together yesterday make me want something pretty of my own to enjoy.

My blank pages can wait a little longer.

Productive procrastination is a nearly guilt-free way of avoiding the blank page. I trot inside, grab my keys, and drive to Weed & Duryea to shop for plants and to people-watch. At least there I won't be assaulted by rave reviews of Ellen's book or by curious literary folk.

A good portion of the parking lot is consumed by dozens of types of flowers and small shrubs, and an equal number of glazed flowerpots. Dazed as a Grateful Dead groupie because I'm surrounded by unfamiliar choices, I mill around with no idea which of these plants are the easiest to maintain.

A diminutive yet stout man with a full beard comes to assist me. Not exactly the stereotype of the gardener a lonely housewife might screw, but that's another clichéd idea to avoid. "Do you know what you need?"

I shake my head. "No idea. My two small flower beds are mostly empty, but I've got a black thumb. Which plants will God take care of best?"

He doesn't laugh at my little joke. Maybe those reviewers are right—cynicism isn't very funny. Crap, all the criticism has burrowed inside my mind like a mole, eating away at my confidence. If I can't root it out, I'll never write anything worthwhile. Will gardening become my backup career?

"Do the beds get full sun or part sun?" he asks.

I grimace, having no idea.

"Which way does the house face?" he asks, trying a new angle.

Again, no idea. "My neighbor's yard has fancy grasses, roses, and hydrangea that look like they're thriving."

"Okay. Well, we have hydrangea over there and roses that way, but if you want a little color for the next few weeks, you might buy some mums."

"Can those go in the ground or only in pots?" A valid question in my mind, but his brows quirk in a way that indicates his conclusion that I'm not too bright.

"Either, but we have some clay pots on sale right there." He points to a set of metal shelves that contain round and square pots of every type.

"Thank you. Do I just grab one of these carts?" I gesture toward an abandoned flatbed wagon.

He nods and then turns to answer another customer's question, leaving me to make my own bad decisions.

Colorful plants would best offset my rental house's dingy shade of white. Roses seem too fussy. Hydrangea look less formal, so I grab four blue hydrangea plants and four buckets of bright orange mums. I impulse-buy four discounted black glazed pots on sale to match the shutters on the house, and wheel my booty to the cash register. Throughout my shopping, I've noted the comings and goings of fortysomething men and women, all of whom look too fatigued to be intriguing. Honestly, it's making me pessimistic about this whole experiment. A younger, beardless man uses some mad spatial skills to load the items into my small trunk.

It's not until I get home and unload my goodies that I remember I don't own a single gardening tool.

I glance at Wendy's house, wondering if she's received my peace offering. I won't ask for another favor until she has. With no further valid forms of procrastination at my disposal, I leave the plants outside and go sit in front of my laptop to think. This work used to be easy. Fun, even.

Now the cursor blinks, each iteration its own insult.

Blink: poser.

Blink: unimaginative.

Blink: self-absorbed.

I close the laptop to quiet my doubts, but the tick of my clock's second hand runs through my thoughts. With a determined shove, I push back from the desk, walk down to the kitchen to get my bottle of Bulleit from the liquor cabinet, and pour myself a glass. Two fingers? No, a sighting of Ellen's book being touted while mine languishes deserves at least three fingers' worth.

After knocking it back like a shot, I repour myself extra for sipping, then begin a slow parade through the small house. Taking deep breaths, I let my boozy brain wander. My editor's "suggestion" and a disgruntled landlord's gossip are all I've gotten in four days' time. I grimace, shamed that I've nothing original to say to the world and am stooping to such depths. Maybe my folks have a point—I should chuck this writing gig and seduce a venture capitalist who can jet me around the world. Yacht clubs, private planes, private rum tastings in the Caribbean—would that be so terrible?

I chug the bourbon and hop around the house, making music with the various squeaking floorboards—because that will surely elicit mad genius.

A knock at the door ends my goofing around. When I answer, Wendy's round blue eyes blink back at me. She's wearing gray slacks, with black flats. A pink long-sleeved top is neatly tucked into her waist with a thin black Chanel belt. It's only eleven thirty in the morning. I can't imagine why she's so dressed, unless she has a part-time job she didn't mention.

"Hi, Wendy." With the empty tumbler dangling from my hand, I lean against the doorframe to counter the effects of the bourbon, which begin to grab hold.

Wendy's shrewd gaze rises from the glass to my face. "Hello, Harper. I came to thank you for the book. I'll be sure to include it in Billy's next care package."

"I hope it helps him. I remember how hard it was to adapt to dorm life." A lie, actually. I took to college with absolutely no homesickness or other strife because freedom had been the best drug on that campus. Is Billy like me—happy to be away from a provincial town and overweening mother? Could this be an interesting point of conflict or story layer? I need more data. "Would you like a drink?"

"Oh, no. Thank you." Wendy pats her chest like one might pat a baby's back to soothe it.

"Oh, come on, Wendy. Have a drink with me. Bourbon is good for the soul." I turn and walk back toward the kitchen, banking on her curiosity to entice her to follow me.

Following a brief silence, the soles of her shoes lightly tap on the floor behind me. "I've never tried bourbon."

"Never?" This is good. It'll loosen her up, although she made free with her opinions easily enough yesterday. I nab a clean tumbler and pour just a finger. No need to waste my supply. "Most people sip it. But if you don't like the taste, go on and belt it back."

Wendy dips her nose into the glass and sniffs, then immediately pulls away. "It smells like cleaning solution."

"Well, it can wipe your mind clean," I tease, raising my glass like a toast. "Bottoms up."

Wendy steels herself and then downs the bourbon like a shot while I sip mine. She sticks her tongue out, grimacing. "My throat's on fire."

I chuckle. "In a few minutes, your whole body will relax." As will her inhibitions.

She's glancing around this old kitchen, her head shaking slightly.

"What's the matter?"

Wendy huffs, still clutching the empty glass, staring at a gash in an upper cabinet door. "Peg would be heartsick by how he let this place go."

"The elusive Peg again."

A bright smile crosses Wendy's face. "Have you had a friend like that . . . someone who really got you? It was always comfortable between us. I should feel sorry for George that she left him, but I'm really angry that he didn't try harder to make her happy." She sighs heavily, like she was the one who got dumped.

"You miss her." Perhaps there is story fodder in that friendship, especially if it was more than mere friendship. Maybe my book should focus on neighbors . . . or on things that can go wrong between neighbors? Why did George think Wendy was hiding something when his wife clearly liked and trusted her? And does Wendy have any idea that Peg shared some of Wendy's background with her husband?

She holds out her glass for more bourbon, which makes me smile. Of course I oblige.

"I do miss Peg, but here's to new friends and new horizons." She thrusts her glass forward to clink against mine.

"To new friends." A sizzle of guilt fires through me. It's not that I don't like Wendy. She seems like a decent person. But my hidden agenda makes our chitchat disingenuous, which erects an invisible wall between us.

If I come clean, she'll clam up and alert her entire mom network. I've yet to generate a single interesting story premise, so I can't risk alienating her. Desperation has damaged my moral compass.

Wendy forces the bourbon down her gullet. "To be honest, I didn't come over just to thank you. I noticed your new plants and thought you might like a hand with them."

This isn't even procrastination; it's character research. "I would, actually. They're sitting out there because I forgot to buy a shovel."

"We can use mine." Her facial expression is already softening from typically being on the qui vive.

"Okay, but there's no rush, right?" I shrug, refilling her glass yet again. "I'm enjoying the bourbon."

That's no lie. Bourbon numbs the painful truth of how my weakened confidence killed my ability to create compelling characters from scratch. Apparently, I've been writing repelling ones instead.

Wendy stares at the glass for a minute as if thinking: *I shouldn't be drinking in the middle of the day, but I've got nothing more pressing to do, and I like making a new friend, so maybe there's nothing wrong with it.*

Before she begs off, I press: "Don't make me drink alone. I don't know anyone else in town and would like the company."

"Okay." She smiles as if I've given her a diamond necklace. "The yard work can wait."

I'm betting a lot on George Durbin's mumbled remarks, so there'd better be more to Wendy than fastidiousness.

I don't want to cause her pain or humiliation. I need only a spark of something original for the kernel of a noteworthy character. In truth, she's using me to replace her friend Peg as much as I'm using her to generate ideas. Besides, she'll never know my character is based on her. I'll change the physical details so that no one else will suspect it, either. And who knows? If she does find out, she might be flattered.

"Let's go sit in the living room. I'll put on music—do you like Dar Williams?"

"I never heard of her."

My turn to grab my chest. "You're in for a treat."

We walk to the living room. While I fumble to turn on my speakers and tell Alexa what to play, Wendy is taking a closer look at my personal items, including a grouping of my dad's handmade votives.

When "After All" rings out from the speaker, I flop onto the sofa and pour myself a smidge more bourbon.

Wendy tentatively tests out my Finn Juhl Pelican chair. "You bought really smart-looking pots for your plants. The yard will look sharp when we're finished."

A little flattery will grease the skids. "Your yard inspired me."

"Thank you." She tucks her chin and smiles, all the while stroking the nap of the chair. "Sorry I'm staring at your stuff, but it's so different from the Durbins' furniture. Modern and fresh. I'd like to redecorate, but Joe's not convinced. He prefers to save so he can retire earlier and we can travel together."

It's not an unreasonable argument, but Wendy's probably deferring to him more than agreeing with him. "I've yet to meet him."

"You've probably seen him jogging. He's a big runner." She makes a funny face. "He likes hobbies like that—you know, the kind where he's on his own."

Hm. Interesting. "He's a loner?"

She takes a healthy swallow of bourbon, no longer wincing at the sting. "Well, not exactly. He likes people fine, but he also likes downtime."

"An introvert?" I lean back and pull my feet up on the cushion, wishing I had a cigarette. The mood strikes at times like this—with the sun and bourbon warming me. I lift my face to enjoy the sun streaming into the room on what will likely be one of the last warm fall days.

"Somewhat, yes. I'm . . . not the same." She laughs to herself, although her forehead is wrinkled as if frowning. Is she concentrating on that bourbon or stifling some thought?

"You don't say?"

Wendy obviously craves connection with people. Her eagerness to befriend me is sweet yet sort of sad. The puzzle is why this attractive, earnest, and helpful woman needs me as a friend, and this mystery gives some weight to George Durbin's french-fry remark. He mentioned her mother's mental health, but it'll take finesse to get to that topic.

"I'm not complaining," she's quick to add. "He's a good father and friend. I'm very lucky."

I have the sense it's not just me she's trying to convince.

At first blush, Wendy seems somewhat interchangeable with my mother. But unlike my mom and her friends—whom I call the "CCs," or Circleville Critics—Wendy's not listing grievances about her husband. The CCs' litany is one of many reasons I see no point in marriage. Because, really, if it always ends with boredom and frustration, why bother?

"You're lucky. A lot of women I know complain about their spouses."

"That's too bad. Your spouse is the person who sticks by you through thick and thin. You shouldn't talk behind their backs, even if you wish they didn't snore or were more interested in sex." She pauses as if catching herself, tipping me off to the fact that those weren't random hypothetical complaints.

Even if George knows about her sex life from Peg, that wouldn't prompt his warning—unless Wendy proposed a three-way because she's not getting enough at home. Doubtful for many reasons. Besides, a cheating spouse is about as clichéd as some of the characters in my last book.

Wendy's gaze wanders through the window. "I've found that negative thoughts beget more negativity. It's better to focus on gratitude, don't you think?"

"I suppose." Begrudgingly, I admire her loyalty to her husband. Perhaps I shouldn't be as cynical about the institution. I frown. No. Even in this era, the average woman still gives up more of herself in a marriage than a man does. Calvin never held that kind of power over me because I wasn't legally bound to put up with him. Then again, if I'd shared a bit of Wendy's attitudes about love and partnership, maybe Calvin wouldn't have been easily bewitched by another.

Eh, screw that.

Wendy's still yammering about gratitude. "That's a nonanswer. Either you agree or you don't."

Maybe it's time to cut off that bourbon. I considered her perspective, so she should consider mine.

"Gratitude is fine as long as it's not a smoke screen for ignoring complaints because you're too afraid to raise them. Or worse, if you don't feel entitled to complain—like your happiness is less important than your husband's."

She leans forward, staring at those patent leather loafers that look spit shined. Her gaze meets mine then, her resolve so strong I sit back in my seat. "It's not about fear. It's about appreciating what you have instead of lamenting what you don't."

Sounds like a rationalization from someone too entrenched in society's expectations to question them—but if her sex life is flagging, how grateful can she really be? "If you say so."

She tilts her head, scratching something behind her ear. I'm guessing she's miffed by my flippant reply, so her composure interests me. "You must've had a pretty easy childhood."

"What makes you think that?" How quickly she believes she can sum up and understand me and my motives. If it weren't annoying, it'd be impressive. But this gives me an opening to discuss her childhood, too, so I let it pass.

"Because your worst complaint is your parents' double standard. Not to minimize that, but I bet you never went hungry, or lacked a ready supply of ironed clothes, or had birthdays and holidays pass without celebration, or suffered from screaming matches between your parents. They probably showed up for recitals or sports or whatnot, and bragged about you to their friends. You never had to walk on eggshells to avoid triggering a major meltdown, or avoid bringing friends home because that caused trouble. When people grow up like you, they take a lot for granted, so practicing gratitude might seem more like a smoke screen than a commitment."

The fact that I'm not instantly dismissing her argument makes me think I've had too much bourbon. Wendy's wistful tone also tells me that her homelife was not stable—supporting George's remark about her mother. Did she have to walk on eggshells? What kinds of meltdowns was she avoiding? Are these things why she doesn't visit her mother more often?

I could share something personal on the chance it will open her up. The idea makes the room feel warmer. I tug at my shirt collar and clear my throat. "My parents covered the basics, but even at this point, they try to talk me into what they think I should be and to want the future they want for me rather than accepting and loving me as I am."

Well, hell, that sounded like self-pity.

Wendy's eyes go wide and her gaze softens, like she's approaching a wounded kitten. She catches her lip between her teeth, and then with a gentle voice says, "I'm sorry you don't feel accepted, Harper. That's painful. I don't know your parents, but as a parent, I feel certain they never intend to hurt you. Parents make mistakes just like everyone else, no matter how hard we try not to. Most of us just want to impart our values and encourage the choices we believe will make our kids' lives easier and happy."

"Isn't there a line, though? A point where a parent accepts that the child has a right to his or her own identity? That everyone's definition of happiness isn't the same?"

Her gaze dips into the empty bourbon glass, and then she frowns as if wishing she had a little left. "Sometimes it's hard to accept choices you consider detrimental. That works both ways, doesn't it? I mean, you have obviously strong opinions about what you view as your mom's compromises."

My lips part when she lands that direct hit. It takes me a second to regroup. I'm not here for therapy. I need information, so it's time to change the subject. "You mentioned before that your mom is in Rhode Island. Is that where you grew up?"

"Yes, in Westerly—not far from the border of Connecticut." Her face is flushed from the alcohol, and her spine appears to be relaxing. "It's a small town like this, but not quite as posh."

"Near Watch Hill?" A city friend from old-money "summers" in Watch Hill. I visited the beach community once. Nice enough but not for me. I prefer Ibiza.

"Right near there. It used to be quieter, before Taylor Swift sightings and such." Her raised brow reveals a distaste for the burgeoning popularity.

It occurs to me she's never mentioned her father. "Your parents must still like it if they stayed all this time."

Wendy squares her shoulders, her expression more stonelike. "My father left when I was young, but my mother won't ever leave. She can't handle . . . change."

Her voice is cool and flat now, indicating her childhood hardship is rooted more in her mother's rigidity than her father's absence. My body whirs as I collect clues to unlocking Wendy—someone who is simultaneously tight as a drum yet doggedly optimistic. A curious, confounding mix. She doesn't seem ready to talk about her mom, though, so I change directions. "Did you meet Joe in Rhode Island?"

"We met through a mutual friend after college, when Joe was getting his master's at UConn." Her face brightens while she reminisces. "I thought he was so handsome—way out of my league. But he was also sweet. He brought me fresh flowers every week that first year. I knew he was the one when I learned about how he looked out for the old man who lived in the lower unit of his duplex—taking out his garbage, sweeping his front walk, picking up groceries. That kindness did it. Once we married, I worked as a real estate broker while he finished grad school."

"I didn't know you were a broker." The perfect job for someone with her chatty demeanor and enthusiasm for new neighbors. "Why'd you quit?"

She freezes for a millisecond, like she's been caught red-handed with something. "It got to be too much—a job, a child, a house to run—so I prioritized my son's needs."

Plausible, but the way she's picking at her lint-free pants suggests that's not the whole truth. "What about going back, now that he's off living his own life? Maybe it's time to rebuild one of your own."

My mistake is apparent when she rises from her chair. "Well, this was lovely, but I'm a little woozy. Perhaps we'll get to those beds later, or tomorrow morning." She gestures outside, not looking all that woozy. "A little effort will make a big difference."

Her genuine anticipation soaks me with guilt for plying her with booze. Am I a bad person or simply someone backed into a corner? Either way, I don't like myself much at this moment.

I stand, too. "You know, I hate to put you out. Maybe I could just borrow your tools and do it myself. I can google how to plant those shrubs."

"No, no. I'm happy to help. I love gardening's instant gratification." Who am I to rob her of easy joy?

"Okay. Let me know when you're up to it." I would take before-and-after pictures for Instagram if I weren't afraid some of those eighty thousand followers might live here and also know Wendy. "Thanks for your help. You're too nice to me, you know."

I feel better—or more honest—after issuing that slight warning. We start for the door.

"It's no problem. I like having a friend next door again." Wendy suddenly grabs me into a quick but sincere hug. My body is still vibrating from the unexpected contact when she steps outside. "I'm planning a small dinner party next Saturday. Would you come? You could meet Joe and a few others in town."

Oh God, that sounds dull. I smile, prepared to suffer for my art, resolving to find some way to make it all up to her in the end. "That's so nice, thank you. I don't cook, but I can bring some booze."

She grimaces. "No more bourbon, please. Maybe some wine? It's not necessary, of course." She skips down the front steps so fast I'm afraid she'll stumble. "I'll check back later to help with the plants, Harper."

"Bye." I wait for her to disappear before going inside, a bit woozy myself.

I take our empty glasses to the kitchen sink before wandering back upstairs. Wendy's beliefs about gratitude keep looping through my thoughts. Is she right? Can we choose our responses to the world around us, and do those choices make all the difference? Mine seem to trample through my brain like a herd of angry elephants, but perhaps Wendy isn't the only one of us who rationalizes her decisions.

The earlier message from my mother cuts through my musing, unraveling the incomplete threads of thought. But it seems like they could be braided into something that might become interesting. A fictionalized and exaggerated version of Wendy requires a dark history. What were those early eggshells about, I wonder? And how did she retain such a strong sense of hope? If she won't open up, I'll have to spin something. She'll also need a name—my antagonist. What is Wendy short for? Gwendolyn? Gwen?

Gwen is good. Solid. Just uncommon enough, too.

So, dear Gwen, what makes you believe in redemption and crave the hope woven into romance novels? What makes you so open on one hand and so skittish on the other?

While making notes and crafting scenarios, I'm avoiding a few nagging questions: What gave Wendy surprising insight into someone like me, and will her dinner party end up hurting me more than helping me achieve my goal? Also, how long can I put off returning my mother's call without being a bitch?

My agent's face blooms on the screen when my phone vibrates suddenly, stopping my heart. I cover my face and inhale sharply before answering. "Hi, Cassandra."

"Harper. How are you?"

Aside from procrastinating away another day I don't have to waste? "Good, good. Settled and sketching out some new ideas." I slouch back in my chair, crossing my ankles as if a relaxed posture will slow my heartbeat.

"That's great. I just hung up with Tessa about another client, and she asked whether you had a new proposal ready."

Even the bourbon fails me now as every muscle tenses. "Not yet, but I'm homing in on something. Not urban. Not twentysomethings. I heard you both loud and clear, and am finding inspiration here in the burbs."

"Can you expound a bit?" She sounds skeptical.

Time to pull something out of my ass. "Something *Stepford Wives* meets a more modern *Revolutionary Road*–ish."

"Hm." Not exactly enthusiasm. "When will I see pages?"

"I'm still working out plot details, but soon." It's amazing that my pants don't immediately catch fire.

"This week?"

Crap. "Maybe."

"We need to get moving before Tessa gets irked. I can't stress enough how imperative it is to hand off a pitch-perfect manuscript this time."

As if I've forgotten. I rub the back of my neck, but it's still tight as hell. "Understood. I'll send you something by next week."

"Great. Well, good luck."

"Thanks. Have a good afternoon." I hit "End" and stare at the ceiling.

A week! My pulse speeds up. I need a change of scenery and coffee, so I pop a K-Cup in the Keurig I've set up on my desk, wait sixty seconds, then take my mug and my notebook out to the porch steps. Surrounded by my potted hydrangea, I listen to the neighborhood kids shouting as they play.

Steam rises from my beverage as Wendy's opinions on marriage and gratitude continue to poke at me. For all their bickering—about everything from how long Mom's mother visited each year to every nutrition fad she made us try—my own parents also work together to manage aging parents and their own minor health issues. None of that changes the lack of support I got. *"Creative writing major? Might as well pick medieval French poetry for how employable you'll be."* I still remember my dad's skeptical expression during that conversation while my mother nervously picked at her fingernails. Meanwhile, Rick's taking six years to finish college was not just tolerated—it was excused. *"It's better that he figures out what he wants now because he'll be doing it to support his family the rest of his life,"* Dad had said. Exactly the kind of double standard that set my course and primed my need to prove my family wrong. Now my career is teetering, and with it my financial independence. Thirty-odd years of choices that brought me here to a place where I'm totally on my own and counting on a near stranger and divine intervention.

There's a story there somewhere. Unfortunately, that'd require me to get honest about myself, and honesty isn't the easiest thing for a paid liar like me.

CHAPTER FIVE

WENDY

Ten days later, Saturday evening

If I could fan myself without drawing attention, I would. As things stand, my silk shirt is clinging to my back. Despite beautiful antipasto and charcuterie platters, a trendy jazz playlist, and some lovely wine brought by our dinner party guests, conversation remains stilted.

Dirk and Sue Wheeler are normally quite boisterous—always teasing each other and those around them. Not tonight. Although sitting side by side, they aren't speaking to one another. The tension between them seems to have paralyzed everyone else's vocal cords.

Poonam Varma keeps trying to engage Sue with little success, while her husband, Praveen, is eating all the grapes. Nate arrived last and, as such, is seated in the chair farthest from Harper, who is beside Joe on the sofa. That wasn't part of my plan, but at least Nate and Harper eyed each other appreciatively when introduced. Harper also wore a bra and makeup for a change. She looks pretty, although her ripped black jeans, black sweater, and heelless black leather bootees don't exactly brighten her face. Mossy greens and rust colors would suit her warm skin tone best. Still, there's a hipness about her that's got its own appeal. No one has ever called me hip.

"Wendy, where'd you buy that gorgeous secretary?" Harper points at the antique mahogany desk in the corner of the living room.

"Oh, that was a garage-sale find I refinished a while ago." I first started refinishing furniture in high school, after my grandmother died and we ended up with some of her old case goods. After a trip to the local hardware store for information, I used those pieces for practice. It gave me an escape from my mom, who rarely entered the "filthy" garage. The meditative state produced by the rhythmic sanding and required attention to detail also helped reduce the stress and frustration caused by my continual anticipation of her triggers. I accepted never being allowed to invite friends over. But the random upheavals, like occasionally being forced to do homework on the porch whenever she decided my "germy" backpack was lethal, or the rearranging of everything in the house "for luck," were more upsetting. In any case, what always made me happy was—and still is—taking an abandoned, unloved thing and remaking it into something beautiful.

"*You* did that?" she asks as if I've delivered the Second Coming of Christ.

"It's a hobby." I clasp my hands in my lap, uncomfortable being the center of attention. Tonight is about introducing Harper to Nate, not about me.

"More than a hobby," Poonam says. "People in town ask her to fix up their old furniture."

"Only occasionally," I clarify.

"Why don't you make it a business?" Harper asks.

Oh God. My last paying job was back when I almost got caught stealing that damn beaded coaster. How could I risk going into other people's homes to assess the pieces and work on them? "I've always been too busy with Billy and volunteer committees."

"Well, that's over now, right? Throw up a Facebook page and website. I mean, that's really beautiful." Harper leans forward. Since replanting her hydrangea and mums last week, we've shared coffee on her porch a few times. She's always asking me questions, which is flattering, but I hardly know anything about her. In any case, her aggressive manners, while no longer a surprise, still put me on my back foot. "I have the ugliest old buffet. Calvin and I tried to salvage it, but we only made it worse. Could you fix it?"

Calvin must be the bad breakup she referenced in passing last week. "Happy to take a look. Let's talk about that later, though, so we don't bore the others."

I cast a glance around the room. Sue is staring into space, paying no attention to any of us, which is odd and concerning. Her set jaw and slumped shoulders tell me she's not just angry—she's hurt. I'd like to help, but what can I do in the middle of a party? And honestly, we're not such confidants that questions wouldn't come off as prying. Meanwhile, Nate is politely sipping his wine as Dirk prattles on about the Giants, so I'm not sure he's even listening to Harper. If this keeps up, my matchmaking is doomed.

Nate is tall, like Joe. Black hair, the darkest brown eyes, and bronzed skin. Best of all is Nate's broad smile, which always elicits happiness in others. He's sharply dressed tonight in khaki slacks, cognac leather sneakers, and an eggplant-purple sweater. He's smart, well mannered, and kind, just like Joe. Honestly, how could Harper not be interested?

In the lull, Nate turns to Harper. "Speaking of work, what do you do, Harper?"

Oh no! This is awkward with her being between jobs. Can I interrupt to change the subject without being rude?

"I work in publishing," she says. My mouth might've just opened and closed from surprise. My ACLU lawyer guess couldn't have been more off the mark. She catches my gaze and adds, "But I'm between jobs right now."

Nothing about her looks or demeanor strikes me as fitting for a professional editor. Perhaps PR or marketing? That would explain why she thinks it'd be easy to throw up a digital store to sell furniture.

"You should join our book club," Poonam says.

"Yes, of course." I nod, still processing the new tidbit about Harper. "We normally meet weekday mornings at Rosie's Café, but I'm hosting early next month after an evening library event with the author."

"Why not?" Harper's grin appears oddly strained. Do people who work in publishing not enjoy personal book groups? More likely she's worried it will be as awkward as this evening. What *is* going on with Sue and Dirk?

I'm about to tell Harper what we're reading when she turns to Nate. "What about you?"

"My job?" he clarifies, and she nods. "I work for Joe in the town's finance department."

"Ah, math." She shudders playfully, a flirty twinkle in her eye. Joe and Nate exchange a knowing look. Their jobs don't sound exciting, but town finance is an important backbone of our community.

"I'm not great at math, either," I say. Like I mentioned, complementary strengths are key, but luckily that thought doesn't tumble out. Mustn't make my plan too obvious.

Conversation flags again. We need an icebreaker. A game perhaps? The acrylic box of Not Your Mother's Dinner Party conversation cards is sitting unused on the bookshelf behind me. Could be sketchy, but I'm desperate.

"Oh, I meant to put this out." I take it off the shelf. "I got these cards at a holiday gift exchange. If everyone's game for trying them out, I'll start." I wait for everyone's consent.

Sue, Dirk, Praveen, and Poonam look indifferent; Harper wipes away her initial grimace; and Joe winks at me.

"I love games," Nate chimes in. "My mom's a fan of family game night."

I knew I liked Nate. A man who enjoys his mother and family time is a good catch, too. And in any case, these cards have to be better than the awkward tension numbing us all.

"This is more a Q and A than a game, but it's all in good fun, I think." I choose a card and read it aloud. "Would you rather have more friends or be closer to those you have?"

"That's easy," Harper says.

"Mm." Not to me. I'd love more friends, but my affliction makes it trickier than for most. Anticipatory panic about slipping, even when I was on the medication that led to weight gain, caused me to decline many invitations throughout the years until most stopped altogether. Peg was the exception because proximity made for frequent impromptu get-togethers. Not that I'll share any of that. I smile at Harper. "Closer to those I have."

"Exactly." Harper nods. "I'm always a little suspicious of people with too many friends."

I expected a different answer, but given her viewpoint, I'm heartened that she's befriending me. Of course, if she doesn't trust people, it'll be hard to become close.

"Why's that?" Nate asks before popping some prosciutto in his mouth. He strikes me as someone who's never at a loss for friends or invitations, which could make them incompatible.

"No one likes everyone, and no one is universally likable. Therefore, someone with tons of friends is probably something of a phony." Harper eats a mouthful of cheese while Nate and I frown. She's so cynical. That Calvin must've hurt her deeply. Does Nate sense that, too, or is he already writing her off? "Even I can do that math," she jokes.

I laugh so Nate doesn't sour on her mistrust.

"That's a pretty big generalization," Joe teases Harper. "I have to disagree, too, because I like most people, and most people like me, but I'm not a phony."

"That's true." I nod. It is. Heaven knows how I got so lucky. He'd say he was drawn to my energy, can-do spirit, and sparkling eyes. He also likes that I accommodate his mother, who lives an hour away yet is still demanding with her requests for rides to doctor appointments and the grocery store. I do it because I'm grateful to her for raising a good, solid man. Also, I had plenty of practice with the most demanding of mothers.

"You do seem genuinely nice, Joe." Harper smiles. "But are you one hundred percent authentic?"

"I am." He humbly shrugs. "The key to my universal appeal is that I'm nonthreatening and a little bland—like vanilla. Not an exciting flavor, but nobody hates vanilla."

When he laughs at himself, others join in. He always takes pride in this analogy. And not only does no one hate vanilla—some of us love it.

"Okay, next question." I pass the box to Harper because Sue doesn't look interested. I wish I knew what was wrong.

Harper pulls out a card from the middle. "What don't women want?"

To be lied to or cheated on. To be ignored. To turn into a younger version of their mothers. The list is endless. I lean forward, curious about my young friend's thoughts.

"Another easy one—women don't want to be controlled by men." Harper sets the card aside.

Oh boy, here comes a big test—how will Nate react to her staunch feminism?

Nate takes the bait, eyes narrowing. "Not all men want to control women."

"Joe doesn't control me." I smile at my husband, who tries only to help me control my little problem, which I welcome.

"It'd be like trying to control a tornado, dear," Joe teases, drawing light laughter from most everyone, principally Harper, to whom he's paying particular attention even though he knows I want her focus to be on Nate. I smile yet nurse a slight sting, telling myself Joe didn't mean to embarrass me.

Meanwhile, Sue chugs half her wine—her grip so tight her knuckles turn white, as if she's irritated by Joe or me or everything. Maybe I should ask her to join me in the kitchen and give her a chance to talk. I'm considering how to do this gracefully when she sets her empty glass on the table, stands, and faces me. "I'm sorry, Wendy. I need to leave. I shouldn't have come tonight, but Dirk insisted . . ."

"Sue, don't do this now," Dirk grumbles.

She whirls around on him. "Don't tell me what to do. Harper's right. I'm my own person—you don't control me. And frankly, I hardly care what you think right now."

Everyone freezes except for the confused glances darting around like laser beams. Shock heats my body. Poor Sue. Whatever's wrong, a public outburst is unlikely to help. I worry she'll regret it tomorrow.

Through gritted teeth, Dirk says, "You're making a scene."

"Wow, have you got nerve. If your reputation's so important, you should've considered that sooner." Her eyes are bright with tears as she looks around the room. "I'm sorry for making everyone uncomfortable, but I can't stay. Please carry on."

Dumbstruck, I'm rising when she strides to the front door and grabs her jacket off the coatrack. "Sue, wait—"

Dirk catches my arm. "Leave it, Wendy. I'll go." He then bows slightly to the rest of the group. "Apologies, all. Please enjoy your night."

I'm torn between wanting to comfort Sue and wondering if she'd want me to interfere. If I were in a spat with Joe, I wouldn't want outsiders nosing around our private affairs. But not everyone is like me.

We all remain silent until we hear the door click shut behind the unhappy couple. Harper then swigs more wine. "Good for her."

I sink back onto my chair and grab my chest. Having never seen Sue make a scene before, I can only assume Dirk did something beyond the pale. "My heart aches for her."

"Why? She stood up for herself instead of suffering in silence," Harper says, as if a long-term marriage weren't at stake.

And yet a little discretion could've spared her some embarrassment, which will only add to her pain later. "I hope they resolve whatever's going on. They've been happily married for eighteen years."

Harper shoots me a disbelieving look. "Appearances aren't always true. Besides, marriage isn't nirvana. It can be a trap for women as much as anything else."

"You're against marriage?" Nate's impish expression implies amusement more than derision.

"Not for everyone. But a satisfying, lasting relationship doesn't require a legal construct. In fact, I enjoyed an open one for years. We didn't need a ring or license to define our feelings. We chose to show up every day. It was perfect."

I'm still stuck on the words "open one" when Nate says, "Until it ended."

Harper clears her throat, her gaze dipping to her feet for a moment. "Everything ends eventually."

Her glib conclusion doesn't hide the anguish beneath her bravado. The only other time I've seen her vulnerability was when she mentioned how her parents made her feel like an outsider. I relate to that, but for totally different reasons.

"Well, his loss will surely be someone else's gain," Nate says, right before reaching for another slice of prosciutto.

Harper blushes. That's almost good enough to make me forget about Sue and Dirk's troubles.

Still, my heart remains somewhat heavy. I hope Dirk didn't risk their entire marriage for some fling.

"Hon?" Joe's voice gains my attention.

"Sorry, I'm distracted. I don't want to see Dirk and Sue split up."

"One argument doesn't mean divorce," Joe says.

"Divorce is common in this country," Praveen adds casually. "Only one percent of marriages in India end in divorce."

"That's not relevant," Poonam says dismissively before turning to me. "I hope they work it out, too, Wendy. It's best for families to stay intact—as long as there's no danger from abuse, of course."

"Not all abuse is physical," Harper rebuts.

"I agree with Poonam," Joe wades in. "Sometimes we hurt those we love. Or take them for granted. But atonement, love, and respect can heal a lot of wounds. Not that there's never a good reason for divorce, but it shouldn't be the first response. I'd hate for Billy to split his holidays and such because Wendy and I wouldn't try to overcome a setback."

I'm smiling, yet my insides churn. Is he confessing something, or have the Wheelers' spat and Joe's missing libido made me paranoid? Does Joe stay with me for Billy's sake? Suddenly the cheese and crackers in my stomach turn to cement.

Nate shrugs. "No one should judge either way. Some people's capacity for forgiveness is huge. Some people have thin skin. Some people's expectations are so low they don't even realize they're being taken advantage of. In any case, let's pick another question to change the subject." He laughs, defusing the heaviness blanketing the room.

"Maybe we've had enough questions." I can't handle any more surprises. "In fact, the lasagna should be ready now, so why don't you all make yourselves comfortable in the dining room, and I'll join you in five minutes." I refill my glass for the third time before heading to the kitchen to pull the pan out of the oven. It smells delicious and looks even better, all browned and bubbly. At least one thing is going right tonight.

While I'm setting it out to cool slightly, Nate shows up.

"Are you looking for the restroom?" I gesture down the hallway. "It's that way."

"No, no. I thought I'd check to see if you needed help." He leans against the counter. "I can tell you're upset about your friend."

What a darling man. His mom did a great job. I hope when Billy outgrows adolescent self-centeredness, he'll turn out like Nate—a man who is independent, compassionate, and loves his mother.

"Thanks for your concern, but I'll be fine as long as everyone else has a nice time. Please go grab a seat next to Harper." I wave him off while retrieving the salad from the fridge and gathering oil, vinegar, Dijon, salt, and pepper to whisk together a quick vinaigrette. "She's new to town and could use some single friends."

"Friends, hm?" Nate shoots me a "jig is up" look above a congenial grin.

My cheeks must be as red as the cherry tomatoes in the salad, but I busy myself with the whisk to avoid direct eye contact. "Yes, friends. But of course, you are two young, attractive, single people, so if there's something more . . ."

His rich, warm laughter fills the kitchen, relaxing my muscles and helping me to let go of the uneasiness that's gripped me due to Joe's musings.

"Don't worry," he says. "I'm flattered, actually."

I look up. "Good. Joe speaks so highly of your work, and I've always enjoyed talking to you. After meeting Harper, I thought perhaps there could be a little spark, but at the very least, everyone can use a new friend."

He nods. "Can I carry the salad to the table for you?"

"Thank you." I push the bowl his way. "Now shoo. I'll be there in a minute."

When he leaves, I release a deep breath. How ironic that I'm making a love match for Nate and Harper while suspecting that my own relationship isn't as steady as I believed.

Joe brings the last of the stemware into the kitchen while I'm finishing loading the dishwasher. My thoughts are everywhere: missing my son, worried for Sue, upset by Joe's casual remarks, and curious if my matchmaking will take root.

"Another delicious meal, hon." He lines the dirty wineglasses up on the counter, so I fill the sink with warm, soapy water.

"Thank you."

"Why don't you look happier? Nate seemed to like our neighbor." Joe leans his butt against the counter, legs crossed at the ankles, arms crossed at the chest. "She's a firecracker. Smart. Confident."

"Young," I quip. My stomach is on fire. Nate isn't the only one intrigued by Harper, it seems. I dunk one glass in the water and start scrubbing. "I'm upset about Sue and Dirk."

"Ah." He nods. "Definitely an off night for them. Hopefully they're working it out now."

"Hmph." I rinse the glass and wash another, glancing at my husband. "Did Dirk cheat on her?"

"I've no idea, but it could be a hundred other things," he says.

I study him but see no signs of guilty knowledge. "So you haven't heard anything?"

"When do I ever hear things before you?" He smiles, then grabs a dish towel and begins drying the crystal. Is he deflecting?

"You're taking it all very lightly." My suspicions return. Playing down Dirk and Sue's spat. Flirting with Harper. Going on about marital rough patches and sticking it out for the kids. Our flagging sex life. I wouldn't believe him capable of such deception, but I wouldn't have thought it of Dirk, either.

"It's none of our business." He takes another glass to dry. "It's between them, and no one wants to be judged or pitied."

After I wash the final glass, I drain the sink. "You seem pretty well versed in all this."

Joe puts down the final glass and stares at me. "Oh, Wendy. You're not seriously accusing me of something, are you?"

"Can you blame me? The way you went on about flaws and rough patches." Shame and sorrow tussle inside, making me shaky. If Joe doesn't love me anymore, I'll be lost.

"For God's sake, you're being silly. I was just talking. All marriages have ups and downs, but what makes you think I'd ever disrespect you or our life together by sleeping around?"

"Is it so crazy? We haven't had sex in three months, and it's been pretty infrequent since last spring." After blurting that out, I cross my arms, feeling anything but strong. If he confesses something now, I'm not sure what I'll do. Scream? Cry? Run out the door?

He clutches my shoulders. "Honey, look at me. I swear, I'm not having an affair. I've never had an affair. And I never will."

The wave of relief is sudden and strong, but recedes as swiftly. "Then aren't you attracted to me anymore?"

He pulls me in for a hug. "You're a beautiful woman."

I love the smell of him—cashmere mixed with bergamot cologne. It's good to be in his arms, but he's not kissing me, or squeezing my butt, or doing anything that could be construed as foreplay. We could be good friends for all the fire in this hug. More questions would hardly create a romantic mood. Better to kindle some heat instead. I crane my neck to reach up and kiss him.

It's warm and familiar but ends rather quickly. "You must be tired after all this work," he says.

I shake my head, running my hands along his back and pulling him closer. The need to touch and be touched, to connect, swells urgently. "Not too tired, Joe."

I kiss him again and untuck his shirt and sweater so that my hands make contact with his skin. It's awkward at first. Clumsy, even. There's no rhythm. We're rusty. Although he doesn't seem particularly eager, he doesn't put me off.

We go upstairs, where we undress each other and fall into bed, our bodies reawakening and remembering each other's preferences and the habits that get created when making love to the same person for two decades, through all the changes that come from being a young couple to being middle-aged parents.

It's not our most combustible night of sex, nor the longest, but it's a start. I can build on this. We can build on it if we make it a priority. No more letting months pass.

Afterward, I curl with my back against his chest and stare at the wall, shivering and unable to fully extinguish my worry. He didn't push me away. He was tender and gentle. He said all the right things tonight in the kitchen. Yet there is so much that feels unsaid, not the least of which is my own secret about losing a grip on my illness.

In the dark, the dread that—like what happened with my mother—my issues will someday push Joe away closes in on me. If I ask, he'll say nothing would make him leave. He said as much tonight. But everyone has a breaking point. If I keep my secret, he won't go. Deep down, I realize that isn't exactly the same thing as him wanting to be here, but that's a question I'm too afraid to ask.

CHAPTER SIX

HARPER

Monday morning

When my agent's name glows on my phone screen, I hit speakerphone
while refilling my coffee mug, having awakened with a sore throat and
mild headache. Mandy would allege that my symptoms are psychoso-
matic, but I don't think so. Prior to April, I loved speaking with my
agent about my work and how to take my career to the next level. Only
since that "next level" unexpectedly became a downgrade have her calls
caused my thoughts to crimp along with the tightening of every muscle in my body. Each time, I suspect she's calling to drop me because I
haven't dazzled her with brilliance.

"Where's your proposal?" Cassandra asks.

It's been almost two weeks since we last spoke. Definitely longer
than the week I promised.

The hot coffee soothes my scratchy throat. "When we spoke before,
I was noodling a character-driven story about the midlife meltdown of
a suburban housewife named Gwen, but now I'm considering shifting
gears. Lighthearted is selling better lately, so what if I lean into external
plot levers instead of focusing on internal, broody introspection? I'm

thinking Gwen gets a new neighbor—Haley, a younger, secretive non-conformist who's everything Gwen is not. Gwen sets out to change her, but then starts suspecting Haley of having an affair with her husband, particularly because Gwen's sex life is on the fritz. Meanwhile Haley has secrets, too. She's not involved with any man, let alone Gwen's husband, but actually suspects Gwen's husband—a sperm donor during his college years—is her bio dad. That way there are hidden agendas on both sides. I'm not yet sure if the guy should be her bio dad in the end, though. Anyhow, the new working title could be *Bedlam on Beach Lane* or *Ladies Who Lunch* or something. I'm still fully developing Gwen's motives and character, but it feels like the right tone as I stretch into new territory."

"What's Gwen's secret?" No praise or overt excitement.

The chill of an executioner and his axe is hanging over my shoulders.

"I don't know yet." Literally true on every level. Wendy's personal stationery, the welcome gifts, her impeccable wardrobe and garden, and the elegant arrangement of the charcuterie tray on Saturday suggest a militant precision in projecting an image. That lends weight to George Durbin's insinuation that she's hiding something, and people only hide things that embarrass them. To date, she's not disclosed any hint of that during our occasional morning coffees. "Something unexpected that she might be ashamed for others in the community to learn, like maybe she met her husband at a frat party where she was hired to strip? Or maybe her son is actually the result of an affair? Obviously it should tie to her goal and arc, which I'm still working out." None of those ideas are terribly original. Dammit. I've lost my gift. Failure looms large.

There's a pause during which every sound in the house reverberates as I brace to be shot down. "That's certainly the different direction we were looking for and allows for your sharp observations. Can you do humor that isn't biting?"

I grimace, grateful we aren't on a Zoom call. Like many, I recognize and enjoy humor, but it's hardly my stock-in-trade—unless you count zingers, which get tiresome to read. Just check the reviews of my last book. "If I'm trying a new direction, I might as well go all in. I'll send you the opening pages in a week and see what you think."

"Excellent. Send those with an outline—even if it's skeletal. We really need to run something by Tessa before the end of the month. Even then, you'll only have about four months to finish the book."

I suppress an inward groan. Condensing a ninety-thousand-word novel into three pages is a ghastly chore, particularly when you've yet to discover your characters' secrets and motivations. Scratch that—stringing together that many decent words in four months might be worse. "I'm on it. I feel good about this. No 'millennial navel-gazing' this time." My shoulders tug at the recollection of that *Kirkus Reviews* quip.

"Given what's happened with your work this year, a hard pivot is the best strategy."

I hold my gut to recover from her reminder's soft punch. "Maybe I should come into the city and meet you for lunch to discuss it."

She hesitates. "My schedule's pretty busy this week, but let's see after I get the pages."

I grip the counter as the spectral executioner draws closer. She could dump me. I've seen it happen to others but never imagined myself in those shoes—another among tens of thousands of authors toiling away in relative obscurity and poverty. How am I so close to blowing it after having had the ultimate success—*New York Times* success? "Guess I'd better get to it, then. I'll shoot you something soon."

"Super. Good luck with it."

Cassandra hangs up without fanfare.

The volume in this old kitchen returns to a normal level. I fill my lungs before blowing out a long breath, shaking out my arms, and rotating my head a few times. The eerie executioner retreats into the shadows for now.

I sip my coffee, thinking of Ellen. She nursed writerly doubts after her debut's rather soft launch. But given her recent release's success, she probably isn't being dodged by her agent or growing an ulcer the size of Brazil.

This current mood reeks of self-pity. Not a good look, I know. At least being holed up in the boonies means no one else will see it.

I walk along the creaky hallway planks from the kitchen to the front of the house and climb the stairs to the spare bedroom that's become my office. My desk—a mahogany live-edge writing desk—sits in front of the open window, where I enjoy a cool breeze and hazy view of the front yard through billowing curtain sheers. Pretty, but I'm still depressed about selling my condo. If my last manuscript had been accepted, I wouldn't have been pressed to unload my home yet. I force that disappointment aside.

No more procrastinating. At this point, I've got photographs of people and places around town, pages of random brainstorming ideas, notes about everyone I've met through Wendy—including a blowup between an established couple about which I could use more deets, and a handful of potential character traits. While a long way from concocting a story with a twist, I open the laptop, set up a new Word document, type the title page, then a hard page break, and type out *Chapter One, Gwen.*

The cursor blinks impatiently. I am equally frustrated. Once upon a time, ideas flowed with abundance and abandon. The days of too many plot bunnies are now distant memories. How arrogant I was to assume they'd continue gushing like an oil well in the Middle East. Now I'm an empty vessel—or one filled with self-doubt—reduced to stealing from real people's lives in a wretched effort to create interesting characters.

Focus, Harper.

The opening. Should it begin with Gwen and her husband, Gary? Or with her meeting her new neighbor, Haley? I should craft Haley to be everything Gwen fears but is drawn to at the same time. This all hinges on understanding Gwen better than mere broad strokes. Who is Gwen really, and what does she crave? What's she hiding? What does she need?

If I can hook into the right opening, words should flow and unlock more ideas. They might all suck, but getting started is half the battle. Once I finish the first chapter, I'll take a stab at fleshing out an outline.

As usual, time bends in half while I'm thinking, typing, deleting, and trying again. I know this because when my phone rings at noon, I blink in surprise at the clock. I don't recognize the phone number, but it's local.

"Hello?"

"Hi, Harper. It's Nate, from Saturday night."

His unexpected call prompts an even more unexpected smile, which I immediately erase. He's got that hot Simon-from-the-*Bridgerton*-series thing going on, but he's also a conventional, mother-loving finance guy from Connecticut. Not exactly my type. "Oh, Nate. Hi. What a surprise."

"A good one, I hope." His rich, earnest voice skims over me like a silky caress. He's so polished. So preppy. And too . . . too nice. God, I'm horrible.

I sidestep his semiquestion. "How'd you get my number?"

Of course I know. Wendy asked me for it last week under the pretext of a "just in case" emergency. In my notebook, I write down *wily* under Gwen's list of traits.

"Wendy slipped it to me when I left the party. Hope you don't mind." Once again Nate's voice sets off a spray of delicious little tingles down my neck. If my book were already written and I were on my way out of town, I could embrace a little diversion. But doing so now would cause a conundrum. I've never been dishonest with someone I'm dating, yet if I tell him my true identity, he might mention it to Joe, who'd tell Wendy.

"Of course not," I lie. Not completely. I'm flattered by his call but hate deceiving him. "What can I do for you?"

My mother would love this guy, which might be another reason to avoid him. Her lifestyle is the opposite of my aspirations. Wendy would say that's cutting off my nose to spite my face. The fact that I'm projecting *and* considering Wendy's advice should perhaps be the most worrisome aspect of all.

Then again, there is something sweet about Wendy and Joe's relationship. While it likely has issues of its own, they seem comfortable together in their "vanilla" life. And yet Dirk and Sue Wheeler prove married people often end up settling in for reasons that have less to do with passionate love than with familiarity and duty. That puts unhappy women lacking financial independence in a weak position, which plenty of men understand and exploit. Ergo, marriage is often a trap.

"Come out with me on Friday," Nate says, interrupting my thoughts. "I have a surprise in mind, if you like surprises, that is."

I do. And I like Nate. He's easy on the eyes and educated. Decent taste in music from what he mentioned during dinner—an absolute must. Wendy wouldn't have introduced me to anyone less than a top-shelf guy. If only he weren't quite so . . . conventional. So not my type. On the other hand, Calvin turned out to be a closet traditionalist, so what do I know?

Nate might also know things about Joe that could spur ideas for my book. Is that bad? It's not like I called him to dig for info, but if he drops a detail here or there, there's no real harm. "That sounds fun, but fair warning, I'm nursing a cold."

"Oh, sorry. Anything you need?"

"Nah. It should pass by Friday. Let's go for it unless I'm coughing up a lung. Is there a special dress code?"

"Wear comfortable shoes—lots of standing involved. I'll pick you up at six thirty."

Standing? A museum, a tour, an evening posing as a nude model for an art class?

"If it's nearby, I'd like to walk. I miss strolling around the city." It's a great way to absorb the energy around me and then funnel it onto the page. Birdsong and children's laughter don't give off quite the same vibe as engines, horns, and the buzz of overcrowded sidewalks. That said, I do enjoy walking through the peaceful wooded trails of the town's three-hundred-acre Waveny Park.

"Sorry. It's about a fifteen-minute drive along roads without sidewalks, so you can't walk there."

Fifteen minutes—so still in Fairfield County. A surprise is a bold move for a first date, I must say. Maybe Nate isn't as conservative as he appears. "Should I eat first?"

"No. You won't go hungry."

A hint, but I doubt going to a restaurant qualifies as a surprise by anyone's standards. Standing around with lots of food . . . A carnival? "No other hints?"

"Hm. There will be weapons involved."

I blink, momentarily thrown, which I suspect is his intent. "Did Wendy lodge a complaint against me?"

His chuckle means I can pull off a little humor. "Quite the opposite, actually. Listen, I need to get back to work, but am looking forward to Friday."

"Me too." It's not even a lie. An adventure with a handsome man sounds like heaven. But the hiding I'll have to do on a date will be hell. "Have a good week."

After we hang up, I stare through the window blankly. An actual date. If you exclude stress-relieving late-night Tinder booty calls, I haven't been on one since Calvin.

Our first date was a poetry slam. To be fair, we met for the first time there, so it didn't start as a date. But we spent the following thirty-six hours together; thus, I count it as one. We were a force of nature, making pancakes at 2:00 a.m., brainstorming scenes in my work in progress or picking apart those in some of his authors' manuscripts, a last-minute trip to Tennessee for Bonnaroo, flying to Nevada in search of the elusive mailbox on Highway 375 near Area 51.

For a moment I had it all—a riveting lover and a stellar career. Then it all went out like a spring tide, leaving me as blubbery as a beached jellyfish. They say insanity is doing the same thing and expecting a different result, so dating a guy like Nate could be a sane choice.

I grab my face while shaking my head, then stand to shut the window in case something about this town's fresh air is infecting me. That's when I spy Wendy striding up my walkway.

The universe is determined to distract me from the task at hand.

I turn and trot down the stairs to greet her, not wholly displeased by another excuse to procrastinate, if I'm being honest. The story opening hasn't sprung to mind yet, after all.

Before she knocks, I open the door. "Hey. Saw you coming up the walk."

Something's not right. Not only is her blouse wrinkled, but her face is drawn despite her best effort to hide that fact with fresh makeup and dazzling diamond studs. Maybe she's coming down with something, too.

"Oh good. I wasn't sure you were home. I thought I'd look at the buffet you asked me to refinish." She smiles innocently enough, but I suspect she's here to ferret out my impressions of Nate. She's a busybody, but an earnest one. What's she hiding? She alluded to a difficult childhood and a mother who can't change—and certain mental illnesses might support both of those claims. Childhood wounds are key to character development, so I should dig around that a bit.

"Right, right. Come in." I gesture for her to follow me to the dining room. Along the way, I rub my throat to see if my nodes are swollen. I can't afford a cold with my agent fretfully awaiting pages. "Like I said, we picked it up at a tag sale, so it isn't any great shakes."

Wendy ignores me as she inspects the buffet's edges, opening its sticky drawers and doors. "This postmodern design is popular again.

It just needs a little love." She caresses the lumpy shellacked top of the furniture like one might stroke the hair of a sick child.

"A lot of love, I think." I eye it skeptically, trying to picture a transformation of the dull brown box on legs.

Wendy straightens up and begins checking out the dining and living rooms more carefully, taking an inventory of my style. Joke's on her! While I might call my taste eclectic, the truth is that my things mostly comprise impulse buys—varied by mood and opportunity.

The black dining room table with a central base, surrounded by creamy upholstered high-back chairs atop a cheap cream shag rug with a charcoal lattice pattern: all plucked from a neighbor's estate sale. The brass lamps are from a quirky shop on Broadway. The wrought iron wall hanging came from a trip to Vermont—my first getaway with Calvin.

"What is this?" Wendy fingers the tacky gold-plated Ferris wheel cupcake holder.

"It's for cupcakes."

She smiles at me. "Whimsical."

"Calvin had an unnatural love for cupcakes, so I bought that for him years ago as a joke."

Wearing a confused frown, she asks, "He didn't want it?"

"I told him it went missing." I don't know why. Spite? Pettiness? I'd prefer either of those to the reason I suspect—the subconscious need to hold on to a reminder of better days.

Wendy's brows rise—not a surprise—but the almost-approving grin is. "You stole it?"

Not the word I would use, but perhaps there's some truth to it. "I guess so. Its only value is sentimental, though. After the way he left, maybe I got a little spiteful."

If I let myself, I can still hear the clack of the door when he left for the last time, see the light in the living room that had shifted as if there'd been a solar eclipse, feel the deep ache in my chest and throat from stifling tears while lying in bed alone that night picturing him kissing another woman.

"You don't need to explain yourself to me."

Her lack of judgment leaves me momentarily speechless—and curious. The least I would've expected was mild encouragement to return it. Instead, she spins back on the buffet, one arm crossed over her midsection, the other hand at her chin.

"This could be stunning done in a champagne metallic paint with a high-gloss black top and black hardware. Maybe we even paint the interior a peacock blue . . . you know, funky, like you." Her pale face lights up. "What do you think? Of course, if you'd rather I simply restore the wood tone, I can do that, too. That would be very stately."

"No, no. Your vision sounds cool." The fab peekaboo color scheme is in direct conflict with her classic style. Another upended expectation. Some part of Wendy Moore is eager to color outside the lines, and I'm game to assist with that.

Her smile widens. "You won't even recognize it when I'm finished."

"How long will it take? And how much will it cost?"

"Maybe a week? And you get the friend's discount." She looks at me expectantly, but I don't understand.

"So how much is that?"

"Free, silly." She elbows me.

"No. I insist on paying for your time." Nothing is ever truly free, and unknown strings are usually a costlier proposition than a cash transaction.

"A lot of the time will be for drying and stuff." She gestures toward the bookshelves behind me in my living room. "Just cover the costs of supplies, okay?" She folds her arms as if closing off further discussion on that point. "On another note, I want to circle back to book club. I sensed your hesitation on Saturday, but to be honest, we mostly drink coffee, eat snacks, and chitchat. You'd be a welcome addition, and your publishing background might elevate the discussion. Do you work in PR—marketing and selling books?"

"Lots of marketing and selling." Strictly speaking, this isn't a lie. I'm constantly pimping my books and making ads for social media.

"I knew it." She claps her hands together. Her pride stabs me with guilt, but this isn't a harmful lie, so I let it go. "So you're definitely coming?"

I can't refuse another chance to study more women in town. From the sound of it, they're not a serious group of readers, so there's little risk of recognition. I clear my throat, coughing a bit. "I am, but I'd also like a favor from you. As a fellow creative and friend, I must encourage you to use your gift for more than a hobby. It's obvious that this stuff fuels you. There's no reason you can't start a little business and use this piece to sell your talent."

Her face freezes for just a second. It dawns on me then that my "fellow creative" remark might've blown my cover. If she asks, I'll mention book ads or something.

"I'm flattered, Harper. Really. I promise I'll consider it." Her conflicted expression then shifts to one of concern. "Are you okay? You look a little peaked."

Funny because I would say the same of her. "My throat's a little raw, so you should keep your distance. I'm fully vaccinated, so it's probably just allergies."

"Or a cold. Do you need zinc lozenges or Cold-EEZE? I can bring you some." Her energy swiftly changes from friend to mother.

"I'll be fine, thanks." A hot toddy and some rest should do the trick.

"All right. Well, can I come back tonight with Joe to move this into your garage so I can work on it this week?"

It makes sense to keep the mess and fumes in there.

"Sure. How is Joe?" He's so relaxed compared with Wendy; in that way they seem an odd pairing. Yet his affection was obvious from the softness in his gaze anytime he looked her way. "I really enjoyed talking with him."

"Everyone loves Joe." Unexpectedly, something flinty sparks in her gaze before fizzling. "He's fine, thanks."

The shortness of tone combined with her tired appearance raises more questions.

"Now it's my turn to ask if you're okay," I say before thinking better about such blatant prying.

She blinks, twitchy. "Yes, why?"

"You look a little tired, maybe? A little edgy . . ."

"Oh." Her shoulders fall and her demeanor turns almost guilty. "To be honest, I haven't slept well since Saturday. And things with Joe, well, I don't know." Her voice wobbles as she grabs her forehead. "I'm worried he might not be happy at home."

Holy hell, what made her drop that bomb on me like we're lifetime besties? Her confiding deep marital shit underscores my deception. Yes, I want to uncover things about *her*, but this intimate show of trust on her part makes me feel like a monster instead of a writer desperate to resuscitate her career. Besides, this isn't the kind of girl talk I'm qualified for, having never understood the institution of marriage.

I hedge. "He seems happy to me."

"He always says everything is fine, but a wife knows things. Notices changes." She rubs her hands over her face, bringing them together to cover her mouth as she stares into some middle distance.

I pat her shoulder awkwardly. "Your imagination's in overdrive because of the blowup between your friends. That's a marriage in trouble."

Instead of comforting her, my words seem to strike her like a hammer and crack her wide open. "That was unusual for them, proving no one ever knows. If Dirk might've cheated, why not Joe, too?"

"Did Dirk cheat?" That was my assumption.

"I don't know. I'm guessing."

"Well, Joe isn't Dirk, you aren't Sue, and you have no tangible reason to think this way. Exhaustion is screwing with you." Please, please let me be right. Being a shoulder to cry on is not in my skill set.

"I do have reason." Her gaze drifts south as she grabs hold of her elbows.

Getting juicy intel should make me giddy, but her distress is dragging at my limbs. Unfortunately, she takes my silence as permission to share more.

"Joe's been . . . physically distant. He's not so old as to have lost all interest in sex, so maybe he's getting it elsewhere." As soon as she says it, she slaps her hand over her mouth. Her neck and face flush a deep merlot. "I'm sorry. You don't want to hear about this—I just, well, you've been a good listener since we met—but now I'm overwrought *and* mortified. Joe is a good man. I can't imagine him lying to me. He's probably not cheating, but that doesn't mean he's happy."

Although I can usually be counted on for a quick comeback, this time I'm pinned between her impression of me and the truth behind my listening skills.

I owe her a kindness. Honest advice that might help her. In my city-life inner circle—an admittedly small one comprising my old neighbor Mina and two writer pals, Jane and Denise—we often blame the men when relationship problems arise. Jesus, we're the unmarried version of the CCs. I shudder as if a spider fell inside my blouse.

This conversation is pushing me through the looking glass. But back to Wendy. What would make a man disinterested in sex?

"Maybe he's having a problem down there and he's embarrassed." Holy hell, I'd give anything not to be thinking about Joe's penis right now.

Her expression tells me that isn't the problem, though. She dabs at her eyes. "I'm sorry for making things awkward. I miss Peg and am hating the empty-nest thing. Having too much time on my hands to think never leads anywhere good." Her voice is hard with self-loathing, but the stab at sarcasm makes us both chuckle, easing the tension.

"All the more reason to start a small business. Not only would it keep you busy, but when you're doing what you love, you'll love your life more. Plus, you could do some of that redecorating you wanted if you had your own income."

She holds my gaze. "It sounds nice, but I'm not a business person or great with social media. I wouldn't know where to begin to advertise and sell my services."

"I could help." Not that I have time, but helping Wendy find the joy and independence she deserves could mitigate my guilt. "And you could be selective about projects so it isn't overwhelming. It would give you a healthy focus—a sense of new purpose."

She is silent and still, her hesitation stretching long enough to lend weight to her next words.

"I don't know. Going into strangers' homes all over Fairfield County isn't safe." She wrinkles her nose. I suppose a petite woman alone could face some risk, but it seems unlikely. I'm about to say so when she adds, "Please forget everything I've said. You're right, Dirk and Sue rattled me, I miss my son, and now I'm exhausted and looking for problems. I've been married for two decades. An ebb in our sex life is hardly the worst problem."

I should leave it at that, but her cloud of sorrow and acceptance press on me. If her instincts are poking her, she shouldn't ignore them. She's chosen to confide in me, so I'll respond with the frankness that deserves. "That's probably true, and yet don't ignore your intuition. Talk to Joe. Face whatever's going on and see what happens."

She hugs herself, shaking her head ever so slightly. "Talking about things doesn't always stop the inevitable."

"What's inevitable?"

A half shrug. "Maybe you've got a point about marriage. Look at my parents. Look at the Wheelers and so many others in town."

Oh no. I don't want to be responsible for destroying her marriage. Funny, because if anyone who knows me well heard me arguing against the inevitability of divorce, they'd never stop laughing. "All I've said is that marriage isn't for me, which isn't the same as saying you should give up on yours. One thing I do know is that talking to me won't solve your problems with Joe. You need to talk to him. He seems easy to talk to."

"He usually is." Her gaze shifts as she delves into her own thoughts. "You know, my father left because my mother couldn't change. Growing up with that experience makes me insecure, like history will repeat itself."

I've no idea why her musings landed there, but we're on to her childhood—the piece I've been missing—yet now I feel like a gravedigger. The pressure of my deadline, my agent's urgency, my reputation, and my family's taunts all climb onto my back and urge me to ask another question. "You've lost me. Did your mom need to change, or was your dad trying to put her in a box to suit himself?"

Wendy is twisting her wedding band now, staring into the middle distance like a child afraid of telling the truth. "She's got issues that frustrated and embarrassed my dad, so he took off before I hit high school. Moved to Atlanta to work for his brother."

"So he gave up on her and left you both?" Asshat.

Her eyes are bright and brimming. "He isn't a bad man. She's . . . really challenging."

"How so?" I hold my breath, afraid one wrong move will shut her down.

There's a thoughtful pause. I know from George that she's talked about this with Peg, but Peg was an actual friend, not a new neighbor who's hardly been forthcoming.

"She suffers with extreme OCD—especially germophobia." She looks away, a slight slump to her shoulders. "Her obsessions overwhelmed every part of our lives."

Huh. Not what I'd been expecting. The way George spoke, I was thinking schizophrenia or bipolar disorder. It hits me then that Wendy brought this up while musing that history would repeat itself. "Like triple-checking locks and shit?"

"That's the compulsion side, and yes, there's some of that. But the severe germophobia is what's most crippling in her case. She barred other people from our house. It often prevented her from touching us, even. Her condition worsened as I went from toddler to teen—she stopped hugging me and holding my hand once I hit school age. It's not so much about dirt you can see but about germs. In her mind, everything—everything—is crawling with deadly, disgusting bacteria and viruses. So, of course, she rarely ventures out. Luckily she was a technical writer and could work from home. Other kids and neighbors would refer to her as 'that crazy lady,' which was cruel. She's actually very bright and informed." Her forehead creases. I can't even process what her life must've been like, but I'm ashamed that George Durbin's rude remark didn't affront me at the time. Wendy looks at me intently. "I always thought it remarkable and tragic that a brain can be both bright yet troubled—unable to let go of destructive thoughts that aren't real." Then her eyes cloud over.

No wonder she thinks my childhood was easy. And not for nothing, but even people who don't have mental health challenges can't always let go of unrealistic, destructive thoughts. Like me and those damn bad reviews.

"Why didn't your dad take you out of that environment?" Any mother who left her child behind would endure ceaseless judgment from everyone, but I bet Wendy's dad moved on without any guilt at all. Damn double standard in action again.

"She wasn't a bad mother. She always took care of me—washed my clothes, kept food on the table, made sure my homework was done. She read to me, and we used to watch and discuss movies at night. I think my dad thought kids belonged with their mothers. Or maybe he thought I'd turn out like her." Her gaze shoots through the window now, as if searching for him or an answer. Meanwhile, she's revealed so much. First, that she hasn't ever asked him, which makes me wonder how often she speaks to him and also explains why she's afraid to question Joe. More interesting, that perhaps she worries about her own mental health, or that she showed markers when she was younger. She is fastidious, but that's hardly a diagnosis. Still, this could be an interesting character trait. It'd require massive research, but I like that.

"Well, I'm glad to hear that, but screw the excuses for your dad, Wendy. He was selfish to walk away and leave you, especially if he thought you were susceptible to similar struggles. He should've put you in therapy, not left you alone to cope with your mom's problems. Have you never confronted him about that?"

Wendy stiffens in the face of my outrage, looking almost guilty as she shakes her head. Have I struck too close to her deepest fears, or hit upon a hidden pain? I sense both her compassion for her mother and a buried river of resentment. Not to mention how her previous offhand comment about tricky relationships between mothers and daughters now takes on new meaning.

As different as we are, we share something in common: a desire not to be like our own mothers. Granted, she has better cause than I do. Either way, Wendy looks wrung out from this conversation, so it's time to turn down the heat.

"Listen, forget about your parents. That's ancient history. Relationships are hard, period. Focus on what you and Joe have in common, but be brave enough to tell him what you need and how you feel." My words don't lift her hopeless expression. It's painful to see—a reminder of that first month after Calvin left me, when I stayed in bed or on the sofa for hours, longing for his company while imagining his new life. Terrible, terrible days. "You know, I talk tough, but Calvin shocked me. Gutted me, in fact. I thought we were happy. He never once seemed bored or expressed dissatisfaction. Always quick with a smile and new idea.

"Just weeks before his big announcement, we'd been planning a trip to Madrid. I never dreamed that a relationship where you didn't have to give anything up to be together would end. Then one day he showed up and started packing his bag. Told me he'd met a woman—his niece's elementary school teacher. He'd gone to a third-grade recital a few days earlier, and then spent the next afternoon and night with the teacher. Boom—there he was, leaving me for another woman—one he decided to be monogamous with because she wouldn't get more involved with him if he was seeing others." Talk about rejection! I pause to swallow that anew. "That really messed with me. Seven years tossed out like an old pizza box. Half the time, I'm pissed at myself for giving two shits. The other half, I wonder if I could've done or said something to make him stay instead of snarkily barking 'good riddance' at his back. Loving someone is a bitch."

When I take a breath, I'm shocked at having shared so much. Wendy's parted lips tell me she is, too. I add, "Not that Joe is Calvin. Hell, I don't know why I blabbed all that. I guess I don't want you to feel uncomfortable about disclosing your personal stuff."

"Thank you, Harper. That's kind, and I'm sorry you got hurt. He sounds selfish and rash, so you're better off now even if you can't see it yet." She eyes me curiously, her cheeks turning pink. "Can I ask a question?"

The way she's wincing tells me what's coming, but I say, "Sure."

"You mentioned an open relationship—like, you could be with other people if you wanted?" Her voice pitches upward.

I nod.

She flattens a hand across her breastbone—a move that I've seen her do often enough that I might need to give it a nickname. "Didn't you get jealous?"

"Not often. I had flings, too. I loved him, but I also loved being honest about the difference between love and sexual chemistry. Being free to explore one without losing the other. The fact that we kept choosing each other despite having those options was actually reassuring. Or it was until his last fling." I laugh at myself for how cocky I was. How self-assured. And then how utterly dismayed. By him, and by my own reaction. I—the person who never needed a man—let my life fall apart over one. Fucking love . . .

"If he'd wanted to marry you, would you have said yes?"

"I don't think so." That's the truth. I loved him but never once daydreamed of a ring and wedding dress or any of that. I liked our life exactly the way it was—equal footing, equal choices. "I know we don't see this the same, but historically the concept of marriage was more about economics and social structure than about love and happiness."

Wendy scowls.

"Anyway, Calvin and I have been over for almost two years. My date with Nate on Friday will be a first in a long time." Apparently I'm ready for something a little more than the mere physical connections the Tinder booty offered. Perhaps the transient nature of my time here makes Nate a safe testing ground—a casual affair with a shelf life.

Wendy's scowl vanishes and her eyes glitter to life. "You're going out with Nate?"

I allow her a moment of glory. In fact, it makes me smile. "On Friday."

"I *knew* you two would hit it off. He's a sweetheart. This makes me very happy." She grasps my forearm in her excitement, then releases me. "Joe and I go up to Colgate Friday afternoon for Family Weekend, but let's get our nails done Friday morning. My treat."

"Why not?" I haven't had my nails done since ninth grade. Franny Bruggio's birthday party. Friday will be another way to observe women in town performing a ritual, and it'll make Wendy happy. She needs some joy now. I'll choose a gray or navy color instead of the french manicure she'll probably get. Can't allow her too much influence, after all.

"Maybe we'll get our eyebrows done, too. I'll set up appointments." She slips that in before I can object. "But for now, I'll leave you to get back to whatever you were doing when I barged in. I'm sorry I dumped so much in your lap. I'd really appreciate it if you'd keep what I said to yourself, too."

I pretend to lock my lips and toss the key.

"Thanks for listening without judging." She looks much more relaxed than when she first arrived. It's satisfying to know that, in some small way, my being a sounding board helped her.

"Don't mention it." Please don't, or I'll feel guilty when some of what I learned seeps into Gwen's character history. I rub my throat, which is even rawer after so much talking. "Go home and get some rest. I'll see you and Joe later. Can't wait to see the refinished buffet. Let me host the book club so I can show it off."

That wrings another smile from her. "Maybe another time. By the way, we're reading Ellen Griffin's new release, *Same New Story*. She's coming to the New Canaan library on November third, so we're starting there and then heading to my house for wine and discussion. Won't that be fun?" Her face is bright with excitement—like Ellen is Bono or something.

"So fun," I fib, my heart now firmly beneath my heels. I'd rather have my period for a month than listen to a bunch of middle-aged women salivate over Ellen's book while I'm struggling to write my own. This isn't envy; it's self-preservation. I'd be better off paying Wendy for the refinishing work than enduring a night that could fully destroy my confidence. And how will I keep Ellen from telling the truth about my identity?

I'll have to come up with a last-minute excuse to bail, I suppose. Maybe this sore throat will blossom into something worse.

"Joe usually gets home by six, so we'll stop over then." Wendy's smile falters slightly at the mention of her husband, which probably reminded her of her confessions and unresolved doubts. Is a sexless marriage worth exploring in my book? It's an emotionally charged subject. Not uncommon, from what I've read, so not as personal as the OCD stuff, and relatable like my agent instructed.

Boring sex is another reason to avoid marriage, for sure. My thoughts flit from Calvin to Nate before circling back to Wendy and Joe. Ideas are percolating now. I need to get upstairs and start spilling them onto the page.

I usher Wendy to the door and wave as she trots down the porch steps, sighing. Whatever transpires in the coming weeks and months, and however I might use some of her personal information, today I helped her. Regardless of where she and Joe end up, Wendy might find her voice because of me. That seems like a fair trade, doesn't it? One that certainly can't hurt her.

CHAPTER SEVEN

WENDY

Later that evening

On my way downstairs, I stop at Billy's bedroom door and then detour into his room without turning on the lights. The hamper is empty. His desk is cleared of books and highlighters. There are no stray socks to pick up or messy sheets to straighten. Only a few photos remain pinned to the bulletin board. AXE cologne no longer permeates the space—a fact that prompts a pang, which is something I wouldn't have bet on.

Lingering in the emptiness of it all, I sigh and then lie back on his bed, staring through the darkness at the ceiling while memories barge in like dear friends. His first wobbly steps, taken in the living room between the sofa and the coffee table. Preschool finger paintings displayed proudly in the kitchen. Mispronunciations when he was learning to talk. Tooth fairies and endless hugs and dimples that melted my heart every day. Smelly sports equipment in my car that even pine-scented deodorizers couldn't cover. Loud, voracious boys in the house eating my cupboards bare while playing video games and leaving a trail of messes behind. I gave my son everything I never had growing up.

In turn, Billy came to me when scared or proud or curious. Even in high school, he sought my advice or opinion. Being counted on like that was a tangible expression of his love and respect—one that kindled the warmth of significance in my soul. It grounded me. The newly severed apron strings have left a cool, empty space in our home and my life, and left me twisting in circles at the end of those threads.

Joe's headlights flash through the windows as he turns into our driveway, so I bolt upright and head downstairs before he catches me in here again. Who needs that pitying shake of his head?

I open the refrigerator to get the pork roast and potatoes I seasoned earlier. Joe enters our house through the back door as I'm putting the roast into the preheated oven. He sets his backpack on the table before kissing my cheek and shucking off his coat. "What's for dinner, hon?"

"Pork roast and fingerlings." I take his coat, my thoughts now circling my unsettling conversation with Harper. Her independence is inspiring in some ways, even though it seems lonely. I half wonder if that's why I confided in her today. Since I left her house, I can't stop questioning whether my problem might have been prevented or at least treated if my father had taken me with him. If I would've lived freely and fully instead of clamping down on every aspect of my life to prevent a slipup.

I burn with anger until I realize that, had he taken me to Georgia, I wouldn't have met Joe or had Billy. Given that, I can hardly regret my past or waste more time on what-ifs.

"Please go change into sweats so we can go next door and move Harper's buffet into her garage." I shoo Joe forward and follow closely behind.

"Can I take a sec to catch my breath and look at the mail?" He glances at me over his shoulder.

"I told her we'd be there around six."

He slows his steps. "What's the rush?"

I gesture to the oven. "Dinner will be ready in forty-five minutes, and I need that buffet to be moved tonight so I can work on it tomorrow."

"Okay, okay. I'll change." He squints at me. "What are you charging her?"

Always an accountant. I wave his question aside. "You know it's a hobby."

"She had a good point about starting a little business. You're so good at it. And it could take your focus off missing Billy." His encouragement makes my limbs prickle—as if my reluctance is unfounded. Then again, he is in the dark about my slipups.

"You know the risks." I avert my gaze, struck suddenly by an unpleasant parallel I've never before noticed: my father abandoned my mother's mental health issues; my husband has whitewashed mine.

"It's not like your broker days, when you were in dozens of houses per week. And besides, you've been so good since that coaster incident. Surely you can relax now that you're mature and in control of yourself."

As if mental health were simply a maturity thing.

I turn my back and fold his coat over my forearm. He's not an ignorant man, so he should have a better understanding of mental illness. And yet my keeping my setbacks a secret enables his fantasy.

Sometimes I blame him for my secret, reasoning that if he weren't so quick to point out how well I'm doing, I could bear to confess that I'm not always okay. Sure, he supported me at the beginning, but would he stay if forced to live in constant fear of my arrest and how that would humiliate our family? That's too much to ask of anyone.

Rather than come clean or argue, I say, "Go on and change so we can move the furniture before the roast is done."

His shoulders sink while he stares at me like his thoughts are racing. Before he turns to go change, he mutters, "You never hear me."

I could say the same thing. It's almost as if he intentionally ignores my concerns about the risk. Even if he can't understand my anxiety, why would he push me into a sticky situation? Not that I haven't been considering it all day. Being considered a "fellow creative" bowled me over in the best way, and it's fun to fantasize about having a little mad money.

While Joe's upstairs, I hang his coat in the front closet and return to the kitchen. I'm tempted to peek inside his backpack in search of evidence to explain whatever is missing between us but hesitate too long, and then he's tromping down the stairs.

When he returns, he asks, "Were you in Billy's room?"

My brows rise. How did he know?

"The door was open . . . ," he adds quietly.

"Okay, Sherlock. You've caught me. I peeped in his room." I raise my hands in the air like a felon, cloaking my embarrassment in sarcasm.

"Peeped, eh?" Joe grabs my shoulders and kisses my forehead. "Honey, I know you miss him. So do I."

We share a silent moment of nostalgia, but Joe can't miss Billy like I do. His daily life didn't revolve around the minutiae of caring for our son. He didn't drive him to school and pick him up from practice, attend every doctor appointment, pick out his clothes, cook all his meals, work on school committees, and fundraise for his teams. Joe's sense of self isn't as invested in Billy's accomplishments. Not that anyone asked or expected that of me, but it happened, so here I am now—a ship without its rudder. If this is what Harper fears, maybe she's got a point.

"I can't wait to see him," I say. "He sounds a little distant lately, doesn't he?"

"He doesn't need us as much, and that's a good thing." Joe shoots me an emphatic look, lest I get an urge to coddle our son.

He's not wrong, but I resent being rushed through this transition phase. "We need to keep up with who's influencing him, like his roommate, the art student from California. Now he's daydreaming about working in the film industry in Los Angeles."

Joe smiles, his expression wistful, as if he's reliving his own youthful fancies. "Dreams are fun."

"Unless they're risky and take you a million miles from home. Then they're nightmares." For me, anyway.

Joe chuckles, although I was only half kidding. "He'll change his mind a dozen times before he graduates. Let him dream and explore. We're only young once."

I frown. The truth doesn't make my insides blister less at the idea of Billy making rash decisions and living thousands of miles away. Of course, my mother lives nearby and I see her only a few times each year. Apparently emotional distance can grow regardless of geography, a thought that settles coldly inside. "Are you able to leave by one on Friday?"

"I think so, but we'll have to play it by ear. The Finance Board chair is coming in, and I'm not sure how long that'll take."

I stiffen. "We have dinner reservations."

"I know, but isn't my job more important than being a little late for dinner? There's a lot going on with the budget—"

"You've known about this weekend since we dropped him off in August." I cross my arms. "Surely you're entitled to a half day off."

Joe's face falls into resignation. "I'll do my best, Wendy."

I turn away, my body hot with disappointment. Each point of friction between us reignites the nagging questions and doubts that are strangling my sense of security like pokeweed.

"What'd you do today?" Joe shifts gears.

"Nothing much." But then I remember the proof that my meddling isn't always a bad thing. "Did you know that Nate and Harper are going out on Friday?"

"As a matter of fact, I did hear about that." He bows slightly, offering a warm smile. "I'll hand you that one. He seems a little smitten."

"He's not the only one, I think." I slide him a knowing look as we exit through the back door and cross the two driveways. It's dark now, but the porch lights hit the angles of Joe's face in a way that obscures any wrinkles and makes him look years younger. He's a quietly handsome man. Unassuming in every way. I shouldn't let my suspicions provoke a fight.

"She's a nice kid, but I'm not smitten. I was being a good host."

"You weren't giving anyone else such undivided attention." He should admit that he enjoyed the little flirtation. What middle-aged married person wouldn't? I wouldn't begrudge Joe a harmless thrill if we were sharing more thrills of our own.

"She was asking me a lot of questions, which felt nice." He shoves his hands in his pockets, eyes on the ground. "I was also trying to distract her from the tension. Speaking of which, have you spoken with Sue?"

Joe has never been one for gossip, so the question causes me to cock my head. "No. It's only been two days, so I'm not sure she's ready to talk about it, and even if she were, she might not choose to do so with me. Even you said it wasn't our business." Not that I strictly adhere to such boundaries, proven by how I blabbed my marital worries to Harper, whom I'm getting to know only recently. Perhaps Sue would like an ear to bend. I should reach out—invite her over for tea or cards to give her an opportunity to unload if she needs one.

"Well, I heard a rumor." He scratches behind his ear as we climb Harper's porch steps. "Lilah in the tax office mentioned that Dirk got caught in a 'compromising position' with a local hairdresser."

I stop now and gape. Not only because I'm stunned by Dirk's audacity but also because Joe was gossiping with some woman at town hall. "Who's Lilah?"

Joe holds my gaze quite intentionally. "The woman from Boston I mentioned back in July when she started working here."

I don't remember that at all. Questions arise now: How old is she, is she married, is she pretty, did he really mention her before? My pulse throbs thickly as I swallow each one of them. "How does she know Dirk and Sue if she's new to town?"

"She doesn't. The 'other woman' is her hairdresser." He winks, but this isn't cute or funny.

"Well, that's just . . . Poor Sue." I ring Harper's doorbell, shaky and needing to escape my own thoughts. She answers almost immediately, thank God, or who knows what I might've said to Joe.

"Come on in, guys." She waves us inside, looking even paler than she did earlier. Her voice is coated with a strong rasp, too. "I've emptied the buffet, so it's ready to go. It might be easiest to take it through the kitchen rather than out through the front and around . . ."

"Probably," I agree.

"Let me help. It'll be easier with three of us," she offers.

"Are you sure? You don't look so good. Maybe you should just rest," I say.

"I'm fine. I took a rapid antigen test this afternoon to be safe. It was negative, so this must be allergies. I'm not used to all these trees and dead leaves." She points toward the middle of the buffet, which Joe is already eyeing as if it is beyond repair. Granted, it's not much to look at in its current state. "Why don't you man that section, and Joe and I can take the ends?"

Joe immediately heads for the far end, so I wedge my hands inside the middle top drawer, and Harper grabs the other end.

Joe counts, "One, two, three, up!"

With a grunt, we raise the buffet off the floor and begin the long shuffle through the house and out the kitchen door directly into the garage.

"Will you start tomorrow?" Harper's eyes brighten for a second.

"If that works for you. I've got everything I need except the special-order paints."

"This is exciting. Thanks again." She turns to go back into her kitchen, so we follow her. "Would you stay for a drink?"

Unconvinced her stuffy nose is from allergies, I opt to keep a little distance so I don't get sick and miss Family Weekend. Plus, my roast will be done soon.

"No, thanks. I've got dinner in the oven, and you need to rest," I say at the same time Joe looks as if he's about to take her up on the offer.

Harper elbows him. "You're a lucky guy—clean house, good food, talented and nurturing wife."

I try not to roll my eyes, but honestly. She said those things for my benefit, not because she believes them.

He nods, squeezing my shoulder. "I am, indeed."

Harper smiles at me, as if his response should allay all my doubts. It's sweet that she's trying to help me feel better, but it isn't working.

"Well, thank you, both. And maybe you'll be lucky in love soon, too." I shoot Harper a saucy look. "Joe, can you tell Harper anything about Nate—you know, likes or dislikes—before their date this weekend?"

Joe slaps one hand against his jaw in thought. "He's a normal guy. I'm sure you'll have a pleasant night."

This time I can't stop my eyes from rolling upward. He might as well have said Nate sleeps in flannel pajamas for how much that endorsement will rouse Harper's interest.

"I think Wendy's more excited about this date than I am," Harper teases. "Please keep her from picking china patterns."

"Ha ha." I haven't known Harper long, but we've developed a certain rapport. Her pointed questions and opinions make me feel freer with mine. I haven't had that transparency with many women in my life, so I don't take it for granted.

And I'm not about to rush her into anything, but Nate's ten times the man that Calvin was. Now if only I could help her get a new job. Do I know anyone who works in PR?

"Uh-oh. I know that face," Joe says. "Whatever you're plotting, stop. Let those two find their own way."

"I wasn't even thinking about Nate," I reply. "But, Harper, in case this isn't an allergic reaction, try to drink lots of liquids and take vitamin C tonight."

"Okay, Mom," she teases.

Joe nods, underscoring his perception that I can't help myself.

"Sorry to run, but I need to check my roast. Have a nice evening, Harper. I'll pop by midmorning to get started and check on how you're feeling."

"Great!"

Did I detect a note of sarcasm? Harper waves before closing the door to her house, so we wander back to ours.

I pull the roast partway out of the oven and stick the meat thermometer into it. Ten degrees shy of perfect.

"Wendy, would you be open to some advice?" Joe asks, standing by the sink.

I push the rack in and close the oven door. "About what?"

"I know you miss Peg and like the idea of a young new friend, but if you push yourself into every aspect of her life, you might send her running." He folds his arms, his chin dipping as he quietly adds, "No one wants someone else telling them what to do all the time."

A rash of heat causes me to bristle. "I'm not crowding her. She asked me to work on that buffet. And Nate called her—I didn't force him."

There's a moment of hesitation in which Joe is looking at me as if expecting me to come to some realization. Then he sighs in that resigned way of his.

"All right, but don't say I didn't warn you." He picks up an apple from the fruit bowl, rubs it on his sleeve, takes a bite, and walks away.

"Don't ruin your appetite!" I call after him, then sink onto the chair and stare out the back window, wondering why my kindness could get turned against me. I almost follow him to ask, but then the phone rings. "Hello?"

"Wendy. You didn't call me this morning." Tension edges my mother's voice.

"Oh gosh. Sorry, Mom." How did I forget? Every Monday, 9:40 a.m.

"I've been worried all day."

My oversight would've prompted a repetitive series of rituals and whole housecleaning that would rival that of the guys from Servpro. "I'm really sorry. I've got a lot on my mind with our upcoming trip to visit Billy at college, and a furniture-refinishing project I'm undertaking for my new neighbor. Now I've got pork roast coming out of the oven."

"Organic meat, I hope?"

"Nothing but," I fib. Sometimes I take what's available and don't overthink it. In fact, sometimes I do it to prove that I'm not like her—rigid in thoughts and proclivities.

"Well, you won't forget to call me on Thursday, right?" Mom asks, uninterested in asking about Billy or Harper while she's obsessing about my missed call.

"No, Mom."

"But you forgot today. I had you dead on the highway. I said the Rosary four dozen times."

Her concern is laughable because I rarely drive farther than the one mile to town center, and she knows this. Harper's right—my dad was wrong to leave me with no buffer or help dealing with my mother's obsessions. He doesn't even know about my own compulsion. I saw him only six times between his leaving and my wedding. A few years later he came to meet his grandson, a visit that caused me a lot of turmoil. I wondered if he'd disappoint my son one day like he did me. He sends Billy occasional cards but hasn't seen him since his tenth birthday.

Fortunately, Billy seems to attribute his grandfather's detached interest to a matter of geography more than anything else. I won't disabuse him of that notion because I'd never want my son to feel unloved by anyone in his family. That's a wound that never heals.

"You can relax now, Mom. Joe and I are fine. Billy is fine. I told you, I was busy with my neighbor."

I hold my breath, mindful that I caused this spinout. She can't help it. Or maybe she could if she'd stuck with therapy. We often manage normal conversations, but today will not be one of those occasions. Instead, we go through four more rounds of reassurances to the point where I'm about to slam the phone against my skull to make it stop.

"You'll set a reminder for Thursday?" Her voice is brittle, like that of a child who's awakened from a bad dream.

"Yes." I nod despite being alone in the kitchen.

"Okay. Tell Joe hi. Enjoy your dinner—make sure the roast is thoroughly cooked so you don't get trichinosis. Talk to you on Thursday."

"All right. Bye." I hang up and rest my forehead against the table. It might be better if she moved close by, but getting her out of her house at this point is a moot argument. In her mind, it is the only clean place in the Northeast—maybe the world.

In the silence of my kitchen, I try to imagine being stuck inside her thought loops. The constancy of it must be exhausting. When therapy helped me, I begged her to go. After the third session, she quit because the entire process—from leaving the house to the germs in the waiting room—stressed her out.

I'm forever grateful Joe helped me find a good therapist and escorted me to my first session. *"Don't be ashamed, Wendy. I love you, and this isn't your fault. If your mom weren't so overwhelmed with her own issues, you would've been in therapy years ago, but there's no reason you can't start now. Let's get a handle on this so we can build the kind of family life we've dreamed about."* It would've been easier for him to dump me and find someone less complicated.

Therapy mostly worked. I've beaten back at least 90 percent of my urges these past decades, although I can't know if that statistic would hold up had I not also avoided most outings to spare myself the challenge. I'm not perfect, but I'm a good person who gives back to friends and my community. I lie to Joe only to protect him from suffering along with my worst impulses.

Every day I show him and Billy that I love them, so why does it feel like they're both pushing me away?

———

With my duffel of supplies and tools slung over my shoulder, and a box of herbal remedies in hand, I march up Harper's porch steps and knock on the door. It's nine thirty in the morning. She should be awake by now.

She answers, tissues sticking out of the pockets of a terry cloth robe that's been gnarled in the dryer one too many times. Her face registers surprise, perhaps because she's never seen me in my work clothes: paint-stained sweats and a long-sleeved T-shirt, with my hair swept into a high ponytail so it doesn't fall in my face all day.

A pink nose and red-rimmed eyes suggest she's been up most of the night fighting off the cold she'll probably continue to deny. "Good morning, Wendy."

"Oh, Harper, this seems like more than allergies. I brought some things to help, just in case." I nudge the box forward, but she doesn't take it.

"Come on in." She leaves the door hanging open and walks back toward her kitchen, so I close it behind me and follow her.

When we get there, I toss my duffel on the floor by the door to the garage and then begin removing supplies from my makeshift medicine box while she pours herself coffee. By the look of things, she hasn't done a dish in two days.

Raising a blue plastic neti pot, I say, "This is a big help with congestion. Just make a little saline solution with boiled water—cooled to room temperature—and a little salt and baking soda. And here are some vitamin C tabs and zinc, both of which help me. I've also brought lozenges."

She's thumbing through the vitamins. "I'll try anything at this point, 'cause I'm too busy to be sick."

"Busy with what?" Did she get a job?

"A proposal." She avoids my gaze.

I should back off, but can't help myself. "Are you freelancing?" I admit, I spent part of last night thinking that if I did start a little business, I could help her by hiring her.

"Yeah." Her vague reply is accompanied by a dismissive wave, so I drop the subject. I get it. It must be stressful to be out of work. It's not the same as losing my daily mothering role, but that emptiness—the long, uncertain days—are the same.

"Oh, I almost forgot." I turn to get my copy of *Same New Story* from my duffel. "I finished this already—couldn't put it down, actually—so you can borrow mine. It's a fun one."

Each of her next moves happens in slow motion—the way she reaches for the book, the awkward smile spreading across her face, the lazy speed at which she scans the blurb.

"You're too thoughtful." Oddly, her tone sounds like that's a bad thing.

"Well, I'll get out of your hair. Do you mind if I occasionally pop in throughout the day to use the restroom or use the kitchen sink to wash up?" Although what needs a good cleaning most is this kitchen itself.

"Make yourself at home. I'll be upstairs all day."

"Sleep will do you a world of good." I smile and then snatch my bag before opening the door to the garage. "See you later. Feel better!"

She nods as she closes the door behind me.

Once alone, I set out my supplies: putty knife and automatic sander, screwdrivers, mineral spirits, goggles, several grades of sandpaper, tack cloths for cleaning the wood. The first step is stripping the original finish and cleaning up this baby; then the fun work will begin.

I'm awaiting the delivery of the specialty paint I ordered, which could arrive by the end of the week. Oh, shoot, that reminds me I forgot to give Harper the receipt so she can reimburse me for those. Later, I guess.

With my goggles in place, I power up my sander. Smoothing away the blemishes and flaws is extremely satisfying work. Seeing the potential in something ugly, stripping this old gal down to her bare bones, and making her beautiful are like magic. The rhythmic work is also calming. The focus helps quiet so many other thoughts and doubts.

Working with furniture is also easier than working with people. A console doesn't talk back or get disappointed. It doesn't expect or demand anything. And by the time I finish carrying out a refinishing plan, it will look and feel exactly as I intend. I love that result most of all.

I try to envision controlling my impulses, taking on more projects, and being like the women on Instagram who make all those cute videos of their own work. But I'm not good at that kind of thing—at selling—unlike Sue, who is effective at whipping up engagement on social media for fundraisers.

Sue. Another reason I stared at the ceiling last night. Dirk and a local hairdresser, for Pete's sake. I'd be heartbroken and humiliated in her shoes. Might even run up to Rhode Island to escape the gossip while I sorted myself out. The thought that she also might feel like hiding out is what keeps me from calling her.

If I start a little business, I could reach out under the pretext of asking for help. Then if she wanted to share, she could.

Making a name for myself as a premier local refinisher—wouldn't Billy be impressed? I've spent so much of our relationship making sure he wasn't ashamed of me, like I sometimes was of my mother, that I've never thought about ways I could make him proud. It'd be nice to be known for being great at something before I die. And Harper's got a point about the emotional charge this work gives me. It might not be the worst thing if I did something for myself once in a while . . .

Ninety minutes later, I'm thirsty as hell and my lower back is pulsing with tension. I stand to stretch before knocking lightly on Harper's kitchen door. When she doesn't answer, I crack it open.

"Harper?" I peek inside. She told me to make myself at home, after all. "I'm just coming in to get a glass of water."

No answer. I'm glad she's napping. I guzzle a cold glass of water and then set it in the dishwasher. Dirty dishes in the sink sit atop dried food stuck to the basin. I could clean this kitchen in ten minutes, maybe fifteen. It's a weird line to cross, but Harper's sick and might appreciate a little TLC.

I work quickly, partly to avoid getting caught in the act, which could embarrass us both. Then again, it's not like I'm snooping—not really. I'd do this for anybody who didn't feel well. It makes me happy to help her. Once everything is loaded in the dishwasher, I make sudsy water and wipe down all the counters and the stove and reorganize the salt and pepper shakers, napkins, and pencils on her small kitchen table before setting out the paint receipt for her to see.

While wringing out the dishrag to hang over the faucet, I notice more of the unusual glass votives that I saw last week in the living room lined up on the windowsill. Each one is different. Some are colorful, some are clear and thin, others thick. She must collect them.

I smile, imagining her searching for vacation mementos, poking around little shops with friends or by herself. Unlike most trinkets, none of these are schmaltzy or bear the name of the location where she got them. A collection like this takes effort, which tells me something about her, too. She's more sentimental than she lets on, for starters.

The gray, smoky one is like her—darkly sexy and different from the others. Suddenly the tingling burst of euphoria surges, and before I know it, I've pocketed the votive. A squeaky floorboard overhead causes me to freeze and start to sweat. Jesus, what am I doing? More movement, this time on the stairs. She's coming! I can't think—ohmigod! I flee to the garage, where I pace with the hand still gripping the votive buried in my pocket. It feels like a hot charcoal against my palm. My stomach burns, too.

Why didn't I put it back as soon as I heard her?

She has so many of them maybe she won't notice. She's hardly an organized person who keeps track of each little thing in her house. Or I could leave it in her garage. No, why would it be out here? That question would lead directly to me. Think, Wendy. Think. Oh, damn. Oh, double damn.

"Wendy?" Harper's rasp sounds behind me, making me start.

"Oh!" I jump, nearly pulling my hand out of my pocket with the votive held tight. "Sorry. You startled me." My smile is too big; I can feel it.

"You cleaned my kitchen?" Her quizzical look is exaggerated by the reddened nose and glassy eyes.

Oh God. I went too far. "I'm sorry—I mean, I thought you might appreciate a little help since you aren't feeling well."

"You didn't need to do that, but thanks." She's still peering at me funny but doesn't look offended. "How's everything going out here? You really worked up a sweat."

The votive is heavy in my pocket. Can she see the lump?

"Sanding burns calories," I cover, my heart galloping. It takes every ounce of strength not to close my eyes and wish I could disappear. "You know, I was just about to run some errands, so I'll work on this more tomorrow. While I'm out, would you like me to grab some soup or something?"

"I don't want to be a bother."

"It's no bother. I'll be at the store anyway." I might be able to slip the votive back without her noticing if I'm bringing in groceries.

"No, really. I'll call for takeout if I get hungry." She's wearing an expression that reminds me of some of Billy's worst teenage days—the ones during which everything I did annoyed him.

Damn again. "Well, see you tomorrow, then. I hope you feel better."

"Thanks. And, Wendy, it was nice of you to clean the kitchen, but please don't trouble yourself with that again, okay?" She smiles, waving as I trot away.

"You got it!" I can't stomach being called nice after stealing from her.

Once inside my own home, I rest my back against the door until my breathing settles. What a close call. This is exactly why I shouldn't work for people. Salty tears sting my eyes.

I need to hide the evidence until I figure out how to slip it back. Or maybe it's not worth the risk of getting caught returning something she probably won't even miss. What to do, what to do? Tears dampen my cheeks. It's getting worse. I've resisted calling Dr. Haertel, partly to avoid questions from Joe, but it'll be worse if I get arrested for stealing. Maybe I could tell him I want help coping with Billy's absence. Joe would support that goal without questions.

I empty my pocket. For a moment, sunlight streaming through the window emphasizes the smoky patterns in the votive's glass. It's unusually pretty. Smooth and heavy. Oddly comforting despite my remorse. I open my workbag and set the votive inside, then zip it tight and take it to the garage.

Truth be told, I like having this little piece of Harper with me. Something and someone new in my life feels crucial when it seems like I'm losing grip on the old, familiar things.

CHAPTER EIGHT

HARPER

That same evening

I lumber downstairs, phone in hand, holding my breath while I click on an Instagram notification. Sometimes these are good things—fans tagging me with a photo of one of my books and a nice comment. Other times the cute book photo is accompanied by a not-so-nice review, in which case I assume the person who tagged me is a disgruntled writer or a nasty asshat.

This time, the image causes me to come to a dead stop midway down the stairs. Calvin tagged me. The photo—him with a galley of his manuscript in one hand and his other arm around a very pregnant Melissa—disrupts my vision like a bright camera flash. The sting of seeing them pricks with less force than a year ago, but my scrambled thoughts must reassemble before I can read his post. The fucker wrote a book—something he talked idly of doing while we were together—and got a publishing contract. I'm among the many people he'd like to thank for inspiration along the way.

I don't know whether I want to throw up because the breakup that tanked my career inspired him to finally write a novel or because he's going to be a father. A baby! I mean, it's no shock that an editor landed a publishing contract. He always was a good, if undisciplined, writer. But a baby? That's lifelong-level commitment with no days off. No breaks. The kind of handcuffs we used to scoff at. He should've used a photo that didn't show off his pregnant girlfriend if he planned to tag me.

Insensitive prick.

Then again, given my attitude about relationships, he probably assumes I moved on quickly. It irks me that I didn't. Worse, that I couldn't. I loved him. I became convinced I'd never meet another man who liked me as I was and wouldn't try to change my views. My ego couldn't accept that, while he seemed perfect for me, I was not perfect for him. Now I wonder if looking for a perfect fit is immature. If Wendy's opinion that any healthy relationship requires some compromise is true.

Compromise—whether abiding an unequal curfew or watching Linda settle for a misdemeanor unlawful sexual conduct charge against Kevin rather than a felony sexual battery charge—always feels like giving up, but there might be some concessions worth considering.

This is not something I'll solve today, so I shove my phone in my sweat shorts without leaving a comment and shuffle to the kitchen sink to fill the neti pot. Salty water and snot spill thickly out of my nostril and into the sink. Gross, but it's helping me breathe easier—a definite improvement over the morning. When I finish, I set the neti pot in the sink basin. One that is no longer home to a mound of dishes, cups, and frying pans thanks to my neighbor's disquieting yet kind behavior.

I twirl around, the rosemary-mint soapy scent faintly detectable. The dated kitchen feels homey when the counters are shining and the dishes are put away. Calvin was as messy as I am, so living in chaos became my normal state of being. An acknowledgment that cleanliness makes me feel lighter and less stressed comes begrudgingly.

Wendy. The thought prompts a sigh. She's so . . . extra. In good and less good ways.

Still, no one has pampered me since I left Ohio, not even when I've been sick. I suffer alone. Almost proudly. I can't remember the last time I asked for help with anything. Calvin brought me funky gifts, planned interesting outings, introduced me to new music—cool life shit—and he was fun and sexy. But domestic god and nurturer he was not. I almost feel sorry for Melissa and their child . . . almost.

My mother coddled us kids. By the time I'd come home from school, she'd have made my bed and removed my dirty clothes from the floor. Freshly ironed laundry would be neatly tucked into my drawers. Sick days elicited the full handmaid service with all my favorites— grilled cheese, Lipton soup, chocolate milk, vapor rub, and unlimited television. Mom baked cakes whenever we made honor roll, and found other ways to celebrate the little victories in everyday life. At the time, I rolled my eyes, even scoffed at how she could be satisfied making her life about serving everyone else in our house. Looking back, I think it must've hurt her that I didn't see the love behind her efforts beam like a spotlight against a night sky.

I frown.

Is it Wendy, or has the character work I've done on Gwen today made me feel nostalgic for the things that used to seem stifling? Could be guilt. I do owe my mother a call.

I grab my cell phone and dive-bomb the sofa, where I snuggle under a fuzzy blue blanket. A handful of my birthday votives are scattered across the coffee table. I like my fifth-birthday gift best despite the air bubbles—because of those imperfections, in fact. Mom always complained about Dad's hobby causing clutter, but I loved its quirkiness. In hindsight, it was probably the hours he spent at the glassblowing facility that bothered her more than the clutter—not that she'd admit that. A quick perusal of various pieces from my collection reveals a marked improvement of his skill and imagination. With a sigh, I dial home.

"Hello, stranger," my mom answers. Dig number one served with her signature cheerful tone. "Are you finally settled in?"

I accept her mild reproach because this call is delinquent. My family knows my last book didn't hit any lists, but they don't know my career is in real jeopardy. Mom just thinks I'm up here for research. "Yes. It took a while to get myself together."

"I looked up New Canaan on Google. So much nicer than your old neighborhood." Again, the smile in her voice contrasts with the criticism—not that she'd see it as criticism.

My mother doesn't appreciate SoHo. Too crowded. Too loud. Too dirty. *"Don't you miss nature?"* she asked the last time she and Dad visited the city, right after Calvin moved out. Come to think of it, she didn't like Calvin all that much, either, or understand our relationship. *"If you're together all the time and in love, why not get married?"* she once asked. I'd laughed at the idea, but now it's obvious that Calvin's opposition to lifelong monogamy wasn't real. My own attitude made it easy for him to stick around until he found "something better." My muscles twitch. Not that I needed a ring. I didn't and still don't. But love is love, and a broken heart hurts like hell.

"It's different." I force myself to focus on my current conversation. "Very clean—which you'd like. Quiet. A family town." One in which I stick out like a flamingo in the Arctic.

"Maybe I should come visit . . ." She's used that hopeful, guilt-inducing tone on us kids from time to time to great effect. But having her meet Wendy would be catastrophic, and not just because Mom would blow my cover. Those two would end up tighter than those chicks in *Steel Magnolias*, and then I'd have two mothers.

"I'm here to work, not sightsee and shop." In the silence that follows, I replay my words, suspecting my tone was abrupt.

"The stress of this career isn't healthy, honey. Maybe now that you've proved yourself, there's something else you can do, like teach? Pass along what you know for a steady paycheck and great benefits."

I laugh, but her silence tells me she's serious. God, I can already hear my brother taunting me with "those who can't, teach" insults.

"I'm a writer, not a teacher. Not to mention that I love my work." Most of the time. "I'm not quitting."

And I'm never teaching. It'd be the worst job for someone like me, who always needs downtime after being with a group of people. The mere thought of that energy drain is draining enough.

"Okay." She sighs, sounding equally frustrated that our conversations all occur on a bed of eggshells. "Hopefully the fresh air will give you a positive outlook. People like to read hopeful stories with less curse words than your last book."

There she goes, defending unbridled optimism like Wendy does. Is everyone over forty unwilling to face some of the naked ugliness in the world and most human beings' ongoing tussle with selfishness? "All my books have curse words, Mom. Even the bestsellers."

"I'm not criticizing. I'm making a suggestion is all," she defends.

Years' worth of invisible yet weighty pressure is piled onto her version of a pep talk. I can clearly picture her worried grimaces, often accompanied by a warning about life in the arts. Conversations that began in high school and continued through college and afterward. They finally stopped when my debut became a *New York Times* bestseller, but they've crept back into our discussions since April.

"Well, I write what I see. People have flaws." I certainly do. "We can be both petty and thoughtful, selfish and generous, envious and magnanimous. And everyone, bar none, lies once in a while. It's okay to be human. Did you ever think that maybe people are popping anxiety pills at alarming rates because they feel obligated to live up to some idealized Hollywood version of humanity? Books that reflect the actual human condition might help silence people's inner critics. In the long run, accepting reality could make us happier than reading about flawless fantasy people."

I cough into the quiet that greets the end of that tirade.

"Well, anyway," Mom segues, "less distractions should help you focus so you don't have to get a real job . . . A normal job, I mean."

At least she caught herself that time.

"I'm making progress on a new idea. We'll see how it goes." My not-so-subtle way of letting her know not to ask about the plot. Talking about it too soon could jinx everything.

"Good. So how are the people in your new town? Connecticut folks always seem cold in the movies and books, with their big houses staffed with nannies."

More proof that stereotypes in fiction aren't good for society.

"I live in a part of town with modest homes and people. Everyone's friendly so far, although I've met only a few folks. My neighbor Wendy is refinishing my buffet."

"You made a friend!" Like that's the most important thing in life. "Is she single, too?"

"Nope. Married. Her son's a college freshman, so she's 'adopted' me. She likes taking care of people." Exhibit A: my gleaming kitchen and the box of medication left behind.

My mother chuckles. "That first year when the kids are gone is tough. Be nice to her."

"I'm always nice," I snap. It's true, despite dishonesty not exactly fitting within the definition of kindness.

Mom pauses. "I didn't mean anything by it."

I grab my face with my free hand. "Sorry. I'm a little grouchy because I've got a cold."

"You never get enough rest or pay attention to nutrition. Drink lots of liquids, take vitamin C, and nap."

I can't help but smile. There must be some handbook all moms get after giving birth. "How's Dad?"

"Outside raking the leaves. He's thinking about retiring early and selling his glassware on Etsy in a 'serious' way." Her incredulous tone tells me she doesn't exactly support his plan.

I shift to a more upright position. On one hand, the hypocrisy is mind-blowing: I shouldn't pursue a creative career, but now he's going to do it? On the other, he's spent decades at a so-called "real job," and his adult children no longer rely on that paycheck. "That's interesting."

"Mm." She clucks. "I guess I can kiss the garage goodbye for good."

That's only a problem on days when it snows, which aren't excessive around Columbus, Ohio. I'll have to shoot my dad an encouraging text. Shifting gears again, I ask, "What have you been up to?"

"Oh, same old stuff." Her voice changes, almost like she's holding back. "Still volunteering at the ABC House twice a week."

A Better Chance is a residential home for underprivileged kids who show academic promise. They live there with a guardian, attend a good high school, and can visit their parents occasionally on the weekends.

"You've been with them a long time."

"A decade." A noise in the background distracts her for a second. "Do you have any plans to come home soon?"

"No. I'm under a deadline." I do feel bad trampling on the hope in her voice. "Sorry. Maybe after I turn it in. Anyway, what else is happening?"

"I babysit for your brother and Heidi three days a week." She's referring to Jim, not Rick. Jim isn't a bully like Rick. Occasionally he protected me from Rick's relentless taunts, but he mostly kept his head down and took care of himself. He's an engineer now and living near Columbus.

"Do they pay you?"

"Of course not." She sounds aghast. "I love spending time with little Jimbo."

I don't doubt that, but it would be nice of Jim and Heidi to offer her something in exchange for that massive commitment. Then again, she raised her sons to expect that stuff from her (and from women in general), so Jim probably hasn't given a second thought to the magnitude of her promise.

"Jim got a promotion last week, did you hear? VP of something." She sounds proud and not the least bit put out even though Jim and

Heidi could obviously afford to hire help. "Heidi's still working with that pulmonary group. Jimbo is a darling rambunctious toddler. His third birthday is next month, you know."

"I do keep a calendar of family birthdays and send gifts." It's a good thing we aren't on Zoom so she can't see my irritated expression, for shit's sake. I also FaceTime Jim and Heidi on occasion, so my nephew sees me now and then. Not in person—at least, not since two Thanksgivings ago. Truthfully, I'm closer to my cousin Mandy and her daughter than to either of my brothers or my nephew.

"Oh good. Did you hear Gemma's pregnant now?"

My oldest brother Rick's wife. Rick the dick. A bully and misogynist. That sounds awful, but he tormented me for as long as I can remember. From locking me in the shed during hide-and-seek to teasing me when I got my period, he never let up. He's not the brightest, but he was smart enough to do most of this outside my parents' earshot so that—like my friend Linda—I was always trapped in a he-said, she-said game with my complaints. When my debut became a bestseller, the bullying changed to "playful" sarcastic deference. "No, I didn't. When did this happen?"

"The other week. I'm sure he'll tell you whenever you catch up. It's been a busy time."

I seriously doubt he'll be filling me in. He assumes Mom will do it for him. That might even be the real reason she called last week.

"I'll shoot them a congratulations note." Only because Gemma is a decent person. Kind and caring and somehow oblivious to Rick's chauvinism. I always thought she'd wise up, but now she'll be linked to him forever. Please, God, don't let Rick have a daughter. Poor thing wouldn't stand a chance.

"That's nice, honey."

An awkward silence ensues, during which I assume she's wondering if I'll ever have a baby. My eggs become less desirable with each passing month, yet I can't see myself as a mother—not yet, maybe never. I've got little practice with utter selflessness, and I enjoy my freedom. Plus, given my DNA, chances are high my kids would be just as quick to point out my mistakes as I have been with my parents. But it wouldn't hurt me to be a better aunt.

Mom clears her throat. "So, have you met anyone special lately?"

I knew it. She's never cared half as much about my career as she does about my love life. A churlish part of me almost holds back, but thinking about how Wendy lives for any news from Billy, I throw my mom a bone. "I'm going on a date with someone Wendy introduced me to, but it's no big deal."

"What's his name?" Her voice pitches into buoyant territory, exactly like Wendy's did.

"Nate. He's in finance—works for the town. Seems nice enough. That's all I know. I don't plan on making New Canaan my permanent home, so don't get too excited. He's someone my age to hang out with for a while." Mostly. Maybe also someone to have hot sex with when I get uptight and creatively blocked, but given my secrets, that's a complicated proposition.

"Is he handsome?" Now she sounds like a teenager. With two sons and a daughter who never shared much, she hasn't had this kind of conversation often, so I indulge her. I'm mildly concerned that my snooping into Wendy's life to understand her motives has turned around to the point that her influence is changing me. There's also the possibility that I might be more interested in Nate than I'm ready to admit.

"He's handsome. Tall. Trim. He's got a great smile and easygoing personality." Not someone who seems to run hot and cold like Calvin did. Or like I can.

"He sounds great. Is he taking you someplace romantic?" Flowers, candles, heart eyes. Gooey love stuff always excites my mom, but you can't force those things. There's no decision tree that guarantees your journey will end there. That's why a person should rely on something other than romantic love for security—like autonomy and individual success. Recognition. Personal power.

"I'm not sure. He said it would be a surprise."

"Well, I can't wait to hear about it later."

Oh snap. Now I'm roped into another conversation about Nate. At least she did a pretty good job of not pushing me hard on the hot-button topics. Has my staying away taught her to respect my boundaries, or is she simply not as overbearing as I remember? I frown. "I'll let you know how it turns out. Anyway, I should probably get back to work."

"It was so nice to hear from you, honey. Thanks for calling." Her sincerity rings clear.

"You're welcome. Bye!" When I hang up, an unexpected tightness knots in my chest. My mom thanked me for calling, as if I'd done something exceptional. My own brother doesn't tell me his wife's pregnant with their first child. And my only nephew knows the other nursery school kids' moms better than he knows me. None of that reflects very well on me.

My entire family is moving on together with me barely tethered by a weak grip on my mom's resilient apron strings.

I close my eyes and rest my head on a throw pillow, uncomfortable that I've gotten to this age without ever stopping to reevaluate my childhood baggage. Calvin would laugh his ass off to hear my thoughts. Or to learn that a near fifty-year-old woman in the burbs is having such an impact on my lens. Or that I'm going on a date with a conventional finance guy. Then again, Calvin moved to Riverdale in the Bronx and is starting a family, so I'm the one who should be laughing my ass off. Yet not even a chuckle stirs in my chest.

Why drive myself mad? Calvin and babies are irrelevant. I'm not here to cultivate a suburban life or a family or the obligations that come with all that, nor am I here to change my entire life. Maybe Wendy's got me thinking about relationship dynamics a little differently, but I still like being a free woman. Spontaneous. Able to switch gears on a moment's notice.

I'm here for one reason: to write a damn book. A book that won't write itself, especially if I let Wendy, my mom, Calvin, and others steer me off course. I should be digging into my characters' lives, not my own.

I lug myself off the sofa with a grunt, then start up the stairs. Better to dump this emotional upheaval onto the pages than wallow in it on the couch.

———

I close out the Word document twelve hundred words later. Five or so pages—not a ton, but a start. The first line is shit, but it's possible the entire first chapter will change midway through the book. It's always this way—things shifting all the time as characters and themes reveal themselves the more deeply I ponder them.

Satisfied, I go downstairs to make peppermint tea. Outside, clouds are rolling in. Twilight reminds me that it's also cocktail hour, so I tip some bourbon into my mug. After another few moments spent scanning the sky, my gaze falls to the windowsill.

Something's off. A missing votive. The red and the navy are there, the clear squatty glass one, too. But where's the gray one? Birthday fourteen. Gray to mark the "dark years," as my dad referred to them then. At that stage, he probably held out hope I'd eventually blossom into a sweet young woman.

I search the counter and table, but it's nowhere to be found. I'm sure I unpacked it. Pretty sure. I make a quick circle around the first floor, but don't see it in any of the other clusters of votives. Did I leave it in SoHo? No one's been here—

Ah, Wendy. Perhaps she moved it when she cleaned, yet I didn't see it when circling the first floor.

Did she accidentally break it and feel too embarrassed to tell me? I move to rummage through the garbage, but the bin has been emptied and a clean liner installed. Maybe she didn't think much of it. It's not like they're Versace crystal. Still, it's odd that she wouldn't mention it. I hate to accuse her . . .

Nothing to do about it now, so I take my spiked tea to the living room, light a few candles, pull up Yumi Zouma on Spotify, and settle back on the sofa. With my feet tucked beneath me and the blanket across my lap, I sip my hot beverage in the silence and stare out the large front window onto the cul-de-sac. Golden porch lights twinkle along the little street. One guy strolls past, briefcase in tow, probably walking home from the train station. Once home, he'll be greeted by kids, a wife, maybe even a dog. People who care . . .

I turn on the lamp to fend off the chilly darkness, a little bored. No nearby bodega. No easy, cheap food delivery. No serious people-watching to speak of. Just me and my thoughts. A sometimes scary prospect. I could binge-watch something, but I'm not really in the mood. My gaze lands on Ellen's book.

The golden paint strokes on its turquoise cover look luminescent in the candlelight. I stretch forward to pick it up, knowing I need to read it. Want to, even, if only to learn something about why it's such a success, which I can then use to inform my work in progress.

With a nervous sigh, I sit back and crack it open.

Caroline Lotz's father had taught her that anything she gave power to would eventually have power over her, but in her bid to win her husband's forgiveness, she'd forgotten that lesson.

Nice job, Ellen. Theme and conflict in the opening line. Reader questions about what she did to upset her husband also popping into place. Rather than put this down and run upstairs to tear apart my ugly draft pages, I force myself to read on. My pages will be there in the morning, and Ellen's first draft would not have been this polished, either. It's time to stop comparing and simply enjoy the escape. Her good prose doesn't make mine awful. A rising tide floats all ships, and on and on go the mental gymnastics I exercise to keep from falling into the abyss of self-doubt yet again.

Five chapters later, I set the book down. So far, it's as entertaining as its buzz suggests. Fun, witty, engaging. I smile. Ellen's wanted to hit a list, and now she has. I'm truly glad for her. It's a well-earned accolade after years of hard work, discipline, and talent.

Rather than hide when she comes to this library, perhaps I should invite her to meet for dinner beforehand. It's been ages since we last hung out—maybe longer. My breakup and bookpocalypse turned me into something of a modern Miss Havisham—bitter and in hiding while pouring that rejection onto the pages. If we met for dinner, I could also ask Ellen to play along with the ruse of my knowing her from the industry in general rather than her identifying me by my pen name in front of Wendy and the others. Controlling the situation instead of being blindsided is my best chance to maintain my cover.

A steady rain pelts the porch roof. I haven't heard that lulling music since I first moved to the city. One doesn't really hear the soothing thud of rainfall on the roof in an apartment building. Listening now, I get nostalgic recalling rainy days in the tree house my dad built when Rick was born. His roof work was stellar, so that tree house stayed dry. Thinking of him reminds me to ask Wendy about that votive when I see her. Now I'm too tired to do anything.

But I need to focus on my book. I close my eyes and try to play out a scene between Gwen and Haley—their first conversation. When nothing solid materializes, I worry that the low rumble of occasional thunder might be portending something.

CHAPTER NINE

WENDY

Friday morning

"Good morning, Dr. Haertel, thanks for getting back to me." I zip my luggage shut and set it beside Joe's bag near the bedroom door. He's at work, but supports my returning to my psychologist to "combat the empty-nest blues." "Can you squeeze me in soon? I've slipped several times this year, and it's getting worse."

"I have some time early Monday morning. Eight o'clock?"

"That should work, thanks. I know it's been a while. Honestly, I'd been doing pretty well until eighteen months ago." If making my life small enough to avoid temptation can be considered doing well.

"Did something change at that time to create unusual stress or otherwise trigger you?"

I think back. "Well, my best friend moved while we were getting Billy ready for SATs and starting to tour colleges, then came all the applications, and now he's gone, so I guess it's been a prolonged transitional time." I don't mention my marital concerns. It's too embarrassing to discuss on the phone.

"And now?"

My face burns even though Dr. Haertel has never judged me. "I'm at loose ends . . . I even took something from my neighbor's house this week."

It's still buried in my workbag in case I have an opportunity to return it. But Harper hasn't left her house this week—not to run any errands or exercise or anything. She's always there, usually in pajamas and braless. What could she be doing inside all day when she doesn't have kids, a husband, or a job?

She never came into the garage on Wednesday, so I assumed she was sick in bed. Naturally I couldn't test that theory and risk getting caught with the votive in hand. She popped her head in the garage yesterday as I was leaving, so I ducked out claiming to be late for an appointment. I'm not going today because of our other plans.

I'll start painting on Monday, after I return from Colgate. Maybe then she'll finally go grocery shopping and give me an opportunity to sneak the votive back into her kitchen. Of course, the woman survives on Uber Eats, crackers, and bourbon, so I'm not optimistic.

"It sounds like we have some work ahead of us." Dr. Haertel's voice brings me back to our conversation. "It's not surprising, given those transitions. I'll see you Monday."

"Thank you so much. See you then." I hang up, tapping my fingers against my mouth. There isn't time to overthink anything with Harper's and my nail appointments scheduled in twenty minutes.

After parking the car in the lot behind the salon, I steel myself to act normal—or as normal as I ever am. There's no avoiding Harper today. Not when this mani-pedi was my idea—my gift, even. I check myself in the mirror, half expecting to see the word "guilty" stamped across my forehead. After a brief huff, I exit my car.

A bell rings overhead as I slip through the salon's back door and walk to the front entrance. Harper's not here. No shock. Someone who rebels against societal expectations isn't someone likely to respect schedules. To me, showing up late is like announcing that your time is more valuable than that of whoever is waiting on you, yet a little part of me envies the lack of anxiety about keeping to a schedule.

When she doesn't materialize, I go back inside to the cubbies where regulars store polishes and choose "Feelin' Poppy"—an orangey red perfect for autumn—from my box. I grip my purse strap with one hand and the tiny bottle with the other to make it difficult to take anything that doesn't belong to me.

Suddenly Harper is at my side. "Sorry I'm late."

My overbright smile, meant to cover any latent guilty expression, might terrify small children. I gesture toward the racks of polishes for public use located beside the personal cubbies. "Which do you like?"

Harper scans the rows and, wearing a sly grin, nabs a gunmetal-gray bottle of polish.

"Pretty." That was stupid. It's hardly a pretty color. Always black and gray and black and gray. I'm starting to wonder if she's color-blind.

I almost suggest turquoise or red, then think better of it. Unlike me, she perceives advice like some kind of "hey, dummy" slap instead of seeing it as coming from a place of genuine caring. "So, where's Nate taking you?"

Solé is reliably good, but South End has a younger vibe and lively bar area. I grin picturing them having drinks: two interesting, attractive young people flirting. A pang of longing for the early days of my relationship with Joe lodges deep inside my chest. Everything still ahead of us . . .

"I don't know. It's a surprise." Her expression is pleasantly intrigued.

"Ooh. That's exciting!" Joe hasn't surprised me in ages. To be fair, I haven't planned any surprises for him since his forty-fifth birthday party a few years back. Even then, he suspected because it was unusual for me to insist on going out, let alone to the Carriage Barn, a local gallery that is also available to rent for private events. "Did he give you any hint?"

"It's within a fifteen-minute drive, I need comfortable shoes, and weapons are involved." When I gape, she laughs. "Any guesses?"

"Weaponry?" What ever happened to dinner and a show? Thank God I was born in the seventies. I blink, flummoxed.

"He's stumped me, too—not that I'm complaining." Her happiness blooms like daffodils after the winter thaw. Apparently Nate read her well. If they hit it off this weekend, at least I'll have done something good for her to offset my theft.

As we walk to the pedicure room, Harper says, "So, Wendy, I meant to ask you something this week, but never got the chance."

She's wearing the kind of hesitant expression I've used on Billy when asking if he studied hard enough for a test or remembered to take out the trash. Oh God! Does she know? My grip tightens around my purse as beads of perspiration begin to gather at my hairline. "What's that?" I croak.

Every muscle is taut enough to snap. Who knew I could hold my breath this long?

She tilts her head, nose wrinkled apologetically. "When you cleaned up my kitchen, did you accidentally break one of my votives?"

"Yes!" I blurt, compounding my first mistake with a second before covering my face as I struggle not to pass out. What have I just done? "I'm sorry." More than she knows. "You were asleep and I was embarrassed." Then I latch on to an opening—a chance to put it back. "I've been searching for a replacement online but can't find that one. Where'd you get it?"

Such a liar! My entire body is aflame—hopefully she'll assume my sweat is from a hot flash. I'm worse than my mother, who never hid her illness from anyone . . . even when I sometimes wished that she would.

Harper shakes her head. "You won't find one like it. My dad blows glass as a hobby. He makes me a new one for every birthday. That was my fourteenth."

A sentimental gift? My limbs tingle as if falling asleep, pinned beneath the weight of my fraud. And this new lie means I can't even return the damned thing. I'm a terrible person. I avert my gaze and fight back the urge to barf. "Oh no."

"It's okay. Really. I'm not mad. It's not like you did it on purpose." Harper chuckles. "I just needed to make sure I wasn't losing my mind, is all."

Her kindness has the opposite of its intended effect, so my tumbling emotional innards churn on. "I feel awful. Really awful about the keepsake."

"I'll be getting plenty more, provided I stay healthy." She raps her knuckles against her head playfully.

Maybe I should come clean. It would be a relief, in a way. She's open-minded about so many things that she might not judge me a wretched thief. It's not like I *want* to steal things. Wait—I can't tell Harper when I haven't even told Joe. He deserves better.

My head is down as we make our way to our seats, then Harper says, "Sue?"

Across the room, Sue Wheeler is watching the technician wrap paper between her toes before helping her out of the chair and to a dryer.

When she sees us, her expression looks as uncomfortable as I feel. It's been almost a week since she stormed out of my house. Was I right to give her space? I'm still so mad at Dirk, I can only imagine how she feels. Did she come here to suss out Dirk's mistress? Joe didn't mention which salon that bimbo worked in, but this isn't a hair salon. She mustn't be here. Oh, poor Sue.

"You look fabulous," Harper tells her.

She does, too. I recall dressing extra nice for weeks my senior year in college after Greg Hobbs broke up with me, thinking it'd make him regret his decision. I hope Sue's plan works better than mine did. Greg was my first real boyfriend, but our six-month relationship meant much less to him. It was just as well that my ploy to win him back failed, because Joe is a much better man.

Sue touches her face, her gaze darting away. "Thanks."

I force a smile, going along with the pretense that she didn't storm out of my house last weekend. This is not the place to invade her privacy, but I could offer an opportunity to unburden herself if she's looking for one. "I've been meaning to call you to get together for lunch," I say cheerily. I consider bringing up the refinishing business, but until I see Dr. Haertel, that idea will remain on ice. "What's your schedule like?"

Sue's polite smile falters. "I'll call you."

"Super." Her obvious tension proves her wounds are still raw. "I'll make that spinach artichoke quiche you loved from the school fundraiser." If she wants to get together, the ball is in her court, and I no longer have to overthink how to be a good friend.

She nods. "Nice to see you both." Before either of us can respond, she hustles to the other room, where she'll sit for what will likely seem to her an eternity, waiting for her toenails to dry.

Harper kicks off her shoes and plops onto one of the open seats. A technician points me to the one beside her.

Harper leans toward me, mumbling, "Have you heard anything more about that situation?"

Fortunately the tubs of bubbling water should drown out our conversation.

I won't disclose what Joe told me, especially not to someone who doesn't care deeply about Sue. Loyalty matters. So does discretion. And if new-to-town Lilah from town hall already has a connection to the unscrupulous hairstylist, perhaps some of these technicians do, too. Dirk's betrayal enrages me. Ironic, given my deceiving Joe and Harper. Still.

Harper's looking at me curiously. I've hesitated too long. "We haven't had a chance to talk yet."

A technical truth. If I were in Sue's shoes, I wouldn't want people questioning me, no matter how well intentioned. Most of us need space to work through our problems without interference.

"Really?" Harper winces and grabs her calf when the technician massages her foot. She must be ticklish. "My friends and I love a good bitch session whenever a man screws up."

"When you're older and married, you learn not to share everything. Marriage is complex. It takes time to fully understand and weigh one's feelings. And even if I did know more, I wouldn't tell anyone. It's Sue's life. She gets to choose who knows the intimate details."

"How very loyal." Harper sounds almost rueful, although that makes no sense. "It's rare to find people who can be trusted with secrets."

Trusted with secrets, perhaps. But not trusted completely. God, it's so hot in here.

"Everybody has a right to some secrets." Instead of being the fun bonding experience I planned, this spa day feels more like the endless agony of a Chuck E. Cheese birthday party. I gaze blankly at the magazine in my lap, clueless about the identity of the young celebrities splashed across the pages.

"Careful, Wendy, or I'll think you're harboring some, too." Harper winks.

I force a light laugh. If she only knew. The votive is like a stick of dynamite waiting to explode my life and destroy this friendship. Why did I lie about breaking it instead of playing dumb?

Dr. Haertel had better help me quickly.

"Well, what are your plans with your son this weekend? Football game, maybe?" She smiles. "I remember my first college tailgate with my parents."

"Oh gosh." Partying with my underage son is not on my to-do list. "Billy's only eighteen."

"He's in college. You know he's drinking, right?" She cocks one eye.

I shake my head. "I don't think so. He'd lose his lacrosse scholarship if he got caught."

Harper laughs—not to be cruel, I know, but she clearly thinks I'm naive. "Well, I don't know him, so maybe you're right. Then again, there aren't many college freshmen who don't indulge in a keg party now and then."

"Even if he does, I wouldn't encourage it." Billy could still develop an illness like my mother's or mine, and alcohol is generally not a good idea for people with impulse control disorders. Not to mention my general belief that parents shouldn't encourage children to break the law. Billy would be as uncomfortable as I, no doubt. Joe, however, might enjoy it.

Harper sighs, giving me a long look. "For what it's worth, the first time my parents let their hair down with me is one of my better memories. It made me feel like they were finally giving me space to make my own decisions and mistakes."

The unspoken message—that I'm still micromanaging my son—is loud and clear. I'm frowning—I can literally feel my brows pulling together. A small part of me knows exactly how Sue felt when she stormed out of my house, unable to keep herself together for one more minute.

A few weeks ago, I assumed Harper would benefit from my good advice. Ha! She couldn't want anything less. It's galling, though—the possibility that Harper's the sage and I'm the know-nothing. And yet I can't deny that she's opened my eyes a bit. The problem is that I'm not sure her "help" won't inadvertently hurt my life.

"At least tell me you took my other advice," she says.

"What advice?" I am antsy now, wishing I'd run off with Sue.

Harper's stare is nearly accusatory, as if I'm purposely playing dumb. "To talk to Joe. You know, about your concerns."

I freeze, horrified that she's airing my marital issues in public. With as carefree a tone as I can muster, I mutter, "No, no. Everything's fine."

She stares at me long enough to make me self-conscious. "You know no one's handing out gold stars for having a 'perfect' life. It's okay if everything isn't always fine. You're allowed to complain and hunger for things you don't have, to be authentic and demand what you need."

True, although a quick scroll through social media proves that most of us want to project perfect happiness, viewing each "like" and comment as a type of gold star. "I hear you, Harper. But sometimes it's also okay to think things through and work them out for yourself rather than create waves, especially when you've got a family to consider."

She leans closer. "I just worry that your childhood conditioned you to put other people's comfort ahead of your own. That's why I want you to get comfortable saying what you really feel when it matters."

Her sincerity creates a real moment between us. If we were alone, I might be more honest and thank her, but the two technicians at our feet are probably eavesdropping. "I'm not holding back." Another lie. "You were right before. I was overreacting."

"If you say so." Harper shrugs before craning her neck to check out her toes, while I deflate from the lost opportunity to connect at a deeper level. "The Wheelers, Joe, your son . . . All that stress is exactly why I am single and childless."

Maybe I can salvage something between us now. I don't care how independent and nontraditional she is—everyone wants to be loved. "Harper, you've spouted this philosophy for a few weeks, yet you'll never convince me you don't welcome love in your life. You wouldn't have been so hurt in the past if that were true. Maybe I could work on being more assertive, but maybe before your date tonight, you could consider being open to a monogamous relationship instead of automatically rejecting the idea."

I brace for a hot retort, but her body remains slack, her eyes focused. "I've been giving more thought to my relationship dynamics, but that's still a long way from shackling myself with a kid."

"Shackle?" I laugh, thinking about my charismatic, energetic, popular, and smart son. He's everything I'm not and never was. I've done my best to ensure that he had two parents to count on, that our home was always open to his friends, and that he knew I was invested in anything that mattered to him, like lacrosse. My nurturing won't necessarily overrule nature, but I did that part better than my parents. I breathe a little easier each year Billy goes without any hint of impulse control issues. Of course, many such afflictions surface in one's early twenties, so he's not in the clear yet. "It's not like that."

"Nap schedules, school schedules, college tuition . . . feels like a lot of chains to me."

"You're leaving out all the good parts. The incredible love and laughter. The pride and joy." I stop myself there and consider her feelings more carefully. "It's a valid choice to remain childless, but don't make your decision based solely on half-informed perceptions."

Nate strikes me as a family-oriented man, so this pairing will likely end up being my first major strikeout. More evidence that I should focus more on my own relationship than on others'.

We fall silent while Harper studies the technician finishing her glossy topcoat.

"Doesn't this seem a bit wasteful?" she says to no one in particular.

"How so?" I admire my shiny, bright toenails.

"A pedicure in October in New England. It's not like we'll be wearing open-toed shoes."

"Pampering yourself is never out of season." Maintenance is important, too. Especially with calluses. I wouldn't want to run a sandpaper sole up Joe's leg in bed—if we were having sex, I mean. Come to think of it, maybe if I scratched him up, it'd stir him to some action.

"Regular upkeep would be pretty pricey."

This is the first Harper's alluded to her finances. New Canaan rent is less expensive than Manhattan's, but it's high enough to burn through some savings. She's probably getting unemployment checks, though. "How's the freelancing going?"

Her confused expression quickly relaxes. "Oh, you mean my proposal. It's coming along. These things take time."

"The publishing industry must be competitive." I stand, relieved to move to the manicurist station and away from discussions about my marriage. "Did you start *Same New Story*? Everyone's excited to have an expert in the book club now."

"An expert?" Harper's reticent smile seems out of character for someone normally quite confident. A hint at hidden depths, yet she remains a bit closed off even when she's being friendly. "Is there such a thing as a reading expert? I mean, yes, some people understand story structure better than others. Some authors write with more eloquence. Editors and PR folks can push what they deem the buzziest books, but ultimately the average reader decides what books sing to them, and that's a good thing."

"But some books *are* better than others."

She hikes one shoulder. "Yet some outstanding books languish in obscurity while some of the most simplistic fly off the shelves. It's more about fit, and whether the consumer expectation is satisfied."

"Literature is art, not a product." Art that takes me away to new places. That makes me feel less alone in the world. That explores relationships in ways I've been afraid to do in real life. It's precious, unlike a bar of soap or coffee maker.

"It's both."

I shake my head. "What I do—cleaning up old furniture—that's a product. Writers create whole worlds from thin air. That's art. But I get your point. In order to sell books, you probably have to approach them like merchandise."

"I definitely do." Her undercurrent of sarcasm is odd considering that I'm agreeing with her, but I don't press. "Merchandise that will appeal to the largest group and offend the smallest."

"Offend?" That doesn't even make any sense. Sometimes our conversations feel like they're happening in two different languages.

"Some books' messaging or social commentary can upset readers who don't share those same views."

I nod. "This is why I prefer books about relationships, not issues."

"Even relationships are affected by politics and other things. But I get it. You like hopeful endings, not tragic ones."

"Definitely not tragic ones. Why read about bleakness and our lack of control over the future? Books are one place where things can turn out the way they should."

"See, you're proving my point. There are terrific books—really poignant ones—that don't turn out hopeful. But for you, that's a bad fit, so you'd call it a bad book."

"Not if it were well written," I defend.

"Mm. Based on everything you've just said, I'm pretty sure that you'd hate a book that ended tragically, no matter how stellar the prose. Besides, who's to say how things 'should' turn out? You? Me? Some author you don't even know?"

Maybe she's got a point. I'll have to think about it some more.

I'm not sure whether the way she always has me questioning myself and my opinions is good for me or causing more stress. It could be both good and stressful. Most change is, and she's definitely pushing me out of my comfort zone. If you look at it that way, it's sort of her fault that I took her votive.

Harper stands once the technician pushes back from the bowl. "What next?"

"Manicures and then eyebrows. You'll be all polished for your date."

"Nate seems great, Wendy, and I'm looking forward to getting to know him. But don't get too invested. I'll be gone in March, so it's unlikely that this will be a lasting love match."

March? I assumed she'd be here at least a year, maybe longer. Suddenly my stomach hurts for reasons other than my theft or Sue's plight. Come summer, Harper will be gone—unless she ends up falling for Nate despite her protestations. Then she might reconsider. It could happen. No one normal turns her back on love. Of course, no one would say Harper was normal . . .

"Even if I were, Nate might not like me." She picks a manicurist station, so I sit at the next one. "Anyway, when do you think you'll finish the buffet?"

"Early next week." My eagerness about it—about everything, really—wanes. Six months isn't enough time to build a real friendship like I had with Peg. Then again, would a year make a difference? Maybe it's foolish to think I can create a richer life with new friends when I'm always dogged by my particular problem.

On top of that, everyone leaves. Dad. Peg. Billy. Harper. Possibly even Joe someday—especially if Dr. Haertel can't help me.

I really ought to start building something of my hobby so I'm not left with nothing at all.

In any case, that votive will be all I have to remember Harper as the years go on. Since I can't return it now, I'll stick it in my drawer as soon as I get home.

"I can't wait to see it." Harper heaves a happy sigh. "When it's revamped, it won't remind me of the past. Onward and upward, right?"

"Right." Most people look out for themselves, forging ahead in search of their own happiness with little regard for anyone else's investment in the relationship. I know Harper's referring to Calvin, yet I can't help but feel like someone who gets casually dismissed and left behind over and over no matter how hard I try to be a good person.

Am I the problem, or are they?

CHAPTER TEN

HARPER

Friday evening

Nate's car pulls into my driveway, so I trot toward the entry to greet him. While grabbing my green utility jacket off the coatrack, I stop in front of the hall mirror. The salon-created "highly alert" expression remains shocking despite my having had hours to adjust to the waxed brows and tinted lashes. What was I thinking letting Wendy talk me into this? I look wired.

I swing the front door open just as he's reaching for the doorbell.

"Well, hello. Good to see you again." Nate leans forward, his lips grazing my cheek. A sweet gesture and the first body contact I've had from any man in a couple of months. I wouldn't be at all surprised if a film crew were in the yard recording the scene on this porch for a Hallmark movie—one Wendy would love. If I'm being honest, I don't hate the delicious bit of sexual tension coiling in my stomach. Good to know it didn't vanish along with my writing talent. "You look really nice."

"Thanks." Not knowing our plans tonight added an extra layer of anxiety to the "what to wear" dilemma. Considering the traumatic experience of choosing an outfit for my first real date in years, I'll take the compliment. Wendy would probably be horrified that I'm not in a dress or heels, but I'm most comfortable with the standard faded jeans, black shirt, and funky turquoise belt combo, topped off with thick silver hoop earrings. The aging pink suede cowboy boots are my most comfortable footwear, and add a bit of unexpected playfulness.

"So, when do I learn where we're going?" I step onto the porch and lock the door behind me.

Nate tips his head toward the car as he makes his way down the few steps to the yard, his hands buried in his pants pockets. I like his snug dark denim and fitted crisp white button-down shirt. Simple. Casual. And the clothes show off his lean build. "I think I'll keep you guessing a little while longer."

"Ooh, you're an antagonist disguised as a good guy?" This is already a little fun, so I relax, now only mildly concerned about the prospect of weaponry.

He holds up his thumb and forefinger. "A little bit, yeah."

He walks around to the passenger side to open my door. I'm perfectly capable of opening my own door, but his gesture is intended to be considerate, so I don't balk.

Once settled in Nate's Audi, I detect a faint "new car" aroma. "You didn't need to buy a fancy car to impress me," I tease.

Nate buckles himself in and deadpans, "Did it work?"

I nod, stroking the charcoal-gray leather seats. "This is a serious grown-up car."

Big enough for a family of five.

He fires up the engine, puts the car in reverse, and smoothly glides out of my driveway and down Crystal Street. "It's the third car I've ever owned, but my first brand-new car. Got it two weeks ago. I kept my last car for eight years, so I wanted to make sure any new car would transition to a family."

With mock horror, I crack, "You should've told me about your pregnant wife when you asked me out."

"You said you were into open relationships." The outer edges around his eyes crinkle as we both laugh. "But seriously, I'd like a kid or two someday."

Although I'm not currently in the market for one, that smile of his might be potent enough to get me pregnant. I'm guessing he's early to midthirties now, so perhaps men have ticking clocks, too—mental ones, anyhow.

"You sure plan ahead. I'm more of a pantser." In life and in my work, not that he'd know that jargon.

"Commitments make you uncomfortable?" Nate's eyes remain glued on the road ahead as we drive down Route 106 South.

I frown. "Not exactly. I'm just not sure the whole marriage-and-family thing is for me."

"People say everything is better when you've got someone to share it with."

"*Some* people. Maybe Oscar Wilde had it right: 'One should always be in love. That is the reason one should never marry.'" I laugh, but Nate slides me a skeptical look. "I'm not against love, just skeptical of a legal promise to love someone forever. I've yet to meet a decades-long married couple that truly inspires me."

"Are your parents divorced?" he asks.

"No. They're coming up on a fortieth anniversary." This conversation feels heavy for a first date. What happened to favorite-foods-and-best-movie-kind-of-get-to-know-you questions?

"That's a big deal. Lots of people don't make it that far."

Proving my point, actually. "My mom is content to let my dad have his way most of the time."

Whether it was the meals she cooked, the vacations we took, or even what they watched together on TV, Dad mostly got what he wanted. I don't care what she says; there's no way my mother enjoyed watching golf. And by the time I left home, we were all sick of sauerbraten.

"Really?" He asks this thoughtfully, not sarcastically.

"Well, it's not like my dad's a control freak. He's a normal guy. An honest one who provided for his family. But his life kept on its basic path—work, bowling league, poker nights, after-work happy hours—while my mom was at home keeping everything running smoothly and juggling important school and sporting events despite her part-time admin job at the local YMCA. Their dynamic was pretty typical in my neighborhood, which suggests most guys assume they keep some freedom even when married."

"My folks never got that memo." He snickers, which is both a relief and a surprise. A lot of men would argue or turn caustic. "But it sounds like your mom is happy with her choices, so why do they bother you?"

I've always assumed she settled for the life she was taught to want rather than choosing a life that called to her soul, but maybe Nate is right. No one has a gun to her head, and yet she stays and keeps smiling. Is it possible she is actually happy and not brainwashed?

Nate adds, "Anyway, I'm glad someone as smart and attractive as you is single."

Okay, points for his slick way of smoothing things over. It's refreshing that he's not completely closed off to my opinions, either. I'm curious about his family, but also reluctant to get to know him too well while I'm hiding the truth about myself. "For what it's worth, I object to the word 'single.'"

This causes him to screw up his face. "Why?"

"When applied to women my age, it often implies a sort of loneliness rather than a choice." I turn my head to look out my window, wondering why I went there. Am I purposely sabotaging this date, or am I truly as bitter as that sounded? *Dime-store fatalism plagues every page of this protagonist's journey.* That one-star-review commentary jabs me in the side so hard I wince.

Nate pulls away from the stop sign and hits his turn signal. "That's not how I meant it. You're hardly someone to be pitied, Harper. It's clear you meet life on your own terms."

Another nice recovery, although I'm starting to doubt my so-called terms. Nate is very comfortable with honest conversation. I love that, or I would if I weren't lying my ass off about who I am and why I'm in town.

To keep things bubbling along, I opt for less personal territory as he heads into a large parking lot. Hiking a thumb toward the office building with a retail first floor in front of us, I say, "I suspected we'd end up at a gun range, but this isn't that. Now I'm officially stumped."

"Gun range?" He bends partway forward with a snort and slaps the steering wheel. "Sorry to disappoint, but we're taking a cooking class. They hold them here once a month. I thought it would be a fun activity and take the pressure off conversation. There're usually several other couples in the class."

A man who cooks is sexy. A man who makes me cook? Not quite as sexy, but I applaud the initiative.

"I've never had a date make me work for my dinner before." I'm kidding around, but I'm also dead serious. If this is a test of my domestic fitness, I'm doomed to be a spectacular failure.

"Well, there'll be wine, if that helps."

"Wine always helps." I smile. "But be warned. My cooking skills are limited to fried eggs, toaster waffles, reheated leftovers, and boxed brownie mix with walnuts."

Nate opens the door to Jane Dean's Kitchens. "Then this will be both a fun and practical experience. Tonight's menu is Japanese. I've never made a Japanese dish, so it'll be a first for me, too."

I stand at the threshold. "You do know we could probably find a dozen sushi restaurants within two miles of here, right?"

When he laughs, his dark eyes shine with genuine mirth, which makes me smile. "True, but dinner dates can get stale. You learn a lot about a person when you cook with them."

Seems we all have hidden agendas, although as those go, his is well intentioned. He gestures inside, waiting for me to agree.

Having just boasted about being committed to spontaneity, I can hardly refuse. "All right, but expect to leave here hungry because I'll likely ruin everything."

He merely snickers and follows me into the "classroom," which consists of multiple kitchen islands with stove tops and prep sinks, each one also set up with groceries, pans, and cutlery. The teacher is off to the right side of the room, talking to another couple. There are two young preppy couples and one group of three middle-aged women in the room with us. They all look comfortable and eager; meanwhile my stomach is doing somersaults.

This domesticity is so not my scene. I'm not just a fish out of water; I'm flopping on land, gasping for air.

Nate takes my coat along with his and hangs them on the hooks by the door, and then we proceed to the open island at the front. I lift the knife that resembles a small axe. "'Weaponry' is right."

"Seeing you wield that is giving me second thoughts about this idea," he teases.

I set it down and give myself a mental talking-to. How bad could this be? I'll spend an hour chopping vegetables and preparing a dinner that I'll never make again. At least we'll be busy enough to avoid awkward pauses and too-intimate conversations. My curiosity about Nate's compelling blend of self-assurance and warmth worries me. Risking real feelings before I can be fully honest feels a bit like a train wreck in the making.

He raises one brow. "You seem a little skeptical. Next time you can make all the plans and I promise not to complain."

Next time?

"Someone's feeling cocky," I jest, flattered that he's already angling to see me again. Of course, "next time" also means keeping up my ruse. Nate, like Wendy, is a nice person who deserves better.

Fortunately, the instructor begins explaining the meal that we'll be making as well as the different types of knives we'll be using and the proper technique for each one. Nate listens attentively. No doubt he was a teacher's pet. The kind of student who not only gave 100 percent in class but also went above and beyond. Unlike me, the naturally bright but lazy kind. The student who doodled in class while dreaming up stories but could cram weeks' worth of studies into a single night to ace a test, and who didn't need SAT tutoring to score in the ninety-fifth percentile.

My novels are the first thing I've ever cared about and poured my soul into, which is probably why my last book's failure seems to have killed something crucial inside me. Unfortunately, this is neither the time nor place for an identity crisis.

As that thought bubble lingers overhead, I notice the teacher has stopped talking and I missed half of whatever she said.

Nate turns to me. "Do you want to chop the onions while I deal with these mushrooms?" He handles the pile of shiitakes.

"Sure." I grab the little axe, but Nate hands me a different knife.

"This one's better for chopping onions," he says, wearing a patient smile.

Already a mistake and I haven't even begun. I cast a quick glance at the neighboring island to see if the onions are being minced or sliced into strands.

"Thanks." I begin peeling an onion's skin, throwing the waxy shell in the trash. Guilt about my deceit keeps me from asking him questions about the Moores. If I get him talking about himself, it'll leave less time for my half truths. "So, tell me more about your game-loving family. Do you have siblings?"

A genuine smile lights his face, making him even more attractive. He's clearly a man who not only loves but also likes his family. I imagine if I were to consider marriage, this would be an important trait in a partner. The kind of man more likely to invest in his wife's and children's happiness than someone like Calvin ever could.

Calvin had a distant relationship with his family, so he never pushed me to make more effort with mine. Sometimes when Mandy would joyfully recount the happenings of a sister or aunt, I'd hang up with an empty, slightly yearning sensation—an acknowledgment of living disconnected from an important part of life. But then Calvin would bring up Rick's politics or remind me that my parents didn't respect our relationship, and that'd reset me back to our "norm." Or it did until he left me to live the exact life he'd always disdained. Bastard.

"Oh yeah, big family. Growing up I shared a house with three brothers, two sisters, my mom, my dad, and my grammy."

"So you know how to share?" I joke. "I had only two brothers and my parents, which was more than enough for me." As soon as I say it, I regret it, and not only because of the dissatisfied quirk of Nate's brow. I don't dislike my parents—I just dislike the way they dismiss my beliefs and my goals.

I return my attention to the onion and slice it down the middle like the lady next to me did.

"You never wished for a sister?" Nate asks.

Still copying my neighbor, I begin slicing through the halved onion lengthwise. "Not really. My cousin Mandy lived in my same town and we're roughly the same age, so we grew up like sisters."

"Where does she live now?"

"Outside Baltimore." I owe her a call. She wants to visit, but that'd mean she'd have to lie for me with Wendy, which she'd hate. My life is so effing messed up right now, so it's not the best time to decide to dip back into the dating pool. I gaze up at Nate while making another slice; then a sharp burn makes me scream. My hand shoots into the air, fingers splayed, blood oozing down my index finger and onto my palm, then dripping onto the sliced onions.

"Oh damn!" Nate grabs my wrist and sticks my hand underneath cold running water to clear and examine the wound. Blood continues to pour out of a deep inch-long cut. He grimaces. "I think this needs stitches."

"Seriously?" I've never had stitches and suddenly feel nauseated, grabbing the edge of the counter with my good hand for balance.

At this point, we've become the center of attention. Lookie-loos stare and whisper as the teacher rushes to us. "Oh, that looks bad. I warned you about the sharp knives."

Straight to defense mode, as if I've summoned a lawyer.

"Don't worry, I'm not blaming you." I eye her in a way to signal my annoyance.

Her gaze flits to Nate. "You should take her to the ER. I'll clean this up." She gestures to the bloody counter and halfway-prepared food.

"Thanks. I agree." He hands me another clump of paper towels and instructs me to hold them tight against the gash, then glances around the room filled with concerned gazes. "Sorry for the disruption, everyone. Enjoy the class, but watch yourselves!"

And just like that, I've ruined this date before it really got started. I should be pleased, considering how unlikely a coupling we are. I'm not happy, though, and not just because of my sliced-open hand. Perhaps this is a punishment—or reminder—that I shouldn't get involved with anyone while pretending to be someone I'm not.

"I'll grab our coats." Nate presses one hand on the small of my back as he guides me to the car.

He's considerate. Pleasant. Full of good humor. Kind. Accepting. It's something of a shock to feel more than a physical attraction after so long. Makes it harder to give him up too quickly.

"I'm so sorry." That class probably wasn't cheap. Nothing in Fairfield County is. "I feel terrible. Let me reimburse you, Nate."

"Don't worry about it." He grins at me as he starts the car. "If I recall, you did warn me you didn't cook. Let's get you stitched up, and then we'll go have a drink and a good laugh." His smile is so warm I can't help but return it.

An unbidden thought about how Calvin might've reacted to this situation comes. He would've been pissy about losing the money and missing the activity, and I probably would've accepted that guilt. That Calvin did exert subtle control over me in ways I never fully realized is another punch in the face—additional pain I hardly need.

While Nate drives me to the hospital, I keep my hand raised above my heart and close my eyes to shut down further introspection. One crisis at a time is my limit.

———

Ninety minutes later, we've left the Tully Center and are driving down South Avenue toward my house.

"Should we go to Gates for something to eat?" Nate asks.

I stare at my damaged finger, worried about how much it will hurt to type tomorrow. "I don't know if I'm up to it, honestly. Kinda lost my appetite."

He nods, turning down my street, then suggests, "A nightcap might numb the pain."

Nice angle for an invitation inside. He's been such a good sport I don't want to be rude. One drink can't hurt. It'll give me an opportunity to say something to turn him off and extricate myself from this sticky situation without making him think it has anything to do with him.

"I've got some Bulleit inside if you'd like a glass." As I turn to him, I'm struck anew by his handsome bone structure and intense eyes. Why couldn't we have met last year, or even next year after my magnificent comeback?

"If you don't mind, I'd like that very much." He turns off the car, already confident that I won't rescind the offer. Confidence is always attractive, dammit.

"Let's go." I exit the car and walk up the walkway and porch to unlock the front door. As we amble inside, I try to see this quirky old rental through his eyes. All the rooms are painted a pale beige, as if the broker told Mr. Durbin to "freshen it up" with neutral tones. The windows lack blinds of any kind but are framed by sheer curtain panels. I've hung only two large pieces of art—a watercolor I picked up in New Mexico and a cool Manhattan skyline in deep impasto—as well as the ironwork from Vermont. "Have a seat. I'll be back with two glasses. Neat or ice?"

"You tell me."

"Neat." I smile before hustling to the kitchen, mentally admonishing myself for flirting. It's fun, though. I'd forgotten how satisfying banter could be. Those Tinder calls never entailed it—being all about a different kind of satisfaction.

I choose the Glencairn bourbon glassware tonight and pour us each a good amount. The caramelly, nutty aroma hits my nose, instantly easing the tension in my back. When I return to the living room, Nate is studying my bookshelves.

"Thank you." He takes a glass and sniffs it before raising it into the air. "Cheers." He takes a sip but, unlike Wendy, doesn't choke or sputter. Instead, he gestures to the books. "Quite a collection."

I enjoy a nice gulp of the bourbon and let the heat in my throat begin to seep through the rest of my body. "Are you a big reader?"

"Maybe a book a month, sometimes two."

Before I wrote professionally, I read more voraciously. But reading these days isn't the same because I can't turn off the editor part of my brain. "What's your favorite book in recent years?"

"*Circe* was fantastic. I'm a mythology geek, so that was part of it. But you'd like the message about the way society treats women—particularly the most talented and passionate." He sips more bourbon and takes a seat on the sofa.

It would be wise of me to sit in the chair, but sometimes wisdom is overrated. I sit on the sofa with my legs tucked beneath me and quote part of that book: *"You threw me to the crows, but it turns out I prefer them to you."*

"Yes!" Nate flashes his brilliant smile, and I'm dazzled anew. "You read it?"

"I liked it, although it wouldn't be my top pick."

"What would be?" He's leaning toward me slightly, gaze fixed on mine and full of curiosity that's frankly a bit dizzying.

"Probably *Untamed*—the Glennon Doyle memoir. Powerful memoir about finding the courage to stop making choices based on others' expectations. To become the person you were before your beliefs were conditioned."

"How do you mean?" He's smiling and not annoyed, yet even I'm exhausted from harping on these issues.

"Well, the idea is that many of us end up living inauthentically because we're trying to fit into the roles we're supposed to want. The ones society at large embraces. Heterosexual. Wife. Mother. Nurturer. Skinny, buxom, and blue-eyed like Mattel's and Madison Avenue's standards of beauty. If a woman is promiscuous, she's a slut, whereas a man's a stud. Those kinds of conversations." I swig more of my drink and sigh. My finger still throbs.

"I know how you feel about 'the patriarchy,' but speaking as a man, I promise we don't hold monthly meetings to come up with ways to keep women down."

Here's my chance to chase him off so I never have to confess the truth or ghost him. This opening doesn't make me happy, though. I stare him down while gearing up for a preachy speech. "Maybe not, but men still hold most positions of power in government and business. They legislate what we can do with our bodies. Even after hashtag-me-too, some still blame our behavior or clothes for their sexual assaults. They promote and compensate aggressive—even abusive—men while labeling competent, assertive women strident bitches. And in homes with two working parents, most of the housework and childcare still falls on the woman. So from my perspective, men who aren't actively helping break down those barriers are complicit." One of my main beefs with my father and brothers is that very thing—the willful ignorance and refusal to help because doing so wouldn't benefit them.

If this conversation brings this date to an end, I can't be sorry. It's basically my truth. Still, part of me might've been willing to suppress it long enough to experience a kiss or more from this particular man.

"That's a fair point. But what about women who shame, blame, and judge each other on some of those issues instead of making room for a different point of view?" Nate asks with utter sincerity. "I know female pro-lifers who feel judged and shamed by friends, and even you judge your mom for her choices."

Oof. I can't deny that, but it doesn't undercut the bigger point. "Don't you think those divides have roots in brainwashing? Generation after generation promoting the idea that women's 'natural role' is to support others' dreams rather than chasing their own. That the ultimate female experience is motherhood. The fact that some women voted for a guy who bragged about past sexual assault and cheated on his many wives demonstrates how deep-rooted this thinking is. Maybe that's why the women who live within those assigned boxes get pissed at the ones who don't and, conversely, why those who don't observe the 'rules' get mad at the ones they perceive as holding back progress."

"I see." He's wearing a confident, somewhat ironic expression.

"See what?" I lean forward to peer deeper into his eyes.

He studies the contents of his glass for a second. "I'm not discounting your thoughts, but your generalizations make it seem like you're more interested in winning the debate than truly considering my points."

"Ha!" I prefer a man who says what he thinks. I do like to win—there's no denying that. Just like there's no denying my disappointment that having sex with him tonight would be a bad idea. "I heard you. I just think that, despite my flaws, I'm not far off base about society."

Nate finishes his drink and sets the glass on the table. I'm prepared for him to rise and say good night. Instead, he sits back and stretches his long legs. "Harper, I can't change the world, but I can promise I'm not interested in controlling you or any other woman."

"I believe that." I swallow the rest of my bourbon in a single shot. Shit, I'm pretty turned on right now. The line I shouldn't cross is taunting me, and like most dares, I'm about to take it.

He stretches one arm across the back of the sofa as he leans in and reaches for my hand. "How's your finger feeling?"

His warm breath heats the back of my hand. My own breathing slows in response. The air around us hums. My respect for him makes all this tension that much more powerful. I've missed this feeling, this intensity of desire fueled by more than mere physical attraction.

"Better after that glass of bourbon." I shift forward, silencing the better judgment in my head and giving in to the yearning.

Few things are more intoxicating than staring into a person's eyes those final seconds before a first kiss. No wonder so many songs, stories, and movies have been written around this single moment. As such, I savor the delayed gratification as my heart pumps hot blood through my limbs, and allow all that heat to pool between my legs.

Nate's eyes—so round and bottomless—hold my attention. I fight to keep my eyelids from closing as our faces inch closer. My gaze dips to his mouth. He's not smiling now. His full lips are parted in anticipation. My pulse thumps in my neck as his hand rises to cup my face.

Unable to bear the suspense any longer, I make the final move.

Our first kiss is hot and wet and slightly spicy from the bourbon. Nate slides me closer, tightening his hold on me. Any resolve to be honorable melts away in his embrace.

He's good at this. Already I'm anticipating the friction of his hands against my skin, those powerful legs squeezing me, the other places that tongue will tickle.

Sinking into a near dream state, I abandon any remaining self-control and let myself go.

Within seconds, we're tugging at each other's clothes, peeling off the layers, racing toward the inevitable like a runaway freight train, pausing only long enough to remember a condom. My finger feels no pain as hormones and pheromones and other moans take over. Nate is a fierce lover—strong and confident yet at times tender.

In the final throes, I make the mistake of opening my eyes to find his boring through me. I want to look away—to hide—but I can't. The room is alive with the sounds of my panting as he gives me the best climax I've had in years.

Only then does he allow himself to give over to the feeling, so we both shudder together on my tired, old sofa, whose joints creak beneath our sated weight.

Nate's head nestles against my neck as my heart rate settles. I'm dazed. Loose-limbed. Who would've foreseen Wendy being responsible for something this combustible? She deserves a bouquet of thank-you flowers.

Boom!

On that note, reality crashes in, causing me to tense. If I'd said good night in the car, I wouldn't have felt this much guilt about allowing him to believe half truths about me and why I'm even in this town. Now my deceit has even more teeth. My desperate ego has turned me into a liar who is being unfair to Nate, Wendy, and even Joe. This is not where I thought my writing career would lead me. This is not who I want to be.

My eyes burn. Good God, if he sees my crying, he'll totally get the wrong idea. I blink while staring at the ceiling, trying to think of anything else. My finger throbs anew.

Nate pushes back onto his haunches. He's quite a sight with that broad, muscular chest and trim waist. Much more fit than I am, so I drag the throw over my squishy midsection. Does he expect an invitation to stay the night? If it weren't for my lies, I might extend one, but I'm currently on the verge of a breakdown.

"That was . . . outstanding," I say, rising to a sitting position and cloaking myself in the comfortable familiarity of emotional distance.

"Give me an hour," he murmurs, his voice purring with satisfaction and pride.

If only I could. I fiddle with my earlobe. "Normally I would, but I, well, my finger does kind of hurt, and I just . . . There's a project I'm doing, plus the temporary nature of my living here. I don't want to be insensitive, but—"

Nate presses his fingertip to my lips to silence me. "No apologies. No excuses. No promises. One date at a time. As long as we're honest with each other, that's enough."

He stands to dress himself, unaware that his words sliced through me like that knife went through my finger. I like him and want to be honest. But I need to write this book—one I've finally begun to get excited about—and am ruthlessly committed to my comeback.

When his shoes are tied, I wrap myself in the blanket and follow him to the door, rising on my toes for a chaste kiss good night. "Thanks again. I'm sorry about the class, and that I'm so . . . peculiar." Peculiar? That's the best I could come up with? No wonder my last book tanked.

"Peculiar is good. I'll call you." He plants a final kiss on my lips before turning to go to his car.

I close the door and lock it—mostly to keep myself from chasing him down and dragging him back—then bang my head gently against it three times. I've certainly complicated things now. But my slack muscles and spent body continue to cheer me on. To prod me with what-ifs.

I stomp upstairs, trying to quiet the circus in my mind. Crawling into bed, I snuggle into the covers and fall asleep reliving that first kiss and contemplating whether it is too selfish to see him again without making a confession.

CHAPTER ELEVEN

WENDY

Friday evening

When Joe asked if we could listen to a nonfiction book about breathing during the four-hour drive to Colgate, I agreed. His book picks always sound boring at first but end up being informative and interesting. However, today it hardly mattered because I couldn't stop thinking about the votive and my subsequent lie. Escaping from New Canaan hasn't helped like I hoped.

When we check into the Colgate Inn, I busy myself with unpacking while Joe uses the facilities. Hotel rooms used to connote something romantic or be indicative of vacation plans. This evening has been rather transactional—not even a bad joke about the hotel bed. My husband hasn't made any sexual overtures since the night of the dinner party. And poor Sue. Seeing her uneasiness this morning broke my heart. I follow up on my promise to invite her to lunch with a quick text. Next, I alert Billy that we've arrived and will meet him at his dorm soon, then put my phone in my purse.

I wait for Joe to finish up, sitting on the bed with my back against the headboard while staring at the staid beige carpet in this relatively bland room that seems indicative of my life. Functionality without a hint of pizzazz. A place to sleep but not to dream.

At least I'll see Billy soon. He's been less forthcoming about his classes, his roommate, or anything else in recent weeks, which has me spinning all kinds of unwelcome scenarios, especially after that D he got.

Joe comes out of the bathroom. "All set."

I slide off the bed and follow him out of the hotel.

"Did you text Billy?" Joe asks as we cross the parking lot to get to our car.

"Yes. We'll meet him at his dorm." I buckle into the passenger seat. "His roommate's parents couldn't make it, so I invited Craig to join us for dinner. Later tonight the school is hosting a trivia night."

"That sounds good."

I stare at Joe's profile—his content expression—with a touch of envy. The careful life I've constructed to control my problem has left me feeling confined and aimless. A dormant volcano ready to explode, powerless to stop the boiling inside. What if I stole Harper's votive as a cry for help—like I want to get caught? I fan myself, but this isn't another hot flash. It's bald fear.

"Your mom's birthday is next month. Are we going to Rhode Island?" Joe asks, oblivious to my mood.

The one time we coaxed my mother into enjoying a night out at a restaurant, what should've been a celebratory event devolved into a trying two hours filled with circular conversations about the kitchen's cleanliness, the freshness dates on the ingredients, and her fear that trying a new sauce or food would trigger an allergic reaction (despite her never having had a single food allergy), and she also went to the restroom multiple times to wash her hands. It's far easier to bring groceries and a cake to her house, though I know that accommodating her concerns only enables her. Another example of how my life is a disconnected pattern of choices and behaviors that aren't helping anyone, least of all me.

"I can go alone. It's never a pleasant visit for you." Nor for anyone, in truth. Her neuroses about company bringing germs into the house and the disruption of her routines set everyone on edge even though she's also desperate to see us—to see anyone.

The rare times my mother's been at peace and relaxed feel more like an old dream than any reality. If only her OCD weren't as extreme, or if her attitude about therapy and the complications of the medication would change.

I've never wanted my life to mirror hers, yet it's trending in that direction. Like her, I've been inconsistent with therapy and medication, thinking I could manage on my own. Like her I've cut myself off from enjoyable activities "for my own protection." And like her, I'm suffering the consequences of those decisions. Dr. Haertel has her work cut out for her, and so do I.

"Honey, of course I'll come. Those visits upset you." He flashes a kindly smile.

Is that love or pity? Maybe both. "Let's talk about it later. We've got a few weeks. Right now I want to focus on Billy. What if he already looks older? Do you think he's excited to see us?"

Joe pats my thigh. "I'm sure he's looking forward to a good meal. Can we keep it fun and light? Let him lead the discussion and share what he wants. Let's not push him too hard for answers you want."

His plea reminds me of Harper's earlier insinuations. "Why does everyone keep telling me how to behave with my own child?"

"Who's 'everyone'?" He frowns.

Ignoring that, I add, "I've raised Billy and know him better than anybody, so I think I can manage our relationship without help." It takes no effort to recall those first days after his birth—my amazement at his tiny pink feet and alert gaze. Or the way I used to piggyback him around Mead Park and sing made-up songs as we walked to the school bus. Or the first time he put on lacrosse pads, looking like a tiny boy playing at being a man. "I'm not a moron."

"Don't overreact." Joe pauses, and it is then that, again thanks to Harper, I recognize that reply as somewhat patronizing. I almost say so, but hold back. Harper may be right about standing up for yourself, but she's not right to never consider the proper time and place to do that. "I know you're a wonderful, doting mother, Wendy. I just think our job as parents has changed. He's becoming a man. Shouldn't we let him find his own way instead of undermining him with 'helpful suggestions'?"

I close my eyes, determined not to cry or to fight, although right now I'm on the verge of both. The truth stings like a swarm of bees. The problem is that Billy will always be my son. I'll always have three decades' more wisdom than him to impart. I'll always want to know how he's feeling and to share in his wins and losses. Bottom line—I don't feel finished mothering him.

My thoughts stir silently while houses and street signs blur past until the car is parked in the rear of Drake Hall. In daylight, the beautifully treed campus must be a rainbow of autumnal oranges, golds, reds, and umbers—all intermingled amid stately old-world buildings and sleek, modern new ones. Tonight the landscape lighting casts long shadows everywhere.

While Joe locks the car, I text Billy to let him know we've arrived.

"Are you okay?" Joe asks as we make our way toward the entrance to Billy's dormitory.

As if we have time to dig into all these feelings here. "I'm fine. I just want to have a nice visit."

"Me too." He takes my hand, which neither erases his earlier judgment nor silences Harper's. Even Billy would wage some complaints about my parenting style, if I'm being honest. Criticism hurts when everything I do is motivated by unadulterated love. I would've given anything for either of my parents' undivided attention at his age, so I can't fathom feeling smothered by love.

When the door opens and Billy is there in person for the first time in seven weeks, my heart expands, heavy with love. He needs a haircut, but otherwise looks healthy and wonderful. I break free of Joe, fling my arms open, and dive in for a hug. With my ear snug to his chest, I can only imagine an embarrassed flush in his cheeks. Boys his age don't want to be a mama's boy, and yet he doesn't immediately push me away.

Holding my son again—the weight of him is safely against me—settles me. I'll never create fine art, cure a disease, or lead a corporation, but my son is tangible, solid proof that I've done something worthy.

As Joe approaches, Billy eases away from me to hug his father. He always has an easy smile for Joe, whereas with me there is sometimes a hint of tension. I may be the first person he turns to when he's in trouble, but Joe is the parent whose company he prefers. I tell myself it's a male thing and leave it at that.

"You look terrific, son," Joe says, rustling Billy's hair. "College agrees with you."

A sheepish smile makes Billy look younger than eighteen. He's wearing khakis and a navy Vineyard Vines sweater instead of his typical sweats, for my benefit no doubt. "I like it so far."

"Good." Joe claps him on the shoulder. "Sorry we're running late. The board chair chose today to pick apart things with the budget. We have reservations at Hamilton Inn, so we should get going."

"Oh, I wanted to run up to Billy's room," I say.

"Er, it's messy, Mom," Billy says.

His not wanting to show it to us makes me think of Harper's innuendo about partying, but I look at Joe and let it go. "Where's your roommate?"

Billy shrugs.

"He's not coming?" I ask.

"Nah." Billy starts walking toward the car.

"Why not?" I hustle to keep up to his and Joe's long strides, worried that Billy isn't getting along with his roommate.

"No one wants to hang out with other people's parents," Billy says.

There goes my chance to get to know Craig better. I exchange a look with Joe, then say, "Surely it beats sitting alone while everyone else is out with their own parents."

"Not all parents came, so he's not alone."

Joe's expression remains placid but he squeezes my shoulder—a signal for me to drop it.

Ignoring the bristling feeling of being managed, I tuck my arm inside my son's and rest my temple against his shoulder. "Well, then, that means we get you all to ourselves for two hours, so I won't complain."

Joe's shoulders relax.

I take the back seat to allow Billy the chance to stretch his legs.

Questions crowd my mind. How are classes? Midterm grades? Any cute girls in the picture? Do you get along with your roommate? Have you been keeping up with your laundry? Do you miss home? That's what Billy expects—Joe, too—so I bite my tongue to prove I'm not so predictable.

The silence in the car vibrates like a living thing. I'm knotting my purse strap in my fingers while tamping my desire to fill the void. Joe has always been comfortable in the quiet. Billy—once a young chatter-box—started taking on his father's trait in tenth grade. The days when he came running to me with all his stories are gone, and the thought slams into me like a medicine ball.

Acceptance begins to seep through the cracks in my heart. It's possible my micromanaging is pushing my son away. I wish there were a switch I could press to turn off the worry and the desire to help him avoid problems. Throwing myself into something else—something new—could help. Befriending Harper was a start, but she has her own life and won't be governed by me or anyone.

Other women have worn these shoes—stay-at-home mothers in need of new outlets for their energy after their kids leave home. Most of them, however, don't have the complicating factor of a little-researched and little-understood yet often-destructive mental illness that could bring shame upon their family if discovered. That more than any-thing—including Harper's insinuations about my past conditioning—makes it difficult for me to do and say exactly what I want. But Dr. Haertel's help might make it safer to transform my hobby into more. Something that Harper might help me with before she leaves town.

My thoughts circle back to my mom's mental battles, which have included suicidal thoughts. She's been waging this psychological war twenty-five years longer than me, and I'm already exhausted.

Billy swivels to look over his shoulder. "Everything okay, Mom?"

"Sure." I force a smile, and stop these thoughts from preoccupying me tonight. "Why?"

"You're never this quiet. I expected at least twenty questions by now." He eyes me quizzically.

That's how everyone sees me. A buzz saw of questions—a walking, talking checklist. No wonder Billy doesn't enjoy my company as much as his father's. "We've got all weekend to catch up. Tonight let's enjoy a nice dinner and relax. I've missed you."

He smiles. "Miss you guys, too."

Billy faces forward again, unbuckling his seat belt the second Joe parks the car. We walk into the restaurant, a cozy dining room with hardwood floors, farmhouse dining chairs, and greens and golds on the walls and drapes. We're seated at a table in the corner by some windows.

I scan the menu, recalling the pumpkin sage gnocchi. Billy will likely choose the bourbon-glazed meatloaf, while Joe might indulge in the rack of lamb. I set the menu down and let the mood and the hum of patrons wrap around me like a warm hug, determined to prove to my two favorite people that I'm able to let go for an evening and laugh.

———

Hours and two glasses of wine later, Joe and I return to our hotel room. Dinner passed pleasantly, although we didn't learn much at all about

Billy's professors or what kinds of clubs he's planning to join. He hung in with us for about forty-five minutes of trivia before Joe released him to catch up with his friends, until we see him again tomorrow.

I toss my purse on the desk chair and kick off my shoes before going to the sink to wash my face and brush my teeth. The greenish-gray light in the bathroom amplifies every sag, wrinkle, and discoloration of my aging skin. I wouldn't mind so much if, along with these battle scars, I'd gotten equally wiser. Instead I'm playing catch-up at least a decade late.

While I'm patting my face dry, Joe surprises me by sneaking up behind me, wrapping his arms around my waist, and resting his chin on my shoulder. He catches my gaze in the mirror. "Thank you."

"For what?" I stare at his image, stunned by his hold on me.

"For respecting my opinion."

I turn toward him, frowning. "I always respect you, Joe."

"You rarely take my advice."

I stiffen. "You make me sound like a harridan."

"You know I don't think that. I understand where you're coming from most of the time, but I really appreciated feeling heard this evening. And I think Billy did, too." Joe cups my butt.

"Joe!" I flush. His playfulness lets me gloss over what he said because it's been forever since he's been the initiator.

He kisses me while tugging me toward the bed.

Questions swirl, but my wine-soaked blood and the need for physical contact shut them down.

There's no denying the zing of excitement. His hot breath and eager fingers have me quickly flinging off my clothes and tumbling into bed. Each brush of his palm and every hungry kiss makes my chest purr with passion that's been absent too long. I'm alive and young again. Hopeful and loved. Needed. Wanted. Accepted.

A heightened need to revel in the warmth of Joe's body, the stubble along his jaw, and the friction of his chest hair pulses through me. We are truly lost in each other for the first time in months. The moments melt together until I cry out with a burst of pleasure. Afterward, we lie together, panting but replete, with the lights still on.

We spoon together beneath the thin cotton sheet and standard-issue comforter, and I sigh happily. "That was a nice surprise. I've missed this side of you."

"Me too."

I smile at first, then find myself frowning because I don't know why he went cold in the first place. Or what turned him on tonight. "I know you said there isn't another woman—"

"There isn't." He nuzzles my neck.

Accepting his nebulous replies will keep the peace, but it won't solve anything. "Well, then, I wish I understood what's been going on with us. You've made excuses about being tired and whatever, but tonight felt like old times. This is how it should always be. So just tell me, Joe. Why have you been so distant?"

Joe rolls onto his back to click off the lamps, dragging me along so that my cheek is on his chest. I'm glad, because some conversations are easier in the dark.

His chest rises as he draws a deep breath. "I don't know that it's been fully conscious on my part, Wendy, but to be honest, I haven't felt as connected to you as I used to. For years now, your two major focal points have been controlling your illness and caring for Billy. I could see you struggling this summer, getting ready to say goodbye to Billy, but I thought his leaving would be good for us. Yet even now, sometimes when I bring up my work or other random stuff, you cut me off or tune me out. I guess it's all left me feeling a little emasculated. Maybe a little resentful." He falls silent but his arms tighten reassuringly around me.

Nevertheless, a chill seeps through my skin. "Why didn't you say something sooner?"

His breath makes some of my hair flutter, but otherwise we both remain quite still. "You're always dealing with so much—with your mom and Billy and your condition. It seemed heartless to pile on when I'm capable of handling myself. And I didn't want to push you in any direction that made it harder for you to manage your illness. I figured eventually you'd relax and it'd resolve itself."

"Except we've both been living a little unhappily together."

"Not that unhappily." He kisses the top of my head. "We can't change the past. Maybe we should enjoy tonight without overanalyzing things. We have a lot to be grateful for. Billy's living his own life now, so let this be the start of a new chapter in ours."

I'm grateful to know what's been wrong between us, yet am a bit hurt that Joe used sex—or rather withholding it—to prove a point. "But this seems like something we should talk about for more than a minute."

Joe's fingers lightly stroke my arm. "Is there more to say? I thought giving you the driver's seat was helping you, but I'm glad to get this out in the open now. Is there something you've been holding back—aside from missing our physical relationship, I mean?"

Here's my chance to confess. Lying to Joe about my illness certainly doesn't make us closer. But I first want Dr. Haertel's advice on how to broach this with him. "Just that I never meant to be dismissive of you or make you feel invisible. I assume that how I take care of you shows you my love . . ."

"It does, Wendy. I've never doubted your love . . . I just felt that everything else took precedence most of the time. But from here on out, let's trust each other and talk about these things before they build up. Maybe you can start to trust yourself more, too. Let your guard down since you haven't slipped up in more than a decade. Let us be a real team like we were in the beginning. That's what I'd like."

"Me too." That's the truth.

On one hand, he's brushing my illness aside again, yet on the other, my lies of omission have fueled his perspective. And given the fact that he's made concessions for so long thinking he was helping me keep my nose clean, he might end up resentful of the truth.

Judging by his loose limbs and slowed breath, honesty seems to have set Joe free, yet a seed of uneasiness plants itself in me.

While tonight marks a turning point for us, it also proves that my husband can bury his feelings deep enough that I can't see them. I don't know him as well as I thought, and given my history with my father and the truth of my illness, that leaves me with little comfort.

CHAPTER TWELVE

HARPER

Monday morning

I'm on Elm Street around nine in the morning, carrying a bag of warm chocolate croissants from Le Pain Quotidien, when across the street Wendy emerges from a door between Manfredi Jewels and an empty storefront. The retail outlets sit at the base of a three-story brick building, which is where that obscured door must lead. Now I know why she wasn't at my front door with a mocha latte first thing this morning to quiz me about my date with Nate.

"Wendy!" I jog across the street without looking. A giant difference from the city, where one takes her life into her hands anytime she steps off a sidewalk. Here cars are required to give pedestrians the right-of-way—and they do it.

She quickly covers her flustered expression with a pleasant smile. "Hey, Harper." Her gaze drops to the bag in my hand. "What'd you buy? I love their apple turnovers."

The fact that her first question isn't about Nate intensifies my curiosity about what's got her preoccupied.

"Chocolate croissants." I nearly slip up with a joke about the writing fuel—chocolate is a key element in my process. "Where are you coming from?"

She waves dismissively, then tucks a loose hank of hair behind her ear. "Nowhere special. Errands."

Except she's not carrying anything, and what kind of errands could she run in an office building? Maybe Joe works there. And Nate. Thinking he is close by elicits a little buzz.

"Will you be painting my buffet today?" I ask.

"I'll be over midmorning, after I hit the grocery store and dry cleaner and then change clothes." She takes a step as if preparing to leave; then her face lights up. "Oh, wait. How was the date with Nate?"

My body awakens at the memory of his hands and tongue, which I've thought about too often since Friday night. When he called yesterday afternoon, I waited two hours before responding, then pretended that I'd been visiting friends in the city. The city had been on my mind thanks to a note from my broker that the condo sale might be falling through. The appraisal came in lower than the purchase price, which could screw up the buyer's financing. If the financing contingency falls through, the sales contract will be voided. That'll squeeze me financially, but on the other hand, if Tessa loves my book idea, then I'll get the rest of my advance in a few months and could possibly hold on to the condo. Either way, my rise from the ashes must take precedence over lust and flirting. Cassandra pinged me yesterday about my progress. While I like what I've got so far, I don't quite trust my judgment.

Holding up my injured finger, I say, "Exciting if you count a trip to the ER."

Wendy grabs my wrist, concern wrenching her elfin features. "What happened?"

"I sliced it chopping onions in a cooking class." With a lazy shrug and wry tone, I add, "I warned him I'm not domestic."

She nods as if this should've been obvious to even a casual observer. "But you'll be okay?"

"Yes. Stitches come out in a week."

"Good." There goes that hand-to-the-chest move that makes me smile. "So how did you like Nate? Isn't he sweet and handsome? Will you see each other again?" The hopefulness from every romance novel she's ever read curls her lips and shines through her eyes.

"He's very nice. And handsome. But he's settled and looking for a real partner. I'm still figuring things out, so I don't know that things will progress much." As honest as I can be without disclosing the whole truth.

Wendy's forehead wrinkles with displeasure. "Or maybe he's the perfect person to help you through this transition phase."

Transition phase? "Desperation phase" feels more accurate, although I've made surprising progress this weekend. Being with Nate unleashed something, somehow restoring bits that made words begin to flow. Ideas began to jell. Now that I think of it, Wendy is right. Nate might be good for me, but that doesn't mean I'm good for him. In fact, I know that I'm not. At least, not unless I come clean. "This is something I need to work out for myself."

She stares down the street at nothing in particular, but I've become accustomed to her habit of letting her gaze wander away with her thoughts. "People always say that, but is it always so noble to work stuff out for oneself? Asking for help takes courage. So does accepting kindness and love from friends and family." Her gaze then homes in on me. "Trust me, Harper, handling stuff on your own usually makes it harder to accomplish."

She's probably referring to her childhood again. That experience isn't broadly applicable, though. "And yet we each have the right to decide for ourselves how to handle our own life."

Her shoulders rise in a resigned shrug. "Well, let me finish my errands so I can get back to your piece."

With a jaunty wave at odds with her distracted mood, she turns and walks up the street toward the store More 'N' More. It's only after she's gone that I realize I forgot to ask about Family Weekend at Colgate.

Once I'm sure she can't see me, I step closer to the door she came through. The brass directory plate on the wall identifies the various offices housed inside. The orthodontist seems unlikely. Same with the architect. The last name is Jane Haertel, PhD, whom I google.

A psychologist specializing in impulse control disorders. Hm. Therapy. I tuck my phone in my pocket and start walking home, sifting prior conversations with Wendy through a new filter. She could need help coping with her aging mother's OCD. Or does she have it, too?

I stop at the corner of Elm Street and South Avenue, ashamed of my snooping. At first my ruse felt like a harmless game. But I know Wendy now. She's trusted me with intimate information and showered me with kindness. I can't deny my affection for her despite our vast differences. I'd like to become worthy of her trust regardless of how our friendship began. Spying isn't exactly a step in the right direction.

And if she's inherited her mother's condition, that's devastating. Being beset by constant worry could explain why she seems lonely and slightly wary. It also makes my landlord's commentary even more insensitive and indiscreet.

I continue my stroll home, passing Saint Aloysius's schoolyard, where kids are playing basketball on the concrete courts. Their laughter explodes into the air, reminding me of the innocent joy of recess and four square and monkey bars.

In grade school, my brothers, neighborhood kids, and my dad and I would play "monster." Dad would chase us all around the street in a raucous version of hide-and-seek. Once, my brother Jim helped me climb a tree to hide. Sitting side by side with him on that limb, watching others scramble below, had been the best feeling. During the following ten years, we went from being those siblings to the kind who poke at each other, particularly once he started craving his older brother's approval.

It was one thing to deal with Rick, who had never really been kind to me. Jim's slow withdrawal—his refusal to step in between Rick's and my battles—hurt more. Then again, it's easy to blame my brothers for our relationship and family dynamic, but part of the problem might also be how I reacted to them. My tendency to mouth off in the moment rather than plot a more strategic response certainly hasn't made anyone's life easier, least of all my own.

By the time I get home, I've devoured one of the croissants, my mouth and fingers now shiny from the buttery goodness. I pour myself a glass of milk and take it and the other pastries upstairs, determined to revise chapter three of my draft. I open the document, take a giant bite of the croissant and chug of milk, and then reread last night's work.

I click off the last page, wearing a smile. It's not half-bad. The small mental win prompts me to send an email I've been considering.

> Hey, Ellen,
>
> I see you'll be at the New Canaan library next week. I'm renting a place up here while I work on my next book and would love to see you. Are you able to come up a little early and meet me for dinner? Let me know.
>
> Harper

I stare at the note, rereading it to give myself time to fully commit to the invitation. It'd be great to catch up, but I'll also have to face my failure with a colleague and risk exposing my identity in public.

Before hitting "Send," I revise the note:

> P.S.—I've not told my neighbors about my career/ pen name, so if we run into anyone, please don't

mention it. People here think I'm a publicist and I'd
like to keep it that way.

That sounds paranoid, which isn't far from the truth. I delete the postscript, deciding to tell her that part in person. After an incident involving a gossipy email to a "friend" about another friend that eventually made its way back to that person, I never put anything in writing that I don't want shared. Holding my breath, I hit "Send."

With that task done, my mind wanders back to Wendy and the PhD, so I google impulse control disorders. The *Psychiatric Times* website offers a list that includes, among other things *pathological gambling (PG), kleptomania, trichotillomania (TTM), intermittent explosive disorder (IED), and pyromania; these disorders are characterized by difficulties in resisting urges to engage in behaviors that are excessive and/or ultimately harmful to oneself or others.*

Wendy doesn't pluck her hair, and she's so buttoned-up I can't imagine her having rage issues. Gambling, stealing, and setting fires . . . None of those seem right, either, although gambling problems would create marital stress. Could there be something there? Did she drag George's wife off to Foxwoods too often for George's liking? Is she spending money faster than Joe can make it? She did grouse about him being a bit tightfisted, if I recall.

Sitting back, I noodle whether giving Gwen a gambling addiction might enhance my story. If I'm going for raised stakes and conflict, the pyromania might be better. I can already picture a climactic scene when Gwen literally burns her house down. It could be a device and a metaphor at once. No, that's too similar to *Little Fires Everywhere*, and I was trying to keep this book on the light side.

Stealing would probably be better. I can have Gwen swiping all kinds of things throughout the book, each time ratcheting up the over-the-top antics to hide her actions from her husband and the community.

If her husband is a personal wealth manager, having a thief for a wife could be a source of marital strife.

After rubbing my hands together, I open my outline documents and a browser window where I can research kleptomania, and begin to type out some notes. Research is always the best way to generate ideas for scenes and characters. I quickly learn that shoplifting is not the same as kleptomania. In fact, less than 5 percent of shoplifters are actual kleptomaniacs.

I'm hardly the most disciplined person—and some might think I drink more than is good for me—but I can't imagine life with obsessive thoughts or compulsive behaviors like stealing or starting fires. At least with gambling there's the potential for reward.

Several pages of notes later, the rumble of the garage door startles me out of my groove. Wendy has come to work on the buffet. Soon it won't remind me of Calvin anymore.

Curious, I go downstairs. When I enter my garage, she's standing by the buffet, gripping a canvas bag, which she raises. "These paints will be gorgeous."

"Awesome."

She seems more purposeful now than earlier. Not at all like someone laboring with a serious disorder.

The only compulsion I've witnessed is her need to help others. That's probably not what most people would call a mental illness.

I fish around a bit. "Was your mom crafty, too?"

"Pardon?" She looks up, puzzled by the non sequitur.

"From what you've told me, she spends a lot of time alone, so I thought maybe she kept busy with projects like this, and then taught you."

She shakes her head. "She had her work until recently, and she likes to read. She bakes, too."

"So she functions pretty well, then, despite everything."

"Most people with OCD have full lives and relationships. The severity of hers is more limiting, but she still manages okay—or at least in a way that she accepts." She pops open the paint and stirs it. "I taught myself to do this. My mom didn't allow other kids in the house, so I spent a lot of time alone. This hobby became my escape, I guess. A silver lining that I really love." Her smile is tinged with a hint of sorrow.

Pumping her for information makes me feel two inches tall, especially in the face of the grace with which Wendy shouldered such heavy burdens. "Well, I'm grateful. Please let me pay you for more than the supplies."

She shakes her head again while unpacking the duffel and laying out her tools. "I want to do this for you—as a friend."

Checkmate. "Thank you. I appreciate that, and I appreciate you."

Wendy stops fiddling with the supplies and looks up, her expression so delighted it shakes me a little. "As I do you, Harper."

A truthful exchange amid my sea of deceit. "Guess I'll get back to my own project now."

"Hope that's going well." Her encouraging smile is something I rarely got from my parents, so I savor it.

"It's got potential," I say. Not a lie.

"Terrific. Don't let me keep you from it." It's unlike her to rush me off, but I take the hint.

I return to my desk, irked for putting stock in George Durbin's gossip. Aside from a few quirks, Wendy isn't short any french fry more than the rest of us. I pray she's getting help to cope with her mom rather than with battling her own mind every day.

Either way, my character research ends here. I cannot continue to treat my friend like an experiment when she's been so trusting and transparent. It's time to get back to the business of fiction. To believe in myself and my imagination again. I'll do additional field research in the community to bring the setting to life. Book club will be a perfect opportunity to observe more of the social constructs and inspire a realistic portrayal of affluent suburban Connecticut.

My email notification pings. Ellen's reply.

> Great to hear from you! Would love to have dinner and settle my nerves with a glass of wine and a good laugh before the library event. Can't wait to hear what drove you to the burbs! Let's meet at the bookstore. Five o'clock work?
>
> XO
>
> Ellen

No turning back now. I'll have to come clean about my editor's "suggestion" and the bad reviews screwing with my confidence. Sharing stuff with Wendy was good practice for opening up. And Ellen should understand my confidence crisis. This isn't a career for the faint of heart, but even those of us with alligator skin can get beaten down by a series of ugly reviews and our editor's rejection. I reply:

> Five is perfect. I'll make reservations at Solé just down the block from the bookstore. My neighbor's book club is coming to see you speak. They're very excited. I'm reading your book now, btw. So great! Happy to see your hard work rewarded. See you soon.
>
> H

I hit "Send," my spine straightening as I take a step toward ending my skirmish with professional envy. I wish it didn't burden me in the first place, but I'm human. At no point have I begrudged Ellen's success. The embarrassment and doubts spawned by my own failure are simply taking too long to shake off. Who doesn't hate failing?

With my new project boosting my optimism—a trait I indirectly attribute to Wendy—I can support Ellen without feeling phony, thank goodness. Too bad I can't share this change of heart with Wendy. She'd be so proud of her positive influence.

Men routinely prioritize career above relationships. Is my guilt a product of conditioning, or is it something deeper? Something personal to Wendy and me? And then there's my pride. If Wendy learns my pen name, she'll search me on Google, see my catastrophic failure, and feel sorry for me on top of everything else. Pity would be unbearable.

That settles it. H. E. Ross will stay hidden until my editor is happy with my manuscript. Time to dig into this synopsis and outline a story worth writing (and reading).

———

I force a fistful of pretzels down the gullet and then pop into the garage to sneak a peek at Wendy's progress.

"Need a break?" I ask.

The buffet cabinet doors are off the hinges and on a drop cloth. The interior of the unit is a dazzling glossy turquoise, as are the insides of the cabinet doors. Meanwhile, Wendy's applying paint to the exterior—a shimmery pale cream. I spy matte black hardware laid out on the drop cloth and can almost picture how it will all look when it is finished.

"Nope. How do you like it so far?" She eyes her work critically, bent on perfection. Invested. Professional. "It's coming out better than I envisioned. Elegant yet funky, right?"

"Totally. I'm tempted to take a picture to send to Calvin."

She scowls. "He doesn't deserve another second of your time, Harper. Better to invite Nate over to dinner and show it off then."

"You're relentless," I josh, although she's not wrong.

Wendy refills her paint sprayer. "Just don't let your ex make you question Nate's goodness. He's the real deal. Besides, I'm talking about a date, not a wedding. What's wrong with dating?"

"Nothing." As long as you can be honest, which is my dilemma.

It bugs me that she might be a little bit right about the aftershocks of Calvin's rejection affecting my attitude about commitment. He and I were committed in our way—one I believed in at the time. That it ended so suddenly and painfully for me makes me question whether it ever was as good as I thought. And if it wasn't, what does that mean for me and dating? I haven't had a monogamous relationship since Tim Jameson in early college. That didn't work well, either. Maybe the lesson is that there is no one rule to follow when it comes to love.

"Anyway, have you given more thought to going pro? If you feel unsafe in strangers' homes, have them bring their stuff to you, or find your own garage-sale treasures to fix and then sell them on Facebook Marketplace. In fact, I just saw an ad for an antique shop in Shelton. Let's ride up on Friday morning to find one or two small spec pieces."

Rather than shoot me down, she sits back on her haunches. "I've been considering it—even thought I'd hire you to do some PR." While I process that twist, she grins. "Let's do it and see if I get inspired. But right now, I need to finish this coat so the paint dries consistently."

"Great!" I'm stoked about her change of heart, except for the part about helping her with PR. I know enough of the basics to fake it, and maybe I owe her that much. If she is successful, she'll feel empowered, which could help her marriage. Speaking of Joe . . . "Before I go, did you enjoy your weekend at Colgate?"

An enigmatic smile stretches across her face. "We did. Billy seems happy. Joe and I had a good time and a big talk, actually."

That reply begs for a follow-up. "Ooh, I want to hear all about it on our drive up to Shelton. But now I'll let you focus on your work."

I leave the garage buoyant and ready to finalize my synopsis.

Later that afternoon, I hit "Send" on the documents to my agent just as Nate calls. Those eyes. That talented tongue. I'm hot all over, then slap my hand to my face, embarrassed.

I can't put him off a second time, so I answer. "Hi, Nate. How are you?"

"Good. How's your finger holding up?"

I stare at it. "Better than expected."

"Glad to hear it. So how was the city?"

I pause, confused until I recall my fib. "Great, thanks."

"You must miss your friends."

"I do." Not a lie. This is good. The fewer lies the better. "What did you do with the rest of your weekend?"

"Helped my brother move into a new apartment on Saturday. Long bike ride and then a family dinner on Sunday."

I paid friends to help me move, and I can't recall looking forward to any dinner with my entire family. Yet he and Wendy have me curious about whether it's worth trying to forge a new dynamic with them. "Sounds productive."

He laughs. "I suppose it was. Next weekend I'd like to have a little more fun, though. I was hoping you might be up for going out on Saturday. You can pick the activity this time—no knives or cooking required."

"Definitely no cooking." Like rolling thunder, the desire to see him crescendos. Could I tell him a version of the truth—enough that I wouldn't feel like a phony? "Nate, I'd love that, but I don't want to mislead you. I don't have long-term plans to stay in town, and my last relationship sort of messed me up. You deserve someone with their shit together, and I'm not there yet. But if you're cool with no big commitments, then I'll plan something fun for Saturday."

A heartbeat passes in silence. "I told you, one date at a time, Harper."

Is that the same as what I'm saying, or is he assuming I'll change my mind? He doesn't strike me as a guy who'd pretend to support me. In the end, I decide his assumptions aren't my concern as long as I've been honest—honest about my feelings, anyway. "Great. I'll call you later this week. I'm going antiquing with Wendy on Friday. I've got her thinking about turning her refinishing hobby into a little business."

"Interesting . . ."

Something in his tone makes me ask, "How so?"

He hesitates. "You don't seem to be someone who likes being told how to live, yet you're not shy about telling Wendy what she should be doing." He chuckles at his "funny" observation, but it hits me right in the gut.

I frown. "I'm not telling her how to live. I'm helping her enrich her life."

"Isn't that what most people think when giving advice? Anyway, we can bicker about that on Saturday. I've got to get back to work now. Have a good day." He hangs up before I can lob another argument at him.

I stare at the phone, his opinion uncomfortably banging around my mind like a ball-peen hammer. As if envy and lying weren't enough, now I'm a hypocrite? All this time I've blamed Calvin for that bomb of a book, but between Wendy's and Nate's observations, it's hard to deny that some of my own perceptions are at least equally responsible.

My email pings. Cassandra.

After shaking out my hands and blowing out a breath, I open the message.

Got the pages. Will read today and get back to you soon.

I sag in my seat, then decide to reward myself with some bourbon. Three chapters and a skeletal outline. More words than I've cobbled together in a while, and I don't hate them. That's a win. My comeback feels possible. Take that, one-star haters. I am kicking ass despite moving out of my comfort zone.

I owe a lot to Wendy, who's not as easy to typecast as I first suspected. A busybody of a sort, sure, but generous and sincere. Fragile in some sense, but courageous, too, with her openness and vulnerability.

I can't remember the last time I let myself be vulnerable. Maybe I lost that ability after years of defending myself against Rick. Huh.

Well, I'm glad Wendy's agreed to go antique shopping with me. I owe her a good deed for not only fixing me up with a truly decent guy but also for transforming my ugly buffet into something beautiful. Without her, I might also still be floundering for an antagonist and story idea.

That last thought ricochets pain through me as if I stubbed a toe. A good writer shouldn't need to resort to trickery. Stories and themes should come from the heart, not from pilfering strangers' private lives.

As I sip my bourbon, new doubts take root. My celebration is premature. Each drop of liquid fire makes it harder to escape a truth: greatness will elude me as long as I refuse to put my own values under the same microscope I apply to Wendy, Nate, and towns like New Canaan. Even more terrifying, real happiness might never come if I refuse to temper anything about myself.

CHAPTER THIRTEEN

WENDY

Thursday morning

I pull up to my mother's tired farmhouse, with its white paint graying around the edges like its owner's hair. Shapeless boxwoods have the look of overgrown Chia Pets, but the yard is otherwise in decent shape. The unremarkable house resembles many others on the block, hiding the troublesome life inside. Viewed through the filter of living through my parents' fights, my mother's torment and anguish, and my own helplessness in the face of it all, the house looks like something of a crime scene.

I shouldn't judge my mom. She made mistakes, but what parent hasn't? Even when I think I've done right by my son, others disagree. Whatever her demons, my mother loves me. My father? Well, that's another story. His rejection of my mother and withdrawal from my life have adversely affected my behavior in my marriage in ways I never realized until recently.

I grab my purse and stroll up the walkway. I open the squeaky metal storm door before knocking on the front door while opening it.

"Mom? I'm here." I step inside and toe off my "filthy" shoes, leaving them on the vinyl welcome mat she keeps near the door for this reason.

It'd be more apt if it read "No Trespassing." I phoned her yesterday to say I'd come visit today rather than call. Seeing Billy last weekend drove home how my own mother would appreciate my company.

"Good morning, honey." Mom steps out from the kitchen with a smile. She's wearing khakis and a pumpkin-colored cotton sweater, with her hair pulled off her face in a tortoiseshell clip, and a light swipe of lip gloss. All dressed up like she's going somewhere, but only I will see her.

She scoots behind me with a Clorox wipe in hand to clean the doorknobs. "You didn't stop for gas or anything, did you?" she asks while locking and unlocking the door four times before locking it for good.

"No, I promise. I came straight from my house." We air-kiss rather than hug. I know the drill. My hands aren't clean yet, so I beeline to the kitchen sink, where I scrub them in hot water and soap for twenty seconds. Light pours through the unobstructed window that allows sunlight to kill germs on the counters.

While I'm drying my hands with paper towels, she nudges me aside to spray the sink with disinfectant and wipe it out. Only then do her shoulders relax.

"I made tea." She pours herself a cup using one of the two she's set out on the counter along with packets of sugar—heaven forbid we share a sugar bowl—and then takes a seat at the kitchen table.

"Thanks." I fix myself a cup and sit opposite her, wondering when she last let anyone else inside.

"I've been worried about you. You've seemed distracted lately, but you look good." She smiles.

"I'm doing better." Those words slip out before I think about them.

"Good, but what was going on?" Her tone tightens like that of any mother concerned about her child. It's always been this way—her tuning into my moods only when they're troubling enough to overwhelm her own issues. Not that she can help it.

There's no point in lying. The truth is I came here because she's someone most likely to understand my conflict. "To be honest, I'm missing Billy like mad, but even before he left, Joe and I were in a rut. The stress of it all did a number on me." My gaze drifts. "I've been slipping up this past year. Taking things."

Just like that I am sixteen again—sitting on the porch steps as Mrs. McCarthy tells my mom that I tried to sneak her seashell paperweight into my backpack while she was getting cash to pay me for babysitting. I think the only reason Mrs. McCarthy didn't make a bigger deal of it was that she—like many neighbors—knew about my mother's mental issues and either assumed I was struggling similarly or took pity on me. After she'd left, my mother turned to me and asked, "Is this the first time, Wendy?"

"No." I looked at my feet while bracing for her reaction.

"Why are you stealing?"

I couldn't bear the worry in her gaze, so I averted my gaze and shrugged. I had no answer when I didn't understand it myself.

"I see." She fell quiet for what felt like an eternity. "No more babysitting for you. You'll have to find jobs that don't put you in jeopardy." She then opened the screen door. "Go change your clothes and wash up."

And that was it. That was her best advice, borne of her own experience and maybe a touch of guilt about how I may have inherited my problem from her.

Now here we are, and not much has changed. A solemn stare is all she offers. I don't expect a quick fix, but after so many decades, some real advice—or at least genuine sympathy—might be nice. "What does Joe say?"

I glance over my shoulder as if he might appear. "He doesn't know."

She exhales. "Good. That's good."

Is it, though? Dr. Haertel doesn't agree.

"I started back with my therapist on Monday—told Joe I'm having empty-nest blues. I was embarrassed to see her, like I'd failed her after all the work we did years ago. But she didn't seem that fazed. We rehashed CBT, particularly the covert sensitivity training that was most effective for me before. But she also encouraged me to come clean with Joe and Billy, and maybe even with my friends." Perspiration breaks out all over my back just like it did on Monday and every other time I've considered that suggestion. If thinking about it sends my heart pounding its way up my throat, doing it could cause a stroke.

"How would *that* help?" Mom's grip tightens around her cup.

"Releasing the pressure of keeping secrets could reduce my stress. Stigma surrounding mental illness has lessened since the nineties, so it might not be socially lethal." Then again, the stigma hasn't reduced around all mental illnesses, particularly not around those as criminal as mine. "I don't slip when I'm with Joe, partly because I know he's aware of the issue. If others knew, maybe I'd be better because they'd be watching, too. I don't know. Apparently, it helped another patient. That woman outed herself on social media." My skin itched while watching that YouTube video, so I can only imagine the anxiety *she* must've felt when posting it.

"Oh, Wendy, don't do that. Trust me, you don't want Joe to know you've lost control of this. All this time he's believed you were managing it. If he finds out it's still this bad and that you've been hiding that from him, he might leave. No one wants to be saddled with someone like us if they don't have to." Her shoulders round forward in the familiar defeated pose she'd adopted even before my father waltzed into this kitchen and announced his plans to leave. She didn't plead or argue then. She accepted his decision as if she—we—deserved it, and so I did, too. Or I did until Harper got into my head.

"Joe isn't Dad." My terse words make her wince, though my snapping like that gives me away. If I truly believed that, then I wouldn't be hiding anything from Joe.

"Everyone has limits." She keeps her eyes downcast while sipping her tea.

"Dad sure did, but he was . . . well, a selfish ass." It's freeing to speak openly. To place blame on him after decades of excuses. This buzzy feeling must be why Harper is so quick to call people out.

Mom's eyes widen. "Your father tried. I make life unbearable, as we both know."

"Dad could've tried harder. We could've gone to family therapy. That might've even prevented my condition from developing, too. At the very least, he shouldn't have abandoned me and rarely looked back. He took the easy out, blaming you for everything, which isn't fair. You didn't choose this condition. And the vows are for better or worse."

"It's pointless to look back." Mom waves a hand. "We can't undo the past. But think about Billy—why burden him with your problem?"

When I think of how often I've wished my mother were "normal" and how I've resented her genes, it devastates me to imagine Billy viewing me that way if he learns the truth.

Does my hiding it make me as cowardly as my father? "Pretending doesn't help me change or manage my problem. I also don't want Billy to be ashamed to come to us if he's struggling with similar issues."

She shakes her head. "You've kept a close eye on him. You'd know if something was up. Don't go confessing." Like that's so easy. Not to mention the irony of that advice coming from a woman who's given therapy only a fleeting chance. "Let Joe live in peace while you get help."

Harper would pounce like a cat on a can of tuna on the suggestion that Joe's comfort is more important than my sanity. Not to mention the fact that last weekend Joe asked for transparency between us.

"It feels wrong to keep secrets from him." Things between us are shifting into new territory, so I'm unsure whether fessing up now is more likely to damage or to help our relationship. Harper would counsel honesty. She's not afraid of truth. She's not one to feel unworthy for any reason, an inspiring trait I admire. And yet the deep-seated feeling that my condition makes me unworthy of Joe's love lurks like an invisible monster in the closet.

"Once you tell, you can't take it back. Especially with anyone outside the family. No matter what people say to your face, that label will stick with you in that town. You'll always be suspect."

The kitchen walls seem to curl around us as the echo of history—the naked curiosity and jeers about my "strange" mom, like the dismissive remarks my tenth-grade Spanish teacher made when my mother couldn't come to the school for a conference—makes me shiver. If I tell Harper and maybe even Sue, would they gossip, would neighbors whisper, would Billy's high school friends make jokes? Even so, should the fear of shame—my own and Joe's and Billy's—stop me from following Dr. Haertel's advice?

It was foolish to think my mother could help me with this decision. She's hardly a poster child for change. I'm not angry, though. Having suffered the cruelty of others, my mother wants to spare me that pain. Despite Harper's positive influence, I'm not as bold as she is. Not yet, anyway. I wince when it hits me that I probably came here to be discouraged.

I sip my tea to cover my thoughts, but set it down because it's cold. "Let's talk about something else. How are you?"

"Fine." She smiles, clearly relaxed thinking she's convinced me not to blow up my life. "Retirement is nice. I'm writing a children's book."

That's a twist I didn't see coming. My lips part with a giddy smile. "That's cool, Mom. When did you start this?"

"I took an online writing workshop I saw on Facebook." She fiddles nervously with her spoon, as if I might poke fun. "I know I'm old and probably nothing will come of it, but it's interesting to learn about."

"I love that you're trying something new. You've always been a reader, so I bet you'll have a knack for this. I'd love to read a draft when you're ready." Without thinking, I reach across to squeeze her hand. She tenses at first but doesn't pull away. Progress.

"We'll see." Her cheeks bloom with color, but her eyes reflect some pride.

"Okay." To fill the silence, I ask, "How's Deidre Barker?"

Deidre's a compassionate neighbor who respects my mother's phobias rather than using them as a reason to avoid her.

"Same as usual. Yesterday I was having coffee on the porch swing, so she sat on the steps and chatted for a while."

I sigh, curious whether there are more compassionate people like Deidre out there than we imagine. If they were the norm, life could be so different for those of us struggling with mental issues. "Mom, why not try medication and therapy again? It's not too late to finally get out in the community and make new friends." Get a new life, like the one Dad built decades ago.

On my fifteenth birthday he flew me to Atlanta for a long weekend. He sent gifts on birthdays and Christmases for the next few years, but I never went back to Atlanta. We spoke less and less, especially once I went to college. I never told him about my arrest, and once Joe and I began building a life together, Joe's mistrust of my father's intentions made it easier to let go and move forward. Still, my hands fist when I think of Dad off boating and traveling while Mom and I continue to fight our demons.

"I'm turning seventy-five. My life is what it is. Besides, studies show that ninety-one percent of people pick their noses—so imagine all those fingers are touching doorknobs, magazines, and chair arms in a doctor's office."

As if she's never mentioned that stat before. I close my eyes instead of insulting her with an eye roll.

"You can bring your Clorox wipes, or try online sessions." I push my teacup aside. "You're healthy—there's so much you might enjoy if you'd get out of this bubble. In-person writing workshops, for starters."

"I don't want to talk about this anymore." Her frosty tone warns me not to press, so I slump in my seat. "How's your new neighbor?"

"Harper?" That wrings a quick smile. "She's different—younger, brazen. Not someone I'd normally seek out, but she's been good for me. We respect each other's opinions. She's even made me reevaluate my perspective on some things. It's not good to stagnate. You couldn't deal with her messiness, but we've become friends. Here are some photos of her buffet that I refinished." I thumb through my phone, swiping through three or four before-and-after shots. If I do start a business, these would have to be the primary photos on the front of any brochure or website.

"Such talent. I still love my coffee table." She smiles at the mention of her mother's cherrywood coffee table, one of my earliest pieces.

"Harper's pushing me to start a business. We're going antiquing tomorrow morning to select some small pieces to refinish and sell online. The excursion should be a good test of the techniques Dr. Haertel and I practiced on Monday."

Mom's doubtful expression snuffs my enthusiasm like sand tossed on a fire. "What if you slip up? She might gossip."

"Maybe." On one hand, Harper's relationship with her family proves she's not afraid to cut ties when she's appalled. On the other, she's so new to town that if she did gossip, it'd likely be with her New York friends. Not that I'd love that, but it wouldn't affect Joe or Billy. And there's always the chance that, as someone so bent on fighting injustice, she'd be compassionate about my illness.

"Is she married?"

"No." She's convinced me she'll never take that step. I wonder how long it will take Nate to realize the same. "She's got a thing against marriage."

Mom's brows pucker. "Why?"

"She thinks it's a trap for women." Details of her open relationship could send my germophobe mother into a deadly fit of hives. My proximity to potential STDs would be all she'd think about for days. "Harper's a puzzle. Unemployed, yet doesn't fret about money.

Convinced she has all the answers, but her life seems unfocused. She's not even close to her family." Harper's wry smile and messy hair flit through my mind. "I've tried to soften her stance on things, but so far she's not persuaded."

Mom swats the air like she's batting that thought away. "You've got your own issues to worry about. Don't stretch yourself thin for her and end up screwing up your own life."

I frown. If only her obsessive thoughts were positive ones, but it doesn't work that way. Always doom. Always warnings. No wonder it's a struggle for me to be carefree for more than a moment at a time.

My knee bounces restlessly beneath the table. We've settled nothing. Had no breakthroughs. The fading herb-print wallpaper is another reminder that nothing here will ever change. "Can I help with anything before I leave?"

There's usually a deep-cleaning project—something that requires two people, like moving heavy furniture—she's got on her mind.

"Would you cut my hair?" She avoids salons for the same reason she gets her groceries delivered and uses gloves to unbox packages from Amazon. But in this case, I don't mind. My cutting her hair is the only consistent physical connection we've shared. The first time she asked me was right after my father had left. Her trust made me prouder than anything. And while it's hardly a snuggle or a long hug, handling my mother's hair feels sacred in its own way.

"Of course I will."

Her smile widens. "Wash your hands. I'll get the scissors and a comb. Be right back."

While she's upstairs preparing, I put our cups and saucers in the dishwasher, wash out the kettle, and spray the sink clean before wiping the tabletop as well. Mom returns with wet hair and a towel. "Grab a kitchen chair to bring on the back deck."

I know the routine. When the weather is agreeable, she prefers the clippings to fall outside—fewer dead cells floating around her house.

Once she's seated on the deck, I take my time to drape the towel over her shoulders—the closest I get to a real hug. As hard as that is for me, at least I get affection from others. It must be achingly lonesome for my mom to go months at a time without any physical contact. "An inch?"

"Let's make it two or three to hold me until February." She speaks calmly, as if she, too, savors our routine.

I gently comb her hair into sections, letting my fingers graze her scalp, stroke the length of her hair, and rest on her covered shoulders. Once I begin snipping the ends, I work slowly with precision. A cool breeze scatters bits of fallen hair like dandelion fluff, so I find myself making a wish for peace in our lives.

When I finish, I comb her out to check for strays. Before I set down the scissors, I lay my cheek on the top of her head and rest one hand on her shoulder. After a breath, I raise my head. "All set."

She holds still. "Thank you, sweetheart."

It strikes me that this is a relatively normal activity for us, but anyone else watching would think it quite odd—me cutting my mother's hair outside despite the chilly autumn day, and that touching my mother's shoulder and head should feel so momentous. Our lives could be healthier and happier if she'd get help.

"Maybe we could show off your new do on your birthday. Seventy-five deserves more than a simple dinner at home. What about reservations at The Bistro?"

"You don't need to spend a lot of money on me." She gives her head another shake to set free any stray hairs before she rises.

As if this is about money. "Wouldn't a change of scenery be nice? Let's enjoy a meal we don't have to prepare or clean up after."

"A hotel restaurant with people from all over? And have you seen the inside of restaurant kitchens?" She spears me with a cockeyed look, rolling her towel. "I do wish Billy could be with us, though."

"If you went to therapy, you could work up to visiting him at college with me." A long shot, but I shouldn't give up on her. I've done that for too long—another unfortunate similarity with my father. Maybe if I hadn't been so preoccupied with limiting my own triggers, I could've coaxed her into therapy years ago.

"If you choose to blow up your life with some therapist's misguided advice, that's your business. I'm content. I haven't had the flu since you moved out of the house. And we can FaceTime Billy." She hooks an arm around the chair to take it with her. "Wait here. I'll get a broom and dustpan as soon as I toss this in the washer." She hustles through the kitchen door.

The small backyard feels like it's shrinking. Aside from emergencies and major milestones like my college graduation, my wedding, and Billy's birth, my mother's adult life has mostly played out in this quarter acre. Meanwhile, my life isn't much bigger. This comparison might be another reason why I've stayed away.

Mom returns with a broom, which I use to sweep up any remaining hair. "Sounds like I'll be bringing food and a cake here, then."

"Thank you." She touches my shoulder—something so rare I freeze. I feel very fragile today . . . like every word and sound and look will sink me somehow. Like every misstep we've taken has us poised at the edge of the proverbial plank. "I know you're trying to be helpful, but I'm fine, Wendy. I don't need to go making changes at my age."

I tip the dustpan upward so the hairs don't fall out. It's unfair to push her when I'm not willing to take brave steps of my own. "Okay."

Inside, I dump the hair in the trash, rinse the dustpan, and then put it and the broom away. I grab my purse off the back of the kitchen chair and fish for my keys. "Guess I'll head home."

Mom crosses her arms, though I know she'll wipe down my chair and the shoe mat as soon as I leave. "Are you sure about antiquing with that neighbor?"

Thinking about rummaging around a huge marketplace makes me slightly nauseated. But if this visit has helped me realize anything, it's that I don't want to wake up at seventy-five having let my mental illness rob me of so much life. "I think so. I'll let you know how it went when we talk on Monday morning."

At nine thirty on Friday morning, Harper jogs across her lawn and gets into my passenger seat. On time *and* wearing a bra! I can't help but smile, proud of my good influence.

As she fastens her seat belt, she asks, "No coat? Aren't you cold?"

"No." Pride flies out the window with that lie, but overcoats have pockets where one can easily hide small finds. Better I do without it this trip. I put the car in reverse and glance in the rearview mirror. "We'll be indoors, so I don't need one."

"Did you show Joe the photos of my buffet?"

My husband is happy for me but couldn't tell an end table from a nightstand. "He's not really that into this stuff."

"But he supports you turning your hobby into an income?" She smiles.

"Yes." He even offered to help me do the books.

I turn right and head toward the Merritt Parkway, anxiety tangling a tight web around each muscle. I need to practice systematic desensitization—the exposure to anxiety-producing stimuli—but relaxation and breathing exercises aren't easy with a passenger at my side.

Harper elbows me. "You mentioned things between you two are better now. What happened at Colgate?"

I flush. I've been concentrating on listening to him. The only thing between us now is my secret. "We had a good talk."

"A talk, huh?" She sits up straight and eager, like a retriever wagging its tail. "So you took my advice."

"Sort of. I let things unfold instead of trying to control everything. Joe liked the change, and it led to a big discussion. I guess my bossiness had him feeling a little . . . emasculated."

Harper frowns. "I didn't figure Joe as a guy who'd punish his wife for asserting herself."

"It's not like that." Or perhaps it was a little, but his reaction doesn't diminish the validity of his complaints. "I haven't been valuing his opinions or considering his needs enough. Marriage requires compromise. Neither one of us should always get our way. But we've agreed to be more open and honest now." A promise I've not fully kept.

She shrugs—her only concession. "Well, at least you confronted things. Good for you for actually taking some advice. Most people never do." She crosses her legs, a self-satisfied expression pulling at her mouth.

Funny remark for someone so dismissive of others' opinions. That fact seems lost on her.

"I welcome advice from people I trust." She doesn't appear to take my hint, given the way she's intently watching the road ahead. "Have you taken any of mine?"

Her head snaps in my direction. "What advice?"

"About your parents . . . or Nate?"

She laughs. "You don't give up easily, I'll give you that."

"I'm older, so I see time differently. One day you'll wake up with another decade gone and no chance to go back and do things over." A sigh escapes. "You're still young, but windows are closing on things like having kids. Your parents won't always be around, either. It's not my business. I get that. But I like you, Harper, so I'd hate for you to end up with regrets. That's all."

Harper wrinkles her nose while biting her lower lip. "I appreciate that, Wendy. Believe it or not, I've given more thought to your perspective on things than you can imagine."

Odd phrasing, but I don't press. "I'm flattered. Now if only my mom would consider my perspective, I'd feel even better."

Harper jumps on the change of subject. "What's up with your mom?"

She already knows about my mother's condition, so there's no reason to obfuscate. "She refuses to try therapy for her OCD."

Harper's eyes narrow. "Why?"

"Anxiety about going to the office outweighs any benefit she imagines getting from 'talking to a stranger.' She says she's content, but I think she's given up." Which is so easy to do, as my choices this past decade prove.

"It can't be easy to spill your guts and be judged." Harper leans closer, peering at me like she's watching for a specific reaction.

Trapped in the driver's seat, I can't back away. "They don't judge. That's the point. They help you analyze your behavior and beliefs so you make better choices."

"Sounds like you have personal experience." Her exceedingly casual tone is at odds with such a personal question.

If I were walking, I might've tripped.

"Doesn't everyone?" I laugh it off to sidestep a deeper conversation. My mother's warnings come like slaps to the head. However breezy Harper might act about things like therapy, I can't predict how she'd react if she learned about my kleptomania. And if I tell anyone, it should first be Joe.

"Truth!" Harper chuckles. "We've all got shit to deal with, even if we hide it. That's why we love gossip. Other people's scandals and addictions make our mistakes seem less terrible."

That's not exactly how I'd put it, but I generally agree with the sentiment. "People are entitled to their secrets as long as they aren't hurting anyone."

"Amen." Harper looks away sharply. She's almost edgy today, but I have to stay focused on myself to get through this test without taking something that doesn't belong to me.

While we whiz up the Merritt, my insides rev along with the engine. Why did I start with such a difficult task—shopping with a friend! Dr. Haertel will expect a full report. I'll need to monitor my feelings at the market without drawing Harper's attention. Can she already sense my nervous energy?

Harper pulls a pair of sunglasses out of her bag and puts them on, then offers me a stick of gum. When I decline, she pops two in her mouth and sets her feet on the dash. Those boots have never been polished. Harper doesn't seem to give much thought to her appearance, her career, or her family, which makes me curious about why my going into business for myself matters to her.

To pass the time, I turn on the radio. Billy Joel's "Only the Good Die Young" fills the car.

"My anthem." Harper turns up the sound and starts singing— badly, loudly, and unabashedly—waving one arm around like a conductor. "Come on, you know the words. Everyone does," she coaxes before crooning the lyrics.

A grin tugs at my lips. Moments later I'm belting the refrain along with Harper. By the end of the song, I'm practically panting from laughter, my cheeks sore from smiling. The last time I sang and laughed with another woman . . . Well, I can't even remember it. That brings tears to my eyes, which I cover with more laughter to avoid drowning in self-pity for all I've missed out on. For days like this.

"How much farther?" Harper asks.

"Not much."

We arrive at Nicky's Attic in Shelton, which is essentially a brick warehouse with a colorfully painted entrance and stairwell. From what I've read, it's more indoor flea market than high-end antique dealer. Perfect for someone looking to give new life to neglected pieces.

Harper grabs my forearm. "I hope we find something cool. Did I mention that my cousin Mandy *loves* the buffet? She might be your first customer if we find something she could use."

"That's nice, thanks." The compliment doesn't stop my stomach from clenching. Beneath the shadow of the massive building, I stop a few yards from the front door, as if standing at the entrance of a horror museum.

Harper is up the steps by the time she realizes I'm no longer behind her. "Come on!"

I nod and approach the stairs, hoping momentum will somehow prevent me from doing something stupid. As instructed, I practice a covert sensitization scenario like Dr. Haertel suggested. First, I imagine the buzz in proximity to a tempting item, and then I picture becoming increasingly nauseous the closer it gets. Finally, I see myself reaching for the item but then vomiting in front of Harper and other shoppers. The image is so vivid and visceral I grab my stomach with one hand while clutching the stair railing with the other.

Once inside, I draw a cleansing breath. I can do this. I must.

Dust kicks up as the door swings closed, causing me to sneeze. Black worn patches and scratches mar the ancient wooden floors. Furniture, junky signs, trunks, cheap dining sets, and lighting fixtures are stacked along walls and strewn throughout the space, forming a sort of maze of abandoned items through which I must escape without getting strung up.

There aren't many shoppers here, which is good and bad. Good because I'm less likely to get caught if I slip, but bad because I'd be less likely to slip if there were a lot of people around who could catch me.

"I'll check out that section." Harper points to the far left. "I'll yell if I see something cool."

"Okay. I'll start here." I watch her leave like she's a rescue boat that's left me adrift.

Focusing, I peruse the aisle, searching for an abandoned piece I can transform into something desirable. The rolltop secretary desk could be gorgeous, but it won't fit in my car. Today isn't about finding the perfect piece. It's about getting through this store without stealing. I need only one or two small items to get started.

Amid the junk, I spy a cream-colored, barrel-shaped side table that reminds me of one my grandmother had ages ago. I open its door, inspecting the interior. Looks like maple wood. If the exterior were stripped down and fitted with funky hardware, it could be a cool retro piece. More important, it will fit in my hatchback.

"Hey, Wendy, what about this?" Harper calls from a distance.

I head in the direction of her voice to find her eyeing a hutch.

"A pie safe." It's at least a century old. Pierced-copper insets give the double doors charm, but blue paint is peeling from every surface. It's probably built from soft pine, which wouldn't be difficult to work with. "I love it."

Harper is fingering the metalwork. "What's a pie safe?"

I open the doors. "People used to cool pies on these racks."

I imagine generations of women baking pies for their family, friends, and churches, and passing down recipes. Bringing smiles to faces of the people they love, celebrating life's best moments.

Harper brings an end to my pleasant musing. "People used to live dull lives. Thank God for bakeries." She flutters her lips as if bored already. "Should we take it?"

I shake my head, regretfully. "It won't fit in my car, and the delivery charge would be greater than the price tag."

"Next time we come, we should borrow a pickup truck or rent a U-Haul."

Next time. Instead of that notion striking terror, a cautious smile grows. This is what life could be. New friends. A shot at accepting invitations to doing things in the world. A business of my own. A stronger marriage. It's almost too good to be true.

"We'll see. I found a small table I like, and might grab one of the framed mirrors hanging around." Uncomplicated and inexpensive items are a safe place to start.

"I think you should go big. Put this on hold until you can come back for it. You know you'd make it look awesome. I don't bake, but I might even buy it when you're done."

"For all those books you have . . ." I consider her suggestion, but the chance that someone will race in here to buy it anytime soon seems slim. "I'm not ready to commit. It'll have to wait."

"Good thing the Durbins' house has so many built-in bookshelves, then." Harper pats the piece like it's a dog we're not adopting.

I turn away before she makes me feel sentimental about it. "Speaking of books, did you read *Same New Story?*"

"I'm almost finished." She follows me back to the other row of items.

"Are you loving it?"

She pauses. "It's entertaining. I see why it appeals to so many readers."

Such a formal reply. Is that a publicist thing? "I laughed a few times, cried once, too. When a book can swing me here and there, *that's* a great story."

"It's a big part of the experience," she muses even as she drifts further away.

She mustn't love the book. Either way, I'm shocked she isn't more direct with her opinion. "Maybe hearing the author talk about her process and why she wrote it will make you like it more."

"I actually know Ellen." Harper says this so nonchalantly I almost miss it.

"You do?" I touch her arm, wondering why she didn't mention it sooner. "That's exciting."

She half shrugs, wearing an enigmatic expression. "Publishing is a small industry."

Maybe this is striking a nerve about losing her job. Still, I can't stop my follow-up questions. "Is she nice? Is she funny in real life?"

Another nod. "Very nice, with a quiet sense of humor."

"I knew it. I always figured a writer's personality bleeds into the work."

With an antique squash racquet held in midair, she cocks her head. "Not always. I mean, it is fiction. Writers make up people that are entirely different from themselves, especially when trying to comment on something in society."

"But I mean in general. Like, the tone and the focus . . . It's not like writers can divorce themselves entirely from the way they see the world."

Harper sets the racquet aside, rolling her eyes. "If it makes you feel better to think that all those romance novels are written by warm, witty women, then go ahead, but trust me, some authors are total divas. Meanwhile, some 'harsh' stories are written by cool-ass amazing people."

"Don't tell me about the divas. Let me live in ignorant bliss." I prefer it, honestly. "But I'd love to be introduced to Ellen."

"I'm sure there'll be a book signing. She'll probably take a photo with you."

"So fun." We arrive back at my barrel table. "I'll take this and that mirror." I point up to a midsize oval mirror with an elaborate frame.

"This?" Harper smirks at the table like some playground bully.

I caress its top. "Picture it stripped down to its natural state—maybe with a ceruse treatment—and then updated with black metal hardware."

"It'll never be as cool as the pie safe."

"Cool isn't everything. Anything can shine in its own unique way." I glance around but don't see any salesclerk. "Can you wait here while I go find someone to check me out?"

"Sure." She sits on the table and pulls out her phone, scrolling before I can blink.

"Be right back." I jog to the front of the store, where I remember seeing a cash register. No one is there when I arrive, but a box of five-dollar silver and copper vintage wax seal rings is displayed on the counter. Some have monograms; others have images of birds and flowers.

I finger a few, too aware of that familiar palpitation in my chest. The vibration working its way through my core and limbs. Dual sensations of fear and excitement compete for my attention. I could snatch one and no one would know.

My fingers begin to close; I force myself to imagine putting it in my pocket but getting caught by a camera or staff member. I let the sense of shame fill me, and imagine Harper's reaction and how it might affect our friendship. I picture Joe answering the call after I get arrested, and then, with control, I fold my arms across my chest with my empty hands buried tightly beneath my armpits. Breathe . . .

Someone touches my shoulder. I yelp with a start, upsetting the entire box of rings, which clatter as they hit the floor. I stoop to collect them, shaking slightly but grateful for the technique that kept me from giving in to my urge. The stranger lowers the box for me to put them in, so I look up.

"Are you interested in these?" asks a heavyset woman with wiry hair and kind eyes.

I stand, shaking my head. "Actually, I was looking for help checking out two things over in that first aisle."

My racing heart is a lingering reminder of the near miss. If I hadn't seen Dr. Haertel this week, I might've been slipping a ring into my pocket as she approached.

"Let's go see what you found." She smiles and follows me back to Harper.

The close call shows I'm capable of control, so going into a business that will require me to shop regularly might not be preposterous. A different buzz now floods my system—a joyful one. Anticipating this outing has been the highlight of my week. I'm relieved by my little win and the idea of expanding my world and maybe helping Harper by giving her a little side hustle until she lands a full-time job.

My next appointment with Dr. Haertel is in nine days. Joe's belief that we've committed to transparency is eating away at me. I'm tired of skipping atop quicksand trying to avoid triggers and truths that could take me under.

Dr. Haertel might be right. Coming clean with everyone might be the only path to a freer state of mind. Perhaps that's worth the risk of scorn?

Harper's leaning against the table, looking at her phone. I open my mouth, then close it before she notices. I'm not ready yet. Joe deserves the truth first. The mere thought of his disappointment makes me strain to breathe.

I will tell him. Eventually, I will.

Just not today.

CHAPTER FOURTEEN

HARPER

Friday, late afternoon

To: Harper Ross
From: Cassandra Thornton
Re: WIP Pages

This is it! Love the zany neighbor—she's a good balance of overbearing and kindness—so I'm rooting for her. I think Haley should be the sperm-donor baby—the stakes are greater that way. But on the topic of Haley, she's a bit standoffish. I know she's got her secret agenda, but does she have to be so cold? It might be more powerful if she cozies up to Gwen before Gwen learns the truth. Overall, it has a nice light tone and is a solid new direction. I'll send this to Tessa with the synopsis. Keep going unless you hear otherwise.

I reread the email a second time before releasing the sigh of relief that's been stuck in my lungs since Monday. Thank you, Jesus or Wendy or Nate, or all the above, for breaking me out of my writing slump. My begrudging migration to New Canaan could pay huge dividends, although I'm conflicted about how much to celebrate. The fact that burb life spawned a story despite suburbs being my decades-long nemesis feels a bit like putting on clothes pulled from the hamper.

I sit back and cross my arms, thinking about Cassandra's opinion of Haley. No shock, really. I've kept her distant and nondescript because my last heroine of a similar age garnered only the most biting remarks about everything from her opinions to her actions. But while vanilla may be the secret to Joe's general appeal in real life, it is never a compelling character trait in a novel.

Haley is walking a fine line to get close to the man she thinks is her father, thus her distant manner. Digging deeper into her psyche— her motives for seeking him out—could help make her more relatable. Making sure she has something important on the line should also keep readers rooting for her.

I arrived in New Canaan planning a book about women who project a perfect life while hiding the flaws, but maybe my story is really about the perceptions that drive us all. Or how they're first formed and then shape our lives. Or am I trying to determine whether perceptions shape families or families shape perceptions? Obviously I'm still a long way from understanding what I want to say with this tale.

The second email is from my real estate broker.

> Deal is dead unless you reduce price by $125,000.
> If you don't, then your buyer pool will be limited to cash buyers who don't need the financing contingency.

I listed the condo at $1.25 million, but it appraised at only $1.125 mill.

I grip the edge of my writing desk, unprepared for this decision. The consolation of feeling forced to sell was getting a great price. Reducing it feels like another hit. Now Cassandra's enthusiastic email has breathed new life into my hopes of saving my career, too. If only I knew that Tessa was on board, I'd be more confident that this beach read could put me back on top, or at least give my rebound momentum.

Is there anything worse than standing at the notorious fork? Reducing the price is the safe move. There'll be another condo down the road if things turn around. When. When things turn around. Yet I can't quit on myself now. Not when I'm feeling close to a comeback. I wish I could ask Wendy her opinion—she's so damn optimistic I'm sure she'd be helpful.

I'll call Mandy.

"Hey, cuz." I swivel my chair from side to side, idly glancing out the window to the neighbor's yard, where a nanny is watching a toddler push a toy mower around the grass. "What's happening?"

"I'm sneaking in some me time—out for a walk by myself. My sitter has Becca for another hour." Her tone is cheerful as usual. Despite an occasional complaint about being tired and overwhelmed by motherhood and work, she wouldn't change a thing, and we both know it.

"It just so happens I've got some me time now, too . . . Oh wait, my whole life is me time," I joke, but neither she nor I laugh with any sincerity. I rub my breastbone. Am I turning into Wendy? I drop my hand to my lap. "Actually, I called for help with a decision."

"Is everything okay?"

"That depends. The condo deal fell through. On one hand, I've moved out and had mentally started to count on that cash, but on the other, this seems like a sign—a second chance to hold on to the place. The broker wants to reduce the price, but I'm not sure. I mean, if I can get what I asked or more, it makes losing my home easier to stomach. Dropping the price makes me feel icky."

"I know you love the condo, but the place has some bad juju thanks to Calvin and the last book and stuff, right? Maybe starting over somewhere new is best no matter the price."

True, and yet it's my home. More than that, it's been a point of pride since I bought it. A mark of my success.

"Hello?" she asks.

"Sorry, I'm thinking." I lean forward with my forehead on the edge of the desk. "My emotions are in full rebel mode despite your logic. I can't imagine handing it off to someone else on the cheap."

"Only you know your true financial situation. Can you afford to hold on to it until your next advance? It's just a condo. There are tons of them in Manhattan if you want to move back there."

My head pops up, and I flop back as if thrown into the chair. "If? Of course I'm moving back."

"Oh. I just thought . . . well, it seems like you're settling into New Canaan a bit. And there's Nate."

"Please don't tell me you're suggesting I arrange my life around a guy? One I barely know, by the way."

"Of course not. But if life is going well there—your work, your stress level, a new relationship—why not consider staying? Choose happiness."

"I was happy in New York."

"Not lately you weren't."

I scowl. Sometimes the truth sucks.

Following a sigh, Mandy says, "If you're not ready to let go, don't reduce the price. You might get a cash offer."

I might. And in a few weeks, I'll have Tessa's feedback on the pages. If she's happy, I can count on the second half of that advance (and not need to return the first half, either). That would be enough to hold the condo at least until I see how my next book launch goes. "Thanks. I think I'm going to gamble on myself and keep the price high."

"That's a good bet. Now, before you hang up, I have a question—and don't bite my head off. When will you see Nate again?"

"Tomorrow. But it could be our last date unless . . . Can I tell him the truth and then ask him not to tell Joe?" The fact that I have to ask makes the answer pretty damn obvious.

"Tell him that you're working on a book, and you don't want others to know because they'll interrupt your flow. Beyond that, you don't owe him details about the plot. You're not a gossip columnist doing a tell-all—you're writing *fiction*."

Fiction about a character who is a near mirror image of a neurotic yet lonely woman who has done nothing but be kind to me. Who trusts and confides in me. Whom I care about. Calvin would say that work comes first, but lately that edict feels as slippery as he was. How can I be a feminist and not consider another woman's feelings about being used without her knowledge?

"My agent gave a thumbs-up on the sample chapters." It's a legit reason to quiet my conscience and keep going. The comeback. The career. The restoration of my reputation and chance to keep my home. All writers take pieces of other people's experiences, after all.

"I know you've been stressed, but I've never had doubts. Every author writes one book that's a least favorite. You've got yours, so it's all blue skies from now on."

An optimistic take, but it's entirely possible to write an even worse book than the last.

"Thanks for the pep talk. I wish I'd had a mom like you in my ear." Mine's always too worried about what could go wrong, which basically proves she has no faith in me. When one's own mother has no faith in you, it makes faith as elusive as a unicorn. The silence on Mandy's end makes me sit up. "Hello?"

"I'm still here." The good cheer in her voice, however, is not.

What just happened? "Everything okay?"

"Yeah, yeah. I . . . well, why are you still so hard on your mom?"

"I'm not that hard on her." Not to her face anyway. And pointing out a fact isn't being harsh; it's being honest. "We even talked the other week, and it went okay."

Mandy's never fully supported me in my rocky relationship with my folks, but she's never taken me to task before, either. "I heard. She told my mom."

As if my call warrants a conversation throughout the family. "See, this is the problem. I bet she doesn't tell your mom about every conversation she has with Jim and Rick. Was she lamenting my risky career? Complaining that it takes up all my time? Wondering why she got stuck with a daughter who doesn't want to give her grandkids?"

"No. She was happy to hear from you and wanted to share that with her sister. If she mentioned Nate, you can't be mad at her—or anyone who cares about you—for wanting you to find love. Sisters talk to each other about stuff, including their hopes and wishes for their kids. I tell you about Becca and Jeff all the time. That's what normal people talk about."

A backhanded way of suggesting I'm not normal. While I'm casting about for some reason to feel righteously affronted, Mandy interrupts me.

"I probably shouldn't mention this, but you should know something."

Whatever this is, it doesn't sound good. Is my mother sick? I'm holding my breath, my chest unexpectedly wrenched with concern. "What's wrong?"

"Nothing's wrong." Immediate relief eases my tension, then Mandy says, "Your mom won a community service award for her decade with the ABC House. There's a ceremony in two weeks, and my mom has organized a celebratory dinner at Tambellini's afterward. Your brothers will be there, and so will I, along with other family and friends. Your mom told mine not to 'trouble' you because—and I quote—'you're too busy working to come home for her little award.' But I think you should decide what to prioritize."

"My mom doesn't want me there?" I blink.

"That's not at all what I said. Honestly, you're too old and smart to play the martyr."

Her impatient tone stabs me like a hot poker, which must be why I jump to my feet. "You just said my mom asked that I not be invited."

"Come on, Harper. Obviously she thinks that you wouldn't think something like her 'little' award is worthy of your time. She doesn't want you to feel guilty about skipping it, or to come but then resent being there."

"So she thinks I'm selfish?" I start to pace between the desk and the closet door, scowling.

"Again, not what I said." She pauses. "Instead of only seeing your side of things, maybe try looking at it from her perspective. How many times have you made light of your mom's choices—to stay at home, to volunteer instead of pursue a career?"

Probably too often, I admit to myself. Seems I've been as judgmental as anyone.

"And when's the last time you visited Ohio?" Mandy continues.

Two Thanksgivings ago. "It's been a while."

"Exactly. You skipped two Christmases and Easters. You didn't even show up for cousin Laurie's baby shower in August."

"In case everyone's forgotten, my life took a massive U-turn that first Christmas, and then the next year my career took another. I've been busy bingeing Ben & Jerry's and hiding in shame." Besides, cousin Laurie is five years younger than me, and we were never superclose.

"Everyone's got a busy life, Harper. And disappointments, too. If anything, you've not only had the most success in our family, but you also have the most autonomy. Would it kill you to show up for holidays or to support other people's little wins now and then?"

I frown. "Wow. You sound exactly like my mom."

"I take that as a compliment. Your mom's caring and considerate despite having chosen a different path than you. She might not have been your ideal mother, but she loves you and tried to give you everything you needed to live your best life. The fact that you've gone out and done just that proves that she did some things right, so maybe it's time to give her a break for not being the world's staunchest feminist."

I stand still, mouth agape, head emptied of any good retort. This is Mandy saying these things, not my dad or brothers or aunt. It's not even Wendy, although I'm sure she'd be nodding in agreement like an emphatic bobblehead.

Strangely weak-kneed, I grip the back of the chair for balance. "Okay. I'll think about coming."

"Great. I'll send you the details but won't tell anyone in case you don't make it. I hope you show up, because I'd love to see you, too." Once the lecturing tone has vanished, she sounds like my favorite cousin again.

"I'll watch for the text." A rush of petulance almost makes me hang up the phone without saying goodbye.

"I know you're miffed at me right now. I'm all for you living life however makes you happy, but that happiness shouldn't have to be mutually exclusive from having a relationship with your own family. If you want support for your choices, maybe you could start by supporting theirs."

"You made your point," I snap, then bite my tongue. Mandy's not mean-spirited. Her opinion isn't even all that surprising. "I'll be there."

"Bring Nate." The smile is back in her voice. "He sounds sexy."

"You're still married, right?" Sarcasm is my fallback whenever my emotions run amok, although it's also troubling that the idea of bringing Nate to Ohio isn't her most terrifying suggestion.

"Doesn't make me blind."

That wrings a slight chuckle from me. "Finish your walk. I've got to work on revisions now."

"Good luck. Have fun with Nate and call me next week."

"Kiss Becca for me."

I hang up, then text my broker to leave the staging and keep the original price. Once I set the phone down, I collapse onto my chair, giving myself a moment to breathe through my frustration. Processing that conversation will take longer than I have time for, so I set it aside to focus on my story. Except I can't, because I'm beginning to suspect that Mandy's take on me has something to do with why I can't—or won't—peel back the armor and let readers get close to Haley.

If Gwen is a form of Wendy, have I subconsciously made Haley in my own image? And if so, am I worried that readers won't like her if they see the truth, or that her actions have been more reactive than proactive? Worst case, it could be both.

That would suck even more than all those bad reviews.

———

On Saturday afternoon, Nate and I follow the tour group down MacDougal Street in the Village—a narrow one-way road lined with a few small trees, dozens of restaurants, and clusters of locked bicycles—having just gorged on Chef Pietro's fabulous Bolognese sauce. It's a gorgeous, if chilly, fall day. The city's heartbeat has perked up mine, despite being occasionally assaulted by unpleasant aromas—greasy ones blown out of the multiple kitchen vents we pass, and sour smells rising from the mounds of trash bags awaiting pickup.

My leather jacket is inadequate in this breeze. When I shiver, Nate throws an arm around my shoulder. It makes me twitchy, which is ridiculous considering the more intimate touching we engaged in the other weekend. Perhaps it's the possessiveness his gesture implies, or the mushiness—although I dig that now and then—or maybe I'm self-sabotaging because of my secret identity. Hard to say, but he must sense my discomfort, because his arm drops away. That should make me feel better, but it doesn't.

"Would you like my coat?" He starts to peel off his barn coat—L.L.Bean, something so preppy only he could make it look masculine and sexy.

"I'll be fine. Our last stop is only a few blocks away." With a mocking laugh, I add, "A walking food tour in November probably wasn't my best idea."

"I'm loving it. I don't get down to the city often enough. Better yet, there's been no detour to an ER!" His broad smile and good humor about our last date make my heart stretch in the best way. If my life weren't so complicated, spending more time with Nate would be a no-brainer. "I didn't realize the area's history would be so integral to a food tour. It's fascinating."

I nod, and we stroll almost another full block listening to our group's guide.

Then Nate asks me, "Did you live around here?"

"No, my place is down in SoHo." I hike a thumb over my shoulder, then quickly return my hand to my pocket.

"Is?" His head cocks as if he's misheard me.

I nod. "Yes. Three years now."

"You still own it?" He nearly comes to a stop, but then takes two big strides to keep up with the group.

"Yeah." I brace for the inevitable questions I'm not sure how to answer.

His financially oriented brain is likely doing all kinds of calculations. "Did you sublet it?"

"No. I sold it—but the deal fell through. It's back on the market, but I've still got keys."

He tilts his head. "Isn't New York real estate, like, astronomical?"

The tour guide drones on about a building we're passing, but the buzzing in my head is due to the collision of my two worlds. "It's a tiny place. One bedroom, but very cool."

After a moment of hesitation that might've been a question he decided not to ask, he says, "I'd love to see it."

It's about a half mile away and would be a quiet place to drink a bottle of wine and . . . well, did I mention the mattress? "We could grab a bottle of wine or something after the tour and hang out a bit before heading back to Sleepyville."

We take a few steps in silence; then Nate asks, "So why are you selling it and living in 'Sleepyville'?"

The tour guide's shut-the-hell-up side-eye silences me momentarily while he continues talking about when Bob Dylan and Jimi Hendrix walked these streets to suck up inspiration, as if good art happened only in the sixties. Contemporary artists still walk around here seeking the same thing. The energy and eclectic nature of the Village and Manhattan feeds creativity. It also offers top-notch people-watching and eavesdropping.

"I'll tell you later," I murmur, knowing the time for keeping my secret is coming to an end.

It's only a second date, but honesty feels like the barest minimum I owe him before we have sex again. And I'm 99 percent sure I want him again. Ten years ago, I wouldn't have thought twice about a sex-based relationship that came without any strings, including truthfulness. Even Calvin and I kept our extracurricular liaisons on the down low. But his leaving me for another woman—and my being blindsided by it all— has me disinclined to repeat old patterns. That plus conversations with Wendy and Mandy have forced me to take stock.

Our group comes to a stop in Washington Square Park. Nate is rapt by our tour guide's current speech, blissfully unaware that my stomach hurts (and not because I overate the pasta). Will Nate dislike me for my lie? Will he keep my secret? I could avoid this conflict by choosing abstinence.

My gaze wanders the width of his shoulders, slides down his back, and curls around his tight ass. Abstinence feels more dreadful than telling the truth.

Sixty minutes and too many Brazilian chocolates later, we're strolling down Thompson Street with a bottle of pinot noir.

"Here we are." I take my keys out of my purse and open the door to my building, a 1920s co-op. "I'm in 1C. It's got a gorgeous, if tiny, private patio. Perfect for having a drink when it's not so chilly."

"Sounds nice." His voice rumbles right through me, heating me up like a good shot of bourbon.

When we get inside my apartment, I try to view its shotgun layout and staged decor the way a potential buyer might. Medium-toned hardwood floors, white painted brick walls. Smoky-gray modern kitchen cabinetry contrasted by stark white counters and a subway tile backsplash. Its small cook space is adequate for someone who orders takeout for most meals.

After a month away, I'm jarred by the unplanned homecoming. When I packed up, I'd steeled myself against tears, reminding myself that practicality should trump sentimentality. And yet here I stand, surrounded by memories—good and bad—feeling the pull of the dream life that I created for myself for a little while.

"The place actually looks sophisticated with coordinated furniture instead of my eclectic things and piles of books."

"Where's the patio?" he asks, taking his time to scrutinize every nook and cranny.

"Through the bedroom." I gesture past the kitchen. "Go take a peek. I'll open the wine."

Thank God for screw caps, since my barware is in Connecticut. I grab two red Solo cups from the sleeve we purchased and pour us each a generous amount of wine. It's weird to be here with Nate. This hippie boho unit suits me, and I love the action outside yet can't wholly deny the charm and friendliness of my Connecticut neighbors, my awesome front porch, and the quaint little village of New Canaan. Two very different existences, both with pros and cons.

Nate returns from his inspection and takes the cup I offer. "Thanks."

We click our plastic cups together. "Cheers."

He takes a first sip, leaning his hip against the counter. "It's nice." His large palm caresses the counter appreciatively, his brows knotting together like they can wrest the answer to whatever question he's gnawing on. "You must be one hell of a publicist to afford it."

He peers at me over his cup. I appreciate him waiting for me to decide to open up. Fuck. Fuckity fuck. Time's up.

"I'm not really a publicist." I blurt it out before losing my nerve, then chug half the wine in my cup.

"Okay." Nate widens his stance, an unsurprised expression in his eyes. "Hopefully you're not a psychotic murderer who's lured me to this empty apartment to steal my liver, or a spy who now has to kill me to keep your cover."

"Oh, that's good. You're a storyteller—a dark one." I smile, recalling that, at Wendy's party, he claimed to be an avid reader. "But you can relax. I'm harmless."

As soon as those words are out there, I wonder if they're true. Mandy doesn't think so. Wendy probably wouldn't either if she knew about Gwen. Even Nate might have his doubts now that he knows I've lied to everyone.

As if on cue, he asks, "So why the lie?"

I release a heavy breath through my nose. "It's complicated. I'm trying to keep a low profile."

He raises his eyebrows as if to emphasize that my incomplete answer still leaves him guessing.

"The thing is, I'm a writer. A novelist who enjoyed a lot of success . . . until I didn't." My face gets so hot it might combust at any moment. "After my recent flop—a humbling and very public night-mare—and a rejected manuscript, my editor pushed me in a new direction and 'suggested' I write for an older crowd. We thought immersing myself in a community like New Canaan would help me get a feel for wealthy suburban, middle-aged women and that lifestyle. I didn't tell anyone because if people act different around me, then I won't get an authentic experience. Also, I'm embarrassed about my last book, so I wanted to stay under the radar." I finish the wine and pour myself a bit more, unable to meet Nate's gaze.

"So New Canaan is kind of like a writing retreat for you. A glimpse at how the other half lives?"

Close enough. "Exactly. I hope to salvage my career and maybe even hold on to this place if no one makes a great offer in the interim. It's a long shot, but I'm not a quitter."

"Guess you write under a pen name?" Thankfully, there's no trace of judgment or scorn in his tone. I peek up at him and nod. He flashes a gentle smile. "Since you feel embarrassed about your last book, I won't ask you to share it. But if you've had success before, maybe you're being too hard on yourself. No one hits a home run every single time."

He sounds like Mandy. That familiarity could be why I'm comfortable around him despite not knowing him very well. "It's one thing to have soft sales, but another to get trounced like I did. The reviews were bru-tal." I think to myself, *Laborious prose and characters so stiff they might be corpses. Not even the author's mother could praise this one!*

"I thought you didn't much worry about other people's opinions." He twists his palm up in the air for emphasis.

I bark a laugh. "That's true."

While there are many areas of my life in which I can dismiss others' opinions, nonwriters can't understand how mentally crippling bad reviews can be. How they burrow deep into your subconscious, turning your brain into an emotional minefield that explodes upon the slightest perception of weakness in one's own work.

"But this is a little different from someone criticizing my hairstyle or even my politics. I put my whole heart into my writing, which makes it impossible not to take the criticism personally, I guess. And the public nature of it . . ." I find myself shaking my head while staring into my cup. "How would you like a bad performance review to be done in front of the whole office, let alone the whole world? And what burns almost as much is knowing that my family, who to this day continues to question my career and suggest a safer alternative, probably secretly thought 'told you so' when that book tanked."

Nate doesn't rush in with platitudes, which I appreciate. He lets my feelings hover between us without swatting them away or minimizing them. It's validating, actually, and almost makes me glad I told him. It's been a while since I've been this vulnerable with anyone new, let alone a man. He finally swallows most of his wine. "Thanks for trusting me with something so important and a little painful. I promise not to spill your secret."

"Wow." I lean against the counter, relief loosening all my muscles. "That was a lot easier than I expected. Thanks for not making me feel like a total shithead."

"Did you think I'd be a dick about it?" He looks almost amused by the idea.

I shrug. "You're so straitlaced I thought you'd feel affronted." He probably would if he knew the full truth about why I first cozied up to Wendy. I doubt he'd be moved by the fact that I genuinely like her now.

"Straitlaced?" He sets down his empty cup, chuckling. "What other assumptions have you made about me based on so little information?"

Not so little, really. I know of his government finance job. I know he likes his family game night and is comfortable spending a Saturday night with people at least a full decade older than him. He also enjoys cooking and bought a car for a family he doesn't yet have. "You want a life like Joe's—a nice guy with a secure job in a safe town, someday with a wife and family and pretty Christmas card photos. Your wife might work but will also be a nurturer, a good cook, and someone who likes to keep the game-night tradition going. You'd like to take an annual family beach vacation but throw in an occasional trip to Europe. You host football games with friends over, and can't wait to cheer for your own kid on the sidelines. You're also the neighbor who'll use his snow-blower to clean off the elderly neighbor's driveway and walk on snowy mornings. How'd I do?" I ask smugly, confident I've hit more than one nail on the head.

He's grinning but shaking his head. "You make me sound like one of those dudes in a Hallmark movie."

I nearly spit out my wine from snort-laughing. "The fact that you know of those dudes sort of proves my point."

He holds up his hands in surrender. "My mom loves those movies, so sometimes they're on in the background when she's cooking."

"And again, proving me right."

"All right. Yeah, I'm a good guy and all those things sound nice, but I like a little adventure, too. I have a motorcycle that I ride up into Vermont now and then. I played guitar for a nineties cover band as a side gig until two years ago, when my bandmate Ronny moved to Illinois. And I'd like to live in France for a few years at some point in the next decade."

"Really?" None of those things fit the narrative in my head, and all of them make him even more appealing, if that's possible. That's not exactly good news for someone who doesn't want to get attached.

"Hell yeah," Nate says. "It's a big globe and there's a lot to experience. I don't plan on making my whole life about one thing—not a career, not a person, not a hobby."

"But you talked about wanting a family—you already bought a car for it."

"That doesn't mean I can't also have an adventure. My someday wife could have a job while also enjoying a good cover band and a few-years stint in Menton. Maybe she'll even ride her own Harley."

I don't have a quick comeback, probably because I'm very turned on. "That sounds . . . fun."

He smiles and steps closer. Heat pulses off his skin, causing my libido to ramp up. "Is making up scenarios about people before you know them a hazard of your job?"

"A little, but mine shouldn't be so one-note. Characters are always layered." A fleeting thought about not heeding this in my last book fizzles because I'm staring at his lips now, my heartbeat heavy in my chest. My inner thighs clench.

"Like real people," he murmurs against my cheek.

I swallow. "Yes."

That came out breathy. Embarrassingly so.

He reaches up and fingers a lock of my hair. "Will I be in your book?"

I'd smile if I weren't hot and bothered. "I'm not writing porn."

He laughs, head thrown back before he brings it close to mine. "Maybe you could throw in one or two sex scenes for the hell of it."

"It could help sales." After all, romance novels rake in a billion dollars annually.

Once our lips touch, there's no more talking. Unless you count horny grunts. His rock-solid chest and arms are so very satisfying to clutch. This is what's going through my mind when suddenly I'm lifted off my feet and carried to the bedroom, where we fall onto the mattress amid a clumsy, quick undressing.

For the briefest flash, I think about Calvin. He's the last person I slept with here—Tinder "dates" were never invited. Nate's different. I trust him enough to let him into my space. That's probably relevant. Important, even. My train of thought quickly dies when Nate's mouth makes its way down my neck.

Oh yes. I purr, my back arching as the tension builds in my core.

Nate's not overly sentimental about sex. He's sensual, intense, and experimental—all totally appropriate considering that this is only the second time we've been together. I could get used to this, except I can't, because regardless of his Harley and his plans to live abroad, I don't see either of us commuting back and forth to see each other once I turn in my manuscript and come home for good. The acknowledgment strikes just ahead of my first orgasm. Talk about whiplash.

I force aside the buzzkilling thoughts, grab Nate's head, and drag him up into a kiss before rolling him onto his back and climbing on top. The appreciative light in his eyes sets off all kinds of heady emotions as I sink into an easy rhythm.

We're sweaty. The strain of self-control tightens his neck and face. "Let go!" I fall forward.

It's not too long before I can roll onto my back. We lie there breathless, the rosy late-afternoon light slipping in through the french doors. Nate tucks me against his side, snatching the sheet with his toes until he can reach it with a hand, wrapping us in a warm cotton cocoon.

The Tinder booty often leaped from the bed to clean themselves or grab a smoke. Nate seems quite content to lie still, eyes closed, a soft smile on his lips. Peacefulness worms through me like warm water, and my breath turns deep and restful. Is it Nate? Is it me? Is it just the result of another hot roll in the hay? Or is it stemming from being more honest about myself, and with myself?

Maybe holding on to this feeling night after night is the reason Mandy and Wendy and so many others prefer a commitment. They take comfort in knowing that even if there's a rough patch, someone has promised to stick it out instead of coming home one day to casually dismiss all they ever said and then turn around to give all their attention to someone else.

Perhaps a little certainty wouldn't be unwelcome at thirty-two, either. I tremble a bit at that notion—the vulnerability it'd require and the autonomy I'd need to give up. But the warmth of Nate's skin and the delicate tickling of his fingers running over my side are pretty powerful pulls.

"What are you thinking about?" he asks, rubbing at the frowny lines between my brows with the pad of his thumb.

I fan my hand across his chest. Vomiting up decades' worth of emotional baggage feels like a wrong move for a second date. "Ohio. My mom's being honored for her volunteer work. I haven't been back in a long while. I should probably go."

"Why have you stayed away so long—or is that too nosy?"

"We got into a bad dynamic when I was young and resented that my brothers didn't get in trouble for not making the bed, forgetting to empty the dishwasher, breaking curfew, or drinking beer in high school, yet I got grounded for every infraction. No 'daughter of theirs' was going to act like a 'harpy.'" I cock an eyebrow, to which Nate responds with a resigned sigh.

The incident that caused a permanent, if quiet, rift between my family and me begs to be told. "Things got worse when Linda, a girl I knew, accused one of my brother's friends of sexual assault. Her older brother—a senior—hosted a party, and my oldest brother and his friends, including Kevin—a popular football player, were there drinking, of course. According to Linda—who was in eighth grade but already quite buxom—she was on the outskirts of the party and drank some beer, but then didn't feel good, so she went to her room. Kevin followed her, uninvited. He was drunk and acting flirty, then pinned her to her bed, groping and kissing her. She struggled, afraid, but he was strong and muffling her voice." Like every time I consider how helpless she was, my entire body bristles. Nate rises on one elbow, grabbing my hand while I finish. "Thankfully, some other drunk teen stumbled in looking for the bathroom. The interruption gave Linda an escape in time to avoid the worst outcome."

Nate blows out a relieved breath. "That's good."

"Yeah. She ran to her brother, who fought with Kevin. But, of course, then some kids took sides and believed Kevin, who said she invited him in and asked him to kiss her. For a lot of people, that made sense—young girl with a crush on a popular older boy. It was bullshit, of course. Then it became a whole debate in town, and Linda suffered more than Kevin. Twice victimized, like a lot of sexual assault victims." I bite my lip, telling myself to relax. Then I look at Nate, who is patiently watching me and waiting. "What killed me most was my own parents. They knew Kevin and Linda but took Kevin's side, saying my friend wouldn't have been in that position if she hadn't gotten buzzed, and that she must've teased him or something. Like her getting buzzed meant she deserved it. Why didn't they rail on Kevin for getting buzzed and groping an underage girl? That's when I realized how entrenched their double standards were. It still makes me angry, the fact that I could never change them."

"Sometimes people only see clearly when the worst happens to them. If Kevin had attacked you instead of Linda, I bet their response would've been different."

Maybe. I shrug, not entirely convinced. "The other big problem has been their lack of support for my dreams. They'd say they've worried because creative writing isn't often a stable or lucrative lifestyle, but that just proves they don't think I'm talented. Parental doubt makes it a lot harder to believe in yourself, you know? It was awesome when my career took off and they had to eat a little crow. But since my last book tanked, I haven't wanted to face them."

Nate bestows a sympathetic smile while taking his time to process what I've shared. "I'm sorry about what happened to your friend. What still happens to women in those shoes. And it's got to be tough to feel disconnected from your own parents—to think they don't believe in you or are unwilling to stay open to your perspective. You're not alone in those things, though. I think each generation butts up against these kinds of differences with their parents in one way or another."

"Not all older people have antiquated views." I can't imagine Wendy making Billy doubt himself, or being closed off to his perspectives.

"Of course not, but I guess what I mean is that I doubt your parents want to hurt you. They just can't see what they can't see. Not yet, anyway. But things will never change if you give up. Maybe that's enough motivation to extend an olive branch?"

"That's why I'm thinking of going home even though I'll have to face the music and the inevitable taunts from my eldest brother."

"Something tells me you're tough enough to take it." His winning grin throws me off-balance.

"What's with that smile?"

"Trying to picture you as a kid."

Oh. I relax against him again. "What'd you come up with?"

He chuckles. "Lots of energy. Short hair—no ponytails. Probably not many dresses or pastel clothing. A bit of a misfit maybe."

I narrow my gaze. "Misfit?"

Nate rolls onto his stomach and kisses my collarbone. "You make a lot of observations and aren't shy with your opinions—probably never were. Kids like that don't usually fit in the same as kids who act their age."

"Well, yes, I was a tomboy. Two older brothers as first playmates sort of helped that along. I wasn't opposed to dresses, but my mother was opposed to microminis, so that was the problem. I had a core band of friends, actually, but definitely did not run with the so-called popular kids."

"I wasn't popular, either. Nor did I care."

I prop myself on a single elbow. "You with the beautiful smile and helpful attitude not popular?"

"Find me a popular high school boy who isn't an athlete. But it's fine. Name someone who got through their teens without emotional upheaval."

My brows rise. While I can think of some people who seem to have sailed through adolescence like an Arcona yacht, none have it easier than the varsity jocks. "Well, at least you got the last laugh. I can't imagine many men who have their shit together more than you do."

"Hm. For all you know, I'm a deranged sex addict who's lured you here, where you're naked and vulnerable, so I could do my worst." There's a little flash in his eye as he bends over to kiss me.

"Well, sir. Do your worst, please."

Conversation dies, and my last coherent thought is that Ohio would be more tolerable if I listened to Mandy and brought Nate along.

CHAPTER FIFTEEN

WENDY

Thursday evening

Normally I don't wear dresses to book club meetings, but Harper's knowing the author means we could get more than a passing greeting, so I want to make a good impression. A wedge rather than high heel dials back the "try hard" look, as Billy and his friends might dub it. Hopefully Joe hasn't left the house for poker night at Frank Barton's yet. His plans give my friends and me the house to ourselves after the library discussion.

"Honey? I need help with my zipper," I call while stepping off the bottom stair tread.

Joe is in the living room in front of the built-ins flanking the fireplace, holding Miné's fancy metal chopstick and Peg's wine charm in his hands. The drawer to my secret stash is open. My stomach drops. "Wendy, what's all this junk?"

In a seventies sitcom, this would be the part when the camera would pan in and out on my stunned face to mimic the dizzy feeling of being blindsided and busted. My scalp breaks out in a cold sweat. Not this. Not now!

"What are you doing?" The terse words fire like a shot; then I immediately regret my defensive tone. I should be contrite, but shame hardens everything.

Joe's expression remains a picture of puzzlement. "You were in the shower. I was looking for my poker chips and found this drawer jammed with random stuff. What's the rest of this?" He gestures vaguely at the drawer filled with trinkets while blinking and glancing back and forth from the items in his hands to me. Then the dawning of understanding tugs at his features, his eyes widening in dismay.

My tongue feels like it's filling all the space in my mouth. A rivulet of perspiration rolls between my shoulder blades. I should've told Joe the truth instead of procrastinating. Now any apology will sound hollow, tainted by lies and secretiveness.

"Wendy." Joe stares at me, his cheeks high with color. "Is this what it looks like?"

Neither of us moves.

"Yes," I mumble. Why didn't I toss the items?

His chin falls, his features screwing up as he begins to puzzle it out. "How long?"

My mind goes blank, and I begin to tremble.

"Wendy." His clipped tone snaps me out of my daze.

My arms reach forward, like they want to hold on to what could be slipping away. "I don't really know—I guess all along, but not very often . . . at least, not until last year. It's gotten worse this year."

He sputters, dropping the items in his hands onto the coffee table. "So this has been going on for *years* . . ."

Ablaze, I stare at the ground to avoid seeing his disillusionment. This is almost as humiliating as when he bailed me out of jail, except that first time he thought there'd been a mistake. After I confessed, he'd hugged me and kissed my temple, assuring me he'd get me help. Confident we'd lick it together. Now he's standing apart stiffly, scowling, exactly as I've feared.

"Why have you kept this from me all this time?" His voice is tight as he crosses his arms and glares at me.

I wring my hands, taking a step toward him. When he steps back, I stop. How can I make him understand? "You're always telling me how proud you are of my progress. Of how I channel energy into positive things for Billy and the community. You've seemed so relieved that I'm 'better,' I couldn't disappoint you." My throat aches from forcing out those words.

"Now it's my fault?" Indignation contorts every muscle in his face.

I raise my hands. "I'm not blaming you, Joe. This is my problem, I know that. But your relief that I was 'cured' made me ashamed to tell you about the urges and slipups."

"Don't pull that." He waves a hand before rubbing it over his face. "No one thinks I'm hard to talk to. Besides, it's hardly fair to throw my happiness for your recovery in my face when your lies perpetuated my false beliefs. All this time you've let me act the fool instead of letting me in."

"I wasn't trying to make a fool of you. I was afraid you'd leave if you knew everything." I want to reach for him but can't make my body move when it's taking all my strength to stand upright. And yet some irony hits me. "Is my keeping my secret so very different from you withholding your feelings and affection all those months without giving me a chance to fix the problem?"

"Hardly comparable. First, it's months versus years of lies. Second, I kept quiet because I worried a confrontation might trigger a setback. Ha! Little did I know that ship had sailed." He gestures to the drawer.

"Anytime I slipped, I'd promise myself I'd get control of it. Most of the time I did, but not every time. I failed, okay? Sometimes I failed."

For a moment I think he might understand, but then he winces at some private thought and thrusts an arm in the air. "You're not seeing

Dr. Haertel for 'empty-nest syndrome,' are you? That's another lie. Meanwhile, I'm the person who encouraged you to go to counseling in the first place, Wendy. You've got no reason to think I wouldn't support that. None at all."

"I wanted to handle this without causing you stress. It seemed the more loving thing to do. I've been working at being stronger. It's why I let Harper talk me into this business thing. With Dr. Haertel's help, I know it's possible." My eyelids grow heavy as the memory of nearly taking a ring from the antique shop resurfaces.

He grabs his forehead and shakes his head. "I thought we were on the same page after our trip to Colgate. You agreed to be equal partners—to be transparent—yet you still kept this from me. Kept me on the outside. You're still controlling me with lies."

That's not true! "How is my getting therapy or stashing an occasional trinket controlling you?"

He straightens his spine, his gaze as baffled as a teacher who can't comprehend why a student doesn't understand the lesson. When he finally answers, he enunciates slowly. "By keeping me in the dark, you take away my choices. Just like before, you're still making decisions that affect our life together while excluding me and my opinions."

"Joe, please. That's not my intention." Not consciously—or maybe it is conscious, but not malicious. "You know my history with my dad walking out. I always worry you'll leave too . . . Can't you understand my side?"

"Your side? Jesus, Wendy. I've spent two decades on your side—giving you control to help you cope with your issue. I did that because I love you and, at the very least, I thought you were being honest with me. Now I don't know what to think."

We stand a few feet apart, yet he might as well be on the moon. I did cut him out. I know that. I've made my choices based on my own assumptions and my past. I've hurt him, and I don't know how to undo it.

The reminder I set on my phone buzzes. Shoot. I have to get Sue.

"Joe, can we please talk about this tomorrow? I have to finish getting dressed, prepare snacks, and pick up Sue by six forty-five." I blink back tears. "You know I didn't keep quiet out of spite. I was trying to protect you."

He scoffs. "You were protecting yourself." Joe shoves his hands in his pockets. "Who else knows?"

"No one." Almost no one.

He gives me a hard look.

"My mother. But I only told her last week, when I asked for her advice. She told me to solve it on my own rather than stress you out."

"Stress me out?" He turns in a circle, arms outstretched as if appealing to an audience of some sort. "Have I ever been particularly unreasonable or prone to anxiety?"

I shake my head.

"Exactly." He crosses his arms. The distance between us deepens, like a canyon splitting the room in two. "What else about our marriage is based on secrets?"

"Nothing! I love you. I've only wanted to keep my illness from affecting you and Billy. I'm getting help for it again. If you can just step back, you'll see my choices really weren't about *you*."

"Everything you do affects me. And Billy. We don't all live in silos. Be honest for once and admit that, dammit." He's practically trembling with fury. I've never seen him this upset. It utterly defeats me.

"Okay." My shoulders slump. My voice is rough from crying. "I'm sorry. I didn't mean to hurt you. I'd never do that on purpose."

We stare at each other: me with pleading eyes, him with frustration. The air around him—humming with resentment—doesn't give me space to draw a breath.

"Whose stuff is all this?" Joe turns and begins emptying the drawer onto the coffee table. He holds up Harper's gray votive. "What's this?"

My arms curl around my waist. "That's Harper's. I planned to take it back, but then she asked me if I'd accidentally broken it and thrown it away. I said yes without thinking and regretted it immediately. Her father made that for her—not that I knew that when I took it. Now I can't even give it back." My nostrils flare as another wave of tears builds behind my eyes.

"Yes, you can," Joe says calmly but firmly. "You can walk over there, confess to her, and give it back."

"Joe! She could have me arrested or tell the neighbors." My heart speeds up again. I know Dr. Haertel thinks this is an answer, but it's still scary as hell to consider.

"She won't have you arrested for returning her votive. And as far as I can tell, she hasn't made many friends in town, so there wouldn't be much gossip, either." He's wearing that tough-love expression he dons when Billy needs to do something difficult.

"Please, Joe." I hug myself. "I swear I've been considering all of this, but can we talk about it when the timing is better?"

"If I leave it up to you, it'll never be the right time." His body looks as rigid as his tone.

I ache all over from disappointment that Joe isn't hearing anything I'm saying. I need time, but I'm running out of it. "I'll think about it, but I need to pick up Sue in fifteen minutes. Please zip up my dress so I can finish the platters before I leave. I'll answer all your questions tomorrow. I promise."

"Promise that you *will* give this votive back." He points at me like a high school principal scolding a truant.

He's adamant in a way I've seldom seen. My world would be empty without Joe. I'm not sure I mean it yet, but I blurt, "I promise."

He tips his head and squints, like he doesn't quite believe me. My heart throbs. Will this be how it is between us from now on—is mistrust the mistress that will tear us apart?

He approaches me. "Turn around."

"What?" I'm off-balance in pain's tight grip.

"You need a zip, right?"

"Oh, yes. Thank you." I turn around and shakily pull my hair aside. He tugs the zipper harder than necessary.

I turn to kiss him, but he steps back. "I need to shower and change before going to Frank's."

"Okay." My body feels as cold as a corpse. "The poker chips are in the kitchen, in the bottom desk drawer."

"Thanks." He turns and heads upstairs. Conversation over. His head must be throbbing like mine. He feels betrayed, and I can't blame him. They may have seemed like harmless omissions to me, but he deserves better.

"Have fun tonight," I call after him. He doesn't answer.

I stand alone in the entry, unable to move except for the trembling in my limbs. Eventually, I put everything but the votive in the trash, then stow the votive in the drawer and close it. I'll deal with Joe and that forced promise tomorrow. Should I cancel tonight? Call and say I'm sick?

Another excuse—more lies. Joe is going out anyway, and I've dragged Harper into the club, so I can't bail. She doesn't know anyone but Sue, and they hardly hit it off the night they met. I'll have to pretend everything is normal. I'm good at pretending. Tomorrow I'll find a way to fix everything.

I grab a tissue off the bookshelf and dab my eyes on my way back to the kitchen. Mindlessly I retrieve the pastel floral napkins and paper products, then go arrange them on the coffee table. The charcuterie board and tray of petits fours get thrown together haphazardly, then I wrap them and stick them in the refrigerator.

Joe is still upstairs, although the shower water isn't running anymore. I walk back to the front of the house to grab my coat and keys, then glance at the top of the stairs. "See you later, Joe. Good luck."

"Bye."

His abrupt indifference sends another shock wave through me. I steady myself on the newel post before going to my car. Maybe we can talk tonight after everyone leaves. It's never wise to go to bed angry. The truth is that I'll do whatever necessary to save my marriage, even if that means enduring humiliation tomorrow by returning Harper's votive.

CHAPTER SIXTEEN

HARPER

Earlier that same evening

I blow out a breath before entering Elm Street Books to meet up with Ellen, who is perusing the new-release shelves near the front of the store. She glances over her shoulder as I approach. Her round baby blues crinkle around the edges as she smiles.

"Harper! You look great." She grabs me into a quick hug.

It's remarkable what a little makeup and a blow-dryer—two things not commonly part of my routine—do for a person. Not that this will become a habit. "Thanks. So do you."

Ellen's dressed in winter-white slacks and a creamy lightweight sweater. She's cinched the ensemble with a wide leather belt, and tied a coffee-colored scarf around her neck. Her blonde hair hangs in a low-slung, sleek side ponytail. A gold cuff bracelet and hoop earrings add a pop of glam, and it's all finished off with a leopard-print low-rise heel. She looks every bit the success she is.

"Thanks." She squeezes my elbow. "I'm so glad you reached out, although I'm shocked to learn you're living here. I never pictured you leaving the city."

"This is temporary . . . for research."

"Oh! How's it going?" Her genuine interest pries me open, probably because it's been ages since I've chatted with another writer about writing. I've missed that.

"Pretty well, actually. Everyone here believes I'm an out-of-work publicist." Well, everyone but Nate. "The community is welcoming. People sit on their porches. They walk, but not hurried—more for exercise or with their dogs and friends—very social. I think some of the stay-at-home moms struggle with empty nesting, like my neighbor, who latched on to me in an instant. She's inspired my antagonist. Partly the stereotypical Stepford Wife you'd expect, but with unexpected layers. Some of her real-life backstory has led me to giving the character an impulse control disorder. There's still a lot of work to do on the story themes and character sketches, so I'm not sure exactly where it will all lead, but I'm aiming for something airy and fun."

To my surprise, a third voice pipes up behind me. "Ellen, I'm Anne, the store manager. We're thrilled to cohost your talk with the library tonight."

Oh shit. Did Anne hear me talking about my book? And if so, how much did she glean?

"Thank you, Anne. I've been looking forward to it," Ellen says. "This is a great store. I know you're busy, but I wanted to introduce myself and see if there was anything you needed from me before we regroup at the library later this evening."

"No, we're all set. In fact, Janet is coordinating with the library staff now, setting up the signing table with all the books. I'll be there around six forty-five."

"Terrific." Ellen then gestures to me. "This is my friend Harper."

"Yes, we met a few weeks ago. I already fangirled over *If You Say So*." Anne smiles. It seems genuine. Maybe she didn't hear much. "Nice to see you again. Could I get a snapshot of two bestsellers in our store today for social media?"

I hold up both hands. "I'm sorry, but I prefer to remain incognito."

"Understood." Anne's expression is unreadable. "Let me get one of you with your book, Ellen. Then, unless you have specific questions, you can go enjoy dinner."

Ellen obliges, and after a couple of snapshots, Anne says, "We'll see you both later. I think there are at least seventy-five registered guests."

A healthy turnout for Ellen—much better than my last book tour. I let the moment of self-pity pass.

"Lovely. I'll see you at the library," Ellen says, then turns to me. "Let's eat."

"Have a good meal." Anne waves us off.

We exit the store and turn right toward Solé, an upscale Italian restaurant encased in white stucco and wood beams, and boasting a lively bar scene most evenings.

"Do you think Anne heard me talking about my manuscript?" I ask.

Ellen wrinkles her face. "I'm not sure, but don't worry. You didn't give away any spoilers."

"True, but I don't want it getting around that I'm here researching the community for a book. Luckily I don't look a thing like my author photo." In addition to the airbrushing that removed most flaws, the publisher hired hair and makeup people who "suggested" I wear a red shirt.

"Who does?" Ellen laughs as she opens the door to the restaurant.

We're taken to a two-top in the bar area, beneath skylights. Only a few diners are seated at this early hour. The pulsing lounge music helps put me in the mood for this evening's events.

"It's really great to see you," Ellen says after we've ordered wine. "I hardly ever hang with friends anymore. People are so busy making up for time lost because of the pandemic. Sometimes it feels like we're all moving from one thing to the next without stopping to enjoy any of it. Sharing a glass of wine with you is a welcome gift."

Ellen has always been disarmingly pleasant and humble. There's no trace of smugness or, worse, of pity for me.

"I'm glad you have the energy. I remember how exhausting book tours can be." I lean forward, reminding myself of my agent's enthusiasm for my recent pages, and that publishing isn't a finite game. One person's success doesn't make another's harder. There are enough readers for all of us. "I'm thrilled to see your book still sitting on the list. What have you done to celebrate getting your letters?"

That's what some call hitting the *New York Times* or other bestseller lists. When my debut hit, Calvin and I went to Montauk for the weekend and rented a sailboat for the day. We drifted around Long Island Sound, listening to Mumford & Sons, eating Manchego and chocolate, and having sex. The photographic evidence of that orgasmic day is tucked away in a photo album he gave me afterward. A reminder—he said—to help cope with a time when the tables might turn.

How arrogant I was to think that my career would be a balloon that never popped or fell prey to rough winds. *Hubris, thy name is Harper.* Now that photo album isn't so much a reminder of the good times as of how Calvin himself—or at least the folly of that relationship—might've been the first pin to my vulnerable balloon.

"I haven't celebrated much." Ellen swirls her wineglass a moment. "My husband got laid off a few weeks before my book released. He's proud of me and relieved that I'm bringing in money at the exact moment we lost his income, but he's preoccupied with a job hunt and might also be a little envious of all the attention I'm getting. I could be overthinking it—he hasn't said that—I don't know. I haven't wanted to make a huge deal of it all when he's been so down on himself."

She says this so casually, like it's totally normal for a woman to make her success small to avoid stepping on a man's toes. I want to toss my napkin at her, but I don't. I think of Wendy and Sue and the fact that I'm not married and am not in a position to understand or judge Ellen's relationship. In truth, it's kind of her to consider his feelings. "That's very sensitive of you. Still, it's important to celebrate your wins, Ellen. You've worked hard for years. Don't let this moment pass without acknowledging it. Take it from me: you don't know when or if it will come around again. Your husband loves you. I'm sure he wants to celebrate with you, just as you would if the shoe were on the other foot."

Ellen is quick to clarify. "Matt bought flowers and champagne after my agent called with the news. He's not dismissive or anything. I just . . . He's struggling with self-doubt. I know how that goes, so I'm playing it cool in front of him, ducking into the closet to dance each week the book stays on the list. Once he's found a new job, maybe we'll take a little weekend trip to the Hamptons or something."

"I'm going to remind you to do just that." On that note, perhaps I, too, should be sure to celebrate my little wins, like the fact that I'm not going to let old wounds control my present and future. "So where have they got you going next?"

"Oh jeez, it feels like everywhere. Boston, Nashville, Atlanta, Miami, Denver, Chicago, Dallas . . . I don't know. It's a steady trek—boom, boom, boom. I'll look a thousand years old by the time it's over. I never sleep well in hotels."

"I'd trade places in a heartbeat. I love book tours." The buzz of the crowds. Exploring new cities before the gigs. Meeting fans. Eating local cuisine. Or rather, I loved tours until the last one. Low turnouts and audience disengagement had a chilling effect on my exuberance.

"You're pithier than I. Everything I say sounds predictable or trite. At any moment someone could stand up, point a finger, and call me a fraud." She releases a half-hearted sigh. "Wouldn't it be great if we could just write the book and let the publisher worry about selling it while we sit and write the next one? The promotion—the humblebrags and all the rest—it's embarrassing and awkward. That's why I do so little of it, much to my publisher's chagrin."

242

"You're not trite." But I know what she means. Her honesty is a gift that's come exactly when I need it most. "And you're definitely not a fraud. You're at the top of your game. Own it, girl!"

"Thanks." She glances at her lap, not owning it at all. "Anyway, enough shoptalk. Tell me, could you see yourself living in this gorgeous little town long-term?"

Like Mandy, Ellen's seeing this place through a certain filter. "I doubt it, but it's not as bad as I thought it'd be. I've gotten to know a few locals this month—my neighbors, their friends, and a guy."

"A guy!" Ellen dips a thick slice of seasoned focaccia bread into the white bean dip on the table. "That sounds juicy."

"It's complicated and very new. Chances are it'll be a couple of months of good sex doomed to fade when I move back to the city."

Ellen laughs, wiggling her ring finger in the air. "A couple of months of good sex is what led to my marriage."

"Diamond rings aren't on my bucket list." Not yet, anyway.

"Well, you don't have to get married, and people do long distance all the time. Zoom sex!" She giggles and sips more wine. "Is he nice?"

I can't believe that two smart, creative, dynamic professional women are sitting at dinner talking about boys. No wonder progress for women's rights moves at glacial speed. And yet I'm not unhappy to continue the conversation. Go figure. "Very nice. Respectable and respectful. A little surprising, too."

"Sounds like maybe there'll be a little romance in this new book." Ellen slides a sly smile my way.

The idea prompts a laugh. No writer less qualified to write about that topic than I am. "No. My story revolves around two neighbors, each with her own secret. It started as something of a romp that would involve a theme about what's hidden behind our social media slash societal personas, but it's turning into a story about family." Or at least about family influences.

"A secretive neighbors' tale that's really about family? Only you could pull that off."

Could I, or is she being facetious? I raise my wineglass. "To long shots and all the best words."

She clinks her glass. "To remembering why we love to write and not worrying about the rest."

Sincerity glazes her clear, bright tone. Ellen has always been a writer wholly invested in the story, and in others' stories. One who revels in a turn of phrase and in the layers baked into a good book. She's rarely complained about not getting enough support from her publisher or a lack of attention for her earlier work, and she acts like each of her books is a great surprise and mystery. I envy her attitude because she so rarely seems racked by frustrated expectations or fear of missing the mark.

"That's a tall order." I sip my wine.

"Which part? Remembering why we love it?" Her sardonic laughter suggests she's thinking about the hours spent agonizing over each paragraph and revision note.

"The not-worrying-about-the-rest part."

With a half shrug, she says, "It's pointless to worry about what you can't really control."

"But I want to be widely read and loved by readers." I avert my gaze after that egocentric admission.

"If you focus on sales and trends rather than what you want to write, you risk losing the heart of what makes an H. E. Ross story an H. E. Ross story, you know?"

"Whether the heart of an H. E. Ross book is worthwhile is a point of debate these days," I joke. I swirl my wine before taking a long pull to fill the pregnant pause in conversation.

Ellen's empathetic expression locks on me. "I know you were disappointed with your last release, but I honestly liked it. Either way, we write the best book we can at the time. That was a time of upheaval for you, so it's not shocking that the book took on darker tones."

A generous take on my downfall. Her sincerity eases my discomfort.

"I suppose." I laugh at myself. "Being an author—this life of uncertainty and constant public criticism—isn't what I'd imagined. I thought getting published and living the writer's life would make me special." Perhaps it had when I was riding high. Nothing has ever felt so good as proving all the naysayers wrong—showing them that my path was valid. Only now do I see how that attitude gave them all power over me. Most important, it stole something fundamental from what I most loved as a ten-year-old with a notebook and pen: the joy of using my imagination to convey messages I thought mattered. That's where my focus should've always remained.

"The most special part of this career is that we can do it in our pj's." Ellen winks and breaks off another piece of bread.

I snicker. "A definite bonus."

The waiter interrupts us to deliver our pasta—mine with the spicy lobster sauce, hers with prosciutto and peas.

"This smells excellent," Ellen says, forking one of her ravioli. "I could get used to living here. Small-town life with lots of trees, shops, and restaurants, yet close enough to a big city to keep things interesting."

I finish slurping in my first bite before answering. "I'm still a city girl at heart." The anonymity some might dislike makes me feel free.

"You are, for sure."

We smile, then I finish my wine and signal for the waiter to bring me another.

She points her fork at me. "You know, you may be a city girl, but make the most of this experience. Branch out and try new things. Meet more people. We can't write about life if we aren't out living it."

Closing myself off was a definite problem when finishing my last manuscript. I hid away, shamefully licking wounds—me, a modern woman depressed over a man. Never before did I feel such a fraud. "You're right. I lost my way for a while, but this change of scenery has helped."

Getting away from the bad memories haunting me since Calvin left was huge. Now I've made a nice new one with Nate in my condo, which feels like a fresh start.

Ellen puts down her fork and dabs her mouth with a napkin. "It's hard to imagine you without confidence."

"Is it?"

"Yes." Her eyes widen to underscore her reply. "You have everything—talent, success, strong opinions. If you get swamped with doubts, the rest of us are doomed."

Lately my certainty about most things is weaker, particularly when it comes to my family. "Well, from where I sit, you're hardly doomed. Destined for great things is more like it."

Color fills her cheeks, highlighted by her discomfort with compliments. "I'm grateful for my book's success, but I'm actually more excited about a different kind of project."

"Oh?" Is she branching into screenwriting?

Ellen nods. "We're talking about starting a family. Next month I'll be off the pill long enough to begin. This might be one of my last drinks for a while." She guzzles a bit more of her wine.

"Have another!" My nervous laughter sounds tinny.

A baby. Most women in their thirties have one or are thinking about it. Some of my single friends have gone the sperm-donor route rather than wait around for Mr. Right. I adore little Becca, but the idea of motherhood is so . . . permanent. Permanence is rather terrifying for someone who has always embraced a single, spontaneous existence.

Why now? I want to ask. Ellen's hitting her stride in her career. Another bestselling book could cement her trajectory, but that requires more tours and speaking obligations. Not great timing if she's pregnant or nursing a newborn. Still, she has her own goals, which don't have to be the same as mine to be valid.

Look at me. I'm growing.

"Is something wrong?" Ellen asks, peering at me as observantly as most writers I know.

"No. I'm just trying to picture you out to here with a baby." I stretch my arms out in front of me.

Her eyes shine with such warmth and hope I'm literally dazzled.

"Don't get me wrong, I love telling stories and am so grateful to have connected with an audience, but writing is only a part of my life. I'm ready to build a family with Matt and see what other things are ahead for us, too. Hopefully I can balance everything." Ellen spears the last ravioli on her plate, using it to scoop up the remaining bit of sauce.

I nod because I'm at a loss for words. My sole mission since Oberlin has been about my career, so I can't relate to her needs. Even so, she's being genuine. If she never writes another bestseller, she'll be okay with that as long as she has Matt and their future children. It's plain on her face. Other things in her life mean more to her than her work. That's not a bad thing. On the other hand, having a life built on only one thing, like mine, might be.

Who would've predicted that my envy of Ellen might end up having nothing at all to do with her bestseller?

She isn't trying to prove anything to anyone. She's simply living her life, doing something she loves with little expectation of reward. Is that the key? When I wrote my early books, I didn't feel pressure—only passion. Only hope. How do I get back to that?

"Oh," Ellen says, glancing at her watch. "Think I'll pass on a second glass of wine to avoid face-planting at the library. I'm sorry to rush, but I want to get there in time to freshen up and review some of my talking points."

"No worries. You go ahead and I'll catch up in a bit. Let me pick up the tab—a mini celebration of your success. That way you don't have to wait around for the check, either."

"That's sweet, Harper." She dabs her mouth with her napkin before removing her purse from the back of her chair and standing. "Let's not go so long without getting together again."

"Done. Hey, one favor. Tonight, when I introduce you to Wendy, can you spare her a few extra moments? She's a huge fan who's so excited to meet you."

Ellen tilts her head to one side, a sweet smile in place. "Look at you. Dressed in black as always, but just a big softy inside."

Me a softy? No. I'm a liar with an increasing guilt complex. But why disabuse Ellen of her idealistic view? It's the heart of her appeal to readers, after all.

I trust her as much as I'd trust anyone, which means I'm only slightly concerned that my cover might get blown tonight. Then again, Nate didn't criticize me. Maybe I should consider telling Wendy. The guilt monkey on my back is getting awfully heavy to carry.

———

The audience claps after Ellen finishes her talk. For seventy-five minutes she discussed the inspiration for her story and its themes, and patiently answered questions, but I missed much of it because I was preoccupied with Wendy's strange behavior.

She arrived tonight with Sue, dressed to the near nines. I expected her to be on the edge of her seat during the discussion, with her hand shooting in the air to ask questions. Instead, she sat, hands clasped as she twisted her rings, staring into space. She barely made eye contact with me or anyone in the group after she'd introduced me to the women I hadn't yet met. Even Sue, who has reason to act awkward around me, has been more relaxed than Wendy.

I lean close to her ear and whisper, "Everything okay?"

She jolts and turns her head in a quick, birdlike manner. "Yes. Why?"

"You seem . . . distant."

She gestures toward Ellen. "I'm fine. Just listening."

Obviously she's not ready to share what's got her preoccupied—or at least not in public—which I suppose makes sense.

As our row rises to walk back to where Ellen is now signing books, I touch Wendy's elbow, hoping to pull her out of her funk. "Would you like me to introduce you to Ellen?"

Wendy starts, as if waking from a dream. She sends a quick smile although her gaze remains hazy. "Oh, yes. Thank you, Harper. That'd be nice."

I follow her out of the row. "Did you enjoy the discussion?"

Wendy nods, but the dearth of excited chatter confirms she tuned out for much of it. Even Sue is studying her with concern, which is significant given Sue's marital status. That probably won't come up tonight, but I hope she's dumping Dirk. Monogamy was never my gold standard, but if you make that vow, you sure as shit had better keep it.

Our group waits in line without much conversation. When it's Wendy's turn, I step up to the table with her. "Ellen, this is my neighbor Wendy. She's a big fan." I step aside, noting Anne looking at Wendy and me.

Ellen dons her friendliest smile. "Wendy, it's lovely to meet you. Harper mentioned you at dinner. Thanks for coming out tonight to support me. Have you read the book yet?"

This personal attention momentarily cheers Wendy. "Oh, I loved this book. I laughed and cried. How do you make up all these people and situations, and then that twist? I didn't see that one coming."

Ellen shrugs humbly. "Some days it's a mystery even to me. I observe people and situations, and then hope that inspires interesting ideas."

Wendy toys with her pearls. "So is this based on people you know?"

"Not precisely, but bits and pieces resemble people and places familiar to me." Ellen then holds a finger up to her lips like they're in on a secret, which of course Wendy eats up.

"Thank goodness I don't know any writers. I can only imagine what they'd write about me." Wendy laughs self-consciously.

While she heaps more praise on Ellen and waits for Ellen to autograph her book, I twist my neck side to side, trying to loosen the tension caused by my own guilty conscience. If I unburden myself now, would it be for Wendy's sake or for my own? My conscience will be clean, but she'll be hurt, and that pain is avoidable if she never knows about my books. If I tell her, our friendship could end, and then what? It's not like I won't finish the book and turn it in. I've got a deadline and a last shot at saving my condo. Besides, I'm not stealing from her life anymore. At this point I'm focusing on Haley's character, which is requiring painful-enough self-examination.

Dammit, this sucks.

Either way, tonight isn't the time for honesty—not in front of Sue and women I hardly know. I stand aside with Wendy and wait for the rest of the group to get their signed copies, at which point Wendy falls back into quietude.

"Are you sure everything's okay?" I murmur.

"Fine, fine." She waves me off. "I'm just a little tired, is all. Long day."

"Maybe we should cut the evening short, then. People would understand."

Her lips part. "Oh, no. I can't cancel last minute. Besides, I've got wine and snacks waiting. I'll be fine, really. I need this night out with my friends."

She drops her gaze—a signal not to ask what that means. The energy around her is equal parts heavy and vibrant with frenetic energy.

I decide to let sleeping dogs lie.

I'll be here a few more months, finishing the draft. That's plenty of time to find the right way to come clean.

CHAPTER SEVENTEEN

WENDY

"I shouldn't have come tonight." Sue crosses her ankles, clutching her purse in her lap as we drive toward my house. "It's still too soon."

"Why do you say that?" I set aside thoughts about Joe to devote attention to my friend. When she made an excuse to push off my lunch invitation, it confirmed my suspicion that she wasn't ready to let me in. But maybe that's changed.

"Gossip about Dirk's affair has made the rounds. Everyone's on edge around me, not knowing what to say. Even you're jumpy tonight." Sue's sagging shoulders belie her blasé tone.

If I were braver—kinder—I'd confess that my mood has nothing to do with her marriage and everything to do with mine. The words tap-dance on the tip of my tongue, but I hold them in.

It's bad enough that I shared my lackluster sex life with Harper. It'd be even worse if everyone learned the full extent of my and Joe's problems. Problems that are only ours to solve. The fact is, when you complain about your marriage to someone, it will take months or even years before they stop wondering if you're *really* happy. Who needs that?

"I'm sorry you feel awkward, but I'm not jumpy because of you, Sue. I didn't sleep well." Vague but true. "I've been having a hard time with Billy gone. It's why I've let Harper talk me into exploring a small furniture-refinishing business."

Sue's side-eye suggests she's still convinced she's the subject of everyone's scrutiny.

"I appreciate what you're trying to do by changing the subject, Wendy. And I'm sorry I put off lunch." She heaves a sigh so heavy it ruffles her bangs. "It's hard to talk about Dirk because I'm torn. Part of me wants to kick him out and take him for every penny. But the devastated part that's invested decades into our relationship? That's raised children with him and looked forward to enjoying grandchildren and family vacations and holidays? That same part still sees the husband I've loved for half my life . . . That part's frozen with indecision. I can't envision life without him, and yet I don't know how to trust him again. Lies—so many lies."

The thing is, everyone lies from time to time. Everyone disappoints someone they love during their lifetime, even if unintentional. Sue is great, but I bet she's made her share of mistakes in that marriage, too. We all do.

I shiver, thinking of Joe. "Marriages are complicated, so are people. Only you know what's right for you and your family. But I'm here for you, whatever you choose. No judgments. Please lean on me whenever you want to talk, okay?"

While waiting for the light at the intersection of South Avenue and Route 106 to turn green, Sue grips my forearm, her eyes dewy and bright. Our gazes lock, silently communicating the shared understanding of longtime wives and friends. "Thank you, Wendy. That helps a lot."

My heavy heart earns a brief reprieve. How many good deeds will it take to undo my bad ones? There's no time to wonder because we're already at Crystal Street and I've got company on my heels and another ninety minutes of book chat to endure. And to think I was looking forward to this for weeks.

We turn into my driveway. Harper pulls into hers while Kendra, Poonam, and Amy pull in behind me. I'd hoped for five minutes to set out the food, but God isn't giving me any breaks today. At least Joe left some inside lights on for us—a considerate thing because he knows I dislike coming home to a dark house.

My friends laugh about something as we cross the yard, but I'm not really listening. I unlock the front door, hang my coat on the rack with my purse, then beeline for the kitchen to grab the snacks while telling them all to make themselves comfortable.

"Let me help you." Sue trails behind me, seeking any excuse to avoid the others and their curiosity.

Despite the warmth of the lamplight, the house feels as if Joe's and my earlier argument has coated everything in frost. I open the refrigerator and remove the snack trays I threw together. The meats aren't neatly fanned, and the cheese isn't layered nor the platter drizzled with honey. Not my best work. The sting of tears threatens, but I blink them back.

"If you take this tray and bottle of wine, I'll grab the rest." I push the Mexican ceramic platter Joe bought for our eighth anniversary toward Sue. Back then I'd been doing well—managing a young child, volunteering, seeing Dr. Haertel monthly. That success had given me false confidence, making me believe I could manage on my own.

If only I'd called Dr. Haertel a year ago.

"See you out there." Sue hefts the platter in one arm and grabs the bottle with the other.

"Glasses are on the bar cart," I call after her while balancing my own bounty.

Thoughts of Joe, Billy, and my mother bounce ahead of me like rubber balls that could trip me up. When I arrive in the living room, I aim toward the coffee table, nearly stumbling when confronted by Harper's squatty votive sitting in its center.

Any hope that she's been too distracted to notice dies when I raise my gaze to find her standing, hands on her hips, frowning at the votive.

My stomach lurches even as everything else in my body contracts, and the bottle of wine fuses in my hand as if encased in bronze.

Joe! When did he become capable of this kind of cruelty—of doing something calculated to inflict pain? My throat aches from strangling an anguished scream escaping from the crack in my heart. I wait breathlessly for Harper to look at me, hoping she'll read the plea in my eyes: *please let me explain in private.*

Instead, she bends forward and lifts the votive. "This is mine."

Her voice is more quizzical than angry. Maybe she'll send me a questioning look but wait until later to discuss it rather than make everyone uncomfortable. I'm stiff with fear, but either way, I can't skirt the truth.

As the gravity of my crime swallows the room, the chatter quiets. My friends' gazes dart from Harper to me. I'm tongue-tied. Everything simultaneously moves too fast and too slow. The temperature of the room rises ten degrees, prompting a childish wish to melt into the carpet and disappear.

"Harper . . ." My voice chips through the silence. I grope for more to say. Trapped. No explanation will stop the shame or ripple of gossip that will flood the community pipeline. My insides are quaking. I can't look at my friends.

"You said it broke." She's cupping the votive now, like a child with a lovey, speaking aloud but not really to me. Confusion has her in its grip. "Why would you lie after I told you my dad made this for me?" Before I can answer, her expression changes, like she's remembered something or found a missing clue. "Scratch that. I know why you took it."

She seems to snap out of the daze when one of my friends gasps. I don't know who because my field of vision is winnowing.

"Let me explain." My arms begin trembling, so I set down the bottle.

Harper's eyebrow shoots upward, as if surprised. There's something behind her gaze—remorse or maybe pity? "Not necessary. Not now, anyway."

Too late for waiting. The situation is beyond my control, and maybe it's just as well.

"It is necessary, Harper." Everyone's still, their eyes glued to me. Burning from their questioning gazes, I cover my face with my hands. They provide no cover at all, only making my guilt more obvious. I drop my hands to my sides. It's a fight to keep my chin up. "I didn't mean to take it."

"I'm sure you didn't." Her tone is even, which almost makes me feel worse for stealing from her and then lying about it.

I lose the battle to keep my head held high. "I took it, but not on purpose. Sometimes . . . Well, it just came over me and was done before I knew it."

"An impulse control disorder," she mumbles, almost to herself.

It's odd that she knows that term, but I'm desperate to make amends, so I let it go. "I wanted to return it before you noticed but got caught off guard when you asked if I'd broken it. I don't know why I said I did. I'm sorry. I planned to tell you eventually."

"Is that why you set it out tonight?"

"No. Joe did that after I left."

"Why? Did he know it was mine?" She narrows her eyes.

"Harper," Sue says. "Give Wendy a chance to finish."

Amy's, Poonam's, and Kendra's heads are bobbing back and forth like they're watching the US Open.

"Sorry. Not to be a bitch, but I'm kinda thrown." Harper turns back to me. "Regardless of why you came into my home and stole this while I was sick, you later lied about it to my face instead of returning it on any of the days before I asked you if it had broken. Meanwhile, all these weeks I've been changing things in my life based in part on your advice about life and relationships, yet now I learn you're not at all what you seem."

My breath catches. Please, God, don't let her start sharing my other problems with my friends.

Kendra asks, "Have you taken things from any of us?"

"Not from any of you, I swear." All I can do now is pray that coming clean will somehow help me as Dr. Haertel suggested. There's nearly nothing left to lose. "I have stolen before. It started in my teens. I was diagnosed with kleptomania shortly after my dad moved away. It's mostly been under control until lately, but I'm back in therapy now."

Perspiration coats my skin, and my knees feel unsteady. I don't make eye contact with anyone but am sure they're reassessing their opinions of me. Deciding whether to remain friends with a "klepto." Viewing me as nothing more than a shoplifter. A pariah. A loser. A thief. A person they'll politely distance themselves from in the coming weeks.

"You shoplift?" Poonam asks gently.

"No." Explaining the difference to others feels impossible when sometimes even I hardly understand it. "The result is the same, but the motivation is different. Shoplifters take things they want but can't afford or don't feel like paying for. I never take valuables. In my case, the urge to take something isn't premeditated or even to get something I want or need . . . I just take something in my vicinity. I'm immediately remorseful and often return items, but not always—sometimes it's just not possible. But this is why I never go shopping with anyone and prefer to host things at my house rather than go to someone else's party. It's gotten worse since Billy left. My doctor thinks that stress is a big factor." The verbal diarrhea leaves me spent yet somewhat relieved, like a parishioner leaving the confessional booth.

Harper sighs, her nose and mouth twitching like she can't decide what to do next. "I think I should go. I'm sorry you have this burden, Wendy. Really. I'm not mad, but this just . . . Well, it feels like a sign.

You've been a kind friend—even an inspiration at times. But the lies—" She covers her mouth with one hand, like she's holding something inside. "I need to think a bit, so I'm going to go home." She wiggles the votive in the air. "I'll be taking this back, too."

I nod, my head throbbing so hard I can't believe it hasn't exploded.

Harper heads toward the door. "Sorry to disrupt the party, but some space is best for us both right now." A cryptic statement, but I don't have the energy to think more of it. "Good night, everyone." She pivots and strides outside without a backward glance.

Once the door closes, I collapse onto a chair and begin to weep. "I'm sorry. I'm so sorry, everyone. There's no excuse . . ."

Sue reaches over and lays a hand on my shoulder. "It's okay. You're with friends."

That's not the reaction I expected, and the reprieve makes my entire body go slack. I swipe beneath my eyes and force myself to face them. "I'm so embarrassed I don't know what to say."

"You don't have to say anything. I understand living with shame you don't feel like sharing with anyone." Sue opens a bottle of pinot noir and pours everyone a glass. "Everyone here knows why, too. But if we can't turn to our friends when we make mistakes or have problems, well, what kind of friends are they?"

The others shift in their seats, each one forcing an awkward smile. Who can blame them? This is an awkward situation. I want so badly to trust in Sue's sincerity, and to believe her compassion will influence how the others feel.

"You're being very gracious, and I'm happy to answer all your questions later, but right now I have a terrible headache and need to lie down." It's been a grueling few hours. "I'm sorry our night got ruined and hope you'll forgive me. Also, I'd appreciate it if for now you'd keep what you learned between us, for Billy's sake. He has no idea, and I'd prefer he hear about it from me than from a high school friend."

"We understand," Sue says, while Poonam, Kendra, and Amy nod in agreement.

"Don't worry—no one wants to hurt you or Billy. For now, get some rest," Poonam adds, rising to her feet. I press my hands to my eyes to stanch relieved tears. "Can we help clean up?"

"No, thanks, but take home whatever you want to snack on." I rise, too, antsy for them to collect their things and leave. My taut skin is ready to split open like a blanched tomato.

I pray that I can trust them. That they'll keep my secret. But their husbands will have questions when they arrive home early, and bit by bit, this kind of thing is sure to leak out. Everyone knows the only way to keep a secret is to tell no one. I'll have to inform Billy tomorrow. The idea of his disappointment—his shame—makes me want to howl into the wind.

My friends make their way to the front door, muttering polite good-nights and well-wishes. When I close it behind them, a soft cry belches its way to the surface. Dammit, Joe. When did you become hateful and heartless? I have no idea where we go from here, if we go anywhere at all.

All the sacrifices made to contain my problem have been for naught. My reputation is besmirched. If I'm lucky, these friends might overlook it, but the general crowd? No way. Look at Harper's retreat. Like my mother warned, this will likely be my label from now on. Most people won't want to associate with me—or possibly with Joe, if we make it past this awful day. And if we don't, that'll lead to more people questioning what went wrong. How uncomfortable will it be to live in this small town then?

My limbs hang like deadweights at my side, so I don't bother cleaning up. Climbing the stairs will take all my remaining energy.

I shed my clothes in the bathroom and step into a hot shower, hoping to ease the tightness in my shoulders. The water sluices over my skin along with more tears as soft moans echo off the tile. My knees buckle—self-pity tugging me to the ground—but I force myself to turn off the water and dry off.

Once in my pajamas with my teeth brushed, I stare into the mirror. Puffy eyes. Deepened grooves around my frown. I pop a sleeping pill before crawling between the sheets and staring at the ceiling. The empty bed feels huge and cold. My thoughts ramble as I try to picture Joe putting that votive on the table. It's too impossible to imagine.

Whatever pushed him there tonight, some part of him probably regrets it already. At least I hope so. My itchy eyelids grow heavy. I should be grateful he's not home yet, because I'm not sure enough of my own feelings to handle another discussion about our marriage. But whatever my sins, I did not deserve his response. That much I've learned.

We'll talk in the morning before he goes to work. Thank God the sleeping pill grabs me and pulls me under.

———

I pretend to be sleeping when Joe whispers my name. The sleep aid saved my sanity last night, but I'm still not ready to face my husband. The mattress shifts as he gets up to shower. Once the bathroom door clicks shut, I sit with my head against the padded headboard, letting myself and the pain from last night awaken. I'm flawed and have made mistakes that hurt him, but what he did last night is still unthinkable. Maybe unforgivable. I've never imagined being the one contemplating leaving.

The pipes clank when he turns off the shower. Soon water splashes in the sink and the *tink* of his razor tapping against the edge of the bowl echoes. It feels like an hour before he steps into the room in search of underwear, his naked body wrapped with a towel at the waist. Joe's fit yet showing signs of his age—patches of gray hair on his head and elsewhere. The early stages of collagen loss soften his skin.

He looks at me sheepishly—unless I'm imagining that part. "Good morning, Wendy."

"Good?" I clasp my hands on top of the comforter, finding it painful to look at him, much less speak. Everything about us feels unfamiliar now. The ensuing silence is fraught, so my next words come out strained. "You ambushed me, Joe. You took our problems public. I've never been more crushed by anyone in my life, not even my father."

He slides his boxers on, then slings the towel over his shoulder, his eyes watery. "I'm sorry. I have no excuse except that, in the moment, I felt betrayed. It seemed like I had no other choice if I wanted things to change. I was trying to make a point, but thought you'd see the votive and stash it before everyone came inside. Worst case, I hoped Harper would question you privately."

"*You* felt betrayed? I've never done anything with the express intention of hurting or humiliating you." My voice quavers, so I take a breath to compose myself.

"You're right. I'm sorry. Please forgive me." He closes his eyes, his cheeks pink with remorse. "I hardly slept last night, trying to figure some way to undo what I did. Judging from the mess you left out, I'm guessing it didn't go well."

In truth, it didn't go as badly as it could have. Still, it sucked to have been forced into that confession rather than choosing it for myself. "Harper took off. Sue and the others acted supportive, but we both know there's no way it'll stay under wraps forever. Billy will hear about it sooner than later." On that note, the tears come. Kids scorn mothers for less, having little concept of the daily sacrifices—large and small—made for them throughout their lives. "Even if there are good reasons to tell him the truth, I still hate that he might be embarrassed by it all. By me."

My tears affect Joe, who sits on the corner of the bed and grabs my calf. "I'm sick about this. Disgusted with myself, too." He looks helpless and heartsick, but I'm too bitter to offer comfort. What about Harper gave him the impression that she'd shy away from a confrontation? He should've considered a worst-case scenario when making such a big decision. "Is there anything I can do to make things right?"

I shake my head. "There's no stuffing this back in the bottle. I have to call Billy."

"Let me tell him what I did so he doesn't blame you."

My instinct is to tell him no—to own this fully. I have stolen from people. I have kept secrets. And yet my mistakes do not excuse Joe's. "Fine. We'll call tonight when you get home."

Joe reaches for one of my hands and squeezes it, though I don't squeeze back. "Can you forgive me?"

Can I?

"I don't know, Joe. Between this and the sexual stuff, you seem like a stranger."

His eyes water again. "That's fair. It hurts, but it's fair."

I don't need his approval to validate my feelings. Harper has taught me that much, which is a small gift this morning. I'm aware that I've hurt him, too. He gave up a healthier social life for the sake of our marriage, believing it was helping me manage my illness. My lack of trust in him all those years must burn when viewed in that light. When all is said and done, my secret was the poison that began eating away at our once-healthy marriage.

Joe rises to finish dressing for work. "As painful as everything is this morning, I'm going to hope that having this out there might be for the best. There aren't any secrets between us now. I'll keep trying to make amends, and hoping we can start over again and figure things out."

"That sounds like you're trying to reframe what you did like it was meant to help us. The truth is that you lashed out, and now our whole family will be in the spotlight."

He nods. "I snapped, it's true. I'm not trying to minimize that, Wendy. I'm just looking for some path forward."

I hug my knees to my chest. "It scares me to know you're capable of that. I wonder what else you might do."

His face falls. "Nothing to hurt you again, I promise. It might not feel like it today, but I love you. I'm going to fight for your forgiveness and for a way we can learn to trust each other again."

On that note, I finally exhale. I'm still raw, but buried beneath my resentment is twenty-plus years of love. A well that might be deep enough to sustain us despite the drought caused by our mistakes.

Joe is buttoning his shirt when he says, "Are you a little relieved that your friends were supportive? Maybe there won't be as much gossip as you think."

One can hope.

"I was surprised. Sue was particularly kind. Maybe Dr. Haertel's right about the growing compassion for mental illness." I don't blame an alcoholic for her addiction, or someone with bipolar disorder for a bout of mania. I didn't ask for this illness, and I'm taking steps to control it.

My husband is nodding. "Maybe I should call off work today. Would you like that?"

"No. I prefer some alone time to think about everything."

After a moment, he leans forward to kiss the top of my head. "I love you, Wendy. It kills me to think you're afraid of me."

I nestle back into bed, drained by our conversation. Yet as Dr. Haertel predicted, forced or not, the confession has hit some kind of internal reset button. I'm still breathing. Life will go on. My friends didn't run away screaming. As long as my relationship with my son isn't damaged, this isn't the end of the world. "All I can promise right now is one day at a time."

Two hours later, I'm finishing dressing to run errands. Heading out is a little nerve-racking, but if last night didn't break me, I suppose I can take whatever comes next.

While in town, I stop at the bookstore to pick up an apology card for Harper. She was hardly understanding last night, but I did steal from her and then lie about it, all while she was being my friend and helping me define a new purpose. I hate that she's lost faith in who I am.

I choose a pretty floral card, then browse the self-help books about forgiveness before going to the cash register. I'm angry and hurt, but I'm not ready to throw away everything with Joe over one awful choice. Dr. Haertel will be shocked on Monday by all I have to share.

"Hi, Wendy!" Anne calls from behind the register. We've gotten friendly after eighteen years of me buying books for Billy.

"Good morning, Anne." I wave, catching sight of a beautiful cover—red with a black mountainside taking half the page. I grab it and walk to the register, grateful there aren't many customers around. "Last night was a success."

"It was. Ellen's lovely."

I was preoccupied, so I didn't fully enjoy the discussion. Hopefully she'll come back after her next release. "We're lucky to be close to New York so big-time authors can easily come up for events."

Anne looks at me like she's debating something. "I saw you with Ellen's friend last night. How do you know her?"

Has Anne already heard about what happened? My smile might've faltered. "She moved in next door last month."

"So you've gotten friendly?"

Anne's interest in Harper seems more than a passing one. "We did. She's a publicist. Have you worked with her on author events?"

"No. I met her a few weeks ago and then again yesterday afternoon with Ellen." She bites her lip, then leans forward. "Just between us, Wendy, she's not really a publicist."

"She's not?" Anne must be mistaken. Harper wouldn't lie about something that silly.

Anne comes out from behind the register, goes to the general fiction shelves, and retrieves a book. *The Hypocritical Oath* by H. E. Ross. She thumbs through it, then hands it to me opened at the author's biography. A little jolt zings down my spine. There's Harper staring back at me—or a version of Harper, anyway.

"Is that really her?" I ask aloud, although I'm speaking to myself more than to Anne. "Why hide this instead of brag about it?"

"She had such success with *If You Say So* and the next, but this book tanked. I overheard her telling Ellen she's here researching a new book. From the sound of it, she's setting the story in a community based on ours and using real people as muses for various character traits. Since you live next door, you might want to be a little circumspect about what you share." Anne's smile is almost apologetic, like she heard more than she's letting on.

My stomach hits the floor.

Conversations drift back, Harper's probing questions and alleged concern taking on a new tone now. Was she was merely getting dirt on me and Joe for her own purposes? Was it all a game? A big joke? I place my hands on the counter when my knees weaken, my mind still racing. I told her about my sex life, she knows about Billy's bad grade, and worst of all, she knows about my mother and my own illness. "I can't believe it."

Anne shrugs. "Eavesdropping is part of many authors' process. Just watch what you say from now on."

"I'm not interesting enough to be a story character," I joke, hoping to sell my casual indifference despite the way every muscle—especially my heart—is tight with pain. Not only did Harper lie to me for weeks, but she's likely been using me, too. Turns out we were never friends at all.

Stealing that votive was wrong, but Harper's stolen something worse and more personal. And like Joe last night, she's been very intentional.

"I'll take Harper's book instead of the card and other book." No need for apologies now. If anything, she owes me one.

I hand Anne my credit card, my mind skipping ahead to imagine the look on Harper's face when I show up at her door with her book in my hand.

CHAPTER EIGHTEEN

HARPER

It's always sickening to delete entire pages of a draft, but this morning's read-through of last night's work demanded it. It's my own fault for attempting to write a new chapter when highly conflicted, which I was after leaving Wendy's.

The words aren't flowing this morning, either. Another forty minutes wasted in front of the keyboard, my thoughts jumbled and straying. Given my initial goal when moving here, I should be celebrating having George's warning confirmed. Wendy's secret is what I've been seeking, so why am I surrounded by several Pop-Tart wrappers and a half-empty bottle of bourbon?

Rhetorical question, Harper. How can I write when any attempt to get into Gwen's point of view triggers memories of Wendy's splotchy, horrified expression from last night?

Her pleas made me realize that giving Gwen an impulse control disorder to inject humor into a manuscript isn't funny at all. It's insensitive at best and downright cruel at worst. But my editor and agent have already approved the idea, so now what? If I go back and ask to scrap it—if I'm unreliable again—Tessa may choose to stop working with me. Bye-bye, career. And even if she doesn't, how will I come up with yet another new idea and finish writing that in only sixteen weeks?

As Mandy might say, this is a real pickle.

If it were only business, it would be easy, but this problem is more personal. Precisely why it's risky to base a fictional character on someone real. Especially when that real person is—or was—a friend who still doesn't know what I've been up to. The way I handled Wendy's confession has left me feeling a bit like a bully.

All this time I've been digging into Wendy and passing judgment on others, when in fact it's been becoming clearer that, in many ways, I'm the hot mess. That bitter cup does not go down easily. Neither does the revelation that my stalled career isn't Calvin's fault. That's all on me.

The doorbell? Good. The distraction should keep me from opening the bag of Oreos.

I jog down the steps and open the door to see Wendy.

Wow, she's brave. Once my shock subsides, I gesture to my two empty porch chairs before taking a seat myself, eager to try to repair some of the damage.

"Good morning. I'm glad you came over," I begin. Wendy's theft wasn't intentional. And now her past statements—like how she wouldn't "feel safe" going into other people's homes—take on new meaning. Since we met, I've pontificated about gender inequalities and other hardships as if she's never known what it means to struggle. Meanwhile, on top of daily coping with her problem, her confession and vulnerability were rather heroic. "I want to talk about what's happened."

"So do I."

Unfortunately the chill out here isn't solely due to the weather.

"I realize I didn't handle things well last night. I should've waited until we were alone to ask about the votive. I'm sorry for being careless, and I hope your friends continue to be supportive. And just to be clear, I understand why you lied about breaking it and I forgive you for that." And not only because I'm living my own lie. Wendy will be stuck here dealing with the ripple effect of the big reveal long after I've returned to New York. So will Joe and her son, Billy. I've potentially hurt them all. My confession would only inflict more pain at this point, and I think I've caused enough damage. My only bit of peace is the memory of Sue coming to Wendy's defense. Perhaps that circle of friends will have more discretion than I had.

I finish my apology with an attempt at a winsome grin.

Instead of sitting, Wendy towers over me. The air around her crackles. Her eyes are bright; her shoulders are thrown back proudly. "Is that all?"

Not exactly the response I hoped for. "Um, yeah."

"There's nothing else on your conscience." She's clutching something close to her chest. "No secrets of your own?"

My grip tightens around the arms of the chair, and my stomach flip-flops, a sure sign that the tables are turning. "Like what?"

I hold my breath. One one thousand, two one thousand, three one thousand . . .

Wendy speaks through gritted teeth. "Like how you've been lying since the day we met. Pretending to be my friend in order to profit from my pain."

Fuckity fuck. "Wendy, that's not—"

She holds up *The Hypocritical Oath*. "I *know*, Harper."

A shiver shimmies down my spine.

It's poetic that she's waving my dumpster-fire book instead of one of the good ones. If I hadn't already realized that my idea for this work in progress is problematic, Wendy's outrage further taints the manuscript.

It's only fitting that I take my lumps. "Yes. I'm a writer. A *fiction* writer."

"Really? Then your current project isn't about a middle-aged housewife with marriage problems and mental illness?" Her face is drawn, jaw clenched beneath wide, dewy eyes.

While her outrage should be what guts me, it's the hope peeking out from behind the pain in her eyes—like she's desperate to be proven wrong—that does it. Even now, she wants to believe the best in me. She wants to believe in our friendship. The fact that I'm about to disappoint her again sinks like a stone in my gut.

I raise a hand in surrender. "There is a character—the antagonist—who might have some of those traits, but she isn't *you*. She's a character. The character I've written so far could be any one of many women around here facing midlife issues in marriage, with kids, and with parents, and so on. That's the point. She's relatable to a lot of different readers."

It's true, but not exactly true. The kleptomania is less relatable to most and very specific to her. I have abused Wendy's trust, and we both know it. Not only am I a liar; apparently I'm also a coward. My head begins to pound, crowded with images of Mandy, my family, and even Nate lined up and shaking their heads.

Leaning forward I say, "What I've done for my work doesn't mean I don't care about you. I do, Wendy. You're generous, gracious, and strong, and you've helped me rethink some things—important things. I never meant to hurt you."

She wipes a tear from her cheek, her mottled face a study of betrayal. With a voice as quiet as a sad child's, she says, "You humiliated me in front of my friends for taking that votive, yet all this time you've been stealing my life and secrets. Intentionally. Maliciously, even."

"Not maliciously." A weak defense, but an honest one. I hug my knees.

"Yes, maliciously. When your book comes out, some people around here will read it. You'll be interviewed, and then they'll also learn that you lived here—*where* you lived here. They'll put two and two together and assume that if one thing about me rings true, everything else about that character must also be true. I assume my kleptomania is in there."

My chin drops. I could use more bourbon right now. She's not wrong, but she's also not entirely correct.

"The book's title is not *The Story of Wendy Moore*." I move my hands to mimic a marquee, defensiveness welling up. To paraphrase the wonderful, wise Anne Lamott, if people want to be written about warmly, they should behave better. Yet even bourbon and a sugar rush don't drown out the little voice screaming that Wendy *did* treat me kindly. The same voice reminds me that I actively stole her personal story because I lacked the confidence to create my own. Weakly, I add, "Even Ellen told you writers use things from their life experiences in their books."

"Maybe so." She glances down the street with watery eyes, her voice quavering. Her poise, however, remains impeccable. "You want to know the worst part? Meeting you was exciting—a breath of fresh air. A chance to make a new friend, which has never been easy for me. I confided in you and took your advice. Introduced you to my friends and to Nate. Even refinished that buffet practically for free—happily. Other than one terrible impulse, every one of my actions was done in good faith because I thought we were becoming real friends. I guess you can add 'fool' to your character's flaws." Wendy's words and sniffles spear me like swords. She turns as if to go, then glances over her shoulder. "But at least now I better understand why you're such a cynic. I'd be one too if I treated people like disposable puppets."

I bite on the inside of my cheek, shakier than I care to reveal. When I look in the mirror she's holding up, I see my brother Rick. To think I could cause another person the kind of pain that could change who she is strikes like something of a death blow.

She continues, "There's probably no legal way to stop you from writing your 'fictional' character. That would only bring it more attention, anyway. And I won't waste my breath asking you to consider my feelings when they've obviously never mattered. At least I know that, whatever my shortcomings, I'm still a better person than you."

With that, she drops my book on the porch and briskly walks away, as if a loaded missile is aimed at her back.

Perspiration rolls down my cheek despite the sixty-degree temperature, my body pinned in place by her sharp observations. A minute or more passes before I finally rise, go inside without the book, close the door, and stand in the entry, flipping the bird—whether at the door or myself is unclear. How'd I get here; how'd I sink this low?

Pivoting, I march toward the kitchen, grab a tumbler, and pour myself some of that bourbon, drinking it in one long shot before slamming the glass on the counter and refilling it. On my way out of the kitchen, I catch sight of the refinished buffet, swallow some more liquor, and continue to the stairs.

I fucked up. I devastated Wendy, and I'm ashamed. I have no idea how to manage all these feelings, and given everything she just said, she's not interested in hearing from me anytime soon. Maybe not ever.

Then there's the manuscript. My career. I've got a deadline that must be met to salvage my relationship with my editor and publisher. They were excited about this story, but maybe there's a way to write it without causing further destruction to the Moore family.

With my head in my hands, I consider the options for modifying what I've written and altering Gwen so she doesn't resemble Wendy as closely. To finish this project with more ethics, integrity, and compassion than I've shown thus far. If I can figure that out without alienating my agent and editor, I might one day make amends with Wendy. When an hour of brainstorming gets me nowhere, I lace up my sneakers and take off for a long walk.

———

Around six o'clock, a car pulls into my driveway. Nate. We planned takeout and a movie—i.e., couch sex. I almost canceled, but I could use a friendly face tonight. How long he'll remain one is up for debate. I owe him the truth—the whole truth—even though my confession will likely bring an abrupt halt to our new relationship, and he'll leave with a bad taste in his mouth.

I still own the condo. I could return to SoHo to finish my book in relative anonymity, away from angry neighbors and prying eyes. By the time it's completed, turned in, and through editing and production, nearly everyone here will have forgotten about me. Including Nate.

I answer the door, summoning courage.

He's strolling up the front walk with takeout from Hashi Sushi and smiles when our eyes meet. My stomach flutters like it always does when he flashes his teeth like some sexy weapon. Dashing in from the cold, he drops a warm kiss on my lips. "Hungry?"

"Sure." I release the breath I'd been holding. I'll wait for the right moment to disclose the whole mess. "Want some wine or bourbon?"

"I got sake."

I grimace, having never developed a taste for that. We grab plates and napkins and take everything into the dining room, where the gorgeous buffet taunts me again. I sit across from Nate, who's setting out the takeout containers. It's not just that buffet. Even Nate wouldn't be here without Wendy. "How was your day?"

"Typical Friday." He hands me a set of chopsticks, then sets his chin on his fist. "Yours?"

That didn't take long. "Not so good. Wendy and I had a falling-out."

Nate narrows his gaze. "I'm sorry to hear that. Do you want to talk about it?"

Not exactly. I can't tell him about the votive without exposing Wendy's illness, so I fudge a little. "Remember how I told you I'm here researching stuff for my next book?"

He nods.

"Well, one of the main characters is based on Wendy—based on information she told me in confidence." I grimace. It sounds so much worse than it seemed at the start, before she let me into her life. Before she got involved in mine.

His mouth falls open.

"What are you thinking?" If he's half as appalled as I am, he's disgusted.

He rubs his chin. "I'd hate to be used that way. Why'd you do it?"

"My reasons made sense at the time. My back was to the wall professionally. I needed a muse—one who met my editor's wish-list criteria. Maybe it wasn't completely ethical, but I never thought anyone would get hurt. That first week, I didn't think we'd become friends or that she'd end up sharing as much as she did. Then when things began to change, I didn't know how to get out of it. At first, I thought helping her with some of her issues would make up for it. Then I told myself no one would ever know or get hurt. I know now that was all horseshit. I was fooling myself—something I do a lot more than I ever realized."

He listens thoughtfully until I finish, then sits back in his chair, arms folded.

I shove a Boston roll in my mouth to avoid his gaze, and wait for him to politely untangle himself from the messy web of my life.

"What are you going to do about it?" he finally asks.

"Do about what?"

"Wendy."

"What can I do? In terms of the work, I've written a third of the book based on the approved concept. I'll try to figure a way to modify the character without upsetting my editor, but I have to turn in a manuscript. I'm under a deadline and have already received half the advance. I can't afford to walk away and pay it back. If I did that, I'd lose my career and my home. I know I've crossed some lines, but ultimately my book is *fiction*." It's all true, and yet it rings hollow like all justifications. I close my eyes to block out that hopeful look in Wendy's eyes from earlier—the agony I can't ignore.

He sits back, palms on the table. "I asked what you plan to do about Wendy, not about the book."

Oh. "I guess I could try to apologize again, but I don't know that it'll make a difference. The damage is done."

"It might not make a difference to Wendy—you don't know until you try. But it could definitely make a difference to you. I can't imagine carrying guilt around makes writing easier."

I stab another piece of sushi. "Unless I can come up with some way to make amends, I'll have to live with the pain that I caused."

"Maybe. I'm not sure I have any suggestions."

"You don't owe me any. This is on me. Besides, I know you care about the Moores, so if you want to break this off, I'd understand. I don't want you to be in an uncomfortable position with your boss, either."

There's a pause during which Nate's gaze lingers on his plate, his right forefinger tapping the table. My eyes prickle, on the verge of tears. I did this to myself, but it sucks to lose the chance to know him better, because he's definitely a man worth knowing.

"It's not my place to judge you, Harper. Everyone makes mistakes, but I think the test of character is whether they learn from them. You seem to regret what's happened. I doubt you'll do it again. That's good enough for me. So how about we take a little break from thinking about all that now." He smiles that great big persuasive grin.

That tips me over to where I can't hold back the tears, although they've become tears of relief. Nate actually listens without telling me how to behave. He sees my flaws and still supports me. This man—not Calvin and his phony feminism—is one I can make compromises for.

My parents would just love him, too. So would Mandy. Before I can stop myself, I blurt, "Well, then, how'd you like to join me in Ohio next weekend for that family event I mentioned? You know the history, and I could use a shoulder to lean on."

"This'll be a rough week for you." He chuckles, then leans forward and reaches across the table for my hand. "I'd like to meet your family someday, but I'll take a rain check this time. You're going there to find some common ground with them. If I come, I'll be a distraction at best and an excuse to ignore the issues at worst."

"Well, I hate that answer, mostly because it's true." I sigh and release his hand. "But thanks for being so understanding. I was dreading telling you everything, convinced you'd walk out the door." The comfort of acceptance is a feeling I should remember the next time I start to judge my parents or anyone else. For the first time all day, my shoulders finally relax.

"You're welcome. Now how about a lighter topic? What do you feel like watching after dinner?" He dips an unagi roll into wasabi-infused soy sauce and then into his mouth, his tongue darting out to capture an errant drop of soy sauce. That talented, talented tongue.

"Porn?" I cock one brow.

He nearly chokes, making us both chuckle. "I'm serious."

"Me too," I say, loosening my collar. "But I'll settle for hot sex while we play whatever movie you choose."

It's fun to make a man blush, and Nate does it so easily. Yet his eyes are also warm, which does delicious things to my stomach. My problems will still be there tomorrow, but right now I appreciate a breather.

Look at me, sitting here in a proper dining room in suburbia with a good man, sharing a meal, harsh truths, and even some easy laughs. I'm hardly recognizable.

When we finish eating, we take our plates to the kitchen, and then Nate excuses himself to use the restroom. I'm rinsing the dishes to load in the dishwasher when, through the rear window, I spy Joe taking out the trash. He looks up, making eye contact with me. I wave, but he drops his chin and returns inside. Apparently even vanilla has its limits.

Not long ago, his behavior would've set me off on a diatribe about judgmental hypocrites and my right to write whatever the hell I want.

But sorrow has shoved egotism aside, leaving me fumbling around and off-balance. It's different from when Calvin left because this time I'm clear about my role in the fallout. I wish I could tell Wendy how grateful I am for her matchmaking. Or how I finally get what she's been saying about some relationships. She deserves to know she was right. At the very least, perhaps questioning myself in the middle of my comeback book will motivate me to dig deeper, and to find a stronger theme within the story that doesn't rely upon Gwen's foibles.

"Harper, how about *Promising Young Woman*?" Nate calls from the living room.

Ha! Something I once considered myself to be. Half a lifetime ago I made up my mind about the world and the people in it. My broad goals aren't bad, nor are gender inequities false, but the course I mapped to navigate them hasn't exactly fixed anything or made me happy. A different approach—an honest and more thoughtful one—is probably the only way to lift this heavy guilt and become a smarter, stronger woman.

"I still vote for porn," I tease, shutting off the light, unable to erase that last image of Joe from my mind.

CHAPTER NINETEEN

WENDY

Friday evening

Billy's last text mentioned that he'd be busy this weekend, working with his study group on a project due Monday. Our news could distract him, which he can't afford after that D. But we've little choice if we don't want him caught unaware by a friend or social media.

Joe returns from taking out the trash, his cheeks drawn, his eyes tired and distant, apparently dreading this as much as I am. He sits beside me on the sofa, settling a hand on my knee. Despite the distance between us, I don't flinch. The set of his mouth is grim but determined. "Ready?"

Aside from a nauseated stomach and a throat that feels rougher than sandpaper? Sure. I shouldn't have hidden this for so long in the first place. Masking it only contributes to the stigma. My son has a right to know about something that could be in his DNA, too.

Joe opens FaceTime and sets the phone vertically on the coffee table. Each ring affects me like an electrical charge. Billy picks up after the third ring. "Hello."

"Hey, Billy," Joe begins, casting me a "here we go" look. "How's it going?"

"Good, Dad." He's got a ball cap on backward, hair curling up around its edges. Salad or flow, the boys call it, though I don't know why. Not that it matters.

"You busy now or can you talk?" Joe leans forward, elbows to knees, hands clasped together.

"You sound serious."

"Well, your mom and I need to discuss something important."

"Is someone sick?" His brows pull together.

"Hi, honey," I interrupt. "It's nothing life-threatening, but there's something I have to share. Gosh, I'm not sure where to begin . . ." I clear my throat, buying time. I'm still so angry with Joe it's hard to sit beside him, yet I won't burden Billy with our marital strife, too.

"Hang on, let me close my door." We hear scuffling sounds and his door click, then the squeak of bedsprings as he falls onto the mattress and rolls onto his side, staring into the phone camera. "What's wrong? Is it something about my tuition?"

"No." A case of nerves rushes off with the speech I'd planned. My skin breaks into a cold sweat. Floundering, I say, "You know how Gram has OCD—the germophobia and tics?"

"Yeah."

"Well, when I was in high school, I developed an impulse control disorder, too—" My heart is fluttering as if I'm dangling from a skyscraper by the ankles. In two minutes, my son might never look at me the same again. I know this because of my relationship with my own mother. I don't blame her for her illness, but her condition colors most every aspect of our life together and the plans we make.

"Mom?"

I barely glance up, awash in thoughts and regrets.

"Sorry. This is hard to say." I take a breath and close my eyes, covering my face like a child. Eventually, I let my hands fall to my lap and force myself to look at the camera. "I have kleptomania. It was much worse when I was your age. Your father got me into counseling before we got married. Since then I've had it mostly under control, but recently I've slipped up—"

"Are you under arrest?" The horror on his face is like a hammer to my chest.

I swallow thickly, fighting to sit up straight. "No. And I never take anything valuable. It's always little things nearby whenever the urge hits. I'm back in therapy now and am already doing better."

His expression turns anxious. "Does anyone else know?"

Joe speaks up. "Well, unfortunately yes, because of me—" He pauses, weighing how detailed to get, shame reddening his face.

I touch his arm and shake my head. Not because I want to protect him, but because I don't like the idea of Billy losing faith in both parents in one blow. But Joe persists. "Without getting into the weeds, I outed your mom last night in front of her book club. It was a horrible, rash decision—but that's no excuse. I'm ashamed, and I hope you and your mom can forgive me eventually."

"What the fu—" Billy pulls himself back in the nick of time, but his gaze is accusing. "Douche move, Dad."

"Language, honey." It's validating that Billy despises Joe's behavior, but no matter what happens between Joe and me, he's still Billy's dad and deserves respect. Meanwhile, Joe's head is bowed, his expression grim.

"I hardly think swearing is our problem now, Mom. You know this'll get around town. What do I say if someone says something to me?" Billy asks.

"My friends promised not to spread gossip, but it will probably leak out at some point. If someone asks, tell the truth. Say your mom has a mental illness and is getting treatment. Just like Gram. It is what it is, and the best I can do is stay in treatment and work the process." I shrug with a sheepish smile. "The bigger wrinkle is that neighbor I told you about, Harper. Turns out she's an author. She came here to research and write a new book. We learned that book will feature a character based on me and my illness." All day the ache from that betrayal and the phony friendship has ebbed and flowed, pulsing in my head, tensing my shoulders, and now sickening my stomach.

"What a bitch." Billy scowls. Joe nods silently beside me.

"Language," I say more firmly, although I'm resentful enough to call her the c-word.

"I'll get all my friends to one-star her books on Goodreads," he mutters, hot with teen indignation.

"Please don't. Vengeance won't help," I plead. "And the truth is that I did take something from her house—a glass votive—and then lied to her when she questioned me. That's what brought this all to a head. I'm very sorry and embarrassed, but mostly I'm sorry that this affects you." I sigh, relieved to have at least had the chance to come clean before he found out from some other source. With it off my chest, my body deflates. I need to sleep—maybe for days. A clearer head will help me figure out a path forward with Joe and in my community.

"Will she turn you in?" he asks.

Stolen items worth less than $500 are considered a sixth-degree larceny (I looked it up), punishable by a fine and up to three months in jail.

"No." I'm certain despite no assurances from Harper. "I know this is a lot, and it doesn't fit with who you thought I was. But I'm still me. My illness doesn't change anything between us, honey. I love you so much and work every day to be a mother you can be proud of."

Joe squeezes my hand; his eyes are watery, his remorse palpable.

Billy's silence creates a lump in my throat. Then he twists his lips. "I'm sorry you have this problem, Mom."

"Thank you, honey," I say, my voice cracking as it pushes through the tightness. I blink my tears away, but no Christmas gift would eclipse his response.

Joe wades back into the conversation. "Do you have any other questions?"

"No." Billy doesn't seem as willing to extend his father kindness yet. Normally I'd smooth things over between them, but I'm not ready to do that today. Billy is my main concern, not Joe. Not even myself.

"Honey, these disorders can be hereditary, so please come to us if you ever have any kind of compulsion." I watch his reaction, searching for clues.

Joe leans forward, elbows on his knees, lips sucked inward, brows pulled tight. I can't blame him for hoping Billy won't spend a lifetime coping with these types of mental issues.

No one speaks for a moment.

"Billy?" Joe prods.

"I don't have those problems. I didn't know I could, though." His gaze is distant. I understand exactly what he's feeling right now because, even before my first theft, I worried I'd turn into my mother. I hate that my son now has this hanging over him, but all I can do about that is love and support him.

"I bet you'll be just fine, Billy, but if not, talk to us and we'll get you whatever help you need," Joe says. "As for your mom, I promise you both I'll do everything I can to support her, particularly if there's any backlash from last night."

"I hope no one else finds out." Billy's worried tone settles around me like ash. "Maybe Mom shouldn't talk about it more if we don't want other people to find out."

Sue already emailed me today with more assurances, but I don't plan on advertising my illness. "For now, my focus is on therapy."

He rolls onto his back, holding the phone overhead. "Well, I'll guess I'll let you know if someone says something to me."

"Thank you," I reply.

"I'm really sorry for letting you both down." Joe rubs his face. "I'm determined to make it up to you."

Billy raises one brow but doesn't say anything. At eighteen, he already knows some things can't be undone. Then another voice sounds behind him. "Hey, my roommate just got back. Talk later?"

"Of course. Good luck with that project," Joe says.

"Love you," I add.

"Love you, too. Bye." I watch the screen go dark, then slouch back into the sofa cushions. I can feel Joe's sorrow hanging heavy in the room like an overpowering deodorizer. I'm still mad—righteously so—but anger won't save this marriage. And like Sue, I'm not ready to make a big decision about us in a matter of twenty-four hours. "Well, that wasn't as awful as it could've been. Do you think he'll be okay?"

"You raised a good kid." He reaches across the cushion but stops short of touching me, like he's awaiting permission this time. "I keep asking myself how I could've done something so nasty. I hate myself a little for it."

"I hate you a little for it, too," I admit with a sad smile. Then another voice of truth sounds off in my head. "But maybe if I'd been less focused on myself, I would've noticed how much you've been repressing in order to help me cope. That pressure had to be released one way or another."

He stares at me, his gaze ripe with hope. "I love you, Wendy, and don't want to lose what we've built. But even if you find it in your heart to forgive me, I don't think we can go on if you keep hiding things from me. We both deserve better. We've obviously got serious trust issues to work through. What do you think about me coming to a few sessions with Dr. Haertel as a start?"

I can't quite bring myself to reassure him of my love, although I feel it there beneath the pain. "I think that's a good idea."

"Okay."

We sit together in silence, each in our own thoughts, or maybe just at a loss for what to do or say next. There's no map to show us how to get through this evening and the ensuing days when so much remains unresolved.

With a sigh, I aim for a bit of normalcy. "Should we get takeout? Or I could whip up a quick pasta marinara."

"I thought you wanted to finish that end table tonight?"

"Yes." I nod, having forgotten about it. Of course, it reminds me of Harper and our antiquing trip, which dampens my enthusiasm. I have to make peace with the fact that she spurred me into taking this chance so it doesn't taint my love for the work itself.

"Why don't you go do that and I'll cook us something?" It's been a while since Joe's made dinner. I see him trying to be helpful, but I honestly have no appetite.

"Thanks. I'm not very hungry, though, so don't make too much effort." I rise to go change into work clothes, but Joe catches my hand again.

"It's been a rough twenty-four hours, but I'm still the man who has loved you for decades. Try to remember that rather than focusing solely on the terrible thing I did."

I nod, grateful that, unlike my father, he has been steadfast and still wants to help me recover. He's not taking off to flee public scorn or unwilling to forgive my years-long lies of omission. "I know that, Joe."

Ten minutes later, I'm in the garage putting a coat of sealer on the vintage end table and thinking about my to-do list for getting "Recovered Beauties" off the ground. My enthusiasm wavers a bit, but regardless of Harper's lie, she wasn't wrong about everything. This will be good for me. It's a talent that makes me feel special. One that could bring me an income. And while some people may not trust me if they learn about my illness, others might be more understanding and look for solutions, like delivering their furniture for me to work on here. Joe already offered to help me with the books. If he'll go antiquing with me sometimes, this venture could even be one way we begin to reconnect.

My broker job was the last time I did anything purely for my own satisfaction. Building something from a beloved hobby is sparking something joyful in me despite the carnage of the day. That seems significant. I can't predict the future or every problem that might surface, but I am confident this can help me and my therapy.

The to-do list is long and daunting: set up an email account and website, create Facebook and Instagram pages, purchase ring lights for taking good photographs, and set up a seller account on Etsy and Facebook.

Yet it's not easy to put Harper out of my mind, because there were moments when I felt a real connection—one that seemed worth building upon. Not knowing whether it was all a ruse nags at me. It could've been both, yet people don't often use someone they like. Not that Harper does anything the typical way.

We're so different it's hard to say what drew me to her in the first place, or why I confided in her so easily. Loneliness, sure, but maybe I wanted to be pushed or envied her devil-may-care attitude. I'd never felt the freedom to indulge in life that way, but there is something enchanting about it—about her.

I feel silly for missing her even a little bit after what she did. Missing something that wasn't even real . . .

When I finish the final strokes, I sit back to admire my work. Although not as spectacular as Harper's buffet, this is my first for-profit piece, which makes it extra special. Part of me wishes Harper could see it, but that's not an option.

The only upside of being outed was that it showed me that I do have a few real friends with whom I could share this milestone. Women I didn't previously trust to become confidantes, but all of whom displayed grace and compassion in my moment of crisis. Another thing I wish I'd known sooner, but better late than never. On that note, I take out my phone to call Sue.

"Hi, Wendy. How are you today?" Her concern is heartening. A blueprint for the next time I have a friend in trouble. That said, I'm not ready to discuss my family matters. Not at this moment, anyway.

"Still embarrassed, but I'll survive." The truth of my response shocks me. For a hot second, I consider outing Harper's real identity, then decide blame and shame won't help me heal like true friendship and a new business might. In fact, my venture could also help Sue deal with her recent setback. "I'm calling with a proposition, actually."

"Oh?"

Sitting cross-legged on my tarp, I take a few minutes to explain my preliminary business plans. "You were always so good at managing the parents' newsletter and making graphics. Any chance you'd be interested in helping me with the social media side of this enterprise—you know, getting the word out, making the virtual pages pop?"

"Really?"

"I don't have money to pay you yet, but we could figure something out—like an hourly rate or a percentage of each sale. Neither of us will get rich, but it could be fun work. Something new to keep us relevant while making a little mad money." I scan the garage while talking, thinking about how to clean and reorganize it to function better as a real workshop.

"That sounds great, Wendy. I'd love to help."

My eyes sting with happy tears for a change. "I'm so relieved."

"Relieved?"

I press a fingertip to the inside corner of my eye. "I didn't know—I mean, you were kind last night, but there are those who'll avoid me after learning about my problem."

"We might both be the subject of unpleasant gossip for a little while, so let's lean on each other. I'm embarrassed by Dirk's fling, but I also know I'm not the only person whose husband has cheated. And you're not the only person in town with a mental health issue. People in glass houses can go screw themselves, you know?"

I smile. "Your support means so much."

"That's what friends do."

Real friends, anyway. Something I haven't had enough of. Another thing I plan to change through therapy. "Speaking of Dirk, how are you holding up? Last night you sounded a little defeated and confused."

"That's about right. Dirk has agreed to counseling, and he's saying all the right things. I owe it to my family to try. Until this happened, I loved him so much. But trust is so tough to rebuild. If I can't honestly forgive him in six months or so, I'll file for divorce. I hired a forensic accountant on the sly to make sure Dirk isn't starting to hide assets or anything—just in case."

I hope she's as strong as she sounds. As distant as Joe and I seem to be today, our trust issues feel fixable. I don't believe Joe will ever repeat the kind of cruelty he displayed this week, especially if I don't continue to lie to him and make him feel irrelevant. "You're wise and brave. Whenever you need to vent, you just call me."

"Why don't I come over on Monday to discuss business ideas. Cute name, by the way. We should start by getting a logo and taking some pictures of you with work you've done to date."

My thoughts flitter to the gorgeous buffet sitting a few hundred feet away in Harper's dining room. I've got the photos I took already. But it would feel weird to use them now, given where things stand with us. "I have a few things here, and I refinished your daughter's desk. I could call Joan Levy, too. I just have to dig out the before photos off the cloud."

"Great. Should I come by around ten o'clock?"

"Sure. I'll make some notes over the weekend."

"I'll do a little research on the local competition."

"Sounds good." A new business and a closer tie with an old friend. A solid building block toward a healthier outlook.

"Before we hang up, have you spoken to Harper today?"

"Briefly. It's over and I'm fine." The details are irrelevant at this point, so I leave it at that. I open my garage door to air it out, picturing

Harper's expression when I confronted her with her book. "It'll be awkward with her living next door, but she's only renting for a few more months." A fact that no longer makes me as sad.

I walk out onto the driveway and look at the Durbins' house, with its neatened flower beds and bright mums. Another little bomb goes off when thinking back to where I thought her interest in gardening would lead us.

Nate's car is in her driveway. I can't believe I hooked him up with a liar. I worry she's writing about him, too, but Joe said Nate can figure things out on his own. I'm not so sure. Love is blind, after all. In any case, it's proof I need to hit pause on my matchmaking.

"She'll be gone before you know it," Sue assures me.

That will certainly help, but I can't ignore the pinch of disappointment that accompanies that truth. When all is said and done, I enjoyed Harper's company and will miss sipping bourbon and arguing about everything from politics to pedicures. I wonder if she'll miss anything about me.

CHAPTER TWENTY

HARPER

A week later, Friday morning
Circleville, Ohio

I haul myself out of the Uber with my carry-on in front of the 1970s ranch home that felt like a bit of a prison for the first half of my life. No one mentioned making updates since my last visit, yet the rustic red brick is painted white, natural wood shutters flank the windows, and it's got a new front portico and porch with wooden posts, resembling every home remodel on HGTV.

Another noticeable change: there are no kids riding bikes down the street or playing in their yards. It seems like parental fear robs kids of the freedoms I took for granted. My own mother always asked my older brothers to "keep an eye" on me. Little did she realize that requiring them to do that gave them permission to torment me the way only big brothers can.

Standing on the stoop, I draw a deep breath. I called my aunt—the party planner—to let her know I was coming but asked her to keep it a surprise. Hopefully it's a pleasant one for my folks. I raise my hand to knock on the door, then lower it. This is my family home. A place where

I should feel free to walk in without the formality of an announcement. I simultaneously knock on and open the door. "Hello!"

"Hello?" my mother calls from the kitchen. She doesn't seem to recognize my voice, probably because she's not expecting me. When she reaches the entry, she stops; both hands clap to her chest, the wrinkles around her eyes turning up at the edges. "Oh my gosh, Harper! What are you doing here?"

It's been less than two years, yet more gray hairs invade her mane, and her waist is an inch or two thicker. Wendy's warning that my folks won't be here forever replays, wrenching me for more reason than one. I drop my bag to the floor. "Hi, Mom. I heard about your award and wanted to be part of the celebration."

The grandfather clock in the hallway strikes a toll, marking the half hour and breaking the brief, awkward silence. As if awakened from a dream, she snaps her arms open and comes forward to wrap me in a hug, her face flushed and grinning. This is not our normal greeting, and when we have hugged, I've usually pulled away first. This time I don't.

"I'm so happy to see you," she singsongs as we ease apart. The usual perfume of Downy and hairspray wafts around us, its familiarity making me smile. Her gaze darts all over me, drinking me in as she fingers my hair and the hem of my shirt. "I can't believe you're really here. Who told you, anyway?"

"Mandy. I hope it's okay that I came."

"It's better than okay, honey. But I know how busy you are with your new book. I don't want my little thing to be an imposition." She pats her cheeks as if she's embarrassed about being the center of attention.

While she might mean well with that remark, the reminder of how often I've used work as an excuse not to visit doesn't exactly make me feel good. "I know I haven't come around often, but I care about what's important to you." Well, not exactly everything that's important to her—but the meaningful things.

"I never said you didn't," she quips. Then, catching herself, she covers her mouth with both hands. "Let's not nitpick."

"I agree. And, Mom, listen." I turn my palms up. "I want to apologize—"

"For what?"

"For all the times I poked fun at your choices, or made you feel like your priorities are less important than mine. Please don't belittle your accomplishments to me, okay? You've spent a decade making this community a better place by helping people. That's a big deal. I'm sorry you didn't feel comfortable telling me about this or inviting me."

"Oh, well . . ." Her posture softens. "What's brought on all this?"

"Turns out my book isn't my only work in progress." I didn't intend to start the visit with this conversation, but I might as well get it over with now. "Looking back I see that I lashed out whenever I couldn't get you to see things my way or felt like you guys didn't support me. I guess I wanted you to feel as small or insignificant as being dismissed made me feel."

Her expression falls. "I'm sorry you ever felt anything but loved in this house. We've always loved you, even when we didn't understand you. Of course, with everything going on in the country these past few years, I've come to appreciate the importance of some of your views." She shrugs like that's not a huge statement, but the overdue validation sets off a shock of joy. "I can't change the past, but I wish I could take away your pain."

Her regret rings clearly.

I wave a hand. "Let's let that all go. Can we just start over here?"

She smiles, opening her arms for another hug. "Love to."

Two hugs in ten minutes. A record for us. A reward for confronting issues without anger or judgment.

When Mom lets go, she resumes her normal chattiness. "Do you need to use the restroom? Are you hungry? Can I fix you something to eat? I just got back from the store, so the refrigerator is full. How about some cinnamon french toast?"

"Actually, I've been up since four o'clock and haven't showered, so I'd love to clean up before seeing everyone later."

"Of course! But we turned your old room into a craft room this summer. Hope you don't mind. Rick's room is still set up for guests, though." She grimaces, probably bracing for sarcasm.

In truth, it's a disappointment. A homecoming isn't the same when you lose your old room. Why didn't they convert Rick's instead? He'll never stay here again because he lives less than twenty minutes away. But in truth, his larger room makes a better guest room than my old shoebox. I've hardly visited enough to warrant keeping mine intact.

"That'll work just fine." After all these years I'm getting what I always wanted, the bigger "kid's room" in the house. Funny how little that matters now. Maybe it never should have.

"Oh good." Mom pats her chest. The nervous gesture reminds me of Wendy, causing a pang. I really hurt my neighbor, a fact I don't wish to repeat with others. I'm here to build bridges, not burn more down.

"I'm glad you made space for yourself to quilt and scrapbook."

My mom's relieved expression is another win. "Well, take your time. I'll fix a little snack so you have something to eat when you're finished." She touches my hair as if making sure she's not hallucinating, then turns and waddles back to the kitchen while I trudge up the stairs with my suitcase, feeling much less brave than I did a moment ago.

Tonight will be the first time I've seen everyone since my book bombed. There'll be no hiding from my public failure, or from the fact that said failure is part of the reason I've stayed away so long.

Rick's room is decorated with the same shag rug, dull brown furniture that could clearly use Wendy's touch, and plaid window treatments. The only difference is the absence of his personal items. No trophies, photos, certificates, or posters. A clean slate, so to speak.

Perhaps that's something everyone in my family could use at this point in our lives.

As I undress, I wonder if the rest of my family will welcome me home as eagerly as my mother. Right then I make the only vows I'm ready to at this point in my life: *I promise to stop myself from reading into my family's comments, to stop taking the bait when my brothers poke at me or make an aside about my absence or my writing or any other thing that normally sets me off, and to seek common ground with my family.* Like with couples taking vows of marriage, I figure I've got a fifty-fifty chance of keeping mine.

———

There are four eight-top tables set up in the private party room at Tambellini's, which accommodates our family and some of my mother's closest friends and their spouses. Many of the older women don flouncy dress wear—some with a little sparkle. My brothers are both in sports coats and ties, their wives in tasteful dresses. On the other hand, I'm in fitted black crop pants, with heeled boots and a gunmetal-gray silk top. I did remember jewelry, although my silver-and-leather choker and bracelet differ greatly from my cousins' pearls.

I'm seated at the family table with Mom, Dad, Rick, Gemma, Jim, and Heidi. They gave the extra single seat to Dad's divorced brother, Uncle Carl. He's actually cool—the man who introduced me to bourbon, in fact, at my college graduation party. Mandy is two tables away, with husband, parents, and sisters.

"Good speech, Ma." Rick slugs back his dirty martini.

She blushes. "Thanks, honey. I tried, but I'm not a good writer. I should've asked Harper for help."

Rick throws Jim a look, muttering, "What does she know about volunteer work?"

Mom's eyes widen into panic mode. Dad swigs his beer, shaking his head but with no real intention of putting Rick in his place. His firstborn son. Boys will be boys and all that bullshit.

Remember the vow. The vow!

"That's true," I say. Everyone's lips part in unison, like I've transformed into a buffalo or something. I must be in shock, too, because my limbs go a little numb. "Besides, it was good, Mom. You didn't need my help."

"Who are you and what've you done with my sister?" Rick shoots our brother a wry look, as if begging him to join in. Jim's refusal is heartening. Does he ever reflect back and regret letting Rick taunt me? Perhaps one day he might even step up and ask him to stop.

Gemma elbows Rick and raises her empty wineglass toward my mother to deflect attention. "A toast to you, Barbara, for a great speech and a wonderful legacy of community spirit."

"Cheers," the table echoes together, each of us downing a cheap chardonnay. I've always liked Gemma.

"I don't like being the center of attention, but if that's what it takes to get all my kids together again, I'll suffer through it. Thank you all for taking time from your busy lives." Mom smiles, her gaze landing on me. I'm sure she didn't intend for her words to get beneath my skin, but the little girl of yesteryear still trapped inside hears them as subconscious criticism and contrasts it against her letting Rick's jabs go without comment. Layered in these thoughts is another truth I can't deny: she will probably always wish I were a little more like Gemma and Heidi, just as I will always wish she would be a little more like Gloria Steinem or Margaret Atwood. What keeps me from falling back on old patterns tonight is a new awareness that this gap doesn't mean we can't still respect each other and value our relationship.

"It's the least we can do, Ma," Jim says.

I choke back a zinger about the free babysitting. Trying to change might kill me, but dammit, I'm committed to circumspection.

293

Dad turns to me. "So tell us about your new book. What's it about?"

Oh hell. I've told them so many times that I don't like to talk about my works in progress.

"It's about neighbors and family." I swallow more wine, preferring not to get into the details, particularly now, when I'm in a frenzy of rethinking the story and ascertaining the heart of the book.

"Family?" Rick scoffs. "Can you write about that any better than philanthropy?"

"Rick, enough," Mom finally says, fingering her pearl necklace. She's hardly ever stood up for me, and to do so in front of everyone is a noteworthy change.

"It's okay, Mom." I turn to Rick. "Let's not get into a battle of words and ruin Mom's night. One reason I didn't come around much these past two years was to avoid this dynamic." I gesture between us. "While it'd be nice if you'd consider your role in that, I'm working on changing mine. No more taking your bait. So get used to the new me, because this is my family, too, and I want to be here."

"Does this mean you'll come home for Thanksgiving?" My mother looks hopeful.

"Well, that's only two weeks away, so I'm thinking I'd rather come back for Christmas." A compromise—one that leaves the door open for an invitation to meet Nate's family at Thanksgiving.

Mom smiles, her hands coming together joyfully in front of her chest. "That sounds great, honey."

My dad covers my hand with his and squeezes it, smiling.

"Dad, tomorrow I want to hear about your plans for your Etsy shop." The mention of it makes me think of Wendy and the whole votive debacle. I hardly saw her last week—only once through the window when she was pruning her shrubs. The metaphor of that depresses me. We'd planted things together, but then the cold weather moved in and required a trimming back. And while I pushed her to be Joe's equal,

I'm concerned about how their marriage is faring since his actions on the book club night. I hope she doesn't lose everything she loves and values because I tinkered with her life. That concern keeps me up nights.

"The garage is full of glassware now. Never mind that my car sits out in the weather," Mom says.

"You've got a craft room. I need the garage," Dad shoots back.

"It's great to pursue something that makes you happy. You never know when you won't be able to anymore." I smile.

"Now there's a topic you could write about," Rick quips, testing my new resolve.

The table goes quiet, waiting for me to erupt. That's fair. As my temperature rises, I think about Nate. About why he didn't come with me, and my own goals.

"Despite my recent setback, I'm still proud of chasing my dream, and of my past success. My next book could mark a comeback, but even if it doesn't, the whole experience has led to some important personal changes. Maybe you should try making some, too." Okay, sure, I got a little dig in. I mean, I can't be expected to be perfect overnight.

Step by step I will learn to maintain my outlook and goals without avoiding my family. Rick is still a dick; that's his problem, not mine. My mom and dad are happily married—it works for them, so the fact that their dynamic wouldn't work for me is moot. Live and fucking let live. I ought to tape that to my laptop.

"I'm ready for cake," Mom says in an obvious attempt to change the subject.

"Cake sounds great." I refill my wineglass and smile at Mandy from across the room. It's the little wins in life that keep us going.

As my family discusses everything from little Jimbo's nursery school to the last time anyone ate a late-night Thurmanator, my thoughts drift again to Wendy. Her influence—the way she would shine a light on the other side of anything I ever said about my parents—is partly what led me here tonight. This hasn't been an unqualified success or quick fix. Real change will take time and effort on all sides. But I've taken the first step.

I'd be feeling terrific about myself right now if it weren't for the knowledge that Wendy's sitting at home somewhat broken because of me, and I'm not sure changing parts of my book will be enough to repair that.

CHAPTER TWENTY-ONE

WENDY

Late Monday afternoon
Dr. Haertel's office

"Based on everything you've disclosed about how you ended up here, I feel there's still a lot of love between you, and that's worth saving," Dr. Haertel says at the end of our session.

I don't realize how stiff I've been until her words unleash a sigh of relief from me that softens everything and sinks me more comfortably into my chair. Joe is sitting back, nodding thoughtfully, one leg crossed with that foot jiggling atop the opposite knee. His gaze is fixed on the doctor as she continues speaking.

"Going forward, we'll work on mindful communication—how to listen better, how to speak up in the moment instead of letting things simmer—and on rebuilding the trust that's been shaken." Dr. Haertel glances from Joe to me. "Between now and our next session, why don't you both keep a journal to note the things the other does to make you happy or make your life easier, as well as the things you think you're doing for the other. That should help us spot disconnects in what you think you're doing and how it's perceived. It should also help you focus on the good things in your marriage. Also, if something bothers you, note how you handled it—did you bring it up and how did that go, or if you buried it, why? That sort of thing. We'll take a look at all that when we meet next."

Joe leans forward now, sliding a hopeful smile in my direction. "Thank you, Dr. Haertel. Like I've told you both, my marriage is a priority, so I'm committed to doing whatever you suggest will help us."

I allow myself to ride Dr. Haertel's optimism. "Me too."

"See you both in two weeks," she says, standing to signal the end of our session.

Joe and I rise and shake her hand before we exit the cocoon of her office. He holds the door for me when we get to the small lobby and head out into the chilly night air. The shops on Elm Street will be closing soon, but restaurants are already buzzing with customers.

"Why don't we make it a date night and have dinner at South End? We can stop at Walgreens after to get little notebooks for our journals," Joe suggests, his brows high and hopeful.

A date night. This is something we could be doing more regularly with Billy out of the house and my therapy in swing. "That sounds nice."

The breeze makes the prospect of walking several blocks less enticing, so we get into Joe's car and drive the short distance down to Pine Street. As we make our way to the entrance, I have a moment of panic. Will I get through the night without slipping? I throw my shoulders back, determined to push forward.

Once we're seated and Joe's ordered a beer, he turns to me. "I like the journal idea—do you?"

"Honestly? It's a bit daunting, but if she thinks it will help, I'll do my best."

"Which will be ten times better than mine because you're more organized and meticulous." He smiles, glancing casually around the dining room; then his brow furrows as his attention turns back to us.

"Do you think Sue and Dirk will try therapy? I can't believe he'd toss his family aside for someone he barely knows."

"They're in therapy now. Sue's giving it some time before making any big decisions. I have no idea what Dirk's thinking, though." It's a bit of a relief to talk about them instead of us, and yet we're struggling just the same for different reasons.

"I haven't spoken with him since the dinner party." Joe shrugs. "But you and Sue, any progress on the website? Weren't you figuring out colors and stuff?"

"Yes. She's registered a website URL and is designing something simple on Squarespace, whatever that means. We aren't live yet because we're still selecting graphics and fonts, but the color palette will be white space with sage green, pale pink, and metallic gold pops. She'll also handle the newsletter and social media. All I'll need to focus on is the actual refinishing work and taking pictures. Maybe you could help me with some video footage, or I can get a tripod. I know you're busy with work."

"We could do both. Invest in some equipment—lights or tripods or whatever—but I can also help when I'm home. Maybe we could even go antiquing together. A weekend in Vermont? Or up along the Hudson?" When the waiter brings his beer, he takes a big gulp and we order dinner.

After the waiter leaves, I say, "That could be fun—the weekend away. We should do that before the weather turns snowy."

"Would you like me to plan that, or would you rather do it?"

I appreciate what he's doing by asking, but my controlling most of our married-life agenda has been part of our problem. "Why don't you do it, and make some time for something you'd find interesting while we're there, too."

"All righty, consider it done." He sips more beer.

Nervous energy emanates around our table. I suppose it will be part of our exchanges for a while to come. Frankly, I've been a little edgy this past week whenever I've come to town for groceries or the post office or to get my nails done. So far, no one has given me a sideways glance or shied away for any reason. It seems my friends have kept their promise, which I appreciate. It won't last forever, but with Dr. Haertel's help, I'll be more confident about handling the scrutiny whenever that day arrives.

Change is hard. Joe and I are sure to trip up now and then, but I do believe we have a lot of love lurking beneath the nerves and shaken faith.

I sip my water and reach across the table for Joe's hand—the first time I've reached for him since our big fight. "Thanks, Joe."

He raises my hand to his lips and then sets it back on the table without letting go. It feels almost like a first date. Maybe going back to the beginning is the best way to rebuild.

CHAPTER TWENTY-TWO

Harper

Friday morning
Manhattan

Cassandra is in the hallway talking to her assistant while I'm seated in her office. Behind her desk is a bookcase containing all her clients' books. Unlike my personal collection, hers is organized alphabetically, so it is easy to locate my books on the farthest right-hand shelf just below the midline.

Some authors have six books; others, only one. I've got three and counting. Even if I never write another word, I've done something remarkable—and not because some of my work garnered critical acclaim and stellar sales. The remarkable thing, I've come to realize, is that I had the courage to follow my dream. I had the resilience to withstand rejection and criticism and all the other roadblocks to getting an agent and then a publishing contract.

I never quit, and my reward is those books and the fan letters that prove my words matter. My perceptions—for better or worse—have affected strangers. The books are also something I can hold in my hands, a part of me that will go on in perpetuity.

If the worst happens and my career never regains its former momentum, my life is not over. It doesn't detract from what I've accomplished, or what I should be proud of. That's a good thing, because I'm counting on this insight to bolster my courage today. At the same time, I've got another offer on the condo to consider. Not full price, but it is a cash offer and quick close.

Cassandra finally comes into the office and sits at her desk. Her auburn hair is pulled into a sleek ponytail, giving her a severe look, particularly when paired with the smart high-waisted black slacks and snug pink cashmere sweater. "Okay, you've got my attention."

For at least ten minutes, anyway.

I stroke the arms of the leather chair, working up to the ask. "I need to change some elements of the synopsis that Tessa approved, and I want you to have that discussion with her."

She sits back, removes her glasses, and crosses her arms. "First tell me what you want to change and why."

"Okay. First, I've realized that using kleptomania for humor is insensitive, and I don't want to be that author. Gwen doesn't need that trait, either—it doesn't fully serve her arc. Also, after considering your earlier notes on Haley, I've decided that, in addition to her investigating her possible connection to Gwen's husband, maybe she also attaches herself to Gwen as a mentor rather than making Gwen an antagonist. Haley's got plenty to unpack in her own right, and her story about finding her bio dad is really more about her trying to find her place in her adopted family and in the world. That and the fact that Gwen is also going through a late coming-of-age phase in her own way could set the story up with more of a *Thelma & Louise* vibe, without the suicide. I think that makes the entire story more upbeat and relatable to readers of all ages—so I can retain my young readers and pull in an older crowd."

Cassandra rocks in her chair, her mouth pursed while she considers my argument. My heartbeat tracks each second, which pass as painfully as time in a chemistry class. "Those are good points, Harper. Can you send me a revised synopsis before I make the ask? Tessa will want to see exactly how you plan to show all that before she approves the new direction."

"I will get one to you by Monday." Part of me wants to jump up and fist-bump her—I'm so encouraged by her support, and glad for the chance to revive my career without hurting Wendy any further.

"Great. It seems like your experiment in the burbs is working out. When will you be returning to the city?"

"That depends." If Tessa approves this direction, then I can count on getting the rest of my advance in April, which means I can turn down the latest offer on my condo. If I can find a subtenant in Connecticut, I could move back sooner than later. But doing so would make it harder to keep things moving forward with Nate, who I'd certainly miss. "My lease isn't up until the end of March, but I might be able to find a subtenant."

"Well, send me the new synopsis. As long as the story conflict remains strong, Tessa shouldn't be troubled by the change. Upbeat fiction—a story of unlikely friends, even—is never a bad choice."

"That's my hope." I hold up two sets of crossed fingers. "Let me get out of your hair. I know you're busy. But maybe we can grab lunch some other time."

"Perfect. I look forward to reading the new vision for the story. Have a good weekend." She stands and walks with me into the hall. "You know your way out, right?"

I wave her off. "Absolutely. Have a good weekend."

I stroll down the hall, noting the posters on the walls—famous quotes in literature and the imprint's top-selling books—and all the young employees with their heads down. Being back in this environment makes me think of Calvin, who is in his own office not many blocks away, busily bringing new sci-fi stories as well as his own novel into the world.

His baby is due any day—maybe he or she has already arrived. That doesn't give me palpitations. If anything, some of my recent soul-searching has made me realize that Calvin and I were never the perfect fit I thought. We weren't helping each other grow. If anything, we held each other back. The fact that he recognized that before I did is irrelevant. He could've been kinder about it, but a fast, clean break can sometimes be for the best. I don't want to live the rest of my life burdened by ill will toward him. It's too exhausting. And as I sit on the cusp of mapping out a new direction for myself, I'm feeling generous of spirit. Something Nate and Wendy exemplify in most aspects of their lives.

When I get outside, I look toward his office building. I could surprise him. Congratulate him on the book deal and the baby. I shove my hands in my pockets and shake my head. I don't need to see him for closure. I've made my peace with that part of my life on my own.

The pulse of the city thrums as confidence from my meeting takes root. I should catch the first train back to New Canaan and start working on that revised synopsis, but the breeze and sunshine call to me. Central Park isn't far—just a several-blocks-long walk to Columbus Circle. Walking always aids my creativity, so the journey might be a perfect way to take in all the energy.

Nate isn't expecting me until seven, giving me a few hours to kill. It's a welcome change to be back in the city and feeling optimistic about myself and the future. Hopeful, like when I first arrived. A few people have helped me with this turnaround, one of whom I've hurt deeply. As soon as I get Tessa's buy-in on story changes, I'll tell Wendy so she can rest easier. Hopefully she won't slam the door in my face.

CHAPTER TWENTY-THREE

WENDY

The following Wednesday

It's not yet noon, but I'm starting the dishwasher's second full load of the day—Thanksgiving tomorrow has made for much prep work. I'm so happy to have my son home and have Joe and me moving in a better direction—it feels like a perfect time for a holiday celebration. I close the appliance door as Billy comes into the kitchen wearing gym clothes and a worried expression.

"Mom, I got a text from Jackson. He made a joke about you—you know, the thing . . ."

I slump onto a kitchen chair, my buoyant mood temporarily deflated. Here we go—someone in my book club or Harper finally told someone else, and now it's out there. Jackson Crawford was always a bit of a shit. The kind of friend who makes himself feel good by one-upping others. I also know his mother, Miranda, from the lacrosse board. A friendly acquaintance, or so I'd hoped.

I close my eyes and breathe, reminding myself my illness does not define me. It doesn't make me a despicable, unworthy person.

"I'm sorry he did that to you. Are you okay?" I search his eyes for the truth, thankfully finding no real pain there.

"Yeah. I've met with Dr. Caputo at the student counseling center twice since you told me everything. He gave me some tips in case this happened." His chin is tucked, like he's not sure how I'll react.

"Oh?" At first I'm crushed that he didn't choose to come to me with his questions, but then I realize that could be uncomfortable for him, especially if he thinks it embarrasses me. I should be proud of him taking action for himself. A sign of growing up. "I'm glad you have that resource, honey."

Billy smiles—that shy smile that resembles Joe's—but I see his relief, too. "I texted Jackson back that it's not cool to make fun of mental illness, then blocked him. But anyway, I wanted to warn you."

"I appreciate that, but I'm okay. Part of my therapy is learning to work through all aspects of living with my illness, including public opinion, but I'm sorry that you have to manage it, too."

"It's okay, Mom. I know you didn't set out to embarrass me."

Quite the opposite, actually. But hiding it so long only led to the public blowup. I'm learning to be honest, and that's the important thing. "I'm glad you're not letting it fluster you or cause problems with your grades."

"I've pulled my English grade up to a B minus so far. We have one more big paper before the semester ends, so I could end up with a B plus in the class if I get an A on that. I'm going in for his office hours before it's due."

I grin. He's growing from his mistakes like Joe promised he would. He's reaching out for help on his own, which takes confidence. And he's being compassionate. Despite some personal missteps, raising Billy is one of the things I've done right.

"Sounds like you've got it all under control." I give him a quick hug, the only kind boys his age seem to like from their moms.

"I'm going to the Y to work out, okay?"

"Of course. See you later." I watch him duck out the back door, knowing he'll cross the backyard and slip through the gap in our fence to shorten his walk.

I'm rising from the kitchen chair when my doorbell rings. An unexpected interruption, but I suppose the Jell-O mold can wait another five minutes.

When I answer the door, the last person I want to see stares back at me. "Harper?"

"Hi, Wendy." She's got her hands shoved in her jeans' pockets. No coat, just a knit scarf around her neck. Any flicker of residual affection is erased when a cold breeze passes through us, particularly on the heels of what Billy told me.

"I don't have it in me to argue today."

She holds up a hand. "If you can spare a few minutes, I'd really like to share some things. Please."

In spite of myself, I'm curious. It's too cold to stay on the porch, so I open the door wide and wave her inside.

"Thank you." She takes a seat on the sofa, loosening her scarf. We catch each other glancing at the coffee table where the votive was and then recoiling from the memory.

Much has changed in the couple of weeks since that night. Surprisingly, almost all of it is for the better. That thought settles me and reframes my mood.

I sit opposite her in a swivel chair. My cheeks feel warm, but I maintain my composure. "What's on your mind?"

Her head tilts to the left, almost in deference or something equally unlike her. "First, I want to thank you for introducing me to Nate. He's great. I thought you should know I told him the truth about how I mistreated you, but not about the votive or anything related to that. I hope that puts you at ease. You don't have to worry that I'll hurt him or out you." She pauses, giving me a second to chime in, but when I don't, she rubs her hands on her jeans and continues. "Also, I went to visit my family last weekend, which is something I probably wouldn't have done had you not helped me see the other facets of my parents. My mom was ecstatic, and it wasn't a horrible time, so a win-win as far as first steps go." Her brows rise expectantly, like I should definitely say something now.

I hesitate, because none of this changes her deception. At the same time, we've all made mistakes. "I'm glad for your mother, and thankful you've been discreet and honest with Nate. Beyond that, I'm not sure what to say, Harper. I'm not in a place to pick up where things left off, if that's what you came here hoping for."

"I didn't expect that, although perhaps one day . . ." The uncharacteristic hopeful expression makes her look ten years younger.

It almost makes me wish I could take that leap, but unlike with Joe—with whom I share decades of history and love—I've known Harper less than two months.

"Anyway," she says into the silence, "I just . . . What I want you to know is that, until I got to know you, I hadn't encountered many conventional women like you—kind, unselfish, and nurturing yet willing to consider other perspectives, and who show integrity even when it's difficult or embarrassing. I admire your bravery, and your consistently good intentions. I'm sorry I let my own desperation justify deceiving you, and I'm sorry I embarrassed you in front of your friends. If I could go back and do things differently, I'd like to believe I would." Her gaze is more vulnerable than I've ever seen it. She's trying, I'll give her that much. But that book—when it comes out, it will likely hurt me all over again.

I look at my hands—two tight fists on my thighs—and relax them. "Thank you. If it helps ease your conscience, my world hasn't imploded. There's a little gossip out there, but we're all handling it well. Joe and I are in counseling, too, so perhaps fate brought you here to force me to make changes before I wasted another decade of my life locked in the prison I built to contain my illness."

"See? You're so good at looking for the positives—the potential in things, Wendy. I've really come to admire that." She lets loose a breath. "On that note, I have news that hopefully proves my sincerity. I'm changing the focus of my story—shifting it to the younger character and her family issues. I've taken out the impulse control disorder, too. My editor and I are working on a different angle to make Gwen quirky in a fun way. I've got four months to finish the book. If I find a sub-tenant for the house, I'll return to the city to finish my work. That way you and Joe can relax and get back to your life without an unpleasant reminder next door."

I should jump for joy, but in truth, sitting with Harper this way makes me mourn the friendship we might've built if we'd both been more honest with ourselves and each other.

"It wasn't all unpleasant." I twist my lips. "Truth is, you helped me as much as you hurt me. You forced me to take stock of my life and make changes. I've even convinced Sue to help me with the refurbishing business, so maybe we can call it even. Or at least call it a truce."

"I'd love that." Harper glances around the living room, her gaze landing on Billy's senior picture for a moment. The pregnant pause is loaded, like neither of us knows quite how to let go. "Wherever we end up, know that, despite how this started, I did come to genuinely care for you as a friend. I will always wish you and your family the best, Wendy. I mean that." She rises, possibly worn thin from all the honesty.

I stand, too, although I'm unsteady on my feet. She breathed new life into my old one, and that's not something I'll forget. "Thank you. It's been . . . interesting. I hope you find what you're looking for from life, too."

We offer each other an awkward smile. A hug would feel inauthentic and a handshake too formal, so I simply follow her to the door with strangely heavy feet.

"Take care of yourself," she says as she crosses the porch.

"You too." I wave once before closing the door, then turn around and lean my back against it, letting her small kindnesses seep into and fill all the tiny cracks inside.

She may not have become the bosom buddy I was looking for, but she left a lasting imprint on my life. I'm stronger for having let her in. I can't control life or whether people will disappoint me, but Harper helped me discover that I can weather those ups and downs. That's a gift worth cherishing.

EPILOGUE

Harper
Sixteen months later
Manhattan

After finishing my read-aloud of an excerpt from *As I See It*, I close the book and set it on the table, then look out into the audience gathered at the Strand bookstore near Union Square. There are easily sixty people or more, which is reassuring. My new release debuted at number nine on the *New York Times* bestseller list last week. My publisher and I hope it will climb or hold awhile, but at the very least, the early reviews are strong. I can breathe a little easier again knowing I'm no longer a has-been who needs to find a new job.

The moderator is thanking everyone for coming, and telling them where to queue up to get signed copies. Nate has been sitting in the second row, far right, beaming at me for the past hour. He came down to support me and to celebrate later in private. Commuting hasn't become a problem for us yet, so things have bubbled along. He's been flexible, so I agreed to monogamy if he could accept my reluctance to make a lifelong commitment at this point—although we have made plans to visit Greece in July.

One by one, I sign books and chitchat with readers. I'd forgotten how much I enjoy this part of my career. How amazing it feels to touch one reader, let alone a dozen or more. I am blessed to do this work, which I won't take for granted. That said, I'm eager to be alone with Nate. The line seems unending until the last person steps up.

"Hello, Harper." Wendy hands me her purchased book. She looks terrific with fresh highlights and a more modern bob.

"Wendy!" The shock of seeing her temporarily paralyzes me. She came all this way to see me. To support me, I hope. I jump up to hug her across the table, which is unlike me yet feels right in the moment. "I can't believe you came."

"How could I not? This book—or rather your writing it—changed a lot for us both. Our book club is reading it for next month's meeting, too." She shrugs with an awkward smile.

"Really?" I try not to wince at the recollection of the book club meeting I attended. "I'm honored." I take her copy and sign it. "How are Joe and Billy?"

"They're good. Billy ended another semester on the dean's list. Joe and I are having fun traveling more."

"And you?" I ask.

"No slipups in twelve months, thanks to continued therapy. And Recovered Beauties is turning a small profit." A proud smile emerges.

"I follow your Instagram account. The before-and-after videos are clever. You look like you're enjoying it."

She looks shocked, then recovers herself. "I love the creativity more than the business, but it's nice to have a little pocket change. Your buffet is still one of my favorite pieces, but I did buy that pie safe."

"I saw! I almost ordered it, but there's no room in my condo."

We stand there in silence with Nate looking on from a few feet away. He's so good about giving people the space they need at exactly the right time.

"Well, I should go before I miss the next train home. Good luck with this one." Wendy wiggles the book in the air and turns toward Nate as she prepares to leave.

"Wendy," I call. She glances back, waiting for me to continue. "Maybe the next time you come to the city we could grab lunch or a drink."

She cocks her head. "I'd like that, Harper."

Nate steps forward to kiss her on the cheek. "Good to see you, Wendy."

She pats his shoulder, wearing a warm smile. "Nice to know I'm four for four in the matchmaking department."

I can't deny that Wendy knows a lot more about love and the value of compromise than I do, but I'm learning.

———

Wendy

Outside the Strand

As soon as I get outside, I stop, pull the book from the bag, and open it to the bookmarked page. Oddly, Harper signed the dedication page instead of the title page. Her handwriting is even messier than her normal hairstyle, but I can make it out:

Wendy, Thank you for coming to see me tonight. It means more than you know. XO—H. E. Ross

When my eyes rise to the dedication, I flatten my palm on my chest along with a sharp intake of breath.

For Wendy, my gracious neighbor, who not only showed me how to be a better friend but also exemplifies true courage.

ACKNOWLEDGMENTS

As usual, it took an army of people to bring this book to all of you—not the least of whom are my family and friends for their continued love, encouragement, and support.

My agent, Jill Marsal, and my patient editors, Chris Werner and Tiffany Yates Martin, also deserve a hearty round of applause. My editors, in particular, worked miracles to help me refine this book—a story that stretched me into new territory as I tried my hand at a little humor and lightheartedness. And none of my work would find its way to readers without the entire Montlake family working so hard on my behalf. I'm indebted to the PR and marketing staff, the art department, the editorial staff, and the sales team for playing an invaluable role in my career.

I also want to thank my critique partners, Linda Avellar, Falguni Kothari, and Ginger McKnight, for their guidance and enthusiasm as we worked through the chapters. Their keen eyes are a godsend. Additionally, a big thanks to my beta readers, Amy Liz Talley, Sally Kilpatrick, Virginia Kantra, and Louise Foerster, for their feedback on the early draft, as well as hugs for my other dear friends Tracy Brogan, Priscilla Oliveras, Sonali Dev, and Barbara O'Neal, who inspire me on a daily basis and who are always there to talk through plot knots and provide feedback on a chapter or two. Every book I write really is a group project!

I couldn't produce any of my work without the MTBs (Regina Kyle, Gail Chianese, Jane Haertel, Jamie K. Schmidt, and Megan Ryder), who help me plot and keep my spirits up when doubt grabs hold.

Finally, and most important, thank you, readers, for making the time and effort I dedicate to my work worthwhile. Considering all your options, I'm honored by your choice to spend your time with me.

BOOK CLUB QUESTIONS

1. Wendy is experiencing the growing pains of being an empty nester. Have you had this experience? Did it affect your marriage? What did you do with your newly acquired free time?

2. When Harper's stellar career takes a sharp turn, her ego is hit hard. Have you experienced a job loss or setback? Did it create self-doubt? How did you recover your confidence?

3. Nearly one in five adults in the United States lives with mental illness, and nearly half go without treatment (for a variety of reasons, including the cost of medical care). Do you think Wendy's life would've been better if she'd felt free to be honest about her condition with her friends and Joe? What do you think can be done to help those afflicted feel safer being open about their condition? Should our government provide a health care safety net for people like Wendy?

4. Harper is quick to point out gender inequities that exist in our society. Have you experienced any in your family or workplace? How did you handle it? Do you agree with Harper's approach to discussing feminist issues, or do you think there are better ways to foster change? Discuss.

5. After years of loyal support, Joe snaps and treats Wendy cruelly. Is his action forgivable? If you had to choose, would you rather be in Sue's faltering marriage or Wendy's? Why?

6. One of the themes in this story is the idea that things you fear end up having power over you. Do you agree with this concept? Wendy's and Harper's pasts play huge roles in their decisions, particularly in the first half of the book. Has fear ever influenced a major decision about your career or relationships?

7. Wendy is a bit of a busybody, but she means well. Have you had a neighbor like her? How did you handle it?

8. Harper took "borrowing" from real life to new heights in her desperation to conjure a premise for a new novel. Do you think she was in the wrong? Where would you draw the line on what is and isn't fair game for an author to use as inspiration?

9. People joke about sexless marriages, but they account for roughly 15 percent of all marriages. Would you be willing to stay in a sexless marriage if everything else was good (i.e., you felt loved and supported in all other areas of your married life)? Do you think it is possible to be happy with that life?

10. Trust (or the lack and/or betrayal of it) is a big issue in the book. Does Wendy deserve some of the blame in her marital problems because of her own secrets and failure to trust Joe?

11. Harper is a fish out of water when she comes to New Canaan. Do you prefer an urban, suburban, or rural lifestyle? Why? What is one thing from a different type of lifestyle that you might like to experience?

AN EXCERPT FROM

THE BEAUTY OF RAIN

EDITOR'S NOTE: THIS IS AN EARLY
EXCERPT AND MAY NOT REFLECT THE
FINISHED BOOK.

CHAPTER ONE

AMY FOX WALSH

Old Greenwich
A Saturday in late February

Nobody who wins the Powerball imagines such luck will lead to the death of their spouse and only child. Yet it did for me. Even ten months later, the question most often reflected in other people's eyes is *"Oh my God, how do you handle that?"* Well, here's the answer: most days I shamble around like a zombie searching for a reason to keep going, but today I'm throwing a birthday party for my late son, Scotty.

Granted, it's a peculiar twist on my reputation for planning memorable birthday celebrations. One of Scotty's baby pictures sits on the kitchen table, bathed in the harsh winter light spilling through the wall of plate glass windows that frame the backyard's patchy brown grass and the distant, choppy water of Long Island Sound. This weather is the same as it was exactly five years ago today—a date I never want to ignore even though it now wrings new shivers.

I can do this. I must do it. It might be easier if my sister, Kristin, and her husband, Tony, weren't putting a crimp in the festivities by tiptoeing around while silently questioning my sanity. If my extended stay at the Silver Hill mental hospital last summer hasn't already answered that question, they aren't nearly as smart as their multiple diplomas proclaim.

They may find this shindig a bit macabre, but I'm hardly the only surviving parent who's ever planned one. It's quite possible I'll have a meltdown at some point. Probable, even. But this morning was the first time in all these months that I woke up with a purpose, so it can't be my worst-ever idea. No, that honor goes to the overly tweezed eyebrows of my freshman year in high school that earned me the nickname "Plucky" until graduation.

One minute at a time, that's how I'll manage. At this moment, I'm savoring the chocolate and sugar aromas—a rare treat in Kristin's normally immaculate, sleek kitchen. My niece and nephew race to the large quartz island, where I'm layering frosting on the bungled birthday cake. I blame the overpriced, underused oven for the cratered top of the sheet cake, although I can fault only myself for the poorly sliced and reassembled sections that were meant to construct a Piglet confection.

"That's a pig?" Livvy's face puckers with disbelief. She climbs onto a stool, bouncing on her knees, her black-brown curls springing around her face.

I stare down at the lumpy mound that looks like a swollen pink hornet, swallowing the bubble of disappointment rising in my throat. It's nothing like the photograph, but it's too early for me to fall apart.

"Use your imagination a little, will ya?" I slide Livvy a smile before sticking out my tongue. She's been my little savior since I moved into the guest suite in September.

"Scotty loves pigs!" She reaches for the sky with the enthusiasm only a six-year-old can muster.

Loves. "Yes." I rub the ache his obsession with Piglet lodges in my chest.

Luca, who's turning nine in April, swipes his finger along the base of the frosting, less interested in how the cake looks than how it tastes.

Skinny but tall for his age, he's fair like Kristin, with her same pin-straight blonde hair.

"Ah, ah, ah." I shake my head, pointing the spatula at him. "Not yet."

"Sorry," he says matter-of-factly, already showing signs of his father's personality as he turns and walks to the family room, plops onto the enormous suede sectional, and picks up the latest Theodore Boone book—something Scotty will never read.

"What are those presents, Aunt Amy?" Livvy asks, pointing at the boxes on the counter near the toaster.

"You'll have to be patient." I use black M&M's for the pig's snout and eyes, then step back to see if it's made an improvement. Being an avid fan of *The Great British Baking Show* does not, apparently, improve one's baking skills. My "design fail" makes me more sympathetic toward the contestant whose Freddie Mercury bust cake looked like Mr. Pringle, but maybe it's a win to have tried at all.

"Are you bothering your aunt while she's busy?" Kristin asks Livvy when she enters the kitchen to place a card on the pile beside the two gift-wrapped boxes. Even when she's not in the room, she's no doubt checking the Arlo cameras to gauge my frame of mind. Earlier I overheard her whispering to Tony about my manic mood.

"No!" Livvy frowns at her mother. "I'm good company."

And a good mimic, repeating the exact words I tell her on the mornings when she crawls into bed with me before sunrise.

Kristin ruffles her hair. "How about you go find Daddy? I think he's on the Peloton. Tell him we'll be serving lunch soon."

At that I turn my back on them, pretending to need something from the refrigerator. What I actually need is a breather. Kristin means well, but her careful language hit a nerve. Not that it's hard to hit one lately. Nor can I fault her apprehension. But really, can't we call this a birthday party? It's got all the trappings. Her professionally decorated family room now looks like Chuck E. Cheese visited and barfed up streamers and dozens of red, yellow, and blue balloons. The kitchen table is covered with a Winnie the Pooh tablecloth and confetti. The only thing missing is Kidz Bop blaring from the speakers.

"Mom and Dad want us to Zoom when things get underway," Kristin says. That's better than if they'd flown in, as they wanted. The last thing I needed this week was four more eyes anxiously studying my every move.

I grab the pack of American cheese from the refrigerator and put it on the island. "That'll be nice."

"Grilled cheese," she says gently, her gaze soft and fathomless enough to fall into if I let myself. I've spent my life in her shadow. Always a little smarter, a little prettier, and until recently, a lot wealthier than I. Yet she's never lorded anything over me—the opposite, really, as if she knows her advantages and tries to diminish them.

"Scotty's favorite." Another pang prompts me to busy myself with a new task. I open the pantry to get bread and potato chips.

"What else can I do?" my sister asks.

"Maybe grab the paper plates and silverware?" I shrug.

Kristin lays a hand on my shoulder as she breezes past. "Of course."

The gesture makes me stiffen. She wants to be my safe space. To be the person I confide in. She also wants to know I'm okay. When I'm up to any of that, I'll let her know, but not beforehand. And not right now.

While I'm buttering bread and compiling the sandwiches, Tony shows up, his hair still wet from the shower. He's objectively handsome—the classic Italian look with wavy black-brown hair and equally dark eyes, a strong nose and chin. A major contrast to the slightly dorky looks of my husband, Tom. Medium brown hair and fair skin. A bit elfin, but sincere and approachable, like I prefer. I miss that face and smile.

"Let's see that cake." Tony glances at my attempt and then, like a kid afraid of getting in trouble, avoids all eye contact. One hand covers his mouth, but his torso trembles as he holds back inappropriately timed laughter—the kind of giggles that attack in church or a classroom. The situation makes me snicker, at which point he and my sister relax long enough to laugh.

"Well, the taste is all that matters," he says. Like his son, he can't resist sampling a bit of icing. "Want me to grill the sandwiches?"

His energy returns to edgy restlessness like Kristin's. His initial concern about today's event revolved around the negative impact a ghostly birthday might have on his kids. But he's been patient with me. More than patient. What man wants to indefinitely live with his sister-in-law underfoot?

"No, I'm fine." I shoo him away. "Go spend time with Luca. Let him tell you about that book he's reading."

I turn to the stove, but not before catching his nonverbal exchange with Kristin. The arch of his brow tells me he's annoyed by my suggestion. It also indicates they've talked about this kind of thing before. I'm not sorry, though. Promotions and business deals come and go, but childhood is fleeting and can never be recaptured. They should understand that as well as anyone, given what we're doing today.

Twenty minutes later, the remnants of our greasy lunch lie scattered across the table like branches felled by a storm.

"Cake now?" Livvy claps.

"Let's do cards first to let our tummies settle," I suggest, although it's doubtful my stomach will stop churning soon.

Tony rises to collect the dirty napkins and paper plates. He's been quiet throughout lunch, almost as if to avoid accidentally saying something wrong. Restraint is unusual for him, which is why I notice.

Kristin touches my hand. "Should I grab the gifts?"

I shake my head. "I'll do it, but why don't you fire up Zoom since Mom and Dad want to participate."

"Oh gosh, I nearly forgot." She pushes back from the table and trots to the den, returning in seconds with her iPad before logging on. I hear Mom and Dad peppering Livvy and Luca with questions while I'm getting the cards.

Kristin moves the iPad to the far corner of the table and then suggests we all scoot our chairs around the opposite end so our parents can see everything at once.

"Hi, Mom. Dad." I briefly make eye contact, but it's difficult to watch them struggling to feign happiness. I can't let anything derail this celebration for Scotty. With effort, I don my best Vanna White smile. "Shall we jump in?"

"Me first!" Livvy says, stretching across the table to grab the card she made.

"I'd expect nothing less." I bop my finger against her nose before she opens the envelope.

With great flair, she unfolds her artwork and displays it to everyone before turning it to face me. "This is one time when Luca, Scotty, and me were at the beach—"

"Scotty and I," my sister corrects.

Livvy scowls, and I might've, too. I refocus on the artwork, which depicts two figures in the water (Luca and her, I assume) and then, slightly off-center by himself, is a boy in socks piling rocks on the beach. "Scotty didn't like the water, but he really liked the rocks. He kept piling them and knocking them over and piling them again. Like, forever. That was so funny." She giggles, her head bobbling from side to side. "Then we all had ice cream sandwiches for lunch. It was a fun day."

I remember that day at Tod's Point, too. Two years ago. Scotty had been three and a half. He didn't like sand between his toes, so he wore socks on the beach. I thought it was cute, especially when Tom nicknamed him Two Socks. That day I'd driven down from Stamford, borrowed Kristin's pass, and taken the three kids there, but none of us could coax my son into the water. At one point, Livvy sat beside him and built a rock creation of her own. She'd always tried to connect with him, treating him like a baby brother she wanted to protect.

"That was a fun day." I reach across to squeeze her hand. "Thank you for reminding me."

My gratitude earns me her winning smile. She's innocent and unaware that my insides feel like a piñata defending against an angry batter.

We proceed around the table, with everyone sharing a memory of Scotty. Luca wrote a letter updating Scotty on his soccer team's record. My mother's voice cracks on her turn. So does Kristin's. Tony and Dad muscle through like newscasters reading a teleprompter. Everyone has their own way of dealing with discomfort. I understand. My request wasn't an easy one for any of us, so we do what we can to get through.

When my turn comes, I say, "For mine, we need to go outside."

"What about those presents?" Livvy asks.

"That's next, but go grab a coat." I stand to get my coat and retrieve the floating paper lanterns I've hidden.

Within two minutes, the family is reassembled in winter coats and hats near the sliding doors. I hand everyone a lantern, grab a pack of matches and the iPad, and go out onto the deck. While I reposition the iPad, everyone unwraps their lantern and waits for my speech.

I should've planned something, but anytime I tried, I ended up tossing it in the trash. I'm no Jane Austen. I couldn't find words that held the depth and complexity of my love and yearning.

I sniffle before clearing my throat. "Thank you, guys, for helping me mark this day. I know it might seem strange, but even though Scotty's in heaven, he's still my baby, and I'm still his mom, and a mother can't ignore her child's birthday."

My sister dabs her eyes and then grasps her husband's hand. I miss that, too—the support of a loving partner. The kids are standing dutifully, like they do at Easter mass, waiting for instructions.

It takes several seconds for my throat to loosen enough for me to speak again. "He can't be here with us today, but I thought we could send these lanterns up to him so that, in some way, he's part of our celebration."

Tony's face is splotchy, yet his lips are pressed tight, as if he's zipped up his emotions.

"Let's take a second to light these, and then we'll let them go at the same time and make a little wish, okay?" I look at Livvy and Luca because they, more than anyone, keep me grounded. Livvy nods, her dimples fixed marks on her cheeks. I love her and Luca, and am blessed to be as close to them as I am. Yet I can't deny some envy that they have their lives ahead of them. They will learn about the world and themselves as they continue to grow, graduate from high school and college, find jobs, fall in love. All the things my little boy will never experience.

It's quiet except for the chattering of teeth. The breeze makes lighting the lanterns tricky. We all huddle with our backs turned against the wind to create a barrier, and then we release our offerings.

As they rise, I say, "I miss you so much, my baby, and can't wait for the day when we'll be reunited." My voice catches. "Until then, keep building rock castles in the sky."

With my face lifted to the sun, I watch the brightly colored lanterns drift inland on the wind.

"Mine's the fastest," Livvy announces while pointing at the green lantern charging ahead of the rainbow-colored pack.

My nose is runny as hell and my eyes burn, but I remain rooted there until the last lantern disappears from view.

"I'm cold," Luca says.

"Yes," I answer, a small pit opening inside because my big idea didn't mitigate my loss one bit. "We can go inside now."

"Cake!" Livvy runs ahead and throws open the door before ditching her coat on the floor and sidling up to the table.

Kristin grabs me into a hug before I reenter the house. A silent, tight hug that squeezes out of me the tears I've been holding back. As we ease apart, she grabs my face, her gaze searching mine. I wait for her to say something, but she can't or decides not to. She drops her hands and picks up the iPad before following me inside, where Tony has already put the candles on the cake.

"Oh boy. It really is hideous," I croak, half laughing, half crying, which makes everyone else go still, as if movement or sound will make me implode.

Livvy's small hand slides around mine then. "You always say it's the effort that matters. Good effort, Aunt Amy."

And just like that, she defuses the sorrow gathering around us. We sing, and then the kids slice gigantic pieces of cake for themselves. My appetite is gone, but I force myself to take one bite to honor the custom.

Suddenly the exhaustion of holding myself together cascades like a waterfall, and my head begins to pound.

"I'm sorry, but I need to lie down." I stand, surprising everyone.

"What about the presents?" Livvy asks.

"Those are for you and Luca. You can open them without me, okay? I have a bad headache all of a sudden."

Kristin's hands flex. "Can I do anything? Advil?"

"I have what I need in my room, thanks. Leave the mess. I'll clean it later."

"I'll take care of it," Tony says. "Don't worry about it."

I nod. "Thank you." Before I leave, I turn to the kids. "Don't suck the helium without me!"

"Okay," Luca promises before sneaking a second sliver of cake onto his plate. I kiss both kids on the head and wave to my parents.

"Thanks so much, everyone. I love you all." My eyes are awash in fresh tears and my throat aches, so I dash up the stairs and close the door to my room. Kristin was right—I was riding a strange high this morning, a brief return of the me from before the accident. But reality always catches up sooner or later. The *Winnie-the-Pooh* quote *"How lucky am I to have something that makes saying goodbye so hard"* comes to mind like a message from beyond.

Luck. Something most people pray for. Something everyone cheered about when I won all those millions. Good luck. Dumb luck. Blind luck.

Bad luck.

I flop onto the bed, curl around a pillow, and cry myself to sleep.

When I awaken, the sun is low in the sky and my room has grown dim. The cashmere throw from the chair is swathed across me, letting me know my sister checked on me at some point.

I sit up and catch a glimpse of myself in the mirror—so thin and sallow—then decide to take a bath. Steam fogs up the bathroom as the soaking tub fills. When I disrobe, the scars on my wrists are a permanent reminder of my all-time low point. Of my desperation to escape grief and remorse. Of my inability to turn back the clock and not purchase that lottery ticket.

It should've been me in that boat. Not my son. Not my husband.

And now I'm alone to live with the consequences of my choices. To plan parties that the guest of honor can't attend. To mark time against one cruel twist of fate.

Or not.

I take my nearly full bottle of doxepin from the vanity drawer and set it on the side of the bathtub before I settle into the water.

After Kristin picked me up from the hospital in September, she told me how much she loved me and that she was glad I was doing better. Then she said, "We want you to come live with us for a while, but I have to ask for a promise."

I didn't want to go to my empty home with all its ghosts. "What promise?"

"Please promise you won't harm yourself again. Especially not in my home. I love you, but I don't want Luca and Livvy to witness something no child should see."

I dropped my chin, letting the weight of her words and the pain I'd already caused my family sink in. It wasn't an easy oath to make, but armed with antidepressants and fresh off a month of daily therapy, I said, "I promise."

The time between then and now is like a long, indistinct smudge of getting from sunrise to sunset by making myself useful—doing the family laundry, tidying up, making dinners, and even dismissing the nanny now and then to ferry the kids around to playdates and after-school activities. But the holidays were brutal. I flew to Arizona to stay with my parents rather than ruin Christmas for the kids. At least out west, nothing reminded me of home.

I've done my best to heal, but any joy is fleeting. I'm still stuck and can't find my way forward. Even if I could, I'm not sure I deserve to be happy. Not really. Not when I didn't appreciate what I had until I lost it.

I grip the bottle of pills.

If I took them and went to bed, no one would find me until morning. Everyone might think I had a heart attack. Even once Kristin learned the truth, the kids would never need to know. I don't want to hurt my sister or parents, but they'd survive because they have everything to live for right here under this roof.

A knock at the bedroom door startles me, causing me to drop the bottle. "Shit," I mutter, reaching for it.

"Aunt Amy, can you come play dolls with me now?" Livvy yells.

She obviously likes her new American Girl doll, as I knew she would. That's good.

"Where's your mom, pumpkin?"

"In the office, working."

Naturally. Weekends don't mean rest in this house. Tony's and Kristin's jobs are rarely far from their thoughts. And so, once again, Livvy unknowingly keeps me from checking out.

"Give me five minutes to dry off and get dressed." I toe the drain lever and let the water swirl around me.

"Okay. I'll be in my room."

While I towel off, I consider whether it's time to move out. I've overstayed my welcome, for one thing. And if I'm no longer living here, then I'll no longer be bound by that promise. I could settle my affairs—that damn money—and then choose for myself whether to keep going or to quit.

ABOUT THE AUTHOR

Photo © 2016 Lorah Haskins

Jamie Beck is a *Wall Street Journal* and *USA Today* bestselling author whose realistic and heartwarming stories have sold multimillions of copies. She is a two-time Booksellers' Best Award finalist and a National Readers' Choice Award winner. *Kirkus Reviews, Publishers Weekly,* and *Booklist* have respectively called her work "smart," "uplifting," and "entertaining." In addition to writing novels, she enjoys hitting the slopes in Vermont and Utah and dancing around the kitchen while cooking. Above all, she is a grateful wife and mother to a very patient, supportive family. Fans can get exclusive excerpts and inside scoops and be eligible for birthday-gift drawings by subscribing to her newsletter at https://bit.ly/JBeckNewsletter. To learn more about the author, visit her at www.jamiebeck.com.